the Blood of Zealots

BY
WILLIAM J. ATKINS

This book is a work of fiction. Names, characters, places and in-
cidents are product of the author's imagination or are used ficti-
tiously. Any resemblance to actual events or locales or persons,
living or dead, is entirely coincidental.

Copyright © 2011 William J. Atkins
All rights reserved.
ISBN: 0615447996
ISBN 13: 9780615447995
Library of Congress Control Number: 2011922398
Point Comfort Publishing, LLC
United States

ACKNOWLEDGMENTS

Many people helped coax this story out of me, but special thanks and undying love go to: My amazing wife, Betsy, for our incredibly durable partnership that inspires me every day. My stepdaughter, Grace, who dared to read the first draft and edit the entire manuscript; I could not have done it without you, Gege. My daughter, Becca, for her remarkable sense of humanity, giant heart and, of course, Hannah. My son, Nik, for his beautiful soul and love of all things family. And finally, my father, Atty, for being crazy enough to marry a thirty-year-old divorcee with three children and a Florida brown-pound-hound..

For Mother, your bravery, compassion and love made everything possible

Chapter 1

He awoke not knowing who or where he was. Negotiations between his cobwebbed conscious and physical predicament ensued. After a moment of deliberation, he determined he was Trey Cowens, lying on the ground under a tangle of thorn branches. The early morning light allowed a view of a skyscraper's upper windows aglow in direct sunlight. Trey looked at his watch only to find a naked wrist with razor-thin cuts all the way up his arm. He tried to sit up, but the bush had him trapped. He crawled from the edge of the shrubbery onto the grass. He got to one knee and realized he'd better sit back down because his pants and underwear were around his ankles. Not good.

How did his trousers get pulled down? What happened last night? Trey tried to reconstruct the events of the previous twenty-four hours as he hurriedly re-dressed and stood up. Katie had broken up with him. He had made a complete fool of himself, leaving her in a rage and him on a mission to get trashed. *Success,* he winced, based on his current plight.

Trey remembered going to a seedy tavern in Midtown Manhattan with a plan to get blotto without seeing anyone he knew. He drank there until the work crowd arrived. Then he left and went to a shadier establishment where the patrons were unemployed dock-workers and criminals. It surprised him how comfortable he felt in their company. He remembered meeting a man and a woman seated next to him at the bar. He recalled being helped from the dive by someone and put into a cab around midnight. After that, a complete blank. Trey had blacked out, not remembering a thing after he got into the taxi. It had happened again; he had lost a big chunk of time to his overindulgence. The promise not to drink himself into oblivion was a total joke. He was half naked and cut up on a Tuesday morning; or was it Wednesday?

Trey continued to take inventory of his condition as he made the proverbial walk of shame back to his flat. With no watch, he guessed the time to be a little after seven. People passing him on the sidewalk just accepted him as part of the homeless landscape as they rushed to their important jobs. His pants were grass stained and bloody; his torn shirt hung off one shoulder revealing more abrasions. His head hurt as if an ice pick were impaled in his temple. He still had his keys, wallet, cash, and credit cards. Why hadn't they been stolen? Weird.

Trey let himself into his building, craving a safe place to hide as he tried to remember what had befallen him the previous night. A flashback gave him a flickering view of the proceedings. The smell of stale beer and the amber arms of a man with a Hispanic accent filled three of his senses. He was face down on a padded table with colorful designs covering the walls and bright lights heating his skin. Then the image left as quickly as it had arrived.

Trey peeled off his clothes and fell into the shower. He turned the hot water on high and let the healing river run down his back. An intense pain shot up from his ass. He turned to see what it was and caught a glimpse of something dark on his behind. Trey turned off the water, and grabbed a hand mirror from the counter. Positioning the glass so he could get a good look, he saw it; a small tattoo of a Chihuahua humping a skunk embellished his left hindquarter. Even swollen and red, one would never mistake the disfigurement for a butterfly.

Trey found himself in a place all too familiar of late, the couch of Dr. Rachel Kohen, a respected hypnotherapist. Dr. Kohen and Trey had been working together for more than four months. His longtime business partner had recommended he try "life regression therapy." He had pondered the pros and cons of going until his breakup with Katie and the fateful morning under the thorn bush. This was the most recent in a long string of failed relationships and crapulous episodes. Trey could always move on after these events, which occurred not only between him and his ex-lovers, but also with friends and coworkers. His ability to cut off any feelings and erase the person from his thoughts had served him well until now. These cutoffs started to pile up, and the accumulated experiences became a toxic pit of remorse. Trey began acting out in destructive ways, sabotaging relationships: big, small, professional, personal, erotic, and otherwise.

He thought a few trips to Dr. Kohen would make him as good as new. Now, many visits later, he knew the journey was going to be much longer. The regression work led him back to his earliest childhood memories. Along the way he relived the major events of his life, good and bad, trying to uncover the root cause of his relational retardation. His inability to empathize and love had brought him unhappiness, which he had buried in his subconscious for over thirty years. Hypnosis flung the root cellar door open, and Trey climbed down some rickety steps to find a dusty trove of memories, previously redacted, begging for analysis. Dr. Kohen was happy to accommodate him at $350 per hour.

The doctor had the body of a personal trainer and a nice natural rack that he estimated to be in the range of 34 C. An impressive ass and beautiful legs all fit nicely into a rather expensive business suit that complimented her petite frame. Her tortoiseshell glasses and deep brown eyes gave off an aura of authority and intelligence. Her black hair was on the verge of escaping from the barrette that held her locks in place. From his horizontal position on the couch, the musculature of her upper leg was exposed by a creeping hemline. The tops of her ample breasts were visible through a sheer white blouse, unbuttoned enough to permit her well-tanned traits to be viewed in a quasi-professional way. His obsession with boobs was a classic symptom of a bottle-fed male. His fixation with female breasts was borderline psychotic, but his admiration of Dr. Rachel Kohen's assets provided him with an additional enticement to keep coming back.

Trey's current life drama had drained him emotionally, intellectually, and physically. As he approached middle age, he had no prospects for a soul mate, family, or self-love. However, these sessions were giving him hope. Trey longed for the mature, rewarding relationships he had witnessed but never experienced. He needed to gut it out.

Under the doctor's spell during the previous hour, Trey had recalled his nanny robotically fulfilling daily chores. Changing, feeding, and playing became scheduled events, as were visits with his elderly grandparents. Once a day, after his bath, the nanny presented him for inspection in the drawing room during cocktail hour. His memory of those visits included an overwhelming smell of tobacco and distilled spirits accompanied by a total absence of intimacy.

"Trey, I think this was a breakthrough session." The doctor said, astonished at his ability to recall events from toddlerhood with such clarity. Dr. Cohen scribbled on her notepad, *Raised by subcontractors, hardwired to accept neglect.*

"I'm pretty screwed up, eh, doc?" Trey countered.

"I've seen worse, but that's not the challenge here. You have a long way to go to catch up with Danny Bonaduce and Tatum O'Neal, but your past is riddled with potholes, for sure. What we've accomplished over these last weeks will lead us to concrete answers about why you're rejecting companionship and may help us find some leads on your biological father."

In all the years since his father left, no one in Trey's family had ever spoken of him without prodding. His grandmother seemed terrified by the prospect of opening that chapter in their life all over again. If he pushed her too hard, it would trigger a weeklong fugue followed by hysterical acts of self-preservation, like drinking at nine a.m. and staying in bed for days. As a result, Trey's knowledge about his father came from meager bits of information shared by other relatives and a shoebox of pre-wedding love letters given to him by his grandmother.

"I'm also going to recommend you have a simple DNA test to determine your genetic family lineage. DNA is one tool available to find relatives in situations where the family is unable or unwilling to provide any help. Now that your grandparents are deceased, your options are limited, but DNA along with our regression work can open new doors. There's no guarantee, but I've seen families reunited as a result of these tests." She studied Trey's reaction, looking for a positive response.

Trey thought he would love to swap some DNA with this stunning, smart, single shrink. His DNA had been widely distributed throughout the boroughs of New York City, but none had ever been scientifically analyzed.

"Let's do it," responded Trey, willing to try almost anything at this point.

Chapter 2

Dr. Rachel Kohen, late for yoga class, hurried down Lexington Avenue to the studio. She had stayed after her session with Trey to call her brother, Ari, about setting up a DNA test. Ari had founded a genetic testing lab called Genoshalom Corporation. He, like Rachel, was a doctor of science. Ari had chosen the genome as his area of interest and quickly became a leading authority in the field of population genetics. This new discipline had emerged as a viable science only in the last six years. Deciphering the human genome made it possible to trace humans back thousands of years to a time before writing, agriculture, and domesticated animals. The test could confirm relationships to specific ethnic groups and assist in finding estranged relatives. Rachel set up an appointment for Trey to go in and get the requisite cheek swab later in the week.

As she pounded the pavement on her fifteen-minute walk to 65th Street, she reflected on her session with Trey. What an interesting and attractive man, but his life was a real mess. On one level she felt sorry for Trey; on another she knew him to be a successful investment banker who mingled with wealthy socialites and Ivy League sorostitutes now gracing the New York Times' Society Page. As one of the city's most eligible bachelors, he recently pulled in top dollar at a bachelor auction for AMS. It didn't hurt that he was 6' 2", 185 pounds, and fit as the day was long. She wondered... *how long?*

Rachel arrived at the yoga studio just as the class started. She did her warm-up routine and then joined in as the group moved from the opening Sun Salutation series to a Vinyasa flow. *Concentrate on your breathing,* she reminded herself. *Breathe through your nose, exhale loudly, push the air out, and breathe in, creating room to extend the stretch. Lose your mind to the rhythm of the breath…* His father had abandoned him before he was born. His mother had died during childbirth. His grandparents had raised him until he turned eighteen. He had attended Columbia University and gotten a job as a runner for Merrill Lynch at age twenty-two… *Breathe, Rachel. Concentrate on the pose, hold it, and now flow to the next…* He had passed the Series 7 securities exam, had become a broker by his twenties, had never been married, had never been in a relationship with a man (she hoped), and was not Jewish. Her religious upbringing dictated that she marry a Jew. The pressure was intense for her to find and couple with a man from one of Israel's tribes. Her brother, Ari, the family's relationship despot, was uncompromising in his belief that she had a responsibility to marry within the faith… *Let go of the stress, be one with your breath. Namaste.*

Trey's alarm clock beeped him awake at five a.m. His usual routine included a quick run in the park and a bowl of plain yogurt with granola, orange juice, and a handful of vitamins. He ate breakfast while he read "Heard on the Street." He showered, shaved, and dressed in time to be at the office by seven thirty. He was a creature of habit, some good, some bad, and some downright scary.

Trey was the king of his world once he crossed the threshold into the offices of Trilogica Asset Management, a company he founded after a career as a trader for a number of Wall Street firms. He had already tired of the hectic pace of the trading floor when his largest client approached him about starting their own firm. Trey would run the company and focus on finding, vetting, and investing in hedge funds on behalf of wealthy clients.

His patron provided the start-up capital and remained silent. They were 50/50 partners. Over the years Trilogica gained the reputation of being very shrewd. They never paid more than a 1 percent management fee, always negotiated a lower performance payment (never more than 12.5 percent), and refused to invest if there was a redemption charge. These managers were damn lucky he had called them; his clients were among the biggest, most successful and demanding investors on the planet. At present, Trilogica managed over five billion dollars for some of the world's most influential people. Trey's other job was to kiss their royal asses.

His assistant buzzed in, "Dr. Kohen is on the line for you. Do you want to take it?"

Trey picked up the phone, "Good morning, Doctor. How are you today?"

"Soaked to the bone. I forgot my umbrella, and I had to walk through a monsoon to get to the office."

Trey immediately thought about her drenched blouse and how it would provide a titillating vision of transparency. Thinking about it gave him a minor woody. He forced a picture of Rosy O'Donnell into his head; woody gone.

She continued, "I arranged an appointment at Genoshalom, my brother's company, for a DNA swabbing on Thursday morning at ten. Does that work for you?"

"Sounds good. Where do I go?" Trey asked.

"I'll pick you up in a Town Car outside your office at nine thirty, and we'll ride together. I thought we could take a tour of the laboratory. Ari is doing some innovative work with the genome. I guessed you might be interested," she said with reserved excitement.

"See you then," Trey responded and hung up. He looked at the phone for a lingering second, pondering the meaning of the call, the appointment, and his feelings for this woman.

Chapter 3

Aaron "Ari" Kohen, PhD, graduated from the Rabbinical School of Israel with a fervent passion to return his faith to a proper position of authority in the Middle East. His ultra-Orthodox views were often at odds with those of his classmates and teachers. Frustration with modern Judaism caused Ari to leave the clergy and pursue a life of science. After departing Israel he came to the United States and began his studies in the field of genetics at MIT, where he earned his reputation as a star student and innovative thinker.

During his time at the university, he discovered he was a direct descendent of Aaron, older brother of Moses, who had been chosen by God to be the *Kohen Gadol,* or high priest of the Tabernacle the Jews carried through the wilderness. No wonder he felt so strongly about his Jewishness and the role of Jews in the modern world. Ari's DNA confirmed an unbroken genetic link to the first high priest of the Jewish people, a patrilineal connection spanning over 3,300 years and 106 generations. He, Aaron Eshkol Kohen, was clearly entitled to the job as high priest.

After graduating with honors from MIT, Ari moved to New York to begin his career as a geneticist for a research company. Each Friday at sundown he observed the Sabbath in traditional fashion. One winter Friday in 2001, Ari joined a couple at their Manhattan apartment for a customary Sabbath dinner. They had befriended Ari, the young rabbi/scientist, at the synagogue a few months prior. Moshe Stein and his wife, Ziva, practiced a form of Judaism similar to Ari's. Moshe was much older than Ari and could have been Ziva's father by the looks of him.

They finished the meal, and Moshe got right to the issue that had inspired the dinner invitation. Knowing he was an ordained rabbi and his connection to ancient Aaron, Moshe thought that Ari could help him with a personal problem. In the Jewish faith, having a son was the most important milestone for a man. It assured the continuation of the family line and provided security in old age. Moshe launched into an attack on his wife for her failure to bear him children. Ari was surprised and dumbfounded as his host condemned her in an unrelenting fashion. Ziva sat calmly at the table as her husband catalogued her failings.

"She is a barren bitch, Ari. Look at her; she can't even make a decent brisket. Her oven is defective; there is no more time to waste. And look, she only has one leg." Moshe lifted the tablecloth exposing the crude prosthetic leg that hung beneath the hemline of Ziva's dress. It was an ugly flesh colored appendage that bore no resemblance to a human limb; it was a facsimile of a leg. "Not only is she incapable of bearing me a child, she's a cripple."

Moshe Stein had become rich in the South African diamond trade, and he could not be bothered with those who disagreed with him. His wife was a raven-haired beauty with deep brown eyes that evidenced the pain of the false accusation and reference to her disability.

"Please, Moshe, don't insult our faith and your wife. I'm sure there's a reason for her infertility. Remarkable advances have been made in the reproductive sciences in the last few years. I can suggest a clinic if you're interested," responded Ari, hoping to put the conversation on course to a solution.

Moshe had selected Ziva as his future bride when she was sixteen, arranging it with her father. This was the same father who had caused Ziva to lose her leg. As a rebellious fourteen-year old, Ziva had been caught in the arms of a Gentile boy. Her father had lashed her repeatedly with a *shebet* until open wounds appeared on her lower leg. These gashes went untreated, became gangrenous and had resulted in the amputation of her left leg below the knee. The fake leg did not concern Moshe. In fact, it became a symbol of her obedience to the men in her life. He needed a young baby-maker, not a dance partner.

When Ziva turned eighteen she and Moshe were wed in a traditional Hasidic ceremony. The arranged marriage was a loveless pairing. Ziva was raped countless times at the hands of her much older husband. Some of the sexual encounters were so violent she had suffered internal damage, which likely contributed to her inability to have children.

"I'm not interested in wasting any more of my time trying to fix her. Her infertility is the result of her unfaithfulness to our marriage. It is God's way of cursing me for her actions. I know she has lain with another man. So now must I pay the ultimate price: life without a son?"

Getting more animated, Moshe was pulling at straws seeking to justify his position. With no witnesses to the fictitious acts of extramarital fornication, Moshe was left with Ari as his last hope to jettison this dry well of a woman and start a family with a new wife.

"As a rabbi, I suggest you seek counseling for your marital problems. You can work things out if you give them a chance," offered Ari, in hopes Moshe would agree.

"Better yet, as a rabbi you can tell me it is all right to rid myself of her because she is an adulteress. Then I will go about my business of finding someone who can give me the son I desperately need." Moshe was now pressuring Ari to agree with his findings and give him the religious cover he needed to dump his wife. He wanted Ari to adjudge Ziva guilty of an extramarital affair so he could trade her in for a new one.

Ziva, who had remained silent throughout the entire exchange, spoke up. "I've never been unfaithful to our marriage, or our religion."

With no forewarning, Moshe struck Ziva in the face with the back of his hand, causing her to fall back in her chair and crash to the floor. Ari reacted instantly. He reached across the corner of the table and grabbed the pathetic Jew by the throat. Gasping for air, the diamond merchant tried unsuccessfully to break Ari's hold.

Moshe managed to enunciate a few words even as his Adam's apple was restricted by Ari's grip. "You're no rabbi. You're a fake and a charlatan."

Hearing those words caused Ari to pass to the darkest side of his being. Still holding Moshe around the neck, Ari pushed him, sending them both crashing to the floor. Ari straddled the struggling wife-beater as he contemplated his next move. He had insulted the good name of his wife by fabricating her infidelity, and he had impugned Ari's priestly qualifications.

Once Moshe regained some composure, he realized he was not in charge. Ari decided to let this despicable man humiliate himself. "Why are you doing this? She is the one. Please, I don't understand. I am sorry I hit her. I won't do it again. Just let me go, and we will forget this ever happened. I beg you."

The begging only fueled Ari's fury. Signs of weakness from men who supposedly upheld his faith repulsed him. With Moshe's neck firmly in hand, Ari lifted his head off the floor and smacked it down with the force of a sledgehammer. The exploding thud of Moshe's skull shattering was confirmation that he was dead.

Ziva observed the proceedings through splayed fingers covering her tear-stained face.

Ari turned to her and asked, "Are you all right?"

"Yes, I think so. Is he gone?" she said, hoping that he was.

Ari was surprised at how killing Moshe Stein excited him. His relationship with this woman was instantly galvanized by her relief at the death of her husband and Ari's pleasure in doing the deed. Ari was her hero.

"We need to get him out of here, now. How can I access the basement?" asked Ari.

"It's just four floors below us, and the stairs are outside the door to the apartment," Ziva replied.

Ari wrapped Moshe in a blanket he snatched from the couch. He found his way to the stairwell. Dragging the lifeless body down to the basement, he prayed no one would appear on the stairway, or he would have to kill them too. He was sure that one hundred percent of the building's residents were orthodox Jews and faithfully observing the Sabbath at home. He also knew all of these old buildings were water heated and had a furnace. What he found when he arrived in the boiler room was even better. Most furnaces in New York had been converted from coal to oil or gas. This one was still coal fired.

Ari opened the door of the furnace causing the walls of the basement to take on the rich orange glow of the contained inferno. He lifted the blanket-wrapped human off the floor and fed Moshe into the furnace headfirst. One last push assured the flames would consume the body. Moshe Stein was gone, and Ari was never more alive.

He returned to the apartment and immediately began spelling out what must happen for them to escape blame for Moshe's disappearance. They made plans to meet in one week, knowing phone calls could incriminate them. The thought of seeing Ziva again without her husband excited Ari. He wanted to know her better, and now he would get his chance.

He asked Ziva to repeat his instructions before he left. "Wait for his family and business partners to start calling on Monday morning when he doesn't show up for work. Tell them he went to visit a friend in Connecticut on Sunday and never returned. Say I assumed he went straight to the office on Monday, as he often does."

"Perfect. If you stick to the story, no one will suspect a thing. I'll see you in a week." Ari turned to leave, and Ziva rushed to block his path to the door.

"I…I can't thank you enough for what you've done. I know it sounds strange I'm thanking you for killing my husband, but it is such a relief." She threw her arms around Ari's neck and gave him a big kiss on the lips. He reciprocated, exploring her mouth with his tongue. Ari could taste and smell the beauty of this woman even under such traumatic circumstances. He held her tightly. As co-conspirators in the death of a prominent New York Jew, a silent oath of loyalty bound them never to speak of this incident again. They didn't.

Rachel and Trey entered the Genoshalom building, a new glass and steel structure just off the Long Island Freeway in Levittown that had opened in 2009. A huge, flat-screen monitor displaying a map of the world with numerous colored lines and dots, all emanating from East Africa and eventually circling the globe, dominated the lobby.

A woman approached them from a wall that did not appear to contain an opening. On second inspection, Trey noticed an electronic pocket door disappearing into the adjacent wall structure, leaving no cracks or seams.

"Hello, I'm Ziva Wolfson, Dr. Kohen's assistant. Please follow me. I'll take you to the meeting room."

She led them back through the hidden door to a corridor open to huge skylights at least forty feet above. The hall ended at a set of double doors. Trey was having a momentary sensory overload when the doors slid into the wall revealing a glistening glass conference table encircled by leather chairs.

"Ms. Kohen, would you mind waiting for Dr. Kohen while I escort Mr. Cowens to the lab for a DNA swab? It'll only take about fifteen minutes, and I'll return him for your meeting."

"I'm *Dr.* Kohen also," replied Rachel with an emphasis on *doctor*. "And I would love a black coffee while I wait."

Ziva and Trey departed the same way they had come in, with Trey feeling like he was going to meet the Chairman Mao. This place was amazing, and he was anxious to find out what they did.

Ziva led Trey to an area of the building with more traditional doors and ceilings. Following behind, Trey did a quick ass-check, a perfect ten, made even more interesting by a slight but noticeable limp. She knocked on a door with a sign that said "Sampling." They entered a windowless room that was very similar to a doctor's examination room. Ziva excused herself after telling him to sit on the table and that someone would be right in. He wanted to ask her to join him, but dismissed the thought as stupid. What was it about Jewish women that flipped his switch? Was it their cool intelligence, their dark hair, or simply the fact that most Gentiles didn't stand a chance with these mysterious maidens? Smitten again by the Hebrew gene and what appeared to be a very fit and self-assured woman who had absolutely no interest in him.

A knock on the door was immediately followed by a man entering without waiting for a response. He was an obese gentleman wearing a lab coat that was too tight for his massive frame. He approached Trey with his hand extended.

"Mr. Cowens, welcome to Genoshalom Corporation. My name is Malachi Pinsky, and I'll be taking your DNA sample today." They shook hands, and Malachi reached for a pair of latex-free surgical gloves. He opened a cabinet door and removed two sterile packages, each containing a miniature toothbrush in a vial of clear solution. He asked Trey to open his mouth and proceeded to vigorously scrape the inside of both cheeks. Trey could see that the brush had become discolored with his blood. The lab tech repeated the procedure with the other brush and returned both samples to their individual vials.

"Don't be alarmed by the blood. It's a natural occurrence inside the mouth, much like a vigorous flossing of your teeth that causes momentary bleeding. It has already stopped." Malachi offered a salutation and departed. Trey waited in the examination room, grateful the DNA sampling procedure did not include him squirting his man juice in a cup. If Ziva had stuck around, he would have gladly provided her with a sample.

Just as these thoughts were crossing his mind, there was another knock, the door opened, and the woman in question stood in the doorway. With a serious look, almost like she had been reading Trey's mind, she motioned for him to follow her back to the conference room. Trey sensed a definite attitude coming from her but shrugged it off as being businesslike and professional. Maybe he was reading too much into the vibe of this whole place, but he felt like a lamb among wolves.

Rachel and Ari sat at the head of the large conference table. Ari stood up as Trey entered the room. Ziva left without a word as Ari came around the table and walked toward Trey. Rachel offered a formal introduction, "Trey Cowens, I'd like you to meet my brother, Dr. Ari Kohen. He runs this creepy place."

"Thanks for the sarcasm, Sis. Our guest doesn't need his head filled with your childish views about what I do. She thinks my work with the genome took me away from my true calling as a rabbi." Rachel did not know of his plan to become the high priest of the Temple. For now it had to be that way.

Ari went on. "Here at Genoshalom, we do a broad range of genetic tests related to the diagnosis of inherited diseases. We can also verify paternity to determine the genetic father of an estranged child. Our proprietary ancestry test lets us look back thousands of years thereby connecting each of us with a lost cultural and ethnic past. It can also be useful for the verification of other living relatives besides parents."

Ari wore a crisp white lab coat with his name in script on the breast pocket. His eyes were so brown they appeared black, and his hair was short cropped in an athletic style. He spoke in a quiet, self-assured monotone and made intense eye contact. His piercing gaze was unsettling.

Ari continued to talk as Trey sized him up across the table. "The biochemical tests we use to determine the presence of genetic diseases are cutting edge. We're one of only three laboratories in the world to utilize a method called *histone methylation,* a process that chemically modifies DNA so we can identify which proteins regulate gene behavior. Acting as the body's light switch, these proteins can be turned on and off allowing researchers to experiment with the mechanisms that control human gene expression. Identifying a disease's location at a genetic level reveals the specific biological malfunction and suggests a therapeutic intervention. We are on the verge of major breakthroughs in our understanding of inherited medical conditions and cures for diseases caused by the environment."

Trey considered himself bright, and he always had an interest in science, but this was so far over his head.

Spontaneously Trey said, "Have you ever done any work for the Maury Povich Show? You know, the baby-daddy program where they drag upset people on TV who are stuck in terrible relationships to see if their DNA proves they fathered some child?"

A lingering pause followed the question, as Ari thought, *I should string this fucking Gentile up by his nuts for denigrating my work.* He swallowed the anger, never showing a clue he was upset, and said, "Why no, we've never done any work for Mr. Povich. We'll have to look into that." Pleased that he had masked his annoyance, Ari reached under the table and pushed a button that raised a flat screen TV displaying 3-D images of DNA strands. Pointing at the screen, he began his presentation.

"The human genome is believed to contain twenty to twenty-five thousand genes. Each person carries two copies of every gene, one inherited from the father and the other from the mother. And this is where Genoshalom is doing its most exciting work. It is a new area of genetic investigation called *Deep Ancestry.* Through genetic testing, we can determine from which ethnic and cultural group each individual descended. We go back thousands of years and pinpoint where your forefathers lived, worked, procreated, hunted, farmed, and died.

"About sixty thousand years ago, all of our ancestors left Africa on a quest that eventually populated the world. Each of these individuals, believed to be as few as one hundred people at the time of the migration, is a genetic relative of someone living on the planet today. And yes, we were all once black. Everyone living today in the world descended from a black African woman and man."

As a scientist/rabbi, Ari's "enlightened" Jewish orthodoxy allowed him to believe in the science of genetics while at the same time maintaining his faith in God. Noah and the flood were nice stories, but science trumped allegory in this case. Ari was skilled at redesigning his religious views to accommodate his personal worldview, one where he was above everyone else except God.

He went on to explain Trey's DNA test would uncover his deep ancestry and provide him with a way to scientifically confirm any traditional ancestral research he might conduct. Now Trey's head was really spinning.

"For example, my DNA confirms a direct relationship to Aaron, brother of Moses, the first high priest of the Israelites. The DNA test determined that over the last three thousand years the Kohen's passed down their genetic material to the current generation. Jews always valued marrying within the faith. Marital fidelity is the highest among all known groups in the world at 90 percent, meaning that Jews marry Jews and stay married to them until death. It is this unbroken family chain that enables genetic scientists to tell us definitively where we came from and who we're related to."

Here we go again, Rachel thought. *He's trying to lecture me on the need to marry a Jew, to maintain the purity of the ancestral line.* She hoped Trey was not too put off by his comment.

"I have to go to a meeting now," Ari said unapologetically as he stood to signal the end of the presentation. The door opened right on cue, and Ziva appeared in the hallway. Ari shook Trey's hand, kissed his sister on the cheek, and left the room.

Ziva motioned for Rachel and Trey to follow her back the way they had come in. She led them through the reception area to the front door. With a stern good-bye, she turned and departed. Trey experienced an unexpected sense of relief once he was able to take his first full breath of outdoor air. There was definitely an unusual energy in that place. Rachel wondered why she never got the coffee she had requested from Ziva.

Chapter 4

Trey waited for Dr. Rachel Kohen in one of her session rooms. As instructed during the previous appointment, Trey brought the box of his parent's love letters given to him by his grandmother just before her recent passing. Trey avoided reading them until now for fear of what he might find. Rachel convinced him it would be constructive if they reviewed the letters together.

"Good day, Mr. Cowens," said Rachel as she breezed into the room looking as beautiful as ever. "You brought the letters; let me have a look."

Trey handed the tattered box to the doctor who lifted the lid and emptied its contents onto a round table next to the couch. Careful not to tear any of the delicate documents, she arranged the letters in chronological order from the date stamps on the envelopes. The oldest and most frayed envelope contained a wedding invitation addressed to Mary Louise Stuart inviting her to attend the marriage of James Dalton Campbell and Jeannie MacArthur Raymond in Washington, D.C., on Saturday, June 6, 1970.

"I assume this is your mother's handwriting," referring to the scribble on the back of the invitation.

Trey took a seat at the table next to Rachel and said, "Yes, I think it's hers. What does it say?"

"She wrote William Cowens and a phone number with a 202 area code, which I believe is Washington, D.C.," responded Rachel, hoping to stimulate his interest in the investigation. He appeared more vulnerable than usual on this day and for good reason; they would be lending a voice to his absent parents.

Trey and Rachel took turns reading the love letters in order. She read aloud the ones written by Mary while Trey spoke his father's words. The story of their early courtship and eventual marriage came to life in Rachel's office.

William Joseph Cowens graduated from the McDonough School of Business at Georgetown University on May 1, 1970. A month after graduation, Willy attended the wedding of a Georgetown classmate named James Campbell. At the reception, he met Mary Stuart, an upstate New York debutante attending the nuptials with her brother. Mary had completed her studies in theater and music at the Julliard School in Manhattan the year before. An amazing actress, singer, and musician, Mary also had a gift for writing. Willy was immediately attracted to this beautiful and talented young woman.

During the reception, Mary was at the piano leading a sing-along of popular music and some oldies. A large crowd formed around her as she sang a rendition of "Build Me Up, Buttercup." The alcohol-loosened gathering contributed a cacophonous refrain with the words they knew, basically the chorus. Once the noise subsided, Willy chimed in with a request for Gilbert and Sullivan. Mary and Willy became attached at the hip on the piano bench for the remainder of the evening.

The duo went their separate ways after the wedding, but the memory of the weekend planted a seed of interest in both of their hearts. Eventually, Willy made a call to the New York City flat Mary shared with another Julliard graduate. She was busy as the stage manager for her uncle, Frank Stuart, an accomplished Broadway actor. He was appearing in Neil Simon's *Prisoner of Second Avenue* at the Eugene O'Neill Theater on West 49th Street. Willy had called unexpectedly, and it excited Mary. They planned to meet the following Friday at the theater.

Willy arrived in New York by train from Washington at around six p.m. Curtain was at seven thirty sharp. He went to will call and picked up the complimentary ticket Mary had left for him. They had agreed on the phone to meet at Sardi's on West 44th after the show. Willy found his seat along the right-hand side of the main floor and witnessed an amazing performance by Mary's uncle Frank. He expertly played Mel Edison, the out-of-work, nervous, broken-down New Yorker who is eventually conjured back to reality by his family and loving wife, Edna, during a summer of discontent.

The show concluded with the crowd standing and saluting the amazing cast with a lengthy ovation. Willy filed out with the other theatergoers and made his way to Sardi's around the corner. The maître d' greeted him immediately and led him to a booth in the back of the restaurant. His drink came, and he waited for Mary, taking in the multitude of movie star caricatures on the walls. Lost in a meditation on Jimmy Durante's nose, Mary's sudden appearance surprised Willy. Brimming with post-show adrenaline, Mary planted a quick kiss on his cheek and inquired whether he liked the show. Delighted by how forward she was being, he put on his best Irish response by taking a swig of his drink and offering her a wonderful review.

After Willy's complimentary critique, Mary continued, "Isn't Uncle Frank just marvelous in the role of Mel Edison? I'm so proud of him. You know he's nominated for a Tony Award, and he just might win one this year." She was nervous, making some small talk to calm herself.

"I loved the whole play. Thank you for inviting me." Willy flagged the waiter and they ordered a late dinner.

Mary and Willy enjoyed a meal of oysters and Dover sole washed down with Bombay martinis. They shared alcohol-inspired kisses on the subway ride from the restaurant. Those kisses turned into passionate petting on the living room couch back at Mary's apartment.

Mary Louise Stuart and William Joseph Cowens were married the following April in a large Catholic wedding in Buffalo, New York. The Stuart family owned and operated the Carborundum Corporation, a prominent local manufacturer. Willy accepted a job in the sales and marketing department at the company. The young couple bought a house not far from Mary's parents. They settled down with plans to start a family.

Reading the letters aloud for the first time was emotional for Trey, but gave him the ability to create a mental picture of his parent's relationship that transcended the written words. Rachel could sense his vulnerability as she returned the correspondence to the box and shut the lid.

"What an amazing love story," she said after a moment of reflection.

"I guess they were in love, but that makes it harder to understand why he left," said Trey, trying to reconcile the letters with the reality of his early childhood.

"Only your father knows why he left. One day, if you find him, he'll tell you the whole story. I'm just happy you have these letters, because they demonstrate an honest, loving connection between your parents. Every child wants the comfort of knowing his mother and father loved each other, clearly yours did," Rachel concluded, trying to focus on the positives while bringing the session to an end.

Chapter 5

A simple e-mail from Genoshalom directed Trey to a website where he found the results of his mtDNA test tracing his mother's, mother's, mother's direct maternal line without any influence from husbands. His options for matching his traditional genealogical research with a DNA sample were greatest on his mother's side. It annoyed him that her relatives clammed up with any mention of his father. Numerous skeletons must inhabit the old family closet, or at least some gruesome crime photos, judging by the stonewalling he encountered.

Hopes of discovering family members on his mother's side were rewarded with some basic research on the Internet. He traced her family line back to Ireland. No surprise. He had classic Irish traits and facial structure, not to mention love of drink, song, and laughter.

With a DNA test kit number and a temporary password, he logged on to the Genoshalom website and his own personal webpage. A chaotic mass of information appeared before him containing complex numbers and cryptic abbreviations. Understanding the results of the genetic test would require a major commitment.

He found an explanation of his mtDNA test through a link along the left hand toolbar that took him to information about his *haplogroup*. He learned that haplogroup is a name used to signify your mother's or father's genetic family. Haplogroups could be traced all the way back 120,000 years to Africa and a common female ancestor called Mitochondrial Eve. Her line led to ground zero for the earth's entire population. Along the way, one of Mitochondrial Eve's female descendents met a man called Y-DNA Adam. That became the marriage of genetic Adam and Eve. According to the web page, their offspring survived a migration out of Africa sixty thousand years ago.

We are all descended from a black couple in Africa. Take that Mr. Grand Dragon of the KKK. You were once a black man, Trey thought with a grin.

He dug deeper. A link called "Test Results" led him to specific information about his genetic family's migration route. He was part of Haplogroup J. He knew his most recent ancestors lived in Ireland and kept digging.

A vast majority of Europeans descended from one of seven women often referred to as the Seven Daughters of Eve, six of them born in Europe, and one in modern day Syria. The population genetics community calls her Jasmine (J), reflecting her Middle Eastern roots. Her genetic heirs brought farming and agricultural knowhow to the hunter-gatherer communities of Europe during the Neolithic or New Stone Age period. No wonder he liked to garden and grow things.

Haplogroups, a general designation, can be broken into haplotypes, or what some refer to as haploclans. Trey's mtDNA test further broke his J classification into a clan referred to as J1c1. Jasmine and her family of farmers left the Fertile Crescent in the Middle East ten thousand years ago and eventually found their way to the coast of Norway, boarded ships, and sailed to Scotland. Now he was getting somewhere, because the genetic line found its way to Northern Ireland from Scotland by crossing the Ulster Sea. This was Trey's genetic family. He didn't mind the wind, rain, and cold. He loved to fish, hunt, and hike. Could those traits and preferences be transferred in DNA?

The moment of truth arrived. The next option for drilling down into the mtDNA results was to look for a specific match. He held his breath as he clicked on the link labeled "Matches." The web page loaded slowly, indicating a large amount of data transferring to the screen. A list of names and their country of residence appeared. His eyes immediately went to the surname Tone, his grandmother's maiden name. He clicked on the name, and a complete family tree appeared before him.

With each click, Trey refined his electronic journey. He discovered a link between a person his mtDNA matched and the name Tone. Her name was Grace Kinney from Dublin and her e-mail address appeared under the section for "Exact Matches."

He clicked on the electronic address, and his e-mail program loaded it into the "Send To" field, another decisive moment. Should he send her an e-mail indicating his findings and request information about her family genealogy? Trey always had the courage to execute a stock trade when things on the floor of the exchange were the craziest. Outside the workplace, when it came to matters of family, he normally froze.

Trey was in Rachel Kohen's office lying on the couch when she came in. She asked him to get up and join her at the conference table in an adjacent area separated by floor to ceiling glass. They had never used the table. She offered him something to drink. He declined, not wanting to interrupt the flow of a session headed in a new direction.

Rachel took a seat at the head of the table and started, "Trey, I think this concludes our work together. You've had over twenty sessions during the course of your treatment, and we've made some interesting discoveries about your past. The regression work was remarkable, because men rarely have the ability to recall past experiences in such graphic detail. The transcripts of the sessions make up part of your patient dossier. These, along with my comments, will assist you in understanding how those experiences play a role in your adult behavior patterns." She pushed a thick bound document across the shiny conference table.

Trey didn't move to pick up the opus. He stared at Rachel, not sure if he was happy, sad, or indifferent at being told they would not be continuing. "That's it? No more sessions? No more prying into every single emotionally traumatic experience in my life? No more lectures on intimacy, commitment, and being an only child? No more discussions of abandonment, alcoholism, and drug addiction? What will I do for entertainment?"

"You're ready to find out who you are; don't accept who you've become. Seek out specifics about the past you've avoided until now. The work we've done, along with the DNA results, will give you a starting point. I can refer you to psychiatric generalist if you want to keep seeing someone. I specialize in regression therapy and the hypnotic sciences; I've done all I can professionally to help you find your way. Unless you want me to keep charging you $350 an hour for no good reason, it's time for you to move forward on your own. You can always contact me if you like."

Trey thought for a second and asked, "How about personally? If our professional relationship is over, how about having dinner with me?"

"Trey, I can't. I've been treating you as a patient for some time, and it would be a breach of ethics if I saw you socially."

"Come on, Doctor. What would be wrong with a simple dinner, and then we could see where it goes from there?" Trey submitted with the look of a sick puppy.

"Alright. If after six months you still want to take me to dinner, give me a call," she said sternly, but with a wry smile.

Not totally discouraged, Trey thought, *Why is it that men always have to put themselves out there first? Women act as if they're not as interested as the man; that's bullshit. She wants it as badly as I do; and furthermore, she breached the whole professional ethic thing by taking me to meet her brother. But I'll play along.*

"I guess I should be thankful you didn't say no. Based on my screwed up life, I wouldn't be surprised if you called building security," said Trey, trying to relieve any tension.

If he only knew the sick morons she saw every day. His life was worth saving. Many of the other schmucks should be euthanized.

Her attraction to him was real; she worried he would not call in six months. She couldn't take the chance of polluting her practice by jumping in bed with a patient the day after she terminated their sessions. She would stick to her guns and run the risk.

Trey grabbed the file, stood up, and approached Rachel's end of the table. He extended his hand and gave her a big smile, thanking her for all of her help. As their hands touched, a prickling sensation told him he would indeed be calling in six months. He hoped she would be available.

After Trey's departure, Rachel sat back down at the lightly used table to contemplate what just happened. She sensed darker places in Trey's life she had not explored; contrarily, her interest in him increased. He probably wouldn't call. It would be for the best, considering Ari would never approve of their relationship.

Chapter 6

Trey woke to the howl of the wind blowing over the slate roof of his cottage. The symphony of morning sounds included the wind's gale, the baa-baa of sheep, the tinkle of their bells, and a rooster's crow thrown in here and there. He was no longer in New York. The sounds of spring came from the Irish countryside. He had been there for almost a month, but every sunrise was a surprise as he got up and remembered, like Dorothy, that Oz was nothing like Kansas. He threw off his sheets and pivoted his feet to the stone floor. The chill of a new day reminded him he would have to get some throw rugs. He wrapped himself in a large, stretchy wool blanket and slipped on Crocs for his shuffle to the kitchen. Strong coffee and a fire were the rule of each morning. A brief meditation reading from a book of proverbs, given to him by Rachel, completed the ritual.

Trey had negotiated a leave of absence from Trilogica. His partners were supportive of his decision to go. Undeniably at a breaking point, Trey needed to sort his personal problems and return to work with a new enthusiasm. He would continue to receive his full partner share each quarter, and they expected him to return for the annual partners meeting each November.

Thinking of his New York life, a flashback invaded his tranquility. The night of his blackout had been appearing to him like scenes in a movie, each one more graphic than the one before.

He remembered the pain of the ridiculous tattoo on his butt. He ignored the other tragedy between his ass cheeks. Something terribly wrong had gone on back there, and he did not want to know what. He flashed on a feeling of someone pressing down on him in an unnatural way. The smell of alcohol, a putrid human odor, and a well-fertilized lawn came back to him in a rage of recollection. Why was he face down in the grass? Was his mind making this shit up to fill vacant memories of that night?

County Donegal in Northwest Ireland is the most rugged and isolated part of the country. The Gaelic language and Irish culture thrive in its towns and cities. Trey found a traditional Irish experience in the hills of Donegal. He had come to Ireland three and a half weeks earlier. Through his communication with Grace Kinney in Dublin, he had determined his mother's paternal ancestry led back to a famous Irishman named Theobald Wolfe Tone. He founded the Society of United Irishmen in 1791; the formation of this revolutionary group marked the beginning of the end of English rule over all of Ireland. Changes in leadership, name, and purpose over the decades eventually led to what is today the modern Irish Republican movement.

From this thread, Trey had pieced together enough information about his mother's family to convince him that Ireland was where he should go. He leased a cottage in the countryside not far from Letterkenny. The stone structure sat on fourteen acres of rolling hills. Built in the late eighteenth century, the house had two bedrooms, two baths, an open living area, kitchen, and dining area dominated by a large hearth. At this elevation, the town lay out before him in the morning sun, and the glistening bay beyond reflected a diamond-like image back to his doorstep.

He was meeting with local historian and genealogist Seamus O'Neil, who planned to accompany Trey to Dublin. They met at the quay in Letterkenny where they boarded a floatplane to the Irish capital, about a one-hour plane ride away. Only half full, the twenty-passenger DeHavilland Twin Otter taxied from the dock and turned into the wind. After taking off to the north, the plane made a steep banking turn to the southeast on a heading for

Dublin. The blue water of the bay gave way to the vibrant emerald green of the countryside. Flying at a low altitude, they could see herds of sheep sauntering along the road to their morning grazing pastures. Miles of ancient stone walls separated family properties. On this day, with the help of Mr. O'Neil, Trey would immerse himself in all things Wolfe Tone.

October 12, 1798, Wolfe Tone was aboard the *Hoche*, a French warship that made its way from France to the entrance of Lough Swilly on the coast of Northern Ireland. The voyage had cost the fleet several ships; the British captured many, and others were lost to the sea in a terrible storm. Five thousand French soldiers planned to enter the north of the country where they counted on the support of thirty thousand Irish dissenters. Theobald Wolfe Tone recounted the fateful invasion from his prison cell in Dublin:

> *We had been at sea for twenty days after leaving France. Our ship evaded the British blockade, which along with the weather reduced our fleet by half. The seas were rough on the journey to the north of Ireland. We arrived at the mouth of Lough Swilly accompanied by three French warships, the Loire, the Resolue, and the Biche, with too few men and arms to execute the plan of invasion.*
>
> *So what has become of our effort? What I have given to the cause of Irish independence cannot be measured in mortal terms, but my suffering is minor compared to the wretched existence imposed on three million Irish who persist under the yoke of an oppressive English authority. I left my family in the safety of the United States and returned to France to press the French Directory on a plan to invade Ireland. It has been over four years, and through one failed expedition after another, until that fateful day on Lough Swilly; I have lived as a beggar, an Adjunct General in*

the French armed forces, and now I am a prisoner in the country of my birth. I single-mindedly pursued this cause on behalf of the Irish people at a cost to my family greater than I ever could have imagined.

My wife, Matilda, and children have been forced to live off the charity of friends and fellow Irish immigrants in Princeton, New Jersey. I subjected them to a life in America where the reasonable thinking of civilized men has been suspended, and the greed of an emerging free market democracy has caused them to value money over life and respect for their fellow countrymen. My guilt is increased with the knowledge that Irish in America are regarded as second-class citizens, and my family must bear that indignity because of my decisions. Matilda has never complained, nor has she wept in my presence. She has only encouraged me to follow my heart and pursue a course of action defined by my commitment to Irish independence. How can I be a good father, husband, and provider while at the same time fulfilling my destiny to bring an end to British rule over the land of my ancestors? This is my greatest sorrow.

News of our arrival reached the British. Three English warships and a frigate were spotted by our sentry boat, which rushed back to the Hoche with the report. These four sails and most likely others would bear down on us in a matter of hours before we could disembark our ships.

Another invasion foiled? Less than two years before, winter weather thwarted our expedition to Bantry Bay in the south of Ireland. The day after Christmas in 1796, we pulled anchor and sailed away from the coast of County Cork, Ireland, without setting foot on land because of gale-force winds and violent seas. Seeing the lights of the seaside cottages and village wharf disappear as we left is my second greatest sorrow. The sacrifice of my service to the Irish cause can be counted in years of passionate hatred for the British, the source of all things evil in Ireland; a just cause for an investment of my years.

I heard the men preparing for the attack. Their boots shuffled along the deck above as they rolled munitions to there standards in preparation for the fight that would follow within the hour. I donned the uniform of my adopted country and accepted the challenge of the British onslaught with the dignity I have always shown in the face of danger. A call from the crow's nest confirmed the British had discovered our presence, bearing down on us under a favorable wind.

A knock at my cabin door alerted me to the impending confrontation. The admiral's aide came to beseech me to leave the Hoche and board the Biche, which was preparing to flee the British and return to France with news on the attack and its likely outcome. He encouraged me to go, because he feared if I were captured, I would be tried as a traitor, not a prisoner of war, and be hung and disemboweled for an act of treason. This was a likely outcome, but I didn't fear whatever sentence they might decide. My motives were pure, my cause just, and the outcome was not for me to choose. Further, I refused to leave the French to fight the battle for Ireland without me; it was my cause and passion that led us to this moment.

As the men of the Hoche prepared for battle, I left my cabin and emerged on deck as member of the French Navy. Stepping on deck for the first time in a day, I saw things were very different, a taste of fear and impending doom in the air. The British were excellent warriors on the water. The French are passionate, and what they lack in bravery, they make up with vanity; it just looks bad to lose. I took my position at the port side battery, which included three cannons—two eleven-pounders and one fifteen—and ten seamen. If we had been on land, I fear our ranks would have been depleted greatly by desertion, but the French are not natural swimmers.

The British attacked with the full force of their armaments and inflicted heavy damage on all three French ships. The Biche had fled to sea. We returned fire from our cannons, some of the rounds finding the hulls of the attacking ships, others falling harmlessly into the sea. I beseeched the men to fight harder, to send more rounds, to shoot with accuracy. The British fleet encircled us, and their measured blows landed in chaotic blasts on the decks of the ships. We retreated to shallow water to defend our position. Within six hours the Hoche had been demasted and floated aimlessly near the bay's coast. The Loire and the Resolue were barely visible through the smoke that attached itself to the morning fog causing the rising sun to cast a rose color over the entire bay of the battle. The other two boats also lost their sea legs and drifted toward shore under the prevailing northern breeze.

I could not imagine a positive outcome, but I had to fight on. In a final effort, and with little regard for my own life, I ordered the men to attach their bayonets and prepare to defend the ship from the approaching British. Soldiers populated the entire starboard battery of one ship; its size dwarfed ours, and the number of their men was four times our count. Our cause was honorable, but little could come of a defense at that point other than inflicting more death upon our soldiers. The admiral made the decision for me by ordering all of the men to lay down their arms.

Once aboard, the British secured all the guns and munitions. They ordered us into the ship's hold and locked below deck for the better part of a day while they towed us into port. Upon landing, we were marched to Letterkenny and placed in the courthouse jail, pending our final disposition. The next day all of the officers were transported to Lord Cavan's castle in nearby County Derry for a luncheon with local British magistrates. As prisoners of war, the officers were accorded the respect of our British peers and treated with the dignity deserving of military men. The reason for this lunch was more nefarious. The British had been advised through their spies in Paris that I was aboard one of the French warships and must be found and brought to trial as a traitor in Dublin.

The luncheon began, and I sat with the French officers at Lord Cavan's table. In the uniform of the French Navy, there was nothing remarkable about my appearance. I pretended not to know the language of my captors, and the lunch passed without incident until the door opened and in came Sir George Hill. Sir George, a former classmate at Trinity College, was familiar with my politics and me. Lord Cavanaugh in Dublin sent him to determine if I was part of the captured group, he immediately recognized me.

"Mr. Tone, I am so happy to see you," Sir George said.

I rose from my seat at the table, extended my hand in friendship, and looking him straight in the eye, I responded, "Sir George, I am so happy to see you too. How are Lady Hill and your family?" They removed me from the dining room and escorted me to an adjacent area where I was placed in leg and hand irons for transport to the Dublin Prison, where I sit today awaiting my trial.

Eternally Faithful to a United Ireland,
T. Wolfe Tone

Found guilty of treason in a Dublin court on November 10, 1798, Tone was sentenced to be hanged in two days. He pleaded with the magistrate to be executed by firing squad, the traditional method for soldiers captured during a military action, but was denied. On November 11th, it is said, Tone could hear workers constructing the gallows from his jail cell. A prison guard discovered Tone bleeding from the throat at four a.m. the following morning. He had secreted a penknife into his cell and attempted to take his own life by cutting the side of his neck rather than face the humiliation of being hung in the public square of his hometown. He missed the carotid artery, so death was not immediate. Doctors bandaged his wound and told him not to talk or he would certainly die, to which he responded, "So be it." Theobald Wolfe Tone died shortly thereafter as a martyr for the cause of

Irish Republicanism and became a potent role model for an independent Ireland.

Trey and Seamus were pouring over the writings, memoirs, and
historical records pertaining to Wolfe Tone at the Trinity College
Library in Dublin. They discovered over forty volumes containing
mountains of information about his life, his cause, and his tragic
suicide in prison.

"This is amazing, Seamus. I had no idea he was such an important man in Irish history. I'm dumbfounded by the fact he was a
Protestant yet he worked so hard for the rights of Catholics. What's
the deal?" Trey asked.

Seamus pondered his response as he stared at the pile of books
before him. They had selected a nook on the second floor giving
them access to all of the important Tone volumes on the shelves
surrounding their table. Their six-hour effort unearthed political
writings, letters to family, and many published works by both allies
and foes.

"It was never about religion for Tone. His cause was defined
by a deep-seated hatred of the British and their treatment of common Irish people. Only landowners had the right to vote in the
election for the Irish Parliament; a government made of men who
agreed with the English policy of taxing and oppressing those who
didn't own land. The Irish Parliament was a proxy for all things
British, and it never reflected the true desires of over three million
Irish. Catholics and Protestants were equally excluded from par-
ticipating in the affairs of their government," Seamus said, smiling
with an emotional twinkle in his eye. "This spark ignited the Irish
passion for freedom. While it didn't arrive in full force until many
years later, Tone's words, efforts, and sacrifice laid the groundwork
for what is now the Republic of Ireland."

Wolfe Tone was a major player in the Irish independence movement that eventually gave people like Seamus the same rights as

Irish landed gentry and the British interlopers. Grateful for the opportunity to share the Tone discoveries with someone as knowledgeable as Seamus, Trey also felt torn and angry about the discovery. Why had so much information about his family been hidden? If not for his wealth and ability to invest time in the discovery process, he may have gone his whole life without ever knowing about this important figure in his family's history. A kernel of resentment festered within Trey's psyche, and it was growing.

"I think we've done enough for today. It's time to return to the wharf for our plane ride back to Letterkenny. All of these volumes can be accessed online with your library membership. I wanted you to come to Dublin and touch the books for yourself," Seamus said while closing the Tone memoir. "Walking the same hallways Tone did as a student gives you a much better idea about the importance of the man."

Trey had hoped to meet Grace Kinney on this trip to Dublin. Other business required her presence on the Continent. She was an accomplished corporate attorney who assisted foreign corporations establish and maintain a presence in Ireland. She, like Wolfe Tone, was a graduate of Trinity College Law School. Trey looked up her bio during a break from his work on Tone. Her credentials included magna cum laude in undergraduate studies plus a high-honors designation for her study of the law. She had a striking picture. The headshot was of a woman with bright blue eyes, strawberry blonde hair, and a beautifully soulful face. He wondered about the rest of her.

Their twin-engine floatplane made its final approach for a landing on Lough Swilly into a stiff northeast wind. Trey looked out the window to see whitecaps on the bay. Wolfe Tone fought the last battle of his very young life on this water, knowingly risking his life fighting a much larger British force with little or no hope of success. Yet he fought on in the face of that adversity, knowing his life would be given to the cause; he would never lay eyes on his family again. Trey wondered if he could exhibit equal courage under similar circumstance.

Their plane taxied to the wharf terminal. They disembarked onto a floating platform and walked up a steep gangway to the permanent dock. Peddlers greeted them with offers of boat rides and visits to historic landmarks. Seamus pushed through the crowd of hawkers and straight to the front door of Angus Mae's Pub, right in the heart of the docklands. The establishment had a handful of people sitting and milling around the bar.

"What are you drinking? It's my treat," said Seamus.

Trey had not drunk a drop of alcohol in over a year. The memory of that unspeakable night after his breakup with Katie continued to haunt him. The thought of drinking caused his mind to race back to the murky events of that evening. He knew, with certainty, he had awoken under a thorn bush pledging never to drink again; he had kept that pledge until now. A world away from his troubles in New York, Trey thought, *What's the harm in sharing a beer with my new friend Seamus?*

"I'll have a pint of stout," Trey replied.

Seamus ordered the beers at the bar and brought them to a nearby table. As they sat and enjoyed the first sips of the locally brewed fare, the establishment started to fill up with local patrons just getting off work. Were these his people? It sure felt like home, and the effect of the beer confirmed his intuition. A gentleman from across the room hailed Seamus in a loud voice.

"Hey O'Neil, what happened to your team yesterday? They got their arses kicked by County Clare in the open hurling match. Your man O'Malley was a total no-show. They routed your boys pretty good," the red-faced man boasted.

"Clare had the bloody referees in their pockets the entire match. Our boys never had a chance. You wait until we have them up here for the match next month. Our lads will crush them." Seamus continued, "I'd like you to meet my friend Trey Cowens from the States. He's here for a few months, and I'm helping him with some genealogy. He's a direct descendent of Wolfe Tone on his mother's side. We've just come back from the Trinity College Library where we discovered some amazing information on Tone, some things I didn't even know."

The man immediately turned to the room and said in a loud voice, "Hey, everyone, this bloke is a direct descendent of Wolfe Tone!" The entire pub broke out in song...

> *In childhood days I loved to sit upon my father's knee,*
> *And hear the hates of Granuaile and the days that used to be.*
> *I loved to dwell on what he'd tell, a story of his own*
> *About a hero brave and true. His name was Wolfe Tone.*
>
> *His many deed of bravery, the battles that he fought,*
> *And how he died in prison cell, I saddened at the thought.*
> *It left a spell. How can I tell of tears when all alone*
> *With childish grief in true belief, I prayed for poor Wolfe Tone.*
>
> *In that sad, uneven struggle of the weak against the strong,*
> *When the anguished cry went to the sky, "How long, oh God, how long?"*
> *An Empire's fate decreed a fate that made our people moan.*
> *You did your best; with God you rest, Indomitable Tone.*
>
> *A little grave at Bodenstown close by an ivied wall,*
> *Where the dust of one of Ireland's best awaits the angels call.*
> *And with God's Will he'll guide us still 'till all our land we'll own.*
> *Then swords of flame shall trace the name of our unconquered Tone.*

Once the singing stopped Seamus turned to Trey and said, "We all learned the song in school. It's an Irish anthem known by anyone who grew up in this country. Tone inspired the likes of Michael Connelly and other warriors for Irish independence since his death in 1798."

The beers really started to flow after the serenade. Trey was surrounded by all of the patrons in the pub. Each had a story about Tone they learned in school or heard at home from an elderly relative anxious to share the courage of Tone with a new generation. Trey suspected that much of the talk was part of the national myth, but many stories rang true with his research. Each pint of stout heightened Trey's sense of family; these were his people.

The clock struck eleven p.m. Trey rose from the table, thanked his host and the crowd still encircling them. He walked through a gauntlet of well-wishers, suffering their backslaps and breath fouled by the excessive drinking of the last six hours. He cautiously made his way to the curb outside the pub and hailed a taxi.

Trey arrived at his cottage around midnight, enjoying the alcohol high in the privacy of his own home. He found his bed, grateful to have made it home safely without any new tattoos. In this relaxed state, memories of the morning in the bush returned. He immediately forced a picture of Tone aboard the *Hoche* into his mind. He didn't want to spoil a perfectly good high with recollections of that perverted night. Tone's bravery, the certainty of his convictions, and his selfless acts were inspirational. He questioned whether he could ever be that brave or adopt a cause for which he would give his life.

Chapter 7

Dr. Rachel Kohen was hard at work at her office in New York completing session reports when the phone rang. She picked up on the third ring not recognizing the number on caller ID.

"Dr. Kohen. May I help you?" she said professionally.

"Rachel, Trey Cowens, your ex-mental patient. How are you?" he said in a controlled voice, barely concealing his enthusiasm for the call.

"Hello Trey, I'm wonderful. How are you?" delighted to hear from him, but trying to mask her excitement.

"Still as sick as ever, but very much in love with Ireland," he offered, hoping to spark a conversation.

"Well, I've never been there, but I understand Ireland is lovely this time of the year." She was vibrating in all the right spots as the phone call continued.

Why did this man get under her skin so easily? Handsome, rich, articulate, funny, and afflicted all came to mind. As she thought about the question, she realized the answer was obvious. His wealth and looks were a bonus but her real interest in Trey sprung from a need to save him. She had pursued a career in psychiatry because of her family's history of mental illness. She had dedicated her career to finding out why someone became detached from reality and rejected family life in favor of self-destructive behavior.

Even though she was an accomplished woman of science her daddy issues still raged within. The elder Dr. Kohen had a classic case of borderline personality disorder causing him to idealize and demonize people at the same time. His frequent and sometimes violent mood swings triggered periods of isolation. Rachel and her brother did not approach their father during these episodes, which became more common as he aged. The unfortunate result of his sickness was suicide. Ari had found the body in their basement laboratory one Sunday morning after a violent episode of paranoia the night before. Once over the shock and sadness, her father's death inspired her to learn all about personality disorders and family illness.

"Rachel, it's been six months to the day since we said good-bye in New York. I'd like the opportunity to get to know you better. My psychiatrist says I have to act on these impulses because I don't want to regret not doing so down the road. This is an invitation to come visit me at my stone cottage in the Irish countryside. We could have a wonderful time experiencing the history of Ireland, eating local fare, and hiking in the hills."

Rachel contemplated his offer. His directness and honesty took her aback. Her experience with Jewish men taught her to expect subterfuge and whining. Trey was pursuing her with the subtlety of a nuclear bomb. It turned her on.

"Trey I would really love to, but—"

Trey interrupted before she could complete the sentence. "Look, Rachel, I know it's a big deal to fly across the ocean to visit a man you know professionally as a sicko. That didn't come out right, but you understand what I'm saying. You encouraged me to seek answers about my family through genealogy and to have a DNA test. Here I am on the verge of some major breakthroughs, and all I can think of is sharing the experience with you." Trey took a deep breath and waited hopefully for a positive response.

After a tantalizing moment Rachel said, "Let me review my schedule for the next two weeks and see if my partner can take the sessions I can't cancel. If I come, it won't be for just a long weekend. So be prepared to be my tour guide, because I've always wanted to see Ireland. I should be able to have things sorted out by the weekend." Saying these words, she thought about how uncharacteristic it was for her to fly off to be with a man she barely knew, or rather, whom she knew in all of his twisted bareness. Rachel cringed as she pictured her brother's face when he found out she was planning to jet off to be with a Gentile. Should she run the other way, or be impulsive for once and ignore the family pressure?

Rachel's plane was scheduled to arrive at the Dublin International Airport at ten a.m. Trey arranged for one seat on the Twin Otter's seven thirty flight from Letterkenny quay to the commuter terminal at the Dublin docklands. He would catch a cab to the international airport and they would return to the Dublin quay by noon. Knowing she would be tired after her transoceanic trip, he arranged for Seamus's wife, Clarice O'Neil, to make lunch at the cottage. She also prepared the guest room for Rachel. He wasn't sure if this was for Mrs. O'Neil, who was a devout Catholic, or because Clarice knew Rachel would appreciate the option of her own room. Trey hoped the spare bed would not need to be made again.

As he boarded the Otter from the floating platform, he noticed the cabin was full of business people in suits and ties. Some were reading the Financial Times; others tried to catch a morning nap, or just stared at the sunrise over the bay. Trey was the last to board the packed plane. He found the one remaining seat next to a large man trussed up in a seatbelt extension. There was no hope of lowering the armrest because the man's stomach and hips flowed into Trey's space. Thankfully, he was on the aisle and the flight was just under one hour. The seatmate gave Trey a fat, friendly nod and folded his arms over his substantial belly in preparation for a nap. He had been through worse situations in the United States where most people had trouble fitting into airplane seats. If Wolfe Tone faced down the British, surely he could gut out a one-hour plane ride with Shamu. So he decided to shut his eyes and meditate on Rachel's arrival.

Trey tried to remember what she looked like. Six months had passed, and his mental image of her had faded. He constructed a picture of his former therapist, her legs, her cleavage, and her dark hair. His thoughts led him back to their sessions. He constantly pondered the discoveries from the regression therapy. He tried to face these revelations in a responsible way through diligent research of his family and with daily meditation sessions. Today he wanted to cleanse his mind of anything that resembled a professional relationship with Rachel. Her time in Ireland was for them to be a man and a woman, to discover whether they had a future together. Something deep inside of Trey told him it was not going to be easy.

He paid the cabby at the curb outside the arrival level of the terminal. Running a little late because of the Dublin rush hour traffic, he made a mental note not to schedule his trips to the city right before or after a workday. He rushed to the waiting area, where arriving passengers would flow out of the security zone after landing and clearing customs. He checked the electronic board for her flight. MyAir Flight Number 60 from JFK landed ten minutes ago, and the passengers were currently clearing customs. Trey felt a jolt of emotion charge through his body. Was she really here? Would he kiss her, shake her hand, or just give her a hug? He was nervous as a sixth grader playing his first game of *spin the bottle*. She was here on her own free will, and that scared the living daylights out of Trey. She had flown 3,200 miles to be with him. Talk about pressure.

The security door from the international arrivals area flew open, and there she was, the first passenger out of customs. He was barely ready to greet her having just contemplated his dilemma. Their eyes met. She immediately recognized him in the crowd as she pushed her cart through the mass of limo drivers holding signs for other passengers. Trey did not have a sign, but his face had a nervous smile a mile wide as she approached. Sensing his discomfort, she immediately kissed him on the cheek and gave him a long look in the eyes before saying anything.

"I got upgraded to first class at JFK, row one, seat A. How about that for luck? I slept most of the way because I wanted to arrive fresh enough to keep up with you until sundown," she said with a smack of her lips and a smile that indicated to Trey that she was happy to be there. She appeared to be up for an adventure, and so was Trey.

Rachel couldn't believe she had finally made it to Ireland. She hoped it was not a mistake being here; she had acted on an urge to be with a man who did not fit into her family's plan for her. Screw them; Rachel had her own life to live. Ari would have to accept her choice to be with a man outside the faith if it came to that. She was in Ireland with an attractive and attentive man whom she intended to get to know very personally.

"Great news, first class. Unfortunately, you have one more flight on your itinerary today, a short hop to the quay in Letterkenny. All the seats have a first class view of Ireland." Rachel seemed excited about flying in a floatplane.

"Lead the way."

Chapter 8

Ari had come to Israel to complete the construction of Genoshalom's new laboratory located in an industrial zone in Upper Galilee near the town of Beit Jann. The area was perfect for his plan to expand operations into the Middle East. The move was inspired by work Genoshalom was doing with The National Genographic Society in the field of population genetics. The Society had designated Genoshalom as the primary laboratory in this geographical area for the collection, analysis, and reporting of DNA results. The Society chose Israel as a location because of its highly developed infrastructure, educated workforce, favorable tax laws, and access to the target population groups.

The mission was to collect a multitude of DNA samples from indigenous populations to provide a comprehensive map of human migration out of Africa. With larger numbers of specimens collected from groups inhabiting the same land for tens of thousands of years, geneticists could pinpoint mutations within the genome and geographically plot the journey of clan members to new locations. The results of these investigations would allow scientists to chart the flow of populations around the globe and eventually connect everyone to their deep ancestry.

Being in the land gifted to his forefathers by God was a splendid cover for Ari. Ancient Jacob, grandson to Abraham, the father of monotheism, bore twelve sons. Eleven were bequeathed territory in Canaan, today known as Israel. Naphtali, one of his sons, inherited the region of modern day Galilee. Ari had selected this location for its historical significance and remoteness. It was a fitting site for his plan to return the children of Israel to the territory of their birthright. While collecting and analyzing genetic material, he would continue to pursue his goal of creating a new Israel based on the "Word of God." As a descendent of Jacob, his role had been predetermined by his DNA.

According to the Torah, the third son of Jacob, Levi, would not inherit land from his father because the Lord God of Israel himself was his inheritance. The Tribe of Levi became the priestly class. They staffed and managed the Tabernacle and then the Temple while ministering to the needs of the other eleven tribes. They received tithes and payments of grain and meat for performing the necessary ritualistic and judicial services on behalf of the others. Moses, descendant of Levi, spoke with God often. The Lord ordained through Moses that his brother, Aaron, be the first high priest of Israel. This priestly class became known as the Aaronids. They were charged with the responsibility of upholding the laws of the land and were the custodians of all religious objects in the Tabernacle's sanctuary. Along with the spiritual gift of God's commandments, the Aaronids received forty-eight cities so they could minister to the people throughout the land of Israel, not just in Jerusalem. In Ari's mind, Beit Jann represented a modern version of an ancient municipal gift. He had been plotting his next move for years and needed to put the plan into action.

Ziva accompanied Ari to Israel as his administrative assistant and lover. Their partnership was professional and physical at the same time. They began to think each other's thoughts, but Ziva never completed Ari's sentences, as he constantly did hers. She worshiped him resolutely and lived to satisfy him completely even in the face of his rudeness and disrespect for her talents.

Ari was also driven to be with Ziva because of the challenge of using genetic science to grow her a new leg. Through advances in stem cell research many human organs could now be manufactured in a laboratory, but making a human limb would be the crowning achievement of regenerative science. Ari was committed to being the first to accomplish this feat.

Ziva also had plans of her own; she was not just along for the ride and a new leg. She believed that God had selected Ari to become the High Priest of the Jewish people, and she was destined to be by his side. In the meantime, her uniquely competent style in the workplace gave her a mystique that garnered respect from her employees and the attention she craved from Ari. She oversaw the hiring of local staff.

The genetic testing laboratory was housed in structure thirty feet from the administrative building. The lab was the most modern DNA testing facility on the planet. The concrete and epoxy structure had no windows. The interior and exterior walls were a pleasant cream color, and the only connection to the outside world was a door at the end of the walkway and numerous circular venting pipes protruding from the flat roof.

Guarding the entrance was a dual security system requiring both a retina and fingerprint scan to gain access. Visitors and employees found themselves in a decontamination area immediately upon entering the building. Sterile shoe covers, lab coat, and hairnet were necessary to proceed onto the laboratory floor. Visual confirmation from the security officer was required before being granted access.

Ari was conducting a tour of the laboratory for a group of new field workers who would be collecting DNA samples on behalf of the project.

"You will notice the left side of the lab is a mirror image of the right. We installed two of everything to support Genoshalom's Dual Process Protocol. We divide each sample in half for independent testing by two teams of scientists, thereby confirming results with the utmost accuracy. Two Biomek 3000 purification machines lyse the sample so the DNA can be released, beginning the process. This machine also removes proteins, fat, and other cellular material so they don't contaminate the DNA. The remainder of the sample is combined with special reagents for final testing. The system is entirely automated. These robots can process up to 354 DNA tests at once while also reducing the possibility of human error and sample mix-ups." Ari paused and asked if anyone had any questions before moving to the next station. They all looked stunned. Ari's command of the science had put the group under a spell; no one spoke.

He continued in a professorial tone. "These are the DNA gene amplification machines. They actually enable us to copy and magnify specific portions of the DNA molecule for further analysis. Once the sample has been copied and magnified, we pass it to another area where we conduct the quintessential step in our DNA testing, *capillary analysis.* The actual DNA molecule is examined using *CAPAN,* which produces data allowing us to determine identity, lineage, and family relationships. The information is then loaded into our proprietary software where one of our PhDs will ultimately make the scientific determination regarding the sample. These determinations will assign haplogroup, haplotype, and haploclan designations to the samples. Two teams examine the same DNA, and if they confirm their findings are identical, the results are added to our vast database."

Pausing again for questions or comments, Ari caught the eye of a young man who had a curious look. "My name is Gabriel, and I have a question," he said. "Many of the people I've approached are fearful their DNA sample will be used for something other than these population and migration studies. How can we assure them their DNA will only be used to determine their ancient ancestry and not for things like human cloning?" Everyone shook their heads in the affirmative. Ari needed to address this point of contention.

"Once the DNA samples have been processed, analyzed, and reported, they are destroyed so no further genetic testing or manipulation can ever be conducted. We keep thorough and verifiable records on each sample from cradle to grave." As he finished answering the question, his mind wandered to the other side where all promises could be nullified if they interfered with his primary objectives. He didn't give a shit about the field workers or their subjects. His work with these people was a stepping-stone to fulfilling his destiny and returning the Jews to their rightful place.

"Collecting DNA samples is important for the future of our world. Understanding where we come from can only lead us to a better place tomorrow. Your efforts will contribute mightily to a call for peace by uncovering the close kinship existing between all humans on the planet today. In the meantime, we can unlock the vault of time and peer into our ancient past in ways that we never could have imagined. I thank you, Genoshalom thanks you, the whole world thanks you for the work you will be doing."

Ari turned to the door that opened automatically as he approached. He handed the group off to an assistant waiting in the decontamination room and returned to the laboratory. He was the only one in the lab. Security cameras were limited to the decontamination area because the additional static electricity they emitted interfered with the operation of the testing equipment. He was finally alone with the mechanical monster he had spent years creating. In a few short weeks all of the systems would be operational, and the real work that brought him to the Motherland could begin.

Ari abruptly turned around and walked down the aisle to the end and stopped ten feet from the outer wall of the laboratory. He stood staring at his shadow on the vertical slab. His image took on a ghostly appearance. His lab coat made him look like he was wearing a full-length gown. His head was in a druid-like point as he held his arms out to either side; there was something otherworldly about his form. Raising his hands over his head Ari began a low, monotone chant lasting almost two minutes. The words were unrecognizable, but his face betrayed the seriousness of the undertaking. His soul had been kidnapped by his plan. He had ransomed every last ounce of his spirit for the life force he sought. The mandate must be fulfilled, and he was willing to sacrifice his body, soul, and mind in the process. But first he must finish building the second laboratory, the secret lab that only he and Ziva knew about.

Ari raised his voice slightly from the level of the chant and said, "*Mitsvah sheol.*" A square portion of the floor dropped ten inches and retracted under the outer wall, exposing a staircase leading beneath the commercial testing lab. Originally constructed as a safe room for the lab employees, it had been converted into Ari's own private workspace.

Ari stepped down off the laboratory floor onto the first stair. Full of anticipation, he took the next step. The population genetics lab would be closed for the weekend. Within the next forty-eight hours he would finish installing the equipment he had secretly imported with the DNA testing machines. Another step down, and the lights came on in the dungeon. No one except Ziva knew the true purpose of his subterranean activities. Only the construction company knew the "safe room" existed, and he had required them sign nondisclosure agreements. He added the space at the last minute as a precaution because of the lab's proximity to the Lebanon border and its exposure to raids from Hezbollah terrorists.

One more step and his shadow vanished from the upper wall. Once his head cleared the floor, the portal automatically closed and returned to its invisible state. Air pumped into the chamber; Ari could hear the exhaust fans clearing CO_2 from the cave. He fell to his knees and prayed God would bless this place and give him the strength to succeed. His dark, glassy eyes reflected everything in his range of vision, like a robot collecting and analyzing data from his surroundings. The Messianic Age was coming. Ari would be part creator, part priest, part judge, part jury, and all knowing.

Chapter 9

Rachel looked out the window of the floatplane ten minutes after takeoff, relishing the new sights. "Thank you so much for inviting me. I had second thoughts, but now I'm glad I decided to come. The beauty from the air is breathtaking. I can't wait to get on the ground. Look, there's a herd of sheep."

This is going well, thought Trey. She was more beautiful than he remembered. Her traveling clothes were so different from the business suits she wore as a New York City couch doctor. He was ecstatic to have her here in a neutral location, a place where they could explore their relationship without the interference of her work, her brother, and her religion. He wasn't so sure about the last one, because he knew she was culturally disposed to be with a good Jewish man. However, he was convinced that her Jewishness would not prohibit a little fling with a Gentile as an appetizer. Trey's fervent hope was that once he served the hors d'oeuvres she would never be able to return to the sexually retarded intimacy vacuum that defined coupling with the standard Jewish male.

The Twin Otter touched down on Lough Swilly just after one thirty p.m. With the plane tied off at the dock, they walked down the gangway and up the stairs to the top of the seawall. Trey led Rachel between two old stone buildings to the car park behind Angus Mae's Pub.

Trey had purchased a new Mini Cooper "Clubman", an extended version of the classic car that took Europe by storm in the late 1950s. He popped the back hatch with a push of the remote key. The car beeped to life as if to welcome them. He slipped her bag into the boot and they were off. Leaving town on the main road, they made a right turn at the Village of Conwal where they began a long, gradual climb. Stone walls, green fields, and lovely spring flowers filled the windshield. Rachel took in the scenic view, as they turned left onto an unpaved road. Trees lined the sides of the ancient roadway, which led them up a small hill commanded by a church and its steeple.

"Here we are. This is my driveway; hang on, because it's a little rough." The drive became steeper and their speed increased to counter the effects of gravity as they dodged potholes and large rocks littering the approach. Once they arrived at the top of the hill, a stone structure came into full view against the bluebird sky.

"Is this where you live?" asked Rachel, rather astonished.

"Home sweet home," said Trey as he pulled the Mini to a stop in front of the cottage. He jumped out and opened the passenger door. Rachel stepped onto the drive with a schoolgirl gaze plastered on her face; she was entranced by the whole experience. Leaving her bag in the car, Trey led her to the front door, which Mrs. O'Neil had left unlocked. As they pushed through the entrance, the smell of food overtook them both. He had asked Mrs. O'Neil not to make anything with pork or any derivation thereof. She prepared an adaptation of a classic Irish coddle, a traditional baked casserole, using spicy vegetarian sausage, chicken, potatoes, and herbs. The covered, cast-iron pot was in the oven. Along with the homemade soda bread and a couple bottles of Guinness, they had a fantastic lunch all ready to go.

"Wow, what smells so good?" asked Trey's guest. As he explained the meal their eyes met. The scent of the food triggered a subtle aphrodisiac-like response from them both. Trey moved to close the distance between them. He coaxed her gently into his body with his arm around her waist. With no resistance from her, they melted into each other, their lips touching for the first time. They kissed as young people do on the first date, soft lips and a partially open mouth. *Sweet Jesus,* Trey thought, *is this really happening? She hasn't been here five minutes, and I've got an erection for the ages.*

"How about getting my bag out of the car so I can change out of these clothes and put on something more comfortable?"

"Sure." He released her and went to fetch the bag, while thinking, *She's already reading my mind.*

Upon returning to the house, he made a move toward the guest room. Having used the brief moment he'd been away to assess her potential rooming options, Rachel said, "Hey, where are you going? Don't you want some company in there?" She pointed to the master suite on the other side of the cottage.

Trey stopped abruptly in the middle of the living area. He was shocked at her decision, question, or offer, but happy to accommodate.

"Sure, that would be lovely." He turned toward his room with her bags in hand and lifted them onto the collapsible luggage holder he positioned against the wall. He had cleared out two drawers for her use, just in case. They were sleeping in the same bed. Case closed.

This beautiful woman, his therapist from New York was here on her own free will. She had agreed to be alone with him in a two-hundred-year-old stone cottage in the Irish countryside, and now she just asked to share his bed.

Have I died and gone to heaven? Trey asked himself.

As he returned to the main room, she slid past him saying, "Give me a few minutes to freshen up." She closed the door to the bedroom leaving him standing in the middle of the living area.

He heard a cell phone ring after a few minutes and it wasn't his, so it had to be hers. He could barely hear her speaking through the thick wooden door of his bedroom. A couple of minutes passed. Her voice became louder, interrupting the tranquility of the moment. She was upset and talking louder, in a language that was not English, and then the room went silent. The sound of a running shower is what Trey heard next.

Rachel emerged from the bedroom dressed in jeans, a plain white T-shirt, and walking shoes. The smile on her face belied the stress of the conversation she had terminated minutes before. He wouldn't ask about the call but would wait for her to offer an explanation if she chose.

"How about a hike? I need to get my blood flowing after the flight, and I bet we could work up an appetite. Do you have a picnic basket?" Rachel asked in a take-charge manner. "Let's pack Mrs. O'Neil's casserole, the bread, a couple of beers and go out for a picnic."

Surprised at her energy level after a transcontinental flight, Trey was agreeable to the plan. He located the basket Mrs. O'Neil used to carry the lunch from her home, removed the coddle from the oven, wrapped the bread in a kitchen towel, and grabbed two beers from the fridge. He swiped the red and white tablecloth from the table like a seasoned magician and placed it on top of the items in the basket. They exited the cottage and followed the path up a hill. A slight breeze provided a cooling effect as they made their way toward high ground following a single track normally reserved for sheep and herders.

They came to a clearing where a primeval oak tree dominated the entire scene. Trey spread the tablecloth on the ground while Rachel removed the contents of the picnic basket. They both sat, preparing to enjoy a private meal framed by a perfectly serene Irish countryside. The food's aroma filled the immediate area, reminding them of the kiss they had enjoyed back at the cottage. Rachel leaned into Trey and gave him a kiss on the cheek. "That was my brother, Ari, on the phone earlier, calling from Israel. I didn't tell him about my trip to Ireland because I knew he would freak out and try to change my mind." She paused to gauge Trey's impression of her news about the call.

"Go on," Trey responded in a kindly tone.

"He got mad at me, chastising me for leaving New York without telling him. He's acting like my father. He told me I had no business being with you because you were a former patient. What he really wanted to say was that you aren't Jewish, and I'm wasting time I could use to find a good Jewish man." Rachel hoped she had not scared Trey off by being too honest, too soon.

"Must be tough, Rachel," Trey responded.

"He's overly protective. I'm a big girl and can make my own decisions. Sometimes he's just overbearing to the point of exhaustion. I hung up on him when he launched into a tirade about our family and the responsibility I have to the memory of our parents."

"I'm sorry the call ended so poorly," Trey said with a look of concern.

Rachel laid her head on the nape of Trey's neck. He placed his left arm around her tiny waist. Her breathing was elevated either from the walk, the confession, or the pheromones that were thick in the afternoon air. He encouraged her to lie gently on the ground. His right hand traced the outline of her body as he moved closer and leaned in to kiss her. As their lips met, a faint spark of static electricity shocked them as if to confirm their passion. The mid-afternoon sun had begun its diagonal descent over the picture-perfect Irish scene, warming everything below, including the two Americans. They knew not to waste this moment on food or family business. They didn't.

Chapter 10

Trey was alone in his car making his way to Belfast International Airport for a meeting with a client who was visiting relatives in nearby Ballyclare. When negotiating his leave of absence, he had agreed to attend customer meetings to manage relationships and review portfolio results.

Jeremy Gallagher, a very successful lawyer, had earned his fortune as a plaintiff's attorney in Jackson, Mississippi, suing Big Tobacco. His holdings suffered mightily in the last market downturn, but he had recovered almost 100 percent of the losses due to adjustments Trey made in his hedge-fund allocations.

He woke early that morning to study Jeremy's account statements that had been e-mailed to him from New York the night before. *The meeting should be relatively low key*, thought Trey. However, he always prepared himself for the worst case.

The 160-kilometer drive gave him a couple of hours to reflect on the events of the previous day. He had left Rachel sleeping in his bed under a down duvet wrapped in Irish cotton. Trey snuck out of the bedroom on a cold floor clutching his work clothes while she breathed quietly in her white nest. *Their first day together could not have gone much better*, he thought. She had given herself to him freely and with enthusiasm. The walk back to the cottage after their late lunch provided them with some challenges as the evening light descended upon the path. Without a flashlight, she clutched his arm, and they walked shoulder to shoulder down the trail. As they crested the last hill, the lights of the cottage showed the way to the rear door. He started a fire with the wood delivered by a local farmer the day before. Candles were lit and they lay together on the couch, warming their bodies like two Labradors after a day of hunting in the field.

He woke to the chill of the room. The fire had gone out. They had fallen asleep in each other's arms sometime after midnight. He gently roused Rachel and led her to his bed. The effort of her travel and hike had taken its toll. She was fast asleep in seconds, and he not far behind.

Trey made his way toward the airport and his meeting in a buoyant mood. Being happy about having a beautiful woman in his bed at home was a totally new feeling for Trey. He looked forward to having the meeting behind him so he could get back to the house and Rachel.

The airport command center was located on the top floor of the terminal. Belfast International Airport had one of the most advanced security systems in the entire aviation industry. This included a cutting-edge facial recognition system named FACE (Facial Acquisition Confirmation & Execution System) that recorded, scanned, and identified all arriving passengers as well as people entering the terminal through any of the twenty-two public entrances. Critics referred to the system as FARCE because of the numerous false positives the program produced. The software was loaded with pictures of known terrorists, including those on the International and U.S. "No-Fly Lists." Many in the system were local Irish Nationals who broke away from the Irish Republican Army in 2005 when the IRA pledged to cease all future activities and decommission its weapons.

"I can't believe what I'm seeing," said Sgt. Sean McGregor. "FACE just gave me a hit on someone who entered the terminal through number sixteen, and it's telling me it is Donald Murphy."

Murphy, also known as "Mad Dog", was among the most wanted Irish Republican terrorists in the country. His acts of violence had taken many lives over the past decade, the worst being an attack on a Derry church that left a priest and twelve parishioners dead. Murphy was thought to be in hiding under the protection of an IRA splinter group.

Capt. Bryan Flynn stepped forward to peer over McGregor's shoulder. Seeing the image-match in the 3-D system, he immediately called down to the terminal floor, "Quinn, do you read?"

"Yes, Captain," replied Pvt. Quinn without hesitation. He knew contact from the Captain would be a call to action.

"A subject just entered through number sixteen. He's dressed in a dark business suit carrying a silver metal briefcase. Approach, check for weapons, and bring him to the security office immediately."

Quinn called for support and advanced toward the subject, who had just stepped on the escalator leading up to the passenger greeting area. He decided to wait until they both got off the moving stairway to make contact with the suspect. Once at the top, Quinn hurried around in front of the man in question.

"Sir, may I have a word with you please?" Quinn said in an official voice.

"What's the problem, officer?" asked Trey in a matter-of-fact way, never imagining what would result from the encounter. Two officers appeared in support of Pvt. Quinn's mission. Surrounded by three rather large men in police uniforms, Trey didn't have a clue what was going on. The first officer relieved Trey of his briefcase while another did a cursory pat down looking for firearms. The gathering of authorities drew the attention of travelers and airport workers. Some of them covered their mouths and pointed fingers at Trey as if to say, "I can't believe what I'm seeing." Camera phones were taking pictures of the policemen and detainee. The crowd built as the word circulated around the terminal that a police action was underway.

"Please come with me sir," said Quinn after a few seconds. The other officers moved to clear a path in the considerable crowd blocking their way to the elevator.

"What's going on? Where are you taking me?" asked Trey in a restrained tone as the officers grabbed him by either elbow. "I have a business meeting in thirty minutes. What the hell is going on?" No response. Trained for situations like this, the officers looked straight ahead.

Perspiration began to bead on Trey's forehead as he got onto the lift. No longer in charge, he suddenly saw himself under the thorn bush. Going back to that day was painful and infuriating, and the fucking tattoo was a constant reminder of his flawed life. He forced himself to swallow the fear and stuff the anger.

The elevator doors opened on the third floor. They exited the elevator and ushered Trey directly to a door emblazoned with the words "Security Operations Command". After entering a numeric code into the keypad, Quinn pushed through the door into a chiming and buzzing space filled with people and flat screen monitors displaying every nook and cranny in the building. Quinn handed Trey off to Capt. Flynn, who escorted him to a windowless room with only a table and two chairs.

"Who are you, and why am I here?" asked Trey again, this time more incredulous. Getting angry, he was demanding an explanation for his detention.

"I will ask the questions, and you will answer. Do you have any identification?" Realizing he didn't bring his passport, Trey offered up an international driver's license.

The captain studied the driver's license and its photo. He was unhappy this gentleman didn't have a passport; Flynn knew international driver's licenses were easy to forge. Trey knew he didn't need a passport to cross the border into Northern Ireland. All the border control checkpoints had been abandoned some years back. He left his passport with other valuables back in the safe at the cottage.

The captain studied the license and then asked for Trey's U.S. Social Security number so he could run it through the international system and confirm his identity. Normally not inclined to give out his Social Security number, he would this time to stop the madness. The captain left the room with the number. Trey tried to collect himself by closing his eyes and concentrating on his breathing. Fifteen minutes passed before the door opened, interrupting Trey's fitful meditation. Captain Flynn entered with a man in a business suit who introduced himself as U.S. Custom's Marshall John Lange.

Marshall Lange began, "Mr. Cowens, we had reason to believe you were a person of interest to the British government. Upon further investigation we've confirmed your identity otherwise. I apologize for any inconvenience this caused you. I'm sure you're aware that certain elements here in Ireland want the British to leave the island and will do anything to see that happen."

"How can this happen?" Trey asked.

"I really can't discuss the intricacies of the security system, but it appears that your physical traits are similar to a man wanted for crimes here in Northern Ireland," responded Lange.

"What does that mean? Am I on some list or something?"

"Airport security maintains a list of all criminals at large in the country and international terrorists. It's really for the safety of the public including law abiding visitors like yourself," Capt. Flynn said, trying to defuse Trey's displeasure.

"In all honesty gentlemen, I'm not feeling very safe right now. The system is plainly defective and somehow I ended up on a list of criminals. How in the hell do I get off this list? What can I do to avoid this in the future?" Trey's exasperation was increasing with the realization that these men were not going to be able to help.

"I'm afraid there is nothing you or I can do. It is just an unfortunate mix-up. The system does make mistakes," concluded Lange, trying to terminate this session so they could get back to the real work of protecting the terminal and its travelers.

Trey gave up trying to make sense of the situation and asked, "Can I go now?"

"Yes, I'll have one of my officers escort you back to the main terminal floor so you can continue with your business," responded Capt. Flynn. "Again, I'm sorry for the mistake."

The men left the room, and a uniformed officer came with Trey's briefcase to escort him down the elevator. As he exited the lift, he wondered whom he had been mistaken for and what that person had done to cause such a ruckus. These thoughts were fleeting. He was already fifteen minutes late for his meeting with Jeremy.

Trey had arranged for a private conference room inside the President's Club in the main terminal. He tried to collect his thoughts and calm himself for the meeting. He was still feeling the stress of the crazy police action. *What a fucking nightmare,* he thought. He found the club and went to the meeting room where his client waited.

"Jeremy, sorry I'm late. I had a little mix-up on my way in," he said, not wanting to disclose the exact nature of the delay. "Have you been waiting long?"

"No, my plane arrived a little late from Atlanta. I crawled in here about fifteen minutes ago," Jeremy said with a touch of fatigue. "I tried to make some calls but realized it's still early morning back home. I'm supposed to be at my friend's house in a couple hours, so let's get started."

Not one to keep a client waiting, especially someone who was used to making the equivalent of thirty thousand dollars an hour suing tobacco manufacturers, Trey opened his briefcase and began the review. The session lasted just over an hour, with Trey explaining the quarterly results and how the reallocation helped get back all of the losses from the market crash the previous year.

Jeremy received thirty to forty million dollars per year from the global tobacco settlement. The challenge for an asset manager was to deploy the new money in a way that complemented his current holdings. The plan for Jeremy's new money had been sent to Trey via FedEx the week before; it called for the addition of eight new hedge funds, each getting about five million dollars. Jeremy agreed to the recommendations and indicated the new money would be available over the next twelve months in three separate installments. Trey got the signatures required to implement the investment plan and said good-bye to his client as Jeremy rushed to meet a driver. Trey sat alone in the conference room, relieved to have the meeting behind him, but still shaken by the encounter with the police.

Donald "Mad Dog" Murphy accessed the Belfast Daily newspaper online from his hideout in County Clare. He was directed to a story by a local Belfast operative who frequently fed him items of interest. The security event at Belfast International Airport had been mentioned in the local section under the headline "Donald 'Mad Dog' Murphy Look-Alike Causes Stir in Belfast Terminal." A picture of the man was printed right next to the story. Other people at the scene provided comments and additional pictures of the officers and their subject. Murphy studied the pictures, enlarged them for a better look, and printed the one that seemed to be the clearest. He held up the eight by ten inch image of the man in question next to the hallway mirror and studied it.

"Holy Mother of Jesus, that's me!" he shouted out loud.

Chapter 11

Trey arrived home around four o'clock. He couldn't escape the effects of being mistaken for someone the police called "a person of keen interest." As he pulled into the drive, he saw Rachel on the back terrace. She appeared to be meditating, seated Indian style on a pillow. The back of her hands rested gently on her knees.

Trey closed the car door and tiptoed his way around the knee-wall that encircled the terrace at the rear of the cottage. He sat down on the wall behind Rachel. Her hourglass shape was perched on a cushion she had taken from the couch. Her back was straight, her shoulders and elbows forming a perfectly balanced scale. He hoped her thoughts and feelings were in balance with his.

She rose from the cushion, lifted her arms over her head, and bent back all the way to the ground, catching herself with the palms of her hands. She opened her eyes to see Trey sitting quietly on the wall. Still in the back bend she asked, "How long have you been sitting there?"

"Long enough to know you are really good at whatever it is you're doing," he said respectfully. "I like the outfit too, very functional yet sexy. No wonder you're in such great shape. Do you do this every day?"

"It's become an addiction. I prefer to do sitting meditation and a yoga workout in the morning, but I didn't get up early enough today. I had some incredible dreams about being ravaged on a blanket in a field by a handsome prince in a far off country. Then I woke up in a strange bed, realized it wasn't a dream and that you were the prince."

She approached Trey, who was sitting with his legs crossed. Rachel cupped his ears with her hands and kissed his forehead on her way to the back door. "I need to shower and then eat. I haven't had anything all day." She pushed open the large wooden door that anchored the rear of the cottage. Before entering, she turned and said, "Oh, Seamus called for you about an hour ago. He said he needed to speak with you as soon as you got in."

She vanished inside, leaving Trey to speculate on the meaning of Seamus's call. *Probably more information about Wolfe Tone,* he thought as he located the number in his iPhone.

Rachel and Trey were driving to an early dinner meeting with Seamus at the Clanree Hotel. Trey detailed the scene at the airport for Rachel. She asked questions to make sure she understood what sounded like a harrowing experience. He recounted everything, including his detention in the security office and the rush of fear it had caused.

Once he completed his story Rachel thought for a few moments before asking, "My goodness, Trey are you all right?"

"I'm fine, but it was a bit unsettling, especially with all the travel-security alerts at the airports these days. Situations like that make you glad to be a law-abiding citizen, especially when you're in another country."

He paused to see how Rachel reacted to his story. He was fearful of any controversy that would give her cold feet about their relationship. "I assure you I'm not a hunted man, at least not yet," he said with a laugh as they pulled into the hotel parking lot.

Already seated at a table in the corner of the bar, Seamus rose as they entered the room. Trey introduced Rachel to Seamus. Seamus bent at the waist, reached for her hand, and applied a gallant kiss, as he said, "*Dia dhiut.* God be with you." Rachel was immediately smitten with this sixty-year-old stud of a man and noticeably blushing as they took their seats.

"I had a bit of a situation at the Belfast Airport this morning," Trey said trying to break the ice.

Seamus interrupted him in a hushed tone, "I know all about it. Please keep your voice down. I selected this bar because I knew we would be among the first patrons at this early hour. We need privacy."

"What do you mean you know all about it? How could you know what happened to me at the airport? I just got home a few hours ago, and Rachel is the only person I've told," Trey scowled in a low, indignant tone. He didn't like surprises; he never did and imagined he never would. The fact that Seamus knew his business was troubling.

"Trey, there's something about me I haven't told you. In my youth I was a soldier in the Irish Republican Army. Like your famous ancestor, I was committed to kicking the Brits out of Ireland. In the late 1960s, our battle became known as 'The Troubles.' Lethal weapons eventually replaced words and rocks; then the real troubles began." Seamus paused and let his words sink in, hoping he wasn't alarming his new friends.

He shared some background on The Troubles. Those tumultuous times boiled down to a conflict between Irish Nationalists, who might be Catholic, versus the Northern Irish Unionists, who were mostly Protestant and all British. Seamus commanded the Donegal Brigade, which controlled three separate battalions of volunteers totaling 900-armed men. They were trained to protect Irish Nationalists from attacks by British soldiers as well as defend against Unionist groups who sought to silence their cry for full independence.

Seamus stopped talking as the waitress approached to take their drink and food orders. Once she left, he continued, "Our command structure was susceptible to infiltration by our adversaries, and our missions were repeatedly compromised by spying." Seamus appeared to be reliving the events of those chaotic times. His face took on the seriousness of someone in the line of fire.

"The brigade disbanded and formed smaller paramilitary units that conducted their own missions without a central command. I led one, and we sent a network of spies to infiltrate British and Unionist organizations. Many of these undercover agents are still operational today."

"What does any of this have to do with the 'urgent' meeting we're now having?" asked Trey, wanting Seamus to get to the point that had brought them to the hotel.

"This morning I received a message from one of these individuals, who works for us at the airport. He sent a picture and a narrative. I was shocked to see that it was you in the picture. Then it dawned on me why I had always felt I knew you from a previous life. I just wrote it off to your relationship with Tone until I saw the picture and read the report. You look just like Donald Murphy." As Seamus dropped the bomb on Trey and Rachel, he sat back in his chair and had a long draw on his beer.

"Who the hell is Donald Murphy?" asked Trey.

"He's the top commander of the Real IRA," replied Seamus.

"So? A lot of people look alike. You resemble Sean Connery but I'm not going to start calling you Sir Sean. Why are you telling me all of this?"

"One of Donny's people contacted me this afternoon, and he wants to meet with you." Seamus tensed up afraid he'd overstepped his bounds.

"He wants to meet with me. Why?" asked Trey.

"He wants to discuss your relationship with Wolfe Tone," Seamus said meekly as he confessed, "I've shared your quest with a few close friends, and evidently the word got back to Donny. Add that to the situation at the airport, and I guess it motivated him to call me. I'm sorry if you feel I've violated your anonymity, but I never imagined it would come to this."

"Isn't he a terrorist and wanted by the police?" Rachel interjected.

"Donny's a misunderstood patriot who masterminded the shooting of an Anglican priest in Derry. This preacher molested Donny and one of his best friends back in the '80s. His friend killed himself after years of trying to get the pedophile jailed. The priest just converted to the Anglican Church, moved to Derry, and continued in the service of the Lord without as much as a slap on the wrist. Donny avenged his friend's death and his own scars the only way he knew how, a life for a life. Donny is a very intelligent man and a very good person. I think you'd like him very much."

The waitress served their food. Rachel and Trey had not eaten all day. They dug into their sizable entrees without speaking. After the initial rush to satisfy their hunger, Trey spoke first, asking, "So let's say I agree. How would the meeting be arranged?"

"I can organize a safe meeting place. No one will know when and where you're getting together. Think it over, and let me know if you want me to set it up. If not, I understand, but the resemblance is remarkable. Donny is one of the foremost authorities on the early days of Irish Republicanism, including Wolfe Tone. Much of what I know about the movement and its roots comes from my talks with him."

With the dinner completed and the check paid, Seamus rose from the table to say good-bye. "It's been a delightful meal. I enjoyed every minute of our conversation. Even though what I had to say probably shocked you. I hope you won't think less of me knowing something of my history. The truth will set us all free, and all I can be is who I am: an Irishman who believes all men should be free to determine the course of their own lives."

Seamus kissed Rachel's hand with the same practiced panache he had upon their arrival. He shook Trey's hand firmly and held on. His free hand reached into his coat pocket and his penetrating gaze looked into Trey's soul. He removed an envelope, and handed it to Trey.

"I think you need to see this," said Seamus, as he released Trey's hand, turned and departed.

Trey and Rachel sat back down. He opened the envelope, removed a picture and stared at the image before handing it to

Rachel. She looked at the photo and then turned it over to find "Donald Murphy 2009" written on the back.

"Holy crap, he looks just like you," she whispered.

Trey and Rachel arrived back at the cottage after a short drive from the bar in complete silence. In a zombie-like trance, they made their way to the couch in front of the fireplace. An evening chill had invaded the living area.

Rachel broke the spell by saying, "Are you going to meet this person who appears to be your spitting image?" She didn't want to offer an opinion before he did.

"I don't know. What could be gained by going to visit a terrorist who looks like me? I think I'll pass on the meeting," responded Trey, hoping she was in agreement.

"Good choice. I can see that some of my brilliance is rubbing off on you." Rachel smiled evidencing her total accord with his decision.

"I'll give Seamus a call in the morning and let him know."

Trey left to fetch some firewood as Rachel made a feline nest on the couch, utilizing loose pillows and a woolen blanket. Trey returned with a sling full of fuel. He stacked and lit the fire with the skill of an Eagle Scout. Trey added additional logs to create a large heat source and light show in the darkened space. He joined Rachel on the couch. Stealing a corner of her blanket, he inserted himself into her burrow.

Rachel gazed into the fire. The flames illuminated her face and made the back of her head disappear into a shadow. Her face took on the appearance of a light orange Kabuki mask. He noticed a tear on her cheek. As he reached to wipe it away, she turned, destroying the illusion of the mask.

"I don't know why I'm crying. I'm completely happy being here with you, but I'm afraid about what will happen when I leave. I want to hang on to this in the worst way. What are we going to do?" she asked, as the back of her head fell onto Trey's lap.

"We're going to enjoy the time we have together," he offered, caressing the top of her head.

"You're only the second man in my entire life who has made me feel this way. The first was when I was much younger and serving a two-year commitment on an Israeli kibbutz. When it was over, I returned to the states, and he went into the Israeli military. We corresponded for a few months, but eventually fell out of touch." Relieved to have gotten that off her chest, Rachel relaxed a little more.

"I'm honored to be number two. 'We try harder,' you know?"

Ignoring his attempt at rental car humor, she thought for a while before saying, "I'm a creature of my upbringing. As a Jewish American Princess, I was taught that my responsibility is to the family first. I'm expected to be ambitious in my work but deferential to the family, especially the men. Now I think I'm falling for a man who doesn't fit the profile of someone my family expects."

Rachel's head in Trey's lap was beginning to cause a problem. *Little Trey* was reacting to the direct contact with the back of Rachel's cranium. *What a freaking whore-dog I am,* he thought. *She's in an emotional state, now is not a good time.*

He tried to think himself down, but his well-endowed britches were not cooperating. He didn't want to insult the moment by prescribing an erect dick as a solution to her dilemma. A classic battle between a man's brain and his rooted drive to procreate was being waged. The ancient conflict had been fought countless times through the millennium, and the little brain rarely won. If the dimwit did win, victory would be short lived, compounding the emotional distress of the female partner. No luck chopping down the tree, so he decided to buy some time with a trip to the kitchen for drinks. He moved to the open end of the couch and said, "Are you thirsty? How about something to drink?"

She was having nothing to do with it. Logic was suspended as she reacted to his swollen asset. Rolling over on her stomach, she propped herself up on her elbows and dropped her right hand directly on the bulge in his pants and said, "Don't you think we should try this in bed? We've already made love in a country meadow and I've been looking forward to messing up Mrs. O'Neil's sheets. How about getting a couple of glasses of wine and meeting me in the bedroom? I've got to change into something more suitable for the occasion. Otherwise, my trip to Victoria's Secret in New York will have been a waste."

Trey couldn't agree more, however his verbal approval would have been redundant. *Little Trey* had already voted.

Chapter 12

Sitting in his Upper Galilee office, Ari studied the most recent results of an archeological find from the hill country not far from the lab. Ziva's voice broke the silence, announcing a call on line two from Zeke Yastrow, Genoshalom's head geneticist in New York. "Put him through," barked Ari, upset by the interruption.

"Shalom, Ari. Zeke calling from New York. How are you this morning, I mean afternoon where you are?" he said, confused about the time change.

"What do you want, Zeke? I'm busy and don't have time for small talk." Ari's tone reflected his mood, one all too familiar to Zeke. Ari used this hostile approach with all his employees, not willing to invest his time in mindless talk and mundane relationships. His whole scheme could unravel at any time, and he would leave his minions holding the bag. His best defense against an emotional attachment was to keep them at arm's length and manage through threats and intimidation.

Zeke, a little shaken, proceeded with caution. "You asked me to personally call you when we had the final sixty-seven marker Y-DNA results for subject N672309," he offered in a timid voice.

That was Trey's kit number; Ari had it memorized. The original mtDNA test results had been transmitted to Trey only after Ari had reviewed the report and approved its release. He had instructed his chief science officer to conduct the test on Trey's Y-DNA personally, not leaving it to the normal lab tech. This was a necessary precaution in Ari's mind, because his sister was beginning to have feelings for this Gentile, a fact confirmed by her trip to Ireland.

As he thought about the situation, his mood soured even more. Maybe the Y-DNA results would give him something he could use to blow up their relationship. If not, he could fabricate an abnormality to insert into the results indicating a predisposition to some rare genetic disorder. He had unlimited options because he controlled the results. However, he was not prepared for what he heard next.

"Subject N672309 has a Jewish father. His Y-DNA conclusively indicates he belongs to Haplogroup J and he's also a member of the Cohen Modal Haplotype, a Kohanim, which means he's a direct descendent of Aaron, brother of Moses." Zeke stopped and waited for a response, not sure of what was to come next.

Ari responded in a stern voice, "I know what a Kohanim is, Zeke. Run the test again. There must be a mistake."

"I ran the test three times; the results are conclusive beyond a scientific doubt. I would stake my career on these findings." Zeke's boldness surprised even him, but the truth was the truth. He wondered if he'd stepped over the line with Ari.

"Okay, I'll get back with you. Don't transmit the results to the subject. E-mail them to me along with the template we use for communicating the findings." Not wanting to cause any alarm with his chief scientist, Ari added, "The individual is a family friend, and I want to send him some additional information so he can have a broader understanding of what it means to be Kohanim. I'll take it from here."

Zeke confirmed their understanding, although he was thinking this was odd and not in keeping with the controls he and Ari had so scrupulously put in place. However, he wrote it off to just what Ari had said, the subject was a family friend. Zeke hung up and transmitted the e-mail as instructed.

Ari sat in his office pondering the meaning of Trey's Y-DNA test results. How the fuck could this happen? Was this goy really a Jew? Well, not really, because his mother was not Jewish. But if his father was a member of the Cohen Modal Haplotype, then he was dealing with a distant cousin on his father's side and a member of the priestly line of Aaron. How should he deal with Mr. Cowens?

Maybe the best approach was to follow his instincts and eliminate Trey; or he could tell the truth. Honesty was a challenging concept for Ari, but conceivably the truth might be the best strategy in this case. He did not have any more time to consider this subject, because he was preparing for a meeting with an Israeli government operative. He would deal with Trey and Rachel later. He hoped his sister would come to her senses before he had to do something radical.

Trey woke up early to get a head start on the day. After making coffee, he went to his office alcove attached to the kitchen and powered up his computer. He needed to send the documents Jeremy executed yesterday to his office in New York so the investment plan would be ready when the cash arrived. He scanned the original documents with signatures, created PDF files and attached them to an e-mail with instructions on how to proceed with each asset manager. He would call the Trilogica office at the start of their day to confirm everything over the phone. He planned to send the originals via courier later that afternoon.

Having finished his initial task of the day, he checked the e-mails he had neglected since Rachel's arrival. He clicked the inbox and waited for the Internet connection to catch up with his request. He had installed a DigiWeb satellite system immediately upon arrival at the cottage, and the dish was noticeably slower than his cable connection back in New York. As his one hundred plus e-mails slowly downloaded, he freshened his coffee. The window over the kitchen sink was filled with a luminescence of a sun not yet risen on what appeared to be another cloudless day.

Returning to his desk, an undeniable pang of e-mail dread overcame him. This is a well-documented condition whose symptoms are brought on by an accumulated amount of unchecked electronic mail; the longer the period of avoidance, the more severe the symptoms. Back in the States, Trey had always suffered from e-mail dread, but ever since he had moved to Ireland, he had been able to let go of the day-to-day pressure of managing his inbox. He only dealt with communications from his partners and the rare meeting with clients like Jeremy. His staff, headed by a capable junior partner named Bradley Blyleven, handled all new business communications. Bradley and Trey spoke every Friday on the phone for about an hour, just in case he could offer some assistance to his ambitious, young protégé. Those Friday calls gave Trey confidence his sabbatical plan was working and that leaving had been a superb idea on a number of levels.

Scanning his inbox for important correspondence, an e-mail from Ari Kohen immediately attracted his attention. Why would he be e-mailing Trey unless it was to threaten him for being with his sister? He noticed the subject line said "Y-DNA Test Results for Kit #N672309." He clicked the e-mail, which had a few large attachments. The communication took awhile to download, but finally the text appeared on his screen.

> *Dear Trey,*
>
> *I have the distinct pleasure of informing you that your Y-DNA test results have been completed and confirmed. Y-DNA defines maleness and provides us with a unique look into our paternal past. Because the Y chromosome is passed from father to son without much change through the ages, we can use it as a road map to determine our ancient ancestry with surprising accuracy. Changes occurring to the human genome are called mutations. These mutations are rare and help us define the specific hereditary line back to our most distant male ancestors. The combination of these mutations allows us to pinpoint the genetic signature of male ancestry, which defines a haplotype for that individual. Your results follow here:*

Y-DNA Test Results—Kit # N672309—William J. Cowens

Your father and you are members of Haplogroup J, which is prevalent in much of the Middle Eastern population today. Further analysis of the genetic mutations found in your Y chromosome enable us to predict with 99 percent accuracy that your paternal lineage is a haplotype defined as the Cohen Modal Haplotype (CMH). You are a member of the line of priestly Kohanim who descended from Aaron, brother of Moses, beginning over three thousand years ago. Jewishness is defined by your maternal lineage, but membership in the priestly order of Aaronids, within the Tribe of Levi, is defined by your father. The test is conclusive. Your Y-DNA confirms your CMH status and a direct relationship with a most distant common ancestor that led the Jews in prayer, sacrifice, and worship in ancient Israel.

This is a very prestigious status among the modern Jews and has generated much research. To this e-mail I am attaching documents that contain detailed information about the genetic test, what it means to be CMH, and a reference guide with citations from religious texts about the priestly class.

Sincerely,
Aaron E. Kohen, PhD
Chairman & CEO, Genoshalom Corporation

Trey finished reading and shut his laptop without viewing the attachments. He pushed himself away from the desk and walked out the back door onto the terrace with his coffee. He sat down in a cushioned wicker rocking chair. He couldn't believe what he just read. Trey now had a complete genetic picture of his family. His mother was an Irish Catholic from upstate New York, and his father was a Jew from the priestly class of Aaron. He was surprised and inspired by the news of his Jewish heritage as he wondered where the search for his father would lead. He sat still, looking out over the dew-covered fields. For the first time in his life, he knew something concrete about his father; he was a Jew. A search for his mother's family brought him to Ireland. The effort had produced some interesting results. Now he could add his father's family to the quest for answers.

The sun was above the horizon, already heating the terrace stones. The grain field that spread out before him was silent in the dead calm of the morning. Trey captured the landscape as a mental image that could be recalled and used as a reminder of how he felt at this moment. By merely turning his head to the left, he could catch another view of the incredible scene, click, and then to the right, click. He now had a 180-degree panorama in his mental photo album. He was in fucking Ireland, a Jew and a Catholic all at the same time. He had already learned religion did not define a person; their DNA provided the definitive proof of bloodlines and inherited traits. Many wars were inspired by religious beliefs, he pontificated mentally. How ridiculous, considering you could be fighting someone from your genetic family and not even know because they practiced a different religion.

A whole range of emotions flooded Trey's mind. He was angry with his father for leaving, upset at his mother for dying, and frustrated with his grandparents, for never sharing any information. Happiness overtook his anger as he thought about the personal history he had uncovered through his regression work with Rachel. The images of his life discovered under the influence of hypnosis were beginning to crystallize with thoughts of his Jewishness. He conjured up a picture of his father: handsome, strong, and very intelligent. Most estranged sons imagined their lost fathers as heroes, geniuses, and self-sacrificing men who left to fulfill a higher calling. They would return one day with a logical explanation for their absence, recalling deeds of valor and acts of compassion that distracted them from their paternal obligations.

Stepping out of the fantasy, Trey wondered if his newfound Jewishness would diminish his allure as a bad-boy, Gentile in Rachel's eyes. But Trey also thought she might be happy to be dating a half-breed Jew, because it might get her brother off her back. Either way, he had to tell Rachel.

Trey slipped quietly into the bedroom. He climbed into bed with his houseguest and spooned her as she continued to sleep. Her white-as-ivory shoulders stuck out of the sheets beckoning to be kissed. As he moved to apply his lips to her bare skin, she turned to face him, and their mouths came together.

Completing a morning smooch, she said, "Good morning, Mr. Cowens. Where have you been? It's been lonely in here without you, although I didn't forego sleep in your absence. I'm fully rested from my trip and ready to attack another day," she said in a first-words-of-the-morning voice.

"Well I've got some bad news for you. It turns out that I'm not all Irish. I got an e-mail from your brother, Ari, this morning," he stopped there expecting a concerned response, which he got.

Rachel bolted upright in bed and said, "You what? You got an e-mail from Ari? Oh my God. Did he threaten you for being with me? I knew the crazy bastard would go postal once he found out we were together. I am so sorry. I never meant to get you involved in my family's obsession with interfaith relationships. The fact that we're together has caused Ari some major turmoil. I just want to apologize for him and let you know I really care for you. I don't want this to destroy what we could have, and now he's gone too far." She ended her rant and covered her face with her hands. Her fully exposed breasts hung naturally from beneath her elbows, momentarily distracting Trey.

He shook the effects of her splendid protuberances and responded, "He didn't threaten me at all. He sent my Y-DNA test results from his lab."

Surprised but relieved, Rachel exhaled, "So what's in the e-mail?"

"Well it turns out that my asshole father was a member of the tribe," Trey quipped.

"Tribe? What tribe? Native American?" she asked, not making the connection.

"No, a little further east," he responded.

Rachel's look of confusion gave way to a thoughtful expression as she considered the options. Then it dawned on her that by "tribe" he meant the Jewish people. That is why Ari communicated the results and not his laboratory administrator. "Your father was Jewish?" she asked skeptically.

"Well, maybe he's not a Jew, but he's definitely a member of the Cohen Modal Haplotype. And according to your brother's e-mail, the results are verified and certified," he smiled, trying to gauge her reaction.

"You're shitting me, right? You and your father are descended from the priestly class of Aaron, the same Y-DNA that inhabits my brother's body?" She was outwardly excited as she pieced together the connection.

"Yep, I've got the same twisted genetic makeup as your brother. Who would have thought? Trey Cowens is *Jew-ish*" That attempt at humor did elicit a chuckle from Rachel as she got out of bed and put on a robe.

"I need to see the e-mail right now," she demanded, walking out of the bedroom.

Trey followed her to his desk, opened the computer, and cued up the e-mail for her inspection. Rachel's morning ensemble included a sexy pair of reading glasses that she wore before putting in her contacts. She took his seat at the desk and proceeded to read the e-mail from her brother in its entirety. Once she finished reading, she shut the computer and turned to look up at Trey.

"Trey, you are an Aaronid. You are a member of an exclusive group of men who have been given the responsibility of maintaining the flame of the God within the Jewish community. I'm blown away by these test results. How are you feeling?" she finally asked.

"Well, one day you go to sleep thinking you know a little bit about who you are, and then you wake up and find out you're a Jew," he said in a way that confirmed his confusion about the discovery.

"Never a dull moment hanging out with you, Mr. Cowens. I have to be honest, I'm thrilled because it will take some heat off us with regard to my family. But frankly I never cared much for Jewish men," she said sarcastically.

"Too bad you're stuck with me for another week," Trey said in response to her humor. "I guess you'll have to make do as I fumble around trying to please you in my own Jewish way."

This got a smile from Rachel, who responded with, "It has taken Jewish men over five thousand years to perfect their fumbling techniques. I don't see how you could possibly become as inept in just another week."

"With practice I hope I can meet your reduced expectations. I'm thinking about getting one of those nightshirts that has a hole for your manhood, so you don't have to touch your partner during sex." This last attempt at Jewish humor incited an immediate response.

"That's a myth. Jewish men don't wear a sheet with a hole for sex. Don't even think of it, young man, or I'll go Lorena Bobbitt on you," she said with a wry smile.

At eight a.m. on her seventh day they were getting very comfortable with each other. She looked beautiful as she rose from his desk to hug him around the neck. As she lifted her arms, the sash of her robe loosened to reveal her incredible breasts and yoga-flat stomach. He snuck his body into the breach and held her.

"Hey, let me go," she finally said as she turned toward the bedroom. "I need a bath in that wonderful bear claw tub of yours. I brought special aromatherapy bubble bath just for the occasion. Now leave me to my feminine duties."

Rachel seemed to know what to say and when to say it in a way that elevated Trey's spirits. He imagined the smell of bath salts filling the air when she exited the bathroom, spreading a clean aroma throughout the entire cottage. With his olfactory system on high alert, his eyes were happily taking in the view of Rachel's incredible body when she closed her robe and suggested, "Why don't you busy yourself learning how a *Jew-ish* man pleases his Jewish girlfriend? You can Google it." Then she disappeared into the bathroom and shut the door. He stood alone in the bedroom doorway, wondering if life could get any more confusing as he recounted the events of the last few days.

Trey thought about his parents. Their absence had forced him to discover his history one piece at a time. Maybe he should have been more insistent with his grandparents, forcing them to divulge specifics about his father.

If he is alive, why hasn't the jerk tried to contact me for over thirty-five years? Is that a Jewish thing? No way, not based on the reverence they have for their sons, thought Trey.

His confusion didn't diminish his enthusiasm for the challenge of tracking down everything he could about his family. His journey portended to be intriguing and more than a little scary.

Chapter 13

Trey left Rachel at the cottage around noon to slip into Letterkenny for some groceries. McClafferty's Market on Main Street was his favorite place to food shop because it had a selection of American items he couldn't find in other stores. The market was also home to the best butcher in Ireland, John McClafferty, who befriended Trey his first week in Ireland. John was a strapping man who stood about 6' 4" and weighed around 275 pounds. There wasn't a carcass in Ireland John couldn't tame. Trey had alerted John to Rachel's arrival the previous week and the need for some creative meat sourcing due to her pork prohibition. Pork had never been Trey's favorite meat anyway.

Makes sense now, Trey thought.

Trey approached the meat counter, which looked like a museum exhibit of dead animals and their entrails. Most of the specimens had their heads on, with eyes bulging out of the sockets, registering the last moment of life. Coils of black and white pudding sausage hung decoratively around the display case housing all kinds of offerings from the land, sea, and air.

"Hello, Trey, how are you this fine day?" John asked from behind the counter as he wiped his hands on his permanently blood stained apron.

"Very well, John, nice to see you. I came for my salmon and chicken. Is it ready?" Trey inquired, looking askance at the pig's feet before him.

"In the fridge, I'll get it for you. Would you like to try one of our traditional sausages while you wait? I cooked up a batch a few minutes ago." John offered him a plate with the sausages cut into one-inch pieces. Trey poked one with a toothpick and popped it into his mouth. It had a moldy, earthy taste, at first detestable and then surprisingly satisfying. That must be what they mean by "an acquired taste." He imagined that if he choked down ten pieces he would know if it was a taste he could acquire.

John returned with the order wrapped in white butcher paper and tied with a thin piece of brown yarn. He placed the individual packets in a large paper bag and set it on the counter.

"Anything else today, my friend?" John asked with a smile.

"Yeah, how about a veal steak, something I can pound into submission for a scaloppini?" responded Trey, showing off a little for the butcher.

"Bravo, Trey. You're turning into an Italian chef while you're here in Ireland. I can recommend the veal right in front of you, and I'll be happy to flatten it for you." John removed the meat from the case and ran it through what looked like laundry rollers, and out popped the thinned meat. John wrapped it and affixed a price sticker before handing it to Trey.

"Thanks. What was the sausage I just ate?" Trey asked.

"It's a traditional sausage called *drisheen* made of boiled sheep's blood, breadcrumbs, and seasoning stuffed into its intestines. Did you like it?" John asked knowing Americans generally shied away from exotic concoctions.

"A first for me, but not bad. Thanks for expanding my food palate, but I think I'll stick to the parts of the animal I can identify," Trey said, thinking he would throw-up once he was clear of the store.

He collected his meats and said good-bye to the butcher. He picked up a few more items on his way to checkout. Placing the selections on the conveyor, he rolled his cart to the end of the counter and began bagging his own groceries in the cloth sacks he brought. The clerk, a frumpy looking girl in her late teens, offered Trey a cheery smile and thanked him for helping her as he paid the total.

Trey opened the back of the Mini remotely as he approached the vehicle. The rear hatch opened magically. He placed his bags in the netting that kept the groceries from flying around. As he closed the hatch, everything went dark. Trey was momentarily disoriented as he realized his arms were being held behind his back and his head was covered with a hood. He tried to call out, but a piece of cloth was jammed into his mouth. Two people, maybe three, dragged him away from his car. He struggled against his captors, but efforts to free himself caused severe pain. They shoved Trey backwards into what seemed to be a trunk, an intuition confirmed by the slamming of the lid. He tried to make a racket, but the sounds of his struggle were muted by the noise of the engine and tires on the road.

Being entombed brought back thoughts of the dreaded tattoo and the night he had unspeakable things done to him by strangers. He was haunted by the loss of power and authority over his own actions. The combination of his fear and the motion of the car caused his stomach to entertain vomiting, not a good idea considering the blocked escape route. The thought of dying while choking on his own puke gave his sober mind the resolve to wish the sickness away. Getting his shit together, he swallowed the telltale secretions that forewarned an imminent evacuation of his stomach's contents. Unfortunately, he had to taste the sausage for a second excruciating time.

The car moved fast, to where he had no idea. *What the hell is happening to me?* Trey thought as he considered the reasons for his abduction. He had kept a low profile while in Ireland, not wanting to draw attention to his presence and wealth. The ride got bumpy, and his body bounced off the floor of the trunk repeatedly as the car made its way down a country road.

They stopped. He could hear muted talking coming from the other side of the rear seat. Struggling to stay calm, Trey was having trouble catching his breath through the cover over his head. *Don't panic*, he told himself. *Just try to relax. Everything will work itself out, whatever this is.*

The trunk opened. No one spoke as they lifted a hooded Trey out of the trunk and carried him by the legs and arms across some gravel. He sensed a change in the environment as they passed from outside to inside. He detected the scent of coffee and smoke from a fire. They released his bound legs to the floor and placed his ass firmly on a chair. He heard his captors speaking in low voices in another part of the house. He decided to remain seated and calm, offering no resistance.

A shuffle of feet and the screech of a chair being dragged across the floor were the next sounds Trey recognized. Following a moment of complete silence, one of the men spoke with a deep Irish accent.

"I'm going to remove the hood from your head and the sock from your mouth. There's no need to struggle or scream. You're outnumbered, and no one will hear you. You are with friends, and all we want is an opportunity to speak with you. Once we've concluded our interview, you'll be free to leave."

The hood came off, and light attacked Trey's eyes. He tried to blink away the accumulated eye gunk as he focused on the three men seated around him. The man in front of Trey stared into his eyes. Trey was shocked to see himself. He closed his eyes, shook his head and thought he must be hallucinating. He reopened his eyes; the same person stared back at him, but this time his demeanor had softened.

"Who the fuck are you, and where the hell am I?" Trey shouted.

"Calm down, bloke. We just want to have a little talk," said the large, caramel-colored man sitting to Trey's right. He was definitely not from Ireland. Not interested in his family history, Trey wanted to know what was going on.

The man seated in front of Trey spoke. "Mr. Cowens, I understand you've had quite an interesting week, with the airport situation and all. I'm sorry to abduct you like this, but it was the only way we could assure that our meeting would be private. This precaution is for your safety as well as ours. I hope you will accept our apologies for any rough treatment you endured."

Trey studied the face of the man who spoke with a heavy, local accent. Incredibly, except for some extra weight, they appeared to be exact doubles.

"You're Donald Murphy, aren't you?" he asked, recognizing the man from the picture he received from Seamus. Trey experienced a netherworld tug on his psyche. If this was a dream, he needed to wake up; if not, he was looking at his doppelganger.

"Yes I am, and you are William Cowens, the famous terrorist lookalike. I would be remiss if I didn't comment on the similarity of our appearance," Donny remarked as he turned to his accomplices for confirmation. Both men nodded in agreement as Donny stood brandishing a knife he had removed from his back pocket. "If I cut your restraints, will you promise not to try anything stupid? I assure you once our business is concluded, you will be free to go." Trey answered in the affirmative, and Donny removed the plastic straps. Trey attempted to shake some blood back into his hands and feet as Donny returned to his chair.

"I think we both know why you are here. There is a remarkable resemblance between us, so remarkable that it was necessary to meet you as soon as possible. Looking like me in Ireland is not advisable. I am a wanted man and considered by many to be a terrorist. Your detention at the airport caused quite a stir among both my Republican colleagues and the occupying forces," Donny said, mesmerized by Trey's face.

"Why didn't you arrange a meeting through Seamus? He had already told me all about your involvement in the movement. I would have come to have this conversation on more civil terms." Trey's anger built as he considered his situation. He couldn't think of a good reason for the treatment he had received. He was as curious as Donald Murphy about their identical appearance, but come on, man, not like this.

"Seamus is an old blowhard who is watched closely by the enemy. Spies are everywhere. We take extra precautions when we contact those outside our immediate group. We trust no one, not even the other paramilitary groups within the Real IRA. Don't think we're picking on you. We do this to all of our friends," Donny offered with a slight chuckle.

This set Trey off. "What the fuck is the Real IRA? A bunch of crazy nut-bags that go around blowing people up?" Trey's outrage grew; he didn't like Donny's smug attitude about the kidnapping. Trey casually looked away from Donny and then made a violent lunge from his chair. About halfway to getting all knotted up with Donny, the two goons grabbed him in midair and slammed him to the floor. The concussive force of his head hitting the ground caused him to blackout. Trey slowly shook off the effects of the impact. While regaining his senses he noted he had been returned to the chair with arm and leg restraints.

"We're the Real Irish Republican Army," said Donny, as if nothing had happened. "We uphold an uncompromising form of Irish Republicanism opposing any settlement with the British that falls short of complete Irish unity and independence. Our cause defends the freedoms of common people from the British military occupiers as well as those who seek to undermine the financial security of the Republic. Recent financial misdeeds by the banks, supported by Britain, raped the Irish Treasury, throwing Ireland into a depression. Add that to the racism being practiced against the Irish Catholics in Northern Ireland, and you can see we are justified."

"Justified? Are you kidding me? I don't give a fuck about your Rey-Rah bullshit! You think abducting and killing people is the answer to your national problem. You're insane, Mr. Murphy. From what I hear, everyone but you and a handful of terrorists want peace with the British." Trey had lost his patience listening to Donny rationalize his activities.

"I'm not asking for your approval, Mr. Cowens. I'm only interested in your appearance, which you must agree is mystifyingly similar to mine. You'll be free to go after we have our little talk and we take a few pictures. I even shaved my facial hair for a photo shoot." Donny nodded at the third person, who stepped forward.

He went on, "The guy over there is Terrance, and this is Sean. He will be taking some pictures of us with a Polaroid camera so we may both assess the similarities of our appearance. After all, the FACE system at the airport does a pretty good job of identifying people, better than the press would lead you to believe."

Donny scooted his chair next to Trey's, placing himself in the picture. With one photo taken, Sean asked his subjects to turn to the left and then to the right. Three pictures spit out of the Polaroid and Donny stood to retrieve them from Sean. He studied the photos while the two men lifted the chair and carried Trey into the next room.

Donny laid the three pictures on a coffee table. Trey shut his eyes, refusing to look at the pictures as a way of rejecting both the methods and the philosophy of his captors. But shouldn't he give this thug a chance and let him finish his business so he could get the hell out of here? Trey's mood softened a little as he opened his eyes and viewed the photos on the table. He would play their game hoping to speed up his promised release.

"The restraints are cutting off the circulation to my hands and feet. I'll behave if you cut me loose," Trey implored in a defeated tone.

Donny waved his hand as if to say, *cut him loose*. Sean leaned in holding a nine-inch bowie knife. Trey was certain the blade had not field-dressed any game lately, unless you counted *Homo sapiens*. With two precise draws of the blade, the restraints fell to the floor and blood flowed to Trey's extremities again.

The large brown man turned on the lights in the living room so they could see the pictures clearly on the coffee table. They both tilted forward to study the profile pictures; the similarities were remarkable. They were identical in every way except for the extra chin sported by Donny. They continued to inspect the pictures without uttering a word.

Trey broke the silence. "Did you know your parents?" he asked, turning to face Donny.

"Patrick and Mary Murphy were my parents. Well, I should say my adopted parents. They got me from an orphanage in Dublin as an infant and raised me as their only child. I grew up the son of a factory worker and homemaker in Galway, County Clare." Donny trailed off with a tinge of sadness in his voice.

"Did you ever ask them about your biological parents?" Trey asked in a probing yet sensitive way.

"I didn't know I was adopted until my parents died two years ago. I was going through some of their personal effects and came upon a folder from an orphanage. The folder included paperwork from a New York adoption agency stating I had been given up for adoption in Buffalo, New York, and brought to Ireland by an Irish woman who had been working for a wealthy family in Niagara Falls. I found a birth certificate showing my place and date of birth, but all of the parental information had been removed. The Irish woman arranged for me to be brought to Ireland to be with her family, but somehow I ended up in an orphanage in Dublin. That's all I know," Donny concluded.

Lights were going on in Trey's head as he imagined the chain of events that could have separated the boys when they were newborns.

"I was born in Buffalo, New York. My grandparents were wealthy people who lived in Niagara Falls." They both thought the connection was too auspicious to ignore.

"What is your date of birth," asked Trey

"March 12, 1974," responded Donny; registering Trey's amazement that they were born the same day. This confirmed what Trey had suspected. Donald Murphy was his twin brother. But how the hell had this happened?

Trey lifted the photos from the table. They were brothers. The pictures and story confirmed it. As far as Trey was concerned, he had found his twin brother.

Trey turned to his newfound relative, "I think we have some catching up to do." As he said the words, his mind filled with questions. Why had they been separated? Who had done this? And now, how would they get to know one another?

"I guess we do, and I am pleased to make your acquaintance, Mr. Cowens. It's been too long. Where have you been all of my life?" Donny asked rhetorically, punctuating the comment with a nervous laugh. He was smiling at the realization he was seated next to a blood relative. Trey began to relax, realizing he would live through the day.

Fighting back emotion, Trey spoke, "I think we both agree the physical similarities are remarkable and unimpeachable. And the story of your adoption and birth date adds support to the notion we are twins. I suggest we take a simple DNA paternity test to confirm our siblingship."

Donny regained some of his tough guy demeanor. "I can't submit to any test that will create a paper trail as to my identity. I want to verify our relationship, but it's got to be anonymous, and only the two of us can know the results," Donny said, reverting to his military persona.

"Shouldn't be problem," said Trey. "We can both do separate tests, and yours can be under an assumed name. I don't think we even need a full-blown DNA test to prove our relationship. A simple sibling test will do the trick." Trey hoped for a positive response from Donny and an opportunity to scientifically prove their relationship.

"You arrange to get the test kits, and I'll give you what you need, provided I can be assured no one will know it's my DNA being tested. I can't believe this is happening. So many questions are running through my mind. You must leave before someone reports you missing. Within the next two weeks a major operation will change the face of resistance in Northern Ireland. I suggest you leave the country before things heat up."

"Thanks for the advice, but how will I get the DNA test kits to you?" asked Trey as they both got up from the couch.

"I'll send a woman to clean your cottage on Wednesday. She will introduce herself as Sinead and clean your house for three hours. When she finishes her work, you will pay her sixty Euros and give her the test kit I am to use for the sample," Donny said. "I'll return the samples in the same way the following Friday."

"How will I get the results to you?" Trey asked not quite tracking the chain of events.

"Don't worry, I'll be in touch."

Donny was surprised by the emotions he was feeling. For the first time in years he was thinking about something other than the conflict. He basked in the knowledge that he was not alone anymore. He might actually have a family and even a twin brother. The thought of losing Trey rattled him more than he expected. How would he be able to say good-bye to his brother? He had to protect him.

The two brothers hugged for a long time as they stood in front of the couch. Donny felt relieved, happy, sad, and expectant all at the same time. He didn't want to let go of his new brother. Their bear hug became tighter as they prepared to say farewell.

Donny spoke. "You have to go. Your absence could cause some alarm. It's not wise for us to meet in person again, at least until we can arrange for a secure place and time. I suggest you keep our meeting secret, and please do not tell Seamus. He is a wonderful person and patriot, but Big Brother's eyes are on Seamus. His lips have gotten loose in old age."

Go? Now? I've just met my twin brother and now I have to leave? Trey's inner child was screaming at him to stay.

Before turning to depart, Trey bent down and cuffed one of the photos on the coffee table. Donny led him to the door and said, "I hope to see you soon, my brother. Until then, be careful what you look for because you might find trouble in the most unusual and dangerous places."

Trey stopped in his tracks realizing he had forgotten to share his findings about Wolfe Tone with his new twin. "We're related to Wolfe Tone. His blood is running through your veins. Our mother's family comes from the same revolutionary stock that created Tone and now you. It's incredible you have continued his fight some two hundred years later."

Donny thought about the meaning of Trey's words. "And you know this how?" he asked with suspicion.

"DNA science led me to one of his relatives here in Ireland, and I confirmed the findings by tracing our mother's family back to the famous Irishman through traditional genealogy."

Dumbstruck by the information, Donny's brain went into high gear trying to crunch the data. He had a twin brother, and he was related to the famous Irishman he adopted as the model for attacks on everything British.

Walking toward the car, Trey turned to his brother and said, "Oh yeah, one more thing. Your father is a Jew."

Donny reacted to the words with the fierceness of an attacking lion. Terrance and Sean stepped in to keep Donny off of Trey. "What the fuck did you say?" Confused by the reference, Donny reverted to a Jew-hating Irishman.

"Whoa, Donny, no insult intended, just the facts. If we're twins, then your father was or is Jewish, but don't worry, your mother was a Catholic."

"Are you telling me my father was Jewish and my mother was a Catholic who was related to Wolfe Tone?" Donny was now more confused than ever. He never imagined Trey would have so many tricks up his sleeve. He had underestimated this man, his brother.

"Yes, that's what I am saying. DNA tests proved as much, but it does not make you Jewish unless you convert," Trey said, imagining Donny would sooner cut off his dick then become a Jew.

Trey turned with the other men and walked toward the car, leaving Donny to ponder this new information. "What's his name?" Donny shouted to his departing brother.

"I don't know, but I plan to find out, and you will be among the first to know," Trey was feeling more in charge. It was liberating to turn the tables on his sibling. Was this how it felt to have a brother? A healthy rivalry had been sparked as they prepared to say their final good-byes.

Donny hugged Trey again before he got into the car. Holding the embrace for a long time, Donny whispered into Trey's ear, "Be careful Jew boy. I don't want to lose you." They both hoped to be together soon so they could begin the arduous task of piecing together their shared but separate history.

Out of sorts, Rachel had been waiting for Trey to return from the grocery for over four hours. She tried to call Seamus but he did not answer. She left a nondescript message requesting he call her back as soon as possible.

Instinctually she knew the situation with Trey was too good to be true. Subconsciously, she had been waiting for the "real Trey" to come out. Now she saw it in all of its pitiful glory. This man had managed to fool her, an irony not missed by the psychiatrist. Trey had abandoned her in a foreign country with no means of transportation and limited communication. He was probably meeting up with his Irish girlfriend and lying to the slut about his time with Rachel. Regardless, his behavior was selfish and irresponsible. She could have excused him if he was an hour late, but four freaking hours, intolerable.

It reminded her of dating Oedipal Jewish men who, without explanation, drop everything to be with their mothers. Maybe his Jewish DNA was rearing its ugly head in a perverted sort of way. Rachel sensed traits similar to her father's in this newly discovered member of their tribe.

The noise of a car approaching on the driveway interrupted her thoughts. She ran to the door. Trey's car came to a stop in the turn-around at the front of the cottage. He got out of the Mini. Rachel surprised herself by racing to hug him without saying a word. She held him tightly as if to say she was never going to let him go; she realized that her anger was exceeded by her fear of losing him.

"Well this is a fine greeting. I should go to the market more often," Trey said, trying to inject a little levity into what he recognized as a tense scene.

Pushing him away, in a raised voice she said, "Where the hell have you been? I've been worried to death waiting here for over four hours. You could have at least called to tell me you were running late."

"I didn't have a chance to call because—" Rachel cut him off before he could explain what happened.

"Come on Trey, don't give me that bullshit. You have a cell phone," Rachel said emphatically.

Totally frustrated, she went on, "I don't think I can do this, what with all of the drama and intrigue in your life. I thought I would be coming to Ireland for a vacation with a wonderful man whom I could fall for, but now I am officially questioning my decision."

Living up to her status as a true Jewish American Princess, Rachel made Trey feel wanted, but not in the way women wanted him in the past, for his looks and money. She seemed to harbor deeper feelings that made her freak out and say things implying true emotional content in their relationship. *This is really going somewhere,* Trey thought as he said, "I got kidnapped."

"You're a goddamn liar! Don't make a mockery of the situation by joking about me being worried. You were detained by airport security for being a terrorist the other day, so forgive my concern when a little grocery shopping turns into a four hour absence." She turned away in disgust and headed for the front door.

"No really. Donny Murphy had his thugs pick me up in town. They drove me blindfolded to his hideout. We had a two-hour meeting and exchanged information about our families. I have a photo to prove it." He handed the picture to Rachel, who turned to snatch the offering.

She examined the rectangular memento. "That's incredible. He looks just like you." But her thoughts immediately went back to the grandiose excuses her father used when he would disappear for days on end. Her father manufactured the most believable stories to justify his absenteeism. She prayed this was different.

Trey reached for her hand and led her to the back of the car. He beeped open the rear hatch and retrieved the groceries from the Mini. Luckily the temperatures this time of year were cool, and the car had been out of the sun during his captivity. The groceries were fine and ready to prepare for their evening meal. They walked inside carrying the bags and holding hands.

He related every detail of his abduction and the conversations with his alleged twin brother as they prepared dinner together in the kitchen. Trey wanted her to know everything; after all, she already knew more than anyone else did. His desire to be totally open surprised Trey. Normally he wanted to keep feelings to himself, but with Rachel he spoke his mind without the relational filters he usually employed. Trey was used to giving calculated responses to predictable questions. This was different; he was really falling for Rachel.

Marriage was redundant and complicated in Trey's opinion. If you loved someone, why did you need a legal contract to validate the commitment? And further, from what he could tell, marriage was no better than a 50/50 proposition. His mom and dad were estranged; his grandparents got divorced before they died. Hell, his entire known family batted a thousand percent. Marriage always seemed to end up in a steaming heap of emotional recriminations and heartache; few he ever knew came out the other end happier. So he had resigned himself to conducting "enlightened" relationships he could terminate when marriage became the topic du jour. This felt different, not that he wanted to marry this beautiful Jewish doctor, but she was worth fighting for. If having her meant letting Rachel into the deepest recesses of his mind and soul, then he would. However, he would keep the tattoo story to himself for the time being. The shame of that night still weighed heavily on Trey.

"You've had a full day," Rachel said after hearing about his afternoon. "I assume you believe Donny is your twin based on what you're telling me and a DNA test will provide conclusive proof. It must be traumatic to meet a brother you never knew existed, much less finding him to be your identical twin. To me, the picture is all the proof you should need."

Trey listened as his mind wandered back to his abduction. He already missed that crazy-ass terrorist, and they had been separated for only a couple of hours. *Isn't it strange*, he thought, *that the bond of brotherhood could cause these feelings after such a short encounter and long time apart?* He was ready to be a brother to someone, even a man involved in radical shit like overthrowing a foreign power. Donny had probably killed many men in pursuit of his goals, and oddly, that didn't scare Trey in the least. Trey had an untapped reserve of brotherly love for the person with whom he had spent nine months in their mother's womb.

Baffled by what was happening to him, Trey needed to clear his mind and focus on why he came to Ireland in the first place, to find his family. His DNA placed him squarely in the fight for Irish independence. Considering Donny and Wolfe, his bloodline was alarmingly revolutionary; he smiled at the thought. Could someone be hardwired for radical thoughts and actions? Did people inherit traits that induced fanatical acts?

Trey had revolutionized the concept of asset allocation and professional money management by building Trilogica into the preeminent multi-manager investment fund on Wall Street. He discovered he was not so different from those who chose guns and bombs to settle their conflicts. Trey elected to fight his battles on the trading floor and in the boardroom—less blood, same result: someone wins and someone looses.

"What are we going to do?" asked Rachel, concerned about Trey's safety and the role she might play.

"I think I'll take Donny's advice and leave Ireland when you go back to the States. I'm not sure where I'll go, but we can figure that out before you leave." His smile concealed a fear he wouldn't see her again. He wouldn't blame her if she changed her phone number and got a new e-mail address. His life was complicated and controversial. It was clear that all the hoopla had caused doubt to creep into Rachel's mind.

Chapter 14

Yussel "Yussi" Fischer sat in a private office surrounded by a concave wall of computer screens displaying various combinations of live surveillance images and cable news broadcasts. Hard at work doing what he had done every day for the past forty years, Yussi gathered intelligence, countered terrorism, and managed deep reconnaissance missions. His life had been defined on July 4, 1976 when he led an assault team off a C-130 Hercules aircraft at the Entebbe Airport in Uganda to free one hundred hostages who had been hijacked by the Popular Front for the Liberation of Palestine. Yussi's classmate and best friend Lt. Col. Eitan "Etty" Yedidya, was fatally wounded on that day. Yussi recovered Etty's body amid gunfire from the airport rooftops. Etty was the only Israeli to die that day, and his loss was a constant reminder to Yussi of Israel's enormous challenges.

Yussi left the military and formed Fischer Intelligence when it became clear politics clouded the better judgment of Israel's leadership. A completely secure Israel was his goal. Israel would have to embrace its own form of fanatical, militant behavior if it wanted to be free from the continuous threat of eradication by extremists and radicalized elements in the Arab world. Twenty-first-century political decorum required such actions be called "appropriate response units" or "preemptive strike forces", all designed to do one thing—eliminate the threat, perceived or actual.

The modern theater of war had become a game of Whack-A-Radical. Smack one down and another rag-head pops up to take his place. The young Muslim populations were directing the national angst at their countries' dictators and, for once, not denouncing Israel as the root of their problems. Yussi knew firsthand about the patience of radical Islam and never underestimated its ability to lurk in a sandstorm waiting for an opportunity to strike. He would preempt their moves with the best intelligence and weapons money could buy. Yussi's instruments of war included cyber and microbiological technologies, along with traditional incendiary munitions, a cutting-edge arsenal.

Fischer Intelligence received a huge boost when Etty's younger brother became Prime Minister of Israel. Ever since the election, Yussi had been privately briefing the PM, who friends called "Pimi," on all matters related to Israel's security. Pimi made sure Yussi and his team received adequate financial backing from slush funds controlled by the most orthodox, right-wing elements of the Likud Party. These monies flowed freely through offshore accounts directly into the operational budget of a Fischer Intelligence subsidiary. Technically Fischer was contracted to do polling for the party and take the temperature of the Israeli population regarding actions against or in cooperation with Palestinians. This was a brilliant cover for the covert operations Fischer Intelligence performed for Pimi and his cohorts.

Over the past two years a weakness had evolved within the Israeli citizenry relating to a two-state solution with Palestine. A growing majority of Israelis who were prepared to sacrifice portions of their homeland in order to extract a peace settlement thought concessions would lead to stability. Israelis were sick and tired of watching their friends and children get blown up by suicide bombers. They did not want to be perceived as an occupying force any longer. Most Jews hungered to live in peace and reap the rewards of a prosperity they had worked so hard to create. They were willing to give up land and release terrorists from prison to achieve these goals.

Yussi was disgusted by this turn of events. His polling was conclusive. This populist movement had the potential to destroy everything Yussi had worked for over the last forty years. He was committed to fighting the fight even in the face of such resistance. He earned the right to defend Israel through his actions during the Yom Kippur War in 1973, the fight for the Suez Canal & Golan Heights, as well as the Entebbe and Sabena hijackings. He wouldn't let this naive generation of Israelis commit the biggest mistake he could imagine by conceding hard-fought-for territory for the sake of an ephemeral peace. Any sign of weakness would open the floodgates of retaliation by all the radical elements in the Arab world. Their steel-pointed daggers would be plunged into the weakened corpus of the Israeli state. Yussi swore he would not let that happen.

"Good morning, Colonel Fischer. Your ten-o'clock meeting is here," said a female voice from his phone's intercom, breaking the silence of his early morning trance. Not remembering whom he had agreed to meet, he quickly scanned his diary and found the name—Dr. Aaron Kohen. Scribbled next to the name—"population genetics, friend of Buji."

Isaac "Buji" Stahl had been Yussi's second in command at Fischer Intelligence until his retirement last year. He recalled the conversation with Buji regarding his recently arrived guest. *This should be interesting*, thought Yussi.

Yussi commanded the black box on his desk, "Show him in."

"Welcome to Fischer Intelligence," said Yussi as he greeted Ari with a firm handshake and a motion to be seated in a cluster of chairs away from his desk and the wall of computer screens.

"Thank you for seeing me," Ari said, intimidated by the opulence of the office and the rank of the individuals displayed in photos on the wall, all in various states of embrace with his host.

"Buji said I would find your work fascinating, and we should meet to discuss some mutual interests. What are you doing in Israel, Dr. Kohen?" Yussi leaned back in his chair, prepared to listen for as long as it took.

Ari proceeded to discuss his work as a population geneticist and the chronology of his efforts from the lab at MIT to the formation of Genoshalom. He consciously avoided any statements that could be interpreted as political, not wanting to burn any bridges before they were built. He concluded with a story about his recent move to Israel and the construction of Genoshalom's state-of-the-art laboratory in Upper Galilee. A brief history of the field of population genetics, human migration patterns, and indigenous cluster testing led to a discussion of why he wanted to meet with the colonel.

"I've been keenly aware of your involvement with intelligence gathering. I thank you for the work you do so people like me and companies like Genoshalom can prosper amid the chaos orbiting us every day. My work leads me to some very interesting places, but none interests me more than how genetics can assist Israel. On the surface, this might seem like a far-fetched connection, but I assure you that the science of genetics holds one key to Israel's permanent security." Ari fell silent and reached for a notepad in the breast pocket of his suit coat. He wrote a note and passed it to his host still attached to the pad. Yussi read what Ari wrote and scribbled something in return, also answering with a nod of his head.

The note from Ari read, *"Is there somewhere we can talk privately? I know this room is bugged and under camera surveillance."*

Yussi's response, *"Yes, but not today. I will have someone from my staff contact you."*

Yussi stood to say good-bye to his guest. Ari returned the notepad to his pocket and rose to face his new friend. They shook hands. Yussi escorted Ari to the door. They parted with an unspoken plan to meet again in a more private setting.

Ari rode the elevator down twenty-three floors to the lobby. The glass and marble structure was among the newest office buildings in the city. A construction boom was underway in the Tel Aviv metropolitan area, as witnessed by the numerous cranes hanging over the skyline. The Gush Dan, as the entire area is known, had been growing at a steady rate over the last five years. It was counterintuitive to many that a country like Israel, prone to random terror attacks and suicide bombings, would be prospering at all. As a world recession raged on in most parts of the globe, Israel continued to flourish. Many international companies had recently expanded operations in Israel, attracted by a highly educated workforce and a population hungry to prove their mettle on the global stage.

Israel had already proven its skills in the areas of espionage and military technology. The time had come to be recognized as a collective of creative Jewish minds. Ari saw himself as a central player in a fight pitting science against an enemy that had little regard for human life. Science could combat the Arab suicide offensive so damaging to Israel.

Ziva waited in the parking lot for the meeting with Fischer to end. She pulled the company Mercedes into the turn around on the north side of the giant structure as Ari pushed his way through the revolving door leading out of the lobby. Ari slid into the front seat. Ziva accelerated away causing his head to jerk back against the headrest.

"Slow down Ziva! What's the rush?" he said, a little irritated at her abrupt departure.

"I got a call from Lev Wasserman. They've made an important discovery at the excavation site. He wanted me to interrupt your meeting with Colonel Fischer. I told him he would have to wait. He texted me at least three times since the call, each time telling us to hurry," she said, applying additional pressure to the gas pedal.

Dr. Lev Wasserman led a private archeological team sponsored by Genoshalom working in conjunction with the Israel Antiquities Authority (IAA) to unearth a first-century Jewish burial tomb discovered only six months prior. Government bulldozers preparing a new roadbed in the area had uncovered the entrance to a burial tomb by accident. Ari had contacted the IAA and agreed to fund the operation from the Genoshalom budget. Lev's team turned up some ancient Roman coins post-dating the sealing of the tomb.

Based on the coins, the tomb had been looted by the Romans at the end of the first century CE.

The burial site was located outside of Neve Ur, a kibbutz community with 350 residents about fifteen kilometers south of Galilee. The land had been cleared of Arabs in 1948 and quickly claimed by Jewish settlers, who had formed a cooperative agricultural community. Much like the kibbutz dwellers occupying the land today, Labor Zionists had founded the original community during the second wave of twentieth-century immigration to Israel. These settlers believed that success of a Jewish state could not depend solely upon protections provided by world powers such as Britain and the United States. Jews must occupy and farm the land they claimed never produced anything more than skinny goats and anemic sheep. Today, verdant fields spread to the edges of the irrigation areas like badges of success on a once-blighted earth.

Ziva and Ari raced up the highway heading northeast in the black Mercedes. Ari tried to call Lev using the built-in Bluetooth phone system. He did not answer. They would be there in less than two hours, but Ari was anxious to speak with him before they arrived.

The IAA had the responsibility of monitoring all excavation sites in the country. They stationed one inspector at Neve Ur to follow the progress of the university students that Genoshalom hired. The students did the tedious work of separating dirt and rubble from the artifacts. The inspector was in charge of making sure everything unearthed got properly recorded and turned over to the IAA for classification and safekeeping. Ari was interested in the good public relations created by the sponsorship of such a high-profile dig. It also gave him unusual access to a potential gold mine of ancient DNA. His man Wasserman was programmed to alert Ari of anything unique or out of the ordinary.

"What did Lev say, Ziva?" Ari demanded.

"I told you. He said he had to speak with you directly." Ziva was as frustrated as Ari by the calls and text messages. "He was worked up, so I tried to get him to tell me what was going on. When I pressed him, he told me you made him promise not to talk to anyone else about what he finds in the tomb. You need to tell Lev I'm your partner."

Ziva's assertiveness turned Ari on. She had an extraordinary intellect and an incredible body, even with the absent limb. He thought about her demand and said, "I'll talk to Lev."

Ari tried to call Lev again, and this time he answered. "Lev, it's Ari, Ziva said you called." Ari's voice had changed to a calm, professorial tone as he engaged Wasserman in a discussion. He never wanted to appear anxious about the dig. He gave no sign of any ulterior motives when speaking to anyone about the excavation, not even his number-one man.

"It's big, Ari. I arrived alone this morning and decided to enter the chamber to see how much work had been completed last Friday. The students digging along the western side of the main room uncovered some stones that didn't match the rest of the material used to construct the burial chamber. I removed some mortar from the lower end of a stone and, Ari, there's another chamber, obviously a separate room by the odor that came from the opening," Lev paused, out of breath.

"Lev…go on," Ari said firmly.

"OK, sorry…I probed the opening further with an illuminated matchstick video camera, and I discovered a new and much bigger chamber. Ari, it looks like it is undisturbed. I mean we would be the first people in two thousand years to enter this space. What should I do?" As one of the country's foremost archaeologists, Lev had only dreamt of such a find. Locating an undisturbed burial chamber would immediately make Lev a celebrity among his colleagues and secure his tenure at the university.

"Do absolutely nothing until I arrive. And don't tell anyone about what you've found," Ari's voice was becoming more forceful.

"It's spring break for the kids, no one will be here until next Monday. Uzi Rubens, the inspector from IAA, said he would come back then, figuring that no work would be done until the students returned." Lev was silent, waiting for further instructions.

"Ms. Wolfson and I will be there in ninety minutes. Wait for us at the dig hut so you can give us a full briefing. Then we will decide our next step. Thanks for the call. You did the right thing, Lev. This could be a huge discovery for all of us." Ari ended on an upbeat note, hoping to calm any concerns Lev might have.

Ari's work in genetics led him to the emerging field of molecular archaeology. This area of archaeology promised to shape the way humans looked into their past. By harvesting and analyzing small amounts of genetic material from urns, latrines, animal bones, and tools, you could determine what ancient people hunted, ate, and wore. Also known as archaeological chemistry, this new science had the power to definitively establish trading relationships between communities and cultures well before the advent of writing.

But the real thrill for Ari was the availability of ancient, human DNA. If the adjacent burial chamber had not been looted there was a high likelihood, in Israel's extremely dry climate, that human DNA would be available for harvesting. He turned to Ziva and barked, "Go faster."

Ziva accelerated to over 180 kilometers per hour. They passed all the cars on the highway as if they were standing still. The Mercedes and Ziva were up to the task. At this rate, they would be at the site in less than ninety minutes. Ari was deep in thought about how he would handle the situation with Lev. If the find was as important as Ari thought, then Lev would become a liability, one that Ari could not afford. The main goals of his work in Israel were unknown to anyone except Ziva and him.

Chapter 15

Trey was looking out the window of the Hawker 4000 executive jet he had boarded at the Signature Private Jet Terminal next to the Dublin International Airport just an hour before. He and Rachel had driven to Dublin to catch her flight back to the states after a two-week stay at his cottage. Taking Donny's advice, Trey decided to evacuate Ireland for a while.

Trilogica had provided Trey with a NetJets Card as part of his leave of absence agreement. With all of the scrutiny he faced at the Belfast Airport, he decided flying privately would be the best way to go. He contacted his NetJets representative, who arranged for a plane in Dublin. The private jet allowed him to forgo the facial or retina scanning at most European airports. His luggage was x-rayed, and he walked through a standard metal detector to enter the secure waiting area of the private terminal. The plane's pilot met him within minutes of his arrival and escorted him to the aircraft.

Trey was seated in the incredibly luxurious surroundings of Raytheon Beech's finely appointed cabin; eight captain's chairs were outfitted with satellite radio, telephone, and TV. Ignoring the media opportunities, Trey stared out the oval portal onto the European mainland from his perch forty thousand feet in the air. He would be in Tel Aviv in less than four hours.

The DNA tests proved what they already knew; Donny and Trey were twin brothers. His newfound sibling had insisted Trey leave Ireland because looking like "Mad Dog" Murphy would be a risk to Trey's health. While he had hardly scratched the surface of his Irish heritage, the situation in Ireland dictated a temporary change of scenery. The discovery of his father's lineage provided him with a unique opportunity to dig into the Jewish side of his family. Plus, Trey did not want to return to an empty cottage after the incredible two weeks with Rachel.

Trey had submitted his Y-DNA test results to an international study that compared his DNA to other participants. As luck would have it, he got an exact match to a person in Israel. Zach Cohen, a middle aged Israeli responded to Trey's query and agreed to a meeting. The DNA unlocked more than doors into his past. Knowledge of his relationship to Tone and that he was the product of a Jewish father launched his search to the next level. His family tree was filling out nicely.

Trey considered the arc of history that had brought him to this point. He was retracing his ancestor's journey from ground zero, his place of birth in Buffalo, to the homelands of his parents and their parents. He could only imagine the hardships his forefathers had endured over the thousands of years it took for his DNA to reach upstate New York. His journey was facilitated by modern information and avionics technology, but the emotion of discovery was universal and timeless.

All things considered, a trip to Israel made sense. He knew he had to go, or his search for answers would be incomplete. Thoughts of his lineage consumed him for the better part of the next hour as he helped himself to the refreshment center and a cold beer. The captain announced their flight had passed the halfway mark, and there were two hours remaining.

The "Arab Spring" in the Middle East and North Africa was in full swing as Trey made his way to the Holy Land. Modern Israel, the only true democracy in the region, had been rewarded with GDP growth dwarfing its larger neighbors. While Arabs focused on removing calcified kleptocrats, the Jews prepared to increase their advantage. He was adrenalized by thoughts of his heritage and the prospects for a face-to-face meeting with his father.

Trey's brain switched gears and wandered back to his time with Rachel. After his abduction and return, she had not let him out of her sight. Their conversations ranged from the unique to the absurd as they talked about siblings, parents, life, love, and destiny. He had never opened up so completely to anyone before. It cleansed him; she scrubbed away his inhibitions about sharing his deepest and most private thoughts by opening her life to him. The sex was as intense as the personal revelations.

"We will be landing in twenty minutes. Please make sure your seatbelt is fastened," announced the pilot over the intercom interrupting Trey's daydream.

Trey arrived at the InterContinental David Hotel in Tel Aviv after an uneventful limo ride from the airport. He cleared passport control and customs with no problems. He paid and tipped his driver as a valet lifted his one duffel bag from the trunk and followed him through the revolving door into the lobby. Three attractive women staffed the reception desk, all of whom could have been in an alluring advertisement for Israeli tourism. It surprised Trey when one spoke up in perfect English, asking, "Checking in, Mr. Cowens?"

Trey remembered the valet asking for his name at the curb so he could label his bag. They must use some kind of microphone system enabling them to notify the reception desk of an arriving guest. *Stealthy,* Trey thought. *Even the hotels in Israel were getting into spy technology.*

"Yes, checking in. I'll be staying for three nights." Trey pulled out his wallet and produced an InterContinental Ambassador Card and his American Express. The clerk swiped and returned both cards. She gave the computer screen a quizzical look, and said, "It appears your three-night stay will be in an executive suite. You have been upgraded at no cost as an Ambassador."

Trey was led to his room by the same valet who had clandestinely given his name to the receptionist. He unlocked the door to the suite and held it for Trey to enter. A view of the Mediterranean Sea filled Trey's eyes with delight as he tossed his briefcase on the bed and went to open the sliding glass doors leading to the suite's balcony. He ventured to the railing and took in a deep breath of the sea air.

He turned to see the valet placing his duffel on the luggage rack. "Can I get you some ice from the machine?" he asked.

"Sure," replied Trey.

The valet returned with a full bucket and said, "Tel Aviv is a safe city. You may walk around day or night, but always use caution if you plan to leave the immediate business and shopping district. For security purposes, I suggest you let the staff know where you are going and when you will return. Have an enjoyable stay, and don't hesitate to contact the concierge should you need anything." Trey handed him a tip, and he departed with a smile.

Not at all tired from the trip, Trey opened the mini-bar and removed two airplane bottles of Crown Royal. Filling a glass with ice, he emptied both into the tumbler and watched the brown liquid go to work. He located a bottle of sparkling water on the counter and added a splash to his drink before heading out onto the balcony to survey his surroundings.

The comfortable patio furniture invited him to lounge under the warm Mediterranean sun. He began to think about being in Israel and what he hoped to find during his stay. He had only booked three nights in the hotel, anticipating he would need to go to Jerusalem in a few days. Trey did not contact Ari about his trip to Israel. He would leave that up to Rachel after he had briefed her on the first days of his visit.

All of his life, he had believed he was Irish Catholic just like Dave Cowens, the standout Boston Celtics basketball player. Now he was struck by the fact that with a few changes to his name he could also be a Jew. Cowens became Cohen by substituting an *h* and removing an *s* at the end. Did his father change his name when he had come to the United States? Was it because of anti-Semitism? Was he hiding from something? Was Trey barking up the wrong tree? He would find out soon enough, because he was meeting one of his genetic matches in less than an hour in the Executive Club Lounge.

The drink and direct sunlight gave Trey a flushed feeling, reminding him of waking under the bush. Each time he revisited that beastly morning, he recalled a new piece of information. Paradoxically, the alcohol gave him courage to face the fuzzy parts of the incident even though booze had caused the memory loss in the first place. He removed his clothes and went into the shower. The humiliation of that dreadful morning, still fresh on his skin, needed a constant cleansing.

Reenergized by the shower, he left the suite and headed to the club for his meeting with Zach Cohen. Trey took the elevator to the twenty-first floor, where the doors opened directly into the club. A hostess greeted Trey: "Welcome to the InterContinental Executive Club. Please help yourself to any of the food and drink. Let me know if there is anything else you need."

"I'm Trey Cowens, and I'm meeting a gentleman here in a few minutes. He's not a hotel guest. How will he gain access to this level?" Trey inquired realizing that his guest could not get up to the club level without a keycard.

"No problem, Mr. Cowens. I will alert the valet and have your guest escorted to the club. What is his name?"

"Zach Cohen."

"As soon as Mr. Cohen arrives I will make sure he finds his way to the club." She picked up the phone, said a few things in Hebrew, hung up, and gave Trey a nod.

Trey wandered to the self-serve bar and found his favorite brand of rye whiskey. He had started drinking more since his move to Europe. His fear of drink had mellowed. The Europeans drank with such élan and control. Trey thought he could do the same, even if the Chihuahua argued the opposite. He poured three fingers of whiskey into a highball glass already filled with ice, adding a splash of Perrier and a twist of lemon completed the cocktail.

Trey made himself comfortable with a faxed printout of the New York Times at a table near a window with an incredible view of downtown Tel Aviv. Not the least bit drawn to the financial section of the paper, he thought about how his life was changing. He was interested in European news, science, and sports. Trey had entered a new phase of his life where he sought quality, not quantity.

Trey's life was changing exponentially. By making self-discovery a priority, he had learned more about himself in nine months than he had in his entire life. He was still afraid of where the road might lead, but he was getting stronger each day. He was convinced that genetics and traditional genealogy would open a world of family connectedness thus far absent in his life. He was committed to finding answers, and along the way he hoped he would meet some interesting people to call family. He had met his estranged twin brother. Even though their time together was short and tumultuous, he knew they would be part of each other's life.

The hostess approached Trey and said, "Mr. Cohen is on his way up."

The door to the elevator opened, and out walked a man in a dark suit carrying a briefcase. He spoke to the hostess who rose to escort him to Trey's table. Trey stood to greet his guest.

"Zach Cohen. I'm pleased to meet you, Mr. Cowens," he said as he took the seat Trey pulled out for him.

"The pleasure is all mine, Zach. Please call me Trey. Thanks for coming to meet with me," Trey offered, making some small talk.

"Not at all. I work in the district not seven blocks from the hotel. I drove over instead of walking because I have to meet my wife for an appointment at six." Zach had good English, better than Trey remembered from the phone calls. Zach declined the offer of a drink, so they began.

"Like I said on the phone, our genetic tests indicate that we are related through our fathers. I was very pleased to discover that you and I share the same Y-DNA. As you know, this indicates a close familial relationship, one only shared by individuals with the same male ancestry. I'm hoping you can educate me about your male relatives so we can determine where our family histories intersect. I never knew my father. He left before I was born, and my mother died during childbirth. I thought I was an only child, but I have recently learned I have a twin brother. We have been separated since birth. If that's not confusing enough, I learned that my father was Jewish, while I have grown up a Roman Catholic in the United States. So here I am trying to learn about my father and his family." Trey looked at his visitor; Zach was listening intently to every word.

"Mr. Cowens, I mean Trey, I'm stunned you are here and that we are meeting. I never thought I would be sitting with a relative because of my participation in a genetic study. You hear about people meeting lost relatives through long and arduous research of family genealogy and old books. I was thrilled to get your call."

Zach began talking about his family story as Trey listened. His father, Omar Cohen, had been an able-bodied warrior in the fight for Israeli freedom in the 1967 Six Days' War. He had commanded a tank division that helped capture the Sinai and East Jerusalem for Israel. He received the nation's highest military honor, The Medal of Valor, for his actions on the battlefield. Omar attained a rank of Lieutenant Colonel and became a Battalion Commander during the Yom Kippur War in 1973. He retired in 1996 after many years of sterling military service.

Omar had a brother who pursued an academic career, William Cohen. He was named after a British military officer who had befriended his father during the 1936 Arab uprisings in Palestine. After his three years of mandatory military service, William left Israel to pursue a postgraduate degree at Georgetown University in the United States. Uncle William returned to Israel each year to visit family members until Zach was around nine years old. That was his last memory of his uncle, and he hadn't really thought much about him until today. Come to think of it, his father hadn't mentioned his Uncle William in years.

"Is your father still alive?" Trey asked, cutting right to the heart of the matter.

"Yes, he lives in an assisted living center on the outskirts of town. My mother died two years ago, and without her, father started to decline," Zach replied.

"Zach, I have good reason to believe that we are first cousins and that your father is my uncle. Is there any way we can arrange a meeting with him?" Trey's excitement was impossible to conceal.

"I visit him every Sunday. I will ask him if it's okay to bring you on my next visit. I'm sure he will be anxious to see you once I give him some background. He's in decent shape mentally; however, his body has been failing him. I suppose that's the price he has to pay for hard fighting and hard living."

Zach went on, "Somehow he found a Viagra connection at the retirement center, and now I'm getting calls from the center's director about midnight liaisons with female residents." Zach smiled as he related the story about Omar's nighttime escapades.

It was almost five thirty, and Trey remembered his guest had an appointment with his wife at six. "Let me know what your father says about Sunday. I would love to meet him and have a chance to verify our theory that we are related through his brother."

"I'll call him tonight and let you know tomorrow. It's been a true pleasure meeting you, Trey." Zach rose from the table, extended his hand, and gave Trey a firm handshake. Trey watched his new friend-slash-relative enter the elevator and disappear.

DNA testing had produced results. With a little luck, Trey would meet his father's brother in a couple of days. He had been in Israel only a few hours, and he may have made the connection of his lifetime.

Chapter 16

Ziva's speed increased as they raced beyond the city limits. They would be at the dig site within the hour. Ari occupied himself with thoughts of Lev's call and the excitement in his voice. He also ruminated silently about his relationship with Ziva. She had become much more than Ari's loyal assistant. She and Ari had escaped blame for the death of her degenerate husband after a cursory investigation by the police. Ziva joined Ari at his Long Island company where she learned the ins and outs of running a genetic laboratory.

Their close proximity during the workday encouraged a relationship to develop that spilled over into their private lives. Ari's sexual needs were more than satisfied by Ziva's resolute obedience to his instructions. They had agreed on a "safe word" which Ari ignored frequently. He was amazed at how far Ziva would go to make him happy.

"Slow down, you're going to miss the turn Ziva," Ari snapped with a hint of disgust at her driving habits. "You always slam on the brakes at the last minute. What are you trying to prove?"

"Don't have a camel, Ari. I've got it under control," responded Ziva with a rye smile, knowing the exit was further up the road. She had learned his bark was much worse than his bite. She had become comfortable jousting with him when he got too full of himself, but she knew her place.

The dig-house sat on a rise just above the burial chamber. They drove past the site and turned onto a frontage road that led them back to the dig house. Stopping in front of the hut, a plume of road dust swallowed the Benz; Ari and Ziva emerged from the cloud looking for Lev.

Archaeological sites created bumps in the normal contour of the terrain and over the years, accreted soil, mud, dirt, and other material piled up on the ancient structures. They eventually vanished from view, forgotten by local citizens. They became bulges in the land that were plowed over, built on, and normally crushed under the weight of centuries. Ari and Ziva saw the site 150 meters to the south. This tomb had held up structurally under more than ten feet of material for over two thousand years.

A chain link fence, buried three feet in the ground, topped by razor wire and secured by an authoritative gate surrounded the tomb. The IAA took the extra precaution of electrifying the fence, because tomb raiders were skilled at cutting and digging their way into ancient sites. A solid metal door protected the tomb entrance, hung by the construction company the day of the initial discovery. Most Israelis were conscious of their delicate heritage and anxious to preserve everything about their past.

Ziva and Ari went inside the dig house expecting to find Lev. Not there. They hiked down the trail to the burial chamber, thinking Lev would call-out and alert them to his whereabouts. Still no sign of Lev. Ari began to get angry as he thought about the excitement in Lev's voice and the realization he was nowhere to be found. The gate to the fenced area was wide open and the metal door was ajar.

As they bent down to enter the tomb's vestibule, Ari pulled out a small flashlight that was attached to his key ring. A foul odor invaded their noses as they ducked again to enter the central area of the tomb, which had six niches dug into the outer walls. These recesses contained raised benches carved out of the limestone by masons during the first century. In ancient times, being dead did not mean you stayed dead. Deceased Jews were placed in these alcoves to assure they were not buried alive. There were stories of people "coming to life" after being in a coma for a period of days, sometimes even weeks.

The bodies remained exposed, covered only by a linen burial shroud, in the limestone nook for up to a year. When fully decomposed, their bones were gathered and placed in an ossuary, a limestone box, for final burial in another part of the chamber. These boxes were often inscribed with the name of the departed and additional family information.

"Lev, are you in here?" called Ari. No answer. He shined his flashlight into the first niche, empty. He continued to search the tomb with the tiny light guiding the way. In the third recess he found Lev. He was lying on his back with his hands folded over his chest as if taking a nap. The foul odor they smelled upon entering the chamber emanated from Lev's pants.

Ari gasped, "Ziva, come in here right now." She rushed to stand beside Ari as they both looked at Lev under the faint light.

"Is he breathing?" asked Ziva, covering her mouth and nose trying to withstand the putrid stench.

Ari stood beside Lev. He wasn't breathing. He lifted Lev's limp wrist to check for a pulse. Nothing. Closer examination revealed an unknown object in Lev's mouth. Ari directed the flashlight onto Lev's lips as he stuck two fingers into his mouth and pinched out a small cylindrical piece of stone. It appeared to be an ancient roller stamp or seal that was engraved with letters. He stared at the one inch-long seal momentarily before handing it to Ziva for safekeeping. They could study it after they figured out what to do with the dead archeologist.

"What happened to him, and why was that stone seal in his mouth?" Ari asked with a befuddled look.

"Maybe he was trying to hide it from the person who killed him?" Ziva said in an equally confused fashion. "It's been just over two hours since we spoke with Lev. Do you think someone else is here right now?"

"Let's check the other burial niches to be sure." A quick search of the remaining parts of the tomb confirmed they were alone. Ari and Ziva continued to speculate on Lev's demise. They entertained all of the possible scenarios from murder to a heart attack. But they kept coming back to the tiny, barrel shaped stone.

"We need to figure out what the seal says, and if it has anything to do with Lev's death. How can we transfer the message on the cylinder so we can see what is engraved on it?" Ari asked, knowing that in ancient times the relief on the cylinder was designed to produce a three-dimensional image by rolling it on wet clay.

They walked out of the tomb and stood in the scorching light of day. They were both drenched in sweat from the combination of drama and heat. Ziva dried her hands on Ari's shirt and gently retrieved the seal from her bag along with a jeweler's monocle she used in the laboratory. She held the object between her thumb and forefinger as she rotated the diminutive stone in an attempt to see all the characters while peering through the monocle. Ari looked over her shoulder as she carefully studied the miniature seal's three lines. The first line was written in Aramaic, the tongue of Jesus's family. The second line was clearly Greek; the letters of that alphabet recognizable even to Ari. Line three was ancient Hebrew, as different from Israel's national language as were hieroglyphs from modern Arabic. Although the characters of these three languages were identifiable they looked jumbled and out of order.

"This stone stamp may be older than the tomb itself. I'll need to study it with the appropriate reference material."

"But what does it say, Ziva?" Ari asked impatiently.

"I haven't a clue right now, but I think I'll be able to translate it once I get it back to my office and can transfer the words to a legible surface." She could tell by Ari's body language that he wasn't going to be able to wait.

"At least read the Hebrew," he implored her in his nice voice.

"This isn't the modern language we all love to hate. It's first-century Hebrew, and I would rather not speculate." Ziva responded firmly.

"Ziva, we have a dead man with a piece of stone in his mouth containing a message in three separate languages. There must be a connection to Lev's death. Please give me something." Ari was getting an edge; Ziva knew she had to make an attempt.

Ignoring the first two lines, she focused on the old Hebrew. Even under magnification she could not translate the words and then it occurred to her, "These words *are* encrypted", she said with a note of frustration. "I believe it's *mirror writing.*"

Ziva reached in her shoulder bag and removed a little, round cosmetic mirror that she handed to Ari. "Hold this in the shadow while I position the seal in the sun so I can see if a reflection of the stone in the mirror will un-jumble the words." Ari did as instructed while Ziva held the object of their investigation in direct sunlight. It worked; it was a mirror cipher. Viewing the letters in their correct order for the first time, the Hebrew words exploded in her mind like a metaphysical aneurism.

"Yeshua is with us…His body survived," Ziva blurted out, trying to contain her emotion, but the gravity of her translation was written on her face.

Ari reacted in a similar fashion as he queried, "It says what?"

"I'm not a hundred percent certain, but it appears that the message on the seal is referring to the bodily remains of Jesus."

The excitement of the phone call had turned into the tragedy of Lev's death and now the mystery of the miniature stone seal.

Was Lev murdered? Ari asked himself. *Did he tell someone else about the new chamber? And now we have a new tomb containing what might be the physical remains of someone named Jesus. Which Jesus?* Ari wondered, knowing it was a common first century name. *Could it be Jesus of Nazareth?*

Ari knew Lev to be very competitive with other academics in his field. He had mentioned fights over discoveries in the past. The antiquities business in Israel was a blood market, where finding and selling ancient artifacts produced big money. If someone else knew about the secret chamber that would be enough of a motive to kill Lev, but why leave the seal?

"Ari, the murderer might still be here," whispered Ziva thinking the interloper could have hidden in a secret space.

"Where would they be Ziva? We've checked all the chambers in the tomb and no one is in there," responded Ari tentatively, reflecting less than 100 percent certainty.

"Whoever did this must know about the tomb. That's a scary thought," concluded Ziva.

"We've got too much on our hands right now to worry about an imagined killer in our midst. Let's focus on what we have and leave the crime investigation to the police," said Ari hoping to curtail further discussion on the topic.

Ari would have to report Lev's death to the authorities and the university, tasks he resented, because they would distract him from his primary purpose. His thoughts kept returning to the message. Had someone inserted the seal into Lev's mouth, or was he trying to swallow it as he died?

Ari went to investigate what they had come for. He found the stone wall Lev referred to on the phone. The discoloration of the stones was subtle, and would not have been noticeable to an untrained eye. Shining his flashlight onto the block where the mortar had been removed, he squinted into the crack. He could see nothing but blackness. Placing his nose in the space, he inhaled deeply and got all the proof he needed, the unique smell of an undisturbed burial chamber. He fought the urge to conduct an exploratory excavation of the new chamber, knowing any additional digging would alert the authorities to its existence. He assumed Lev's assessment of the hidden chamber to be correct; without further confirmation he crammed small rocks and spit-soaked dirt back into the space. When finished, he smoothed the ground in front of the stone to cover any disturbance. The cracks were completely filled and looked just like the others along the wall and floor. Satisfied with his covert reconstruction, he and Ziva went back to the dig house.

They discussed their options and decided the best course of action was for Lev's body to be discovered by the students or Uzi Rubens, the IAA Inspector, when they returned to the site on Monday. As an unmarried professor who lived alone, coworkers and family would not miss Lev before someone found his body at the site on Monday. With no signs of a struggle, Ari trusted that authorities would determine Lev died of natural causes. He certainly did not have time for a murder investigation.

Lev had hung up the phone following his talk with Ari. The light from outside that had been pouring into the chamber suddenly disappeared. *Someone or something must be blocking the doorway*, Lev thought. He turned to see Uzi Rubens standing at the entry to the tomb. Lev hoped he had not overheard his conversation with Ari, but he had.

"Inspector Rubens, I thought we wouldn't see you until next Monday when the students return from their break. What are you doing here today?" Lev asked, reflecting his surprise.

Uzi did not respond to Lev's question. Ducking his head, he walked into the main chamber allowing the sunlight to once again illuminate the wall where Lev had been working. He slid past Lev so he could get a closer look at the stone block where the mortar had been removed. "What's this all about Lev? You know you're not supposed to do any new or unapproved excavation without me being present. What have you found?"

"Oh, nothing. I was just catching up on the work done last week and decided to take a mortar sample for analysis in the lab. It appears to be a different mixture than the other walls," Lev stated cautiously, not wanting to confirm the discovery of the adjacent chamber.

Uzi bent down to look into the space between the stones. "What's with the matchstick video camera? What's in there Lev? Let me see what you've found," Uzi said forcefully, as he grabbed the video camera from the stone bench and pushed the play button. A fisheye image of the undisturbed chamber appeared on the camera's playback screen. Lev had been caught.

"Lev, I thought you were an honest scientist. Why would you lie to me? This is a terrible breech of IAA protocol," said Uzi as he pocketed the video camera.

"Give that back Uzi. You have no right to take my equipment," Lev demanded, as he reached for the camera in Uzi's pocket. Uzi reacted violently pushing him backwards against the chamber wall, knocking the wind out of Lev's lungs. He fell to the ground gasping for air. Uzi stood over him with one foot on Lev's chest restricting his lungs ability to refill with air. Lev struggled to breathe, but Uzi applied more pressure by standing on him with both feet; the full force of the Inspector's two hundred-fifty pound body was now pressing down on the archeologist. Lev tried to free himself but without oxygen he was helpless. He turned various shades of blue and red before his gasps for air stopped. Eventually, his body went limp. Lev had a heart attack right there on the floor of the tomb.

Lev was dead and Uzi needed to make it look like he died naturally and alone. He moved the body to an alcove and positioned Lev on a limestone bench with his arms crossed on his chest. He found the brush Lev had used to assist with the removal of the mortar. He swept away his footprints and any sign of a struggle from the dirt floor. Keeping the camera for himself he departed the tomb leaving Lev to be discovered by Dr. Kohen when he arrived.

Uzi Rubens knew that the undisturbed chamber would contain artifacts of incalculable value on the black market. He had waited his entire career for a discovery of this magnitude. His salary as an IAA Inspector barely covered living expenses; his normal income would never assure him a comfortable retirement. Over the years he had enriched himself marginally by secreting unrecorded finds from excavations and selling them into the underground market. But this was enormous and he had to find a way to get his fair share of the booty that would surely flow from the new chamber. The only people who knew of its existence were Dr. Ari Kohen and himself. As far as Uzi was concerned that was one too many, a fact he would deal with when the time was right, but certainly before anything was made public.

Lev died of a heart attack that had been triggered by his tussle with Uzi, but not before he had placed the most valuable discovery in his mouth for safekeeping. He did not know what was on the little stone seal, but he knew it was important. The barrel shaped rock had been embedded in the mortar on the lower left corner of the stone he had recognized as different from the rest of the wall. As he carefully chiseled away the mortar, the seal came loose in the space he had created. At first he mistook it for a large stone that had been mixed into the mortar, but as he brushed it off he knew he was holding a message from another time, a communication from over 2,000 years ago. Lev's last act on earth may have been his most noble or nefarious. It would depend on who got their hands on the precious relic.

Chapter 17

"Those stupid wankers. I can't believe the arrogance of Mossad parading around a hotel in Dubai looking like a bunch of silly tourists. What were they thinking?" Donny read a journalist's account of the assassination of a leading Hamas figure in the UAE. Everyone presumed Mossad, Israel's famous security apparatus, orchestrated the killing.

Donny directed his comments to three men sitting around his table sharing in a midday meal. A courier from town delivered a pile of newspapers to the house each day. He read voraciously. He kept up on current events by consuming three papers each morning. The rest of Donny's reading focused on military history and technology. He was among the brightest minds when it came to guerilla warfare, targeted assassinations, psychological terrorism, and other "beyond-the-bomb" tactics.

The Irish passports carried by the Mossad assassins must have come from the same source Donny used to obtain fake identification for his people. His man at the passport office in Dublin had been providing fraudulent Irish travel documents to Donny's team for years. This government administrator was an equal-opportunity criminal.

Before being forced undercover, Donny had trained a number of Palestinian freedom fighters from the PLO and Palestinian Islamic Jihad (PIJ). He coached them on targeted terrorism, the kind used so successfully in Northern Ireland during the 70s and 80s. His heart firmly with the Arabs, he thought the Jews' occupation of Palestine as abhorrent as England's annexation of Northern Ireland. The 1948 agreement that partitioned Palestine and gave the Jews a homeland was largely the work of Britain. He was clearly on the correct side of that conflict.

Could he really be half Jewish? And if he were, would that change anything? He thought not. His political philosophy had been hewn by years of experience, not by his genetic makeup. Knowledge of his Jewishness would not erode his convictions about what was right and wrong. The Jews were evil ingrates who took everything and then asked for more. Donny wouldn't let genes dictate his allegiances.

The deal about Wolfe Tone was another matter. Donny could see how their belief systems concurred. Donny had seen paintings and drawings of his hero; he had even viewed Tone's death mask in Dublin once. Nothing in Tone's appearance physically connected him with Donny. *Maybe DNA defined him in more ways than just his appearance*, he thought. *His politics were a lot like Tone's.*

But he couldn't be bothered right now; there would be plenty of time to contemplate everything after the mission.

"Boys, we have work to do," Donny said to the three men. "Today we let Sinn Fein and the British know we will not allow England to continue its occupation of Northern Ireland. The only agreement we will accept is one giving Ireland full control of its people and land, not these half-ass measures permitting the Brits to continue their domination of our citizens. The targets have been defined, you have your orders, and as my commanders in the field, you will now initiate the next round of attacks on the occupiers. A communication blackout will persist until we are outside the country and safely hidden. Are there any questions?" Donny waited an adequate amount of time for his team to speak. No one did. They had been through the operation plan more than a hundred times.

Each team consisted of four men: the shooter, a lookout, and two drivers. The shooters were selected based on their ability to hit targets at long range. All shooters had obtained the rank of Field Commander because of their keen marksmanship, leadership skills, and loyalty. The shooters would assassinate the targets, meet the first drivers, and be driven to predetermined locations where another driver waited. This second driver didn't know the final destination of the fleeing assassin. He was instructed to follow the gunman's directions. Once the killers were sure no one was on their tail, they intended to sneak out of the country using fake passports. Only the shooters and Donny knew their final destinations.

They would be safe once out of Ireland, at least until the MI6 and their friends at the CIA got involved. Then a whole new set of directives would be initiated. The assassins had to relocate daily and plant false trails. All of this had been reviewed, studied, and role-played. If there were any surprises, Donny was confident they could face them down with the skills they had honed over the years. Their collective resolve was forged in the heat of battle and the bowels of a struggle for full independence. Their devotion to a free Ireland got them off the pot, prepared to shit on anyone who stood in their way.

Donny stood and the three men rose from their seats. The time to renew their revolutionary oath had come. Donny led them in a recitation of the RIRA pledge: "We will never cease our activities until the occupiers have been removed. We will use all means at our disposal to rid the country of the vile forces that control our fate. We will do whatever is necessary to free our people. We will not stop until every British troop has been erased from our island. We will fight to take our country back, or we will die trying."

Never wanting to end a pep talk with the words "die trying," Donny continued. "Remember the sacrifices of Wolfe Tone and don't forget our right to self-determination. Success is guaranteed because you have prepared resolutely. Now face your fears with the knowledge of our ultimate victory. May God accompany and protect you."

When Donny had completed the recitation, he went to each man and gave him a bear hug. Looking them in the eye, he administered a personal blessing, one specific to each man's role in the plan. Not one to become emotional, Donny turned away from his men as a sign for them to leave him the hell alone and get to work.

His words hung in the air as the men gathered their belongings and left the house. Donny was left alone with his thoughts about the plan and his future. If everything went by the book, he may never be able to return to Ireland, at least as a free man. The thought saddened him. British, Irish, and American authorities would pursue him as a terrorist. Living in the shadows was fine by Donny if he could claim a part in the ultimate defeat of the enemy. He had a job to finish, work started by his famous relative over two hundred years earlier.

Donny's thoughts turned to Trey. Where is he? Is he OK? He hoped Trey had taken his advice and left Ireland. He wondered if they would be together again, or if Trey would disown him when he learned of his involvement in the killings. All of these thoughts and more distracted Donny from the job at hand. Shaking off the sentimentality, he kneeled to pray for the mission, Ireland, and his new brother. He went to his computer to draft a letter that would eventually be sent to authorities claiming responsibility for the assassinations.

Chapter 18

Trey called Rachel with the news about Omar and his brother William along with other particulars from the conversation with Zach at the hotel. Rachel was elated at this turn of events and was equally amazed at how easily he had tracked down a genetic match. "I never thought getting a DNA test would lead to success so soon. I'm thrilled for you, Trey. Are you going to visit Omar?"

"Zach called me earlier today and said Omar invited me for lunch on Sunday." Trey started to get butterflies as he verbalized the meeting plan for the first time.

"Wonderful. I can't wait to hear how it goes," Rachel responded.

Trey would meet his father's brother for the first time in less than forty-eight hours. Scary. "To be honest, I'm nervous. What if my father's still alive?" Trey queried, wondering whether he had the guts to confront the man who had abandoned him so abruptly.

"Oh suck it up. You better assume your father is alive and that you're going to find him. And when you do, there'll be plenty of time for being scared, believe me." Rachel remembered how fear of her father increased as she became more familiar with his psychosis.

"Thanks coach, but this is new to me," Trey quipped, trying to shake his anxiety.

"The real jitters will begin when you're face to face trying to decide what to ask him first," Rachel said knowingly.

Trey became emotional at the thought of actually looking into his father's eyes. He had rushed headlong into DNA testing not realizing he might get instant results. He interrupted the brief silence by saying, "You're right, but I'm further along than I had ever imagined I would be after a few short months, and my mind is trying to catch up with my actions. I guess you already knew that, being a psychiatrist." They both laughed, and the mood lightened.

"Come on, mister financial tycoon, conqueror of the markets. You have so much to be grateful for, and plus, you have a woman who misses you very much and wants to know when she will see you again." Rachel confidently turned the conversation to matters of their relationship.

"Soon I hope. I'll be in Israel for a couple of weeks. I want to follow my DNA trail and tour the historical sites." Trey couldn't be sure where their relationship was headed because at this point he would normally pull back and run from the potential long-term commitment. He tried to suppress the desire to psychoanalyze the situation by thinking about their time together at the cottage and the incredible intimacy they had shared while in Ireland.

Beyond the physical attraction, there was a true love distilling in his heart for this incredible woman. Cognitively, he realized he should turn into the skid of an out-of- control car, but intuitively he turned the opposite direction. Trey ran for the hills when a relationship required even the simplest of commitments. Rachel was different, and Trey kept telling himself, *Stay put. Turn in.*

"I want you to know that I'm having feelings for you beyond what a long distance relationship can support," Rachel offered after a moment of silence. "Trey, I think…I'm falling in love with you." Rachel was reading his mind.

"Me too. My body aches for you. You're on my mind constantly, and I miss your voice, your brain, your mouth, your…I've never felt this way for a woman before."

"Have you ever felt this way for a man?" she asked, trying to break the emotional tension that had taken over the conversation. This was not the time to have a heavy discussion about their future. She chuckled at the thought of Trey's facial expression.

"Not for some years now," Trey responded, and both of them cracked up.

"So I suppose that 'Taco Bell' dog on your ass was a heterosexual indiscretion? Could have fooled me."

"Oh, you noticed my little blemish. It's a long story and one I would prefer to share in person. The dog on my ass needs to be petted regularly or he gets lonely. He's sought the company of strangers when ignored for long periods of time." Trey hoped she didn't get a good look at the entire coital scene on his rump.

"We can't have that. Does the dog like talking dirty on the phone?" Rachel's attempt at tattoo-phone sex was pushing the limit of what Trey was comfortable discussing.

The conversation ended with Trey's promise to call as soon as his meeting with Omar concluded. They agreed to defer definite plans to reunite until Trey had a clearer picture of where his investigation would lead. She wished him luck, and they said their good-byes.

Trey hung up the phone and stared out over the blackness of the sea from the hotel balcony. He needed to find a way to get the tattoo off his ass. He would humanely euthanize the dog and skunk as soon as he found the time. His relationship with Rachel had begun to change him in positive ways. A Mexican rat-dog and garbage-eating polecat were not going to be a constant reminder of his imperfect past.

He walked into the bathroom and retrieved an orange prescription bottle containing Ambien from his toiletry kit. He took one 10 mg tablet over to the mini-bar while retrieving two mini-bottles of Crown Royal. He prepared a perfect cocktail, swallowed the sleeping aid with a healthy swig. A self-induced coma would follow, and he looked forward to the dreamless sleep it would provide. He consumed half the cocktail in one gulp hoping to hasten the onset of a semi-vegetative state. The full force of the alcohol arriving in his stomach reminded him it was a drug also, one he needed to keep in check.

Security lights cast shadows across the balcony. A sea breeze rustled the miniature palms adding a soundtrack to the synthetic light show. Sleep found Trey wrapped in the warmth of a properly drugged epidermis, and with a heart that was totally numb.

Zach and Trey were on the way to meet Omar for lunch at the Chateau Tel Aviv Retirement Living Center located on the outskirts of the city. The old man had a turn for the better once they got him off the Viagra. Evidently, the drug interfered with his heart medication. According to Zach, Omar's mood swings were unpredictable, and Trey should not take anything he said personally. Omar complained constantly about the doctors, the nurses, the food, and whatever stuck in his craw, probably a reaction to not being able to get a stiffy.

They arrived at the Chateau around midday, and drove through the security gate that opened automatically in recognition of Zach's electronic pass. The retirement home was among the most luxurious in the world. Its opulent lobby was appointed with oriental rugs, Louis XV furniture, and beautifully buffed marble floors. Trey thought it must cost an arm and a leg to live in this place.

Zach registered at the reception desk and hailed Trey to follow him down a hall to Omar's residence. Zach removed a keycard from his pocket and knocked softly on the door before inserting the plastic card to gain entry. A small hallway led to the living room that was open to the outside through French doors. Walking through the opening onto the patio, they found Omar in his wheelchair beneath the warming sunlight. Zach gently touched his father's shoulder to announce their arrival.

"Shit! You scared the hell out of me! Are you trying to kill me?" Omar protested, having been awakened from a nap.

"Sorry, Dad. I want you to meet Trey Cowens, the gentleman I told you about on the phone." Omar shielded his eyes from the sun by jamming his palm skyward, almost hitting Zach in the nose. Trey saw the deep creases of a full life chiseled into Omar's face. They inspected each other quizzically before Zach suggested they order lunch and have it delivered to the room. Omar didn't respond, his gaze locked onto Trey's face. Omar tried to make sense of the situation as Trey looked silently into the old man's eyes. A tear broke from the corner of Omar's left eye. Trey saw the emotion run down his host's cheek. He moved to block the sun that was shining on Omar's face by bending over the wheelchair.

"Dad, are you OK?" asked Zach, concerned it had been a mistake to come today.

Ignoring Zach and with his eyes locked on Trey, Omar said, "You look just like him thirty years ago. How did this happen? Where did you come from, and where in the hell is my brother?" Omar was crying out of both eyes, moved by the presence of his lunch guest.

"I'm sorry, who do I look like?" inquired Trey.

"My brother, William. You look just like him when we were young men," offered Omar now trying to collect himself. "I haven't seen him since 2001 when he left on a secret mission for the Israeli government."

"What kind of mission?" asked Trey, anxious to engage Omar in a conversation about his father.

"He worked for the Mossad. And now you're standing before me like the ghost of my long lost brother," Omar wiped his eyes.

"Are you sure I look like him?" Trey wanted to confirm his elderly host was not hallucinating

"We have much to talk about, my nephew," Omar moved on confidently. "Zach told me about the DNA tests, but I don't need a test to prove you are his son. My God, the resemblance is remarkable. Look at your chin, your eyes, and your hair."

"Did you say Mossad?" asked Trey, surprised by the reference to the Israeli intelligence agency.

"Yes, he was among the best and brightest intelligence officers in the entire organization. One day he came to me and said he had to leave for a while. It's been over ten years." Omar's sadness was evident as he spoke about his estranged sibling.

Omar instructed Zach to order lunch for the three of them while he rolled his chair back into the residence. He rooted around in the bottom drawer of a desk and retrieved a photo album. Thumbing through the tattered pages, Omar stopped at a picture of a man in uniform. He turned the book for Trey's viewing under the light of the desk lamp. The man in military garb posed for the camera striking a heroic yet humble stance, a classic military portrait. The resemblance was amazing.

"This is William right after graduation from the university, ready to begin his mandatory military service," said Omar with pride. "He served three years with distinction and then entered the world of intelligence gathering and espionage. As brothers do, William shared many stories of his early operations. The top secret missions took him all over the world and, unfortunately, also into the shadows."

Trey saw his father's image for the first time. Momentarily overwhelmed, he struggled to manage his emotions. He wanted to know everything about the man in the picture, his father.

Trey composed himself and asked, "When was the last time you heard from him?"

"I received a hand-written letter from him a few years ago. Whoever delivered it slid it under my door at home. I have it here."

Omar removed an envelope from another drawer of the desk. Taking the letter out, he handed it to Zach who read it out loud, expertly translating it from the original Hebrew.

> *Dearest Brother,*
>
> *I miss you more than I can say, and I am writing you to apologize for being such a bad brother for all of these years. I am saddened by the fact my choices cost the ones I love so much. These choices sentenced me to a life of anonymity and emotional suffering I cannot express in words. We will probably die without being able to see one another. I miss you desperately.*
>
> *My brother, I am incredibly proud of you. I followed your career every step of the way. Your contributions to Israel are inspiring. I only hope I can live up to the standards you set. Most younger brothers look up to their elder*

ones, but my admiration for you greatly exceeds what any other brother could feel.
Love,
Your Brother William

Zach refolded the letter and let it sit on his lap while the words sunk in. Trey yearned for his father's embrace, a few spoken words to temper the pain, or at least an explanation of why he left.

Omar watched Trey's reaction as the letter was read. "What can you tell me about my brother?" Omar asked.

"Nothing, really. He left my mother before my birth, and my mother died in the delivery room. I lived with my grandparents until I went to college in New York City," responded Trey.

"You never met your father?" asked Omar, a little confused.

"No, never even saw a picture until today. My grandparents didn't speak of him. The letter makes it clear that I may never meet my father." Trey began to tear-up as he realized the finality of those words. "I apologize for being such a child," said Trey wiping the tears from his face as the other men looked on through tears of their own.

Zach and Omar said nothing. They comforted their guest with shoulder rubs and pats on the back. Trey felt a real closeness to these men. He needed to collect himself and find out all he could about his father. This was no time for a pity-party.

"What can you tell me about your brother after he graduated from college and married my mother?" Trey said firmly, wanting to avoid another breakdown. "I read the letters he wrote to her before they married and I saw the marriage announcement from the local Buffalo paper. That's all I know."

A knock at the door interrupted their conversation; time for lunch. Zach let the waiter into the residence. He set the dining room table for their meal, complete with a white cotton tablecloth. No one spoke with the waiter in the room. Omar wheeled under the table and invited the other men to join him.

Omar considered how much to tell his nephew about his brother's covert activities. It did not take long for him to decide to throw caution to the wind and tell it all. His nephew deserved to know the truth about his father. Omar swore Trey and Zach to secrecy and began to tell the story of Willy's early life and career.

Beginning at twelve years of age, Willy would leave Israel to spend his summers in the United Kingdom as the guest of his godfather and namesake, Colonel William Riley O'Conner. The colonel and Willy's father, Joseph Cohen, had become good friends through their work together during the 1936 Arab Revolt in Palestine. Joseph Cohen was a commanding officer in the underground security force known as *Haganah,* predecessor to the Israeli Defense Forces. Colonel O'Conner trained and led these Jewish fighters in an effort to protect the United Kingdom's interests in Palestine as defined by the British Mandate after WW I. Their time together in an effort to quell Arab uprisings created an enduring bond, lasting until the colonel's death in 1968.

Young Willy shared a summer home with O'Conner's wife and two daughters in Northern Ireland, where he learned about Irish culture and also to speak the Gaelic language. The colonel, often away on military business, left Willy to find male companionship on his own. He met some young men during those summers who helped him understand the Irish and British way of life: fishing, hiking, horseback riding, and hurling. The colonel's wife introduced him to the writings of Shakespeare, Stevenson, Darwin, and Dickens. The colonel's oldest daughter enlightened him about the delightful world of a young woman's body. His spoken English developed a pronounced Irish lilt that got thicker with each trip. These summer experiences kindled his interests in foreign languages and the female anatomy. He became fluent in Gaelic, English, Hebrew, French, Italian, German, Arabic, Farsi, and erotica by the time he graduated from the Hebrew University.

Willy contacted recruiters from Mossad, after completing his mandatory military stint, to offer his services to the cause of Israeli security. He entered the notorious Mossad two-year training program and received the highest marks ever awarded. His talent with weapons and stealth operations and his ability to think on his feet gained him recognition at the highest levels of Mossad. Willy's ability to speak eight languages fluently was also a big plus as he entered the world of covert operations.

Mossad created a new identity for William Cohen, now Cowens, with the issuance of a forged UK passport along with fake family, education, and work histories. Armed with the necessary training and language skills, Mossad sent Willy to the United States as a graduate student from Northern Ireland. He entered the McDonough School of Business at Georgetown University to pursue an MBA.

Willy lived alone in a one-bedroom apartment, going to classes by day and training at a Mossad safe house by night. After the two-year course of study, he graduated with honors from both programs. Willy assumed his role as a "sleeper *kidon*", a professional assassin who hid in plain view until called into action against the enemies of Israel.

The Munich Olympics were interrupted by the brutal kidnapping of nine Israeli athletes by the Palestinian Liberation Organization's Black September terrorist group, followers of Yasser Arafat. News reports filled television screens as viewers around the world watched in horror. Terrorists killed three Israelis at the Olympic Village. Reporters stated the remaining hostages were alive only to learn later their captors killed all nine when the German police surrounded the airport. Willy's anger grew as he thought about the murder of the athletes at the hands of those Arab scums. Not long after the Olympic carnage, Willy just vanished.

Once Omar completed his rendition of Willy's early years, he realized his guest was a little overwhelmed by the information.

"Are you alright, Trey?" asked Zach, seeing the concern etched into his face.

"I think so," Trey offered in a melancholy tone.

"That's enough for today," said Omar, concerned he had gone too far, too fast.

"I'll be fine. Don't worry about me. I want to learn all I can about him. Thank you for being so honest," Trey said, trying to smile through the emotional turmoil.

"I'll gladly share more with you during your next visit. I hope you will come often,"

Omar reminded Trey their conversation was extremely confidential. He also promised to help Trey track down his father. Omar didn't hold out much hope, because the moat around Mossad was wide and deep. But he would contact people outside the service to determine if anyone could assist in the search. The odds were slim that anybody knew more than Omar, and that wasn't much.

Chapter 19

The Rt. Hon. Robert Weir, Secretary of State for Northern Ireland, had just completed an early breakfast meeting at Stormont House in Belfast. His chief of security escorted him to his car at the rear of the building; only his personal secretary and driver knew his destination. He was meeting a woman with whom he had an affair that was about to become public if he didn't act immediately. Weir had attempted to break off the relationship several weeks back. She had threatened to go to the media if he didn't pay her a monthly stipend so she and her disabled son could relocate to Dublin.

Shaniq Rason, a cocoa-colored beauty of African descent, had captivated the secretary from the first moment they met. She was the personal assistant to John McNally, a software pioneer who ran Northern Ireland's largest computer services company, EmeraldTech. Weir had met his black princess two years before at the grand opening of EmeraldTech's new headquarters. Shaniq served as hostess for the event and Weir represented the UK Government. Afterwards, they made plans for lunch on the pretense Weir's government could assist EmeraldTech gain a foothold in UK markets.

The lunch launched a two-year affair and a relationship with her son who suffered from multiple sclerosis. Weir had been stricken by childhood polio but had regained 95 percent use of all his physical functions by age thirteen. He went on to play rugby and cricket at boarding school, his infirmity undetectable. He had never spoken of it to anyone until his lunch with Shaniq; there was something irresistible about her. They had midday dates at discreet locations around Belfast until Shaniq's actions caught the attention of her coworkers. She confessed to her best friend at work about the affair, and word found its way back to Weir's ears. The meeting with Shaniq had been hastily organized the night before. He trusted he could handle the matter before it sullied his stellar reputation.

Weir got out of his car behind the Merchant Hotel in downtown Belfast. The Merchant was known for its five-star accommodations, gourmet meals, and discretion when it came to business day hookups. As he stepped from the rear door of his government-issue car, Weir's head was blown off by a single shot fired from a vacant office across High Street. Ironically, the location used by the gunman for Weir's execution belonged to Northern Ireland's Victim Outreach, a UK organization with the motto: "Helping People Cope with Crime." The assassin made an impeccable getaway; the police had no leads.

Bridgette Montigue had been Mark Foster's cook and house nanny since his divorce two years before. Foster was the deputy First Minister for Northern Ireland. Sinn Fein selected him to represent the interests of his Irish nationalist brethren in the Northern Ireland Assembly. The executive branch of the government was made up of three representatives, one from each political faction with a dog in the fight for Northern Ireland. Foster's conflicting roles as the titular head of the Irish nationalist movement and deputy First Minister in the assembly caused him major headaches. Each day he tried to balance the need for a peaceful solution to the conflict with the loss of sovereignty over part of his country.

Bridgette, a twenty-five-year-old woman from a working class family in County Antrim, rode the train to Belfast each weekday morning and walked ten blocks to Foster's home. She rarely saw the minister because of the long hours he spent at his job. He left for work before her arrival and came home well after her departure at the end of the day.

This day began like all the others as she gathered up the minister's dirty clothes and started a load in the washer. Her workday continued with a sweep of the first floor, an attempt to tidy up Foster's office and the preparation of his evening meal. Foster usually wrote a note indicating whether he would need dinner that night. There were no instructions today. Bridgette thought it odd but planned a meal anyway, thinking her boss had just forgotten.

As she prepared the dinner she would leave in the refrigerator with instructions for reheating, she heard the crying of wild cats. The neighborhood suffered from an excess of stray dogs and feral cats. At least once a week she called animal control to have them remove one of these reject animals from Foster's property. She feared for her safety some days because the dogs would roam the area in packs.

This was different; the sounds were similar to the primitive, deep moan of a lioness consuming a fresh kill. She left the kitchen and walked to the sliding glass door that led onto the back patio. She opened the curtains to find the window covered in a red liquid. At first she thought some vandals had thrown rotten tomatoes at the minister's home. Then she saw the cats. They were feeding on something just beneath the door while emitting guttural moans. Bridgette grabbed a broom and slid open the door preparing to scare the cats away. Mark Foster was dead on the fieldstone patio. The back of his head was a mess of flesh and bone. Cats fought for an eating position, unconcerned with the maid's presence.

In shock, Bridgette began whacking the felines with the broom to get them off the dead minister. The cats were fully engaged in their meal. Sizing up Bridgette's fearful commitment, they turned on her. One tomcat swiped at Bridgette and got his claws caught on her apron. Pulling away, she attempted to slide the door shut but her sudden movement swung the cat, still attached to her apron, into the living room. Other cats followed their brother inside. Bridgette slammed the sliding door, pinching one cat in the aluminum frame. Almost cut in half, the feral feline screamed bloody murder for the entire neighborhood to hear.

Bridgette turned her attention to the cat in the house that had managed to get free of her clothing. He circled the maid with his yellow eyes firmly fixed on her baby blues. She noticed more cats squeezing into the house through the sliding door that was propped open by the partially severed, howling cat. As they began to stream into the living area, she ran upstairs to the bedroom and locked the door. She dialed 999, Ireland's emergency number, and was connected to an operator.

"Help, please come quickly. There's a pack of feral cats in the house and a dead man at the back." The operator tried to calm her as she confirmed the address and informed her officers were on the way. Bridgette waited in the locked room until she heard sirens and knocking at the front door. Still afraid to leave the safety of the room, she opened the upstairs window and screamed for help. The police broke down the door, rid the house of the wild cats, and freed Bridgette from the bedroom.

A single bullet to the head had killed Mark Foster as he stepped onto his back patio with the paper that morning. The police determined the shooter had been positioned in the woods one hundred yards from the scene. They did not recover the deadly round; it was probably eaten by the aggressively feeding cats. There were no leads and not a shred of evidence that could point authorities to the killer. Mark Foster's assassination occurred within minutes of the shooting of Robert Weir at the Merchant Hotel.

Peter Mallon, First Minister for Northern Ireland, was a member of the Democratic Unionist Party and appointed by the British Prime Minister. Mallon, a glutton in more ways than one, was well known for his love of food and drink; it earned him the reputation as party minister of the Assembly.

Mallon's fondness for young men was not as well known. His relationship with the current UK Prime Minister began at Eton College and continued at Cambridge University, where they shared a passionate love for darts and dick sucking. The two Englishmen went their separate ways after school. One became Prime Minister of England, and the other fell on hard times as his family business went belly up.

Mallon longed for a return to the privileged life he had enjoyed as a young man. He married a homely woman from a good family to conceal his true sexual orientation. He used incriminating correspondences and photographs from their college days to blackmail the Prime Minister into a government appointment. To the complete bafflement of most UK politicians, he became First Minister of the Northern Ireland Assembly. Once the cries of favoritism died down, he got to work.

To everyone's surprise, Mallon did an excellent job. He managed the disarmament of Sinn Fein without incident and drafted a comprehensive power-sharing agreement between the former rebel group and the British. He spoke eloquently about the path to a peaceful solution in the region. However, he could not overcome his love of young men. He had not acted on these urges since university, but recently his mind was gorged with homosexual fantasies. He contacted an escort service and arranged to meet his date at an obscure motel well outside Belfast. Desperate for man sex, Mallon risked everything for the rush of a masculine touch.

He arrived early at the roadside motel. Mallon took a shower and laid his naked, oversized frame on the bed. He was fantasizing about the impending liaison when he heard a knock. He wrapped a towel around his waist and went to unlock the door for his guest. He opened the door; no one was there. He stepped over the threshold to peer down the covered walkway that ran the entire length of the building. Mallon heard a crack, and then felt a pain in his chest. He was shot twice, once in the center of his chest, and once between the eyes. The rounds surgically entered his body milliseconds apart and exited with an explosion of bone-flecked brain matter. Mallon fell onto the concrete walkway with a thud. Blood flowed over the curb and out into the parking area. Two insanely accurate shots from a fair distance had eliminated the minister.

The story of the three simultaneous executions of the leading figures in the Northern Ireland peace process caught fire internationally. Every major news organization, social networking site, and blog carried news of the synchronized assassinations.

"*The work of a genius*," reported one sympathetic daily newspaper.

"*Give them the wretched territory and bring our boys home,*" wrote a London columnist.

"*Where do we go from here?*" was the question posed by a member of the Dublin press.

Shock, disbelief, and sadness pervaded the content of each report. With condolences first given to the families who lost a loved one, the writers launched into rants about the cause of the murders; predictably, these tirades broke out along ideological lines. These factions reverted to talking points as they shouted each other down in public, in print, and on the airwaves. Thankfully, the national debate remained a war of words. None of the warring factions took responsibility for their failure to protect the peace process and its leading administrators. The headline became the failure of Britain and Ireland to resolve the Northern Ireland situation.

Donny read online accounts of the assassinations he had masterfully planned and executed. Seated in the first class cabin aboard an Egypt Air B777-300ER en route to Cairo, he would not know the status of his gunmen until later that day. They had scheduled an online meeting in a predetermined chat room. The men would use code words, and it would take only a few minutes to confirm their condition. According to the papers, they left no clues for the police, but sometimes the authorities fed garbage to reporters in hopes of fooling the perpetrators.

Once they were all safe, it would be time to take credit for the assassinations. He had an elaborate plan to use these murders against the occupiers. He would blame Britain and their collaborators for the state of the Irish economy. London bankers had swindled Ireland, and now they would pay. Pointing to banks as shadow or parallel occupiers was a new approach for the RIRA, but one supported by the fact that unemployment was over 14 percent. New recruits would come from the ranks of the economically disenfranchised. Their numbers grew daily, providing fertile ground for attracting initiates to the cause. Donny and his followers would execute as many ministers and bankers as it took for the Brits to vacate his homeland.

"I guess the 'surgical option' got their attention," whispered Donny to his seatmate. "Beheading the peace process was our only choice. Even though new heads will grow to replace the old, we've established our capabilities at a very high level. We've scared the shit out of the ruling class. They will never again ignore our sovereignty. British politicians and their banker cronies will die one by one if they do."

Grace Kinney, attorney and RIRA loyalist, turned to Donny with knowing eyes and said, "I'm with you to the end; my life is in your hands." She reached her hand under the skimpy airline blanket to hold his, and with three gentle squeezes told him, *I love you.*

He felt her finger, which held a more than ample diamond engagement ring and wedding band. They were now Mr. and Mrs. John Mitchell from Halifax, on vacation to the land of the Pharaohs. Donny's head fell back and his eyes closed as he thought about the events of the last weeks and how life would never be the same. He also wondered where his newfound sibling was and if he was all right. They would land in Cairo in a few hours.

Chapter 20

Ari and Yussi agreed to meet at a busy restaurant in the seaport district of Tel Aviv for lunch. Yussi's assistant had reserved a corner window table in Ari's name, and instructed him to arrive fifteen minutes early and wait for Col. Fischer.

Yussi selected this particular restaurant because the elevated noise levels at lunchtime would allow the men to talk without fear of being overheard by other diners or bugging devices. The restaurant was located just back from the breakwater of the Mediterranean Sea. Floor to ceiling windows gave the patrons a sensation of being on a cruise ship. Ari arrived ten minutes early and ordered sparkling water for the table. He took in his surroundings.

Uzi Ruben, the IAA inspector, had phoned Ari earlier in the day to inform him that Lev's lifeless body had been discovered in the tomb. According to the inspector, Lev looked like he was resting peacefully on a limestone bench in one of the tomb's niches. Once he determined Lev was dead and not asleep, he called his supervisor who immediately phoned the authorities. Ari played the distraught employer, even offering to find and contact family members on behalf of the investigation.

Uzi was dealing with the police, who asked a lot of questions about the site, the sponsor, and how he found the body. He told Ari the authorities would be calling him for an interview later that day. Ari assured Uzi he would come to the dig site directly after lunch, and if they needed anything before, he should call him on his cell phone.

"Good day, Dr. Kohen. I hope I didn't keep you waiting too long. I got stuck in traffic." Yussi greeted Ari with a smile and a warm handshake. He took a seat in the glass corner and faced Ari with a grandfatherly smile on his face. Ari returned the grin with some effort. His mind was still on the dig and the police investigation.

The colonel was a man at peace with himself, exuding confidence without being arrogant. His appearance was understated and comfortable, but beneath this casually friendly demeanor was a warrior of unequaled accomplishments. Colonel Fischer had more battles to win and wars to wage before he hung up his weapons. His brain was still his most potent asset, and Ari saw it working even before their conversation began.

Speaking Hebrew, Colonel Fischer started by saying, "I've just come from my morning briefing at the office. World events are moving so fast we meet twice a day to keep up with the pace of threats. The 'crisis du jour' involves the new Egyptian Parliament which is threatening to rescind the 1979 peace treaty with Israel."

Ari listened as the colonel boasted about his clandestine work with the Israeli government.

Fischer continued, "As you might know, many of our military actions of the recent past would have been impossible without the implicit, if not public, cooperation of Egypt. Our efforts in Gaza were dependent upon Egypt holding a tough line at the border with the Hamas-controlled territory. I understand they are going to open the border crossing. The Egyptians, under the previous regime, provided Israel with just enough political cover to avoid conflict with the moderate Arab nations in the neighborhood."

Yussi let out a sigh revealing the efforts of the morning had taken a toll. "I need a drink. What about you?"

"I'll stick with water if you don't mind, but you go ahead. Lunch is my treat. I'm honored you would take time out of your busy schedule to meet with a lowly scientist," responded Ari, genuflecting with an appropriate amount of feigned respect for his elder lunch guest.

"Not at all. I'm looking forward to our chat. It'll help me get my mind off a morning filled with security and intelligence matters. Now tell me, what you are up to, Dr. Kohen?" the colonel asked abruptly, finished with the small talk.

"Just trying to save the world through science," Ari joked, eliciting a chuckle from his lunch mate. "So far I've only managed to ruin a marriage. However, I'm working on a plan to save all the world's marriages by genetically modifying females to accept the fact men are incorrigible louts." That got a belly laugh from Yussi.

The waiter appeared at the table, and Yussi ordered his drink, a Johnny Walker Black on the rocks with a twist of lemon. Ari consulted the menu while Yussi caught someone's eye in the restaurant and gave a friendly nod. Ari glanced at the subject of Yussi's attention who was a beautiful young woman sitting at a table with an elderly, grandfather type. The waiter returned with the cocktail; they placed their orders and went back to their conversation. Yussi got right to the point alluded to by Ari during their first meeting.

"Dr. Kohen, you said you had some interesting insights to share with me regarding the future security of our nation. We're alone here, in a manner of speaking, so you may now unveil your notions about protecting our country." Yussi sat back, lifting the drink to his lips. He swallowed half of its contents in one swig.

"Colonel, I am a descendent of a long line of priests which you know as the Kohanim. I chose science rather than the synagogue as a way to promote our culture and belief system. In genetics, I discovered a powerful tool that can further our cause on many fronts. One of these is Israel's security." Ari paused to see if the unique connection made sense to Yussi.

"Really?" the colonel responded with a hint of disbelief. "Continue."

"It sounds outlandish to equate DNA to the security of a nation. But I assure you there are both altruistic and evil ways to use genetic science to accomplish this end. My view is the altruistic approach will yield more results and gain the respect of the international community." All crap, and Ari knew it. He was still feeling out his lunch guest.

"What if talking fails and peace can't be negotiated? We've got to prepare for a complete breakdown of the peace process," the colonel said.

"When push comes to shove Israel needs to ignore international condemnation and do whatever is necessary to secure its nationhood," Ari responded without hesitation.

"We agree on that point," said Yussi, gaining interest.

"The fact that I'm a Kohanim requires I do everything in my power to protect the land given to our people." Ari waited to gauge if the theological reference turned off this secular soldier.

"Go on," said Yussi, displaying no reaction to the remark.

"The Order of the Islamic League, OIL, hosts a summit every three years called The Conference of Kings. The organization's stated objectives include the strengthening of Islamic solidarity among member countries, the safeguarding of Holy Places, and the support of the Palestinian people in their effort to recover their 'occupied land.' Anyone with a computer can view this information on the Internet. The unspoken objective, but one known to all of the members, is the complete and total eradication of Israel, to drive the Jews into the sea." Ari punctuated this last phrase to highlight the biggest risk; the end game dreamed of daily by all Islamic turd worshippers.

"So what's new about that, Dr. Kohen? They've been railing against Israel since the beginning of time. Its members speak openly about the destruction of Israel in public forums and at conferences sponsored by Western powers without any repercussions. We in the intelligence community are quite accustomed to the abuse." Another sip of the drink and Yussi went on. "Dr. Kohen, please get to the point because I'm an impatient and busy man who has political conversations all day long with people more knowledgeable than you on this subject."

Not the least bit insulted or intimidated, Ari continued, "Again, I thank you for your time, Colonel Fischer. I know it's valuable. What I'm about to tell you has the potential to surgically eliminate the most radical threats that could evolve from the regime change underway in the region. The Middle Eastern democracy

146 William J. Atkins

movement has created a fertile environment for radical Islam to flourish. The leadership structures of Israel's most important Arab neighbors are in total disarray. The Jewish state needs to be proactive in targeting and destroying threats before they attain critical mass." The waiter appeared with their lunch. Yussi began eating immediately. Ari took a bite of his fish and returned his fork to the table preparing to do all of the talking.

"This year's Conference of Kings is scheduled to take place in three weeks at the Iberotel Grand Sharm Hotel in Sharm El Sheikh, Egypt. The heads of all fifty-four OIL member states will be attending along with some of their terrorist friends. In other words, all of the Muslims who wield any power in the Islamic world will be at this meeting.

Now to the science: population genetics tells us people today have inherited their genetic blueprint from a recombination of DNA when a father's sperm fertilizes a mother's egg. This recombination creates a hybrid individual whose traits are derived from both parents. This gives us our individuality and explains why no two people are exactly alike, even siblings, unless they are a product of multiple births like twins and triplets." He paused to make sure Yussi understood.

"Continue," said Yussi, his eyes betraying a growing disinterest.

"The first part of my plan would be to surreptitiously gather DNA samples from individuals at the conference and analyze them to determine what if any genetic diseases exist within the group. I imagine with all the inbreeding, many of the representatives inherited conditions, some of which would cause them embarrassment if they were made public. I reviewed pictures of the attendees and can say with confidence we will uncover some interesting maladies. Imagine the shock in the Muslim community when they discover their leaders have genetic conditions compromising their ability to lead and govern. Modern science permits us to shine a light on something that is factual and beyond dispute. Disclosing these disorders assists us by temporarily redirecting the focus on their ability to lead. A discovery along these lines would send shock waves through OIL, the United Nations, and all of Islam."

The first part of his plan was on the table, and Ari needed Yussi's network to obtain the DNA required for testing.

"How would you suggest we get these DNA samples?" Yussi's interest continued to wane as he ordered another drink.

"Through your network of field officers and helpers, I'm sure you could engage willing parties who could find their way onto the housekeeping staff at the Iberotel. By knowing the schedule of the meetings and room numbers of the attendees, these agents could harvest hair from a brush or snot from a prayer rug. By marking the samples with the room number of the occupant we would be able to match the genetic results with the individual." Again, Ari waited for a sign Yussi had interest in his plan.

"So you are saying these fucking Arabs may be terminally ill or have some other embarrassing conditions. And somehow this realization will advance our objectives to secure our borders and defeat the enemy? Not likely." Doing what he did best, Yussi challenged the idea to see how the proponent defended his position.

"Yes, I'm suggesting it as a first step in a more comprehensive plan. It will cause nonmilitary chaos within both established and emerging Islamic leadership groups. There's no better way to accomplish this than by exposing some of its leaders as being too sick to govern, or to embarrass them by uncovering sexually transmitted diseases or terminal illnesses. Once the tests conclusively uncover a genetic condition or an environmentally contracted disease, we will tell the world and let the information do its work." Ari's eyes fell to his plate as he contemplated eating the cold entree.

"I am skeptical of your plan, Dr. Kohen. Even if we obtained the necessary samples and uncovered these conditions, it doesn't further our political or military interests." Having consumed his meal, Yussi was in battle mode and ready to fully challenge his lunch guest.

Ari was prepared for the onslaught and did not hesitate to respond. "You are correct, Colonel. The disclosure of medical conditions alone will not permanently change the dynamic of the conflict. It is the first salvo in a number of attacks we can make using this new science."

Still unconvinced, the colonel sat silently with his arms crossed over his considerable belly, impatiently waiting for Ari to finish so he could return to the real work of saving Israel.

A new intensity descended on Ari as he launched into his final pitch for the colonel's assistance. "Colonel Fischer, you have Alzheimer's."

"I what? Did you say I have Alzheimer's?" he asked almost spitting out a mouthful of his drink.

"Yes. I obtained a sample of your DNA when I visited your office last Tuesday. I ran some tests and found a genetic pattern strongly suggesting you suffer from that brain condition." Ari sat back expecting the colonel to lurch across the table to strangle him or have him arrested for stealing his DNA.

The colonel's father had suffered from Alzheimer's. The family specter of the disease reminded him he was a candidate to follow the same downward spiral. Yussi had watched his father go from momentary memory lapses to complete non-recognition of his only son. Was this to be Yussi's death sentence? "You spineless prick. What right do you have stealing and running tests on my DNA without my permission? I'll have you arrested for grand larceny and scientific malpractice. You're way out of line, Dr. Kohen. I think this lunch is over and you will be hearing from my attorney."

Yussi rose abruptly, his belly knocking the table and capsizing all of the glasses in the process. Two waiters rushed to clean up the mess, causing Yussi to momentarily contain his anger as the waiter replaced the tablecloth.

Once the clean linen was in place, Ari beseeched the colonel to sit back down by saying, "Colonel, there is more to the story. Please sit back down."

Not used to taking orders from a civilian, Yussi hesitated but finally relented by taking his seat. The exchange ruined the colonel's scotch buzz but had added a considerable amount of color to his face.

"I'm sorry you are angry, Colonel. I hoped I wouldn't have to resort to trickery during my presentation, but you left me little choice. I never tested your DNA, but I did research your family's medical history in preparation for our meeting. I discovered your father suffered from Alzheimer's and decided to use that knowledge if you were firmly against my plan." Ari waited for the colonel's reaction.

"So you don't know for sure I have Alzheimer's?" asked Yussi, shaken but pleased by the turn of events. Ari had gotten the response he wanted, and now it was time to go in for the kill.

"That's correct sir, but more importantly, I think my point is made; with minimal work we can determine what diseases afflict the families of the Islamic leaders. This information, combined with actual DNA tests, could cause an emotional upheaval infecting the entire ruling population of a particular country. While the leaders are dealing with the odious disclosures and their imminent incapacitation, we will be able to capitalize on the confusion through enhanced intelligence gathering and military action." Ari hoped he had made his point.

The attentive waiter placed another scotch in front of Yussi. A new normal descended upon the table as Yussi said, "I'm not used to being played for a fool, Dr. Kohen, but you made your point. Once these medical conditions are disclosed, especially if they are consistent with family history, there is a potential for a major damage to be inflicted. Let me see what I can do regarding the upcoming conference."

Yussi gave Ari a military glare trying to take back control of the meeting. The scientist's point had been delivered with remarkable precision by provoking an emotional response, making Yussi feel the pain of their potential targets. The colonel was still miffed but also amazed by the resourcefulness of the young doctor.

"Colonel, thank you for being such a good sport. The bigger picture is perhaps of even more interest. The genetic material we obtain will enable us to configure a virus that will attack only the individual we are targeting. This means we can eliminate a high value individual without killing anyone else," offered Ari, hoping to further assuage his lunch guest's anger and plant the hook to the barb.

If Yussi was impressed, he didn't show it, but Ari detected the wheels of wisdom turning. They sat in silence while Yussi sipped his drink and Ari pushed the cold cod around. No one spoke. Both men were aware that the next person to speak would lose the upper hand. Ari gained confidence as the silence continued. He would be happy to let the colonel take credit for any positive outcomes resulting from his genius plan. More importantly, he would be one step closer to creating the proper environment for the construction of the Third Temple in Jerusalem.

"Okay, Dr. Kohen, I'll give you what you want. This information must remain between us, and if others are involved without my knowledge, there will be consequences. What are the next steps?" Yussi asked, still upset but impressed by Ari's underhanded tactics.

"Thank you, Colonel. I'll deliver the sampling equipment. Just let me know where and when." Pleased at the turn of events, Ari kept a straight face as the colonel considered the place and time.

"Bring them by my office tomorrow at two o'clock. I will obtain the samples," Yussi rose from the table to leave. The two men shook hands, and the large Israeli departed.

Still patting himself on the back, Ari's mind turned to the dead body of his colleague at the dig site and the interview he would have to give to authorities. The sooner he spoke with the police, the quicker he could determine what was in the sealed chamber and what the hell those cryptic words on the cylinder meant. He didn't believe in the netherworld of curses and apparitions. As a scientist, he founded his religious faith on a certainty that he was an instrument for God's plan on earth. Through science, he would eradicate the enemies of Israel and position himself for spiritual and monetary riches as high priest.

On top of a seaside warehouse sat microwave antenna MW134, just like the many thousands strewn all over Tel Aviv rooftops, permanently honed onto the windows of a nearby restaurant. The

CIA's Office of Collection Strategies and Analysis (CSAA) covertly placed the small dish on top of the building. Signals collected through MW134 were immediately uploaded to a CIA satellite for transmission to headquarters in Langley, Virginia. The sizable glass exterior of the dining area gave the listeners ample surface area to conduct multiple surveillances at once. The most fertile location was a table in the northwest corner of the dining area where voices resonated within the triangular space. This was the preferred table of the listener's favorite subject, Col. Yussel "Yussi" Fischer. The CIA's code name for the colonel was "Pussi," because most daytime surveillance of the subject included rendezvous with attractive middle-aged women with whom he shared afternoon trysts. Col. Fischer's voiceprint was programmed into the computer-controlled notification system. Once his voice was recognized, the system alerted the day officer responsible for Tel Aviv surveillance.

Special Communications Officer Lincoln Walters got the hit on MW134. Col. Fischer and another gentleman, whose voice was not recognized by the system, were in conversation over lunch. Walters had listened in on numerous lunch conversations between Pussi and others over the last year. The surveillance had provided the CIA with advance notice of the Israeli's attack on Gaza. Pussi, an "old school" spook, did not truly understand the power of new technology. He made the mistake of thinking the noise in the restaurant would make it impossible to eavesdrop on his conversations. Wrong. The U.S. military had the ability to take a room full of noise and strip out everything not related to the target conversation.

An encrypted transcript of the conversation was transmitted to the liaison officer for the Director of Intelligence who coordinated all CIA activities in the region. Goran Frankfurter was the officer in charge of Middle East collection, which included the Israeli file. Activities in his region had gotten hot after the Vice President of the United States was blindsided on a trip to Israel by their decision to expand settlements in East Jerusalem. Goran was called to the Director's office and read the riot act for not forewarning him on Israel's position before the vice president arrived in the country. He took the brunt of the blame within the agency and a formal reprimand from the Director. Goran was still bruised from the encounter that had placed an admonishment in his personnel file. He needed this job and was determined not to allow another lapse in intelligence collection. He redoubled his effort, literally reading every word of intelligence from his region.

Arriving at six a.m. after an intense workout in one of Langley's ultra-modern gyms, he began the review of overnight surveillance. He opened the encrypted file labeled MW134 from the previous day and read the transcribed conversation between Yussi and Ari. The document had been translated from Hebrew to English overnight. Goran was fluent in Hebrew and wanted to listen in the native tongue. He found translators often missed nuances within the dialogue that provided color to the subject matter. His failure to review the audio had caused the oversight on the settlements. It wouldn't happen again.

Goran called up the MP3 file containing the MW134 recordings and dragged it to his desktop. Noting the beginning time on the encrypted memo, he began his review a few minutes before to make sure he wouldn't miss anything. What he heard interested him a great deal. The idea some Arab leaders had diseases impairing their ability to lead got Goran's attention. Genetically proving their sicknesses would take the disclosure of their illnesses beyond the realm of speculation. The plan proposed by Dr. Kohen was bold and scientifically plausible based on Goran's limited knowledge of genetics.

Goran was more skeptical about what came next. Near the end of the lunch, Dr. Kohen offered Col. Fischer an additional incentive to work with him. Kohen outlined a strategy to use the DNA samples to construct a biological weapon that would kill only the intended target. If true, and Goran had his doubts, they could kill someone without injuring any innocents. Goran included details of the meeting in a brief for his boss. He recommended keeping a close eye on the scientist.

Goran's mother, a Syrian Jew by birth, had immigrated to Germany with her parents in the thirties. He never practiced Judaism himself. His grandparents had escaped Nazi Germany, eventually finding their way to the United States in 1944. He began his career at the CIA after receiving a doctorate in communications technology from MIT. Goran rose through the ranks by being smarter than his supervisors, a fact that haunted him to this day. Many people in the agency would like him to fail. His considerable language skills, which included fluency in Arabic, Farsi, French, Hebrew, and German, were usually a ticket to a higher rank in the CIA. Built in anti-Semitism at the agency had limited his upward mobility.

For now he would concentrate on the job at hand. He needed a meeting with Mark Manning, the new Director of Intelligence, so he could relate the contents of the conversation between Yussi and his guest. He would over report news on the Middle East file, not wanting to miss another key event in his region of responsibility.

Chapter 21

Trey continued the search for his father at the Hebrew University in Jerusalem where, according to Omar, William Cohen graduated in 1963. Trey hired a chauffeur through the InterContinental Hotel in Tel Aviv, not wanting to drive himself after witnessing the habits of Israelis behind the wheel. He wouldn't need a car after his arrival in Jerusalem, because the hotel was centrally located just outside the Old City and within walking distance of the university. Trey read the morning paper and enjoyed the beautiful day on the one-hour trip.

As they motored across the 1949 Armistice Agreement Line that supposedly separated Israel from the Arab West Bank, the driver interrupted the quiet. "Mr. Trey, did you know, Prime Minister Rabin was assassinated by his own people?"

"Yes."

"In 1995 he was fatally shot in Tel Aviv after a rally celebrating the Oslo Peace Accord. An ultra-radical, right wing Jew named Yigal Amir shot him." The driver looked in his rearview mirror, hoping to coax Trey into a conversation.

He continued talking in a thick Israeli accent as Trey kept reading the paper. "Jews killing Jews, the lowest point in our history."

Not wanting to engage the driver in a politically charged conversation, Trey made an uninspired response, "That's terrible."

"They caught him immediately. Now, he's in jail serving a life sentence with no chance of parole. Yigal Amir was a Yemeni Jew. Nothing that comes from Yemen is ever good, not even the Jews," he concluded with contempt.

"I hear what you're saying. Hey, can we get some news in English on the radio?" Trey said trying to cut the conversation short before they went any deeper. The driver complied and tuned in the Israel National Radio morning news. They rode in silence as the news informed them of the latest atrocities against Jews and attacks on their homeland. He could see why Israelis were deeply involved in politics, but today his mind was on his father.

Suddenly, "Breaking News" interrupted the report:

> *"The black cloud of terrorism has returned to Northern Ireland with the simultaneous and cold-blooded assassinations of the three men who were leading the reconciliation movement in the region. Mark Foster, deputy First Minister; Peter Mallon, First Minister; and the Rt. Hon. Robert Weir, Secretary of State for Northern Ireland, were all shot at different locations around Belfast yesterday morning. The coordinated attack on the region's highest-ranking officials has left the peace process in question and police looking for answers. No group has taken responsibility for the shootings, but signs point to dissidents from either the Real IRA or the Continuity IRA. Both groups seek the unification of the northern region with the Republic of Ireland. They have each stated publicly they will exhaust all of their resources to derail any arrangement with the British falling short of that goal. Police have no leads at this time."*

Trey was digesting what he just heard when it hit him. Holy shit, this was his brother's work! He never expected Donny's revolutionary calling would include brutally killing the men charged with actually stopping the bloodshed. He tried to get a grip on his feelings for his murderous sibling.

Donny's words had been foreboding. The events reported on the radio explained why Donny insisted Trey leave Ireland as soon as possible. He wondered where Donny was, what he was thinking, and if he was all right. A sense of concern for his brother's safety was at odds with his questions about Donny's acts. Donny promised to "touch base when he could." When that would be depended on circumstances Trey did not control and maybe Donny didn't either.

Arriving at the hotel in Jerusalem before noon, Trey received greetings from the valet as he got out of the car. The driver had phoned ahead alerting the hotel staff of their estimated arrival time. An imprint of his AMEX card and a check of his passport were completed at the reception desk before a dowdy female service associate and a bellman escorted him to his suite. Once inside the suite, the bagman left to retrieve some ice while the service lady quickly reviewed the room amenities. Noticing Trey was not interested in how to adjust the thermostat or hours of operation for the fitness club, she left with the bellman as soon as he returned with the ice.

Trey opened the mini-bar and removed a Diet Coke. He would need a clear brain for his afternoon search of the archives at the Hebrew University. He had contacted the head archivist, saying he had recently found out about his Jewish heritage and was looking for information on a family member who he believed attended the university.

Trey made his way through the urban landscape where the ancient meshed with the new in a compelling combination of metropolitan architectures. He entered the library and went to the administrative office where he asked for Devra Sheraga, the lady he spoke with on the phone. Ms. Sheraga met Trey in the reception area.

They exchanged a cordial greeting, and then she asked, "How may I assist you today, Mr. Cowens?" Ms. Sheraga wore a multicolored *chamsa* on a gold chain around her neck. The amulet looked like an upside-down hand and was worn for good luck. Her *chamsa* was beautiful and so were her breasts, Trey looked away before he could be accused of staring at her boobs.

Trey explained he discovered his estranged father graduated from the university, and he was on a hunt to find out everything he could. He said that his father's name was William Joseph Cohen, and he had graduated in 1963.

"Follow me," said the librarian. They walked back to an area containing university enrollment records. A quick search of the computer database directed them to a wall of books on the second floor. Ms. Sheraga rolled a ladder in front of the floor to ceiling shelving until she located the proper section. She climbed up to within a few rungs from the top allowing Trey a clear view up her skirt, revealing nothing more than some granny panties and further confirmation of his sexual obsession. An unaware Ms. Sheraga located and retrieved the volume. Walking the book to a nearby table, she thumbed through the index finding a page number directing them to a picture of a man in his early twenties. It was him, his father. The photograph was just a headshot, but it was him.

"Is this the person you are looking for?" she inquired.

"Yes it is; I am sure of it. Where else can we look for more information?" Trey asked trying not to act too excited.

After running a photocopy of the page, she returned the volume to its shelf and handed Trey the picture of his father. Ms. Sheraga led him down a long column-lined hall to another room filled with computer terminals. She sat down at one of the workstations and typed some letters and numbers.

She pushed away from the keyboard, saying, "I will leave you to do some searches on your own in our vast database of birth, marriage, and death records. Additionally, you will have access to newspaper articles, book excerpts, and some non-classified government reports. Here is my cell number should you require anything before I return. I'll check back in about an hour." She left Trey staring at the screen opened to a search box and submit button.

He typed in "William Joseph Cohen" and hit submit. The computer took its time extracting results from the database. Clicking on birth records, the program took him to a copy of an Israeli birth certificate. William Joseph Cohen was born January 24, 1940, to Ruth and Joseph Cohen in Tiberius, Galilee. Trey saw the names of his paternal grandparents for the first time. The emotional force of having these names revealed struck him hard. He shut his eyes, trying to imagine what they looked like. The information was powerful. He had done little to prepare himself for the surge of emotions swamping his investigation. Trey shook off the sentiment and refocused on his father.

The birth record contained hyperlinks on the bottom of the page to marriage and death records. In the marriage records, Trey found a certificate listing his father and a woman named Eva Shalom who were married August 11, 1963.

I wonder if my mother knew about his first marriage? Trey asked himself.

Additional links took Trey to the newspaper announcement of the wedding; theirs was a traditional Jewish celebration in Tiberius with family and friends. The photo of the bride and groom was the typical wedding shot of a new couple leaving a synagogue holding hands with broad smiles on their faces.

The link to death records gave Trey a message saying: "No Information Available." He drilled deeper, searching newspapers, magazines, and newsletters that were all linked directly into the university database. He searched "Eva Shalom" and located the same marriage announcement along with additional information about her musical career as a promising classical violinist. Eva's life was cut short by a Palestinian attack on an outdoor concert in 1966, when a bomb exploded under the stage on which she was performing. Authorities never caught the perpetrators, and according to the article, twenty-one people died that night. Eva Shalom Cohen suffered a violent death, and Trey wondered if his father had been in the crowd that night.

Ms. Sheraga returned to offer her assistance, "How's it going, Mr. Cowens?"

"Not bad, but I think I've hit a wall. Every time I try to access details of his work history, college transcripts, and military service, I get 'Access Forbidden'," Trey responded.

"University transcripts, work history, and information on military service are restricted to access by the subject or anyone with written authorization from that party. I recommend you continue your search at the Israel Genealogical Society. All of their records are in the public domain and could broaden your search by expanding the number of family members who might be able to help. My colleague, Sharon Geller, is the head of the IGS. Here is her phone number and the address of her office." She politely asked if there was anything else, turned on her heels, and quickly walked away.

Trey was left holding a photocopied picture of his father, a printout of a marriage announcement, and a business card with the IGS contact information. He'd had enough for today. He would return to the hotel and try to get a workout in before dinner. He thought about his twin brother and wondered if he was safe. He hoped Donny would call soon, because he needed to confirm his involvement in the Irish assassinations.

An alert appeared on Yoshe Barkut's screen from someone trying to access restricted information on a computer located at the Hebrew University. Further analysis of the IP address confirmed the user session took place on a workstation in the Library and Archive building. Yoshe worked for the Collections Department inside the Institute for Intelligence and Special Operations, also known as Mossad—the super-covert Israeli intelligence machine. The signal came from a bugging device installed on all university keyboards. Mossad recorded every keystroke made on the computers. Once a user keyed in words found on the Collection Department's alert list, the system began capturing everything being searched and accessed directly from the server. Today, the name William Joseph Cohen triggered the warning. Based on the information available to the operative, the search was way over his pay grade: Level 5.

Chapter 22

The sun was setting over the hills of Upper Galilee. The sky would remain illuminated for at least another hour encouraged by the sun's reflection off the Mediterranean Sea. Ari would need the extra light to finalize preparations for tonight's mission. From the garage at his understated home, not far from the Genoshalom Lab in Beit Jann, he organized everything to conduct a secret night-time operation.

Ari's favorite Leatherman multi-tool was already affixed to his belt. Laid out on the garage floor were other archeological and construction tools. The considerable selection included a head-lamp for night work; dental cutting and plying tools; a precision drill and saw used by orthopedic surgeons; a masonry drill with a twenty-four-inch bit; a grout router; shovels; a halogen 360-degree work light; surgical gloves; probes; picks; axes; a super silent, light-weight Honda 1000-watt, 220-volt generator; a portable tripod with a winch for hoisting and lifting heavy objects; and finally, a padded titanium Halliburton briefcase that contained other high-tech electronics needed for scientific field work. All of it was neatly organized behind the rear hatch of his black Subaru Outback and covered with a grey blanket that matched the upholstery.

Ari had met with an Israeli police investigator the previous afternoon at the dig house. Sgt. David Latimer asked all of the questions while his able assistant took copious notes. Once Uzi

Rubens discovered Lev's body, he'd called his supervisor, who had phoned the police. Uzi waited at the site for the police and gave them his rendition of the story. The coroner's truck arrived and removed the body after pictures, measurements, and samples were taken.

Sgt. Latimer asked Ari about the last conversations between him and the deceased. Ari related the phone call in which Lev told him about the dig being halted for spring break and that Lev was taking the weekend off to rest from a grueling month-long effort. Lev and Ari agreed to speak again the following Tuesday; they wished each other a pleasant night, and hung up.

His questions followed police protocol to the letter. Latimer wanted to know all about Lev's home life, family, financial situation, university affiliations, other digs, enemies, hobbies, household pets, last vacation, best friend, siblings, and even if he drank coffee or tea. The police were nothing if not thorough.

After the grilling, Sgt. Latimer asked if Ari wanted to add anything. Realizing that less is more in these situations, Ari responded by saying, "He was a good friend and excellent educator. I will miss him deeply."

Latimer robotically terminated the interview by saying, "We are not ruling out foul play in Dr. Wasserman's death. However, our preliminary findings indicate he died by natural causes, heart attack. I'm sorry for your loss. The dig will need to be closed for at least a week so we can return to an undisturbed scene if necessary. We will let you know the exact date you may resume. Here's my card; please call me if you think of anything else that can aid us in our investigation. Have a good evening."

They must memorize these canned speeches in law enforcement school, thought Ari. If he had been upset at Lev's death, which Ari was not, then Latimer's remarks would have provided no comfort at all.

The words, "We are not ruling out foul play," hung in the air as the sergeant walked away. Ari wondered what that meant and if a murder investigation would be forthcoming. If someone murdered Lev, then someone knew something of Ari's business. He would act quickly and decisively before the police or an unknown party discovered the ancient chamber. He imagined Lev might have operated a parallel plan. The big bucks ancient relics commanded on the black market would be enough of a motive.

Ari was headed south for the fifty-kilometer drive to a parking lot in Tiberius where he had arranged to meet Ziva. She would assist him in the nighttime mission. Ziva drove from Tel Aviv, where she had spent two days volunteering at the Babcock In Vitro Fertilization (IVF) Clinic. At the clinic, she counseled women like herself who could not conceive children by natural means.

Ari pulled the Subaru into the parking spot next to Ziva's black Mercedes. They left her car parked there and proceeded south to the dig site. The vehicle's headlights provided the only illumination on the moonless night. Once in the vicinity of the dig, they parked the wagon in a commuter lot used by area residents who worked the graveyard shift in factories to the south. Their vehicle was hidden perfectly in the lot with the other cars for the next ten hours.

Their destination was the first-century burial tomb and the undisturbed chamber. Ari had conceived a plan to enter the companion chamber from the outside rather than going through the door to the established site. It would require some heavy digging and lifting to get down to the tomb from ground level. Ari and Ziva loaded equipment and instruments into two large backpacks designed to hold the excavation tools. Ari hauled the generator, and Ziva carried the titanium briefcase on the fifteen-minute hike from the commuter lot to the dig site.

Ari found the rock he had placed the previous day indicating the approximate location of the hidden chamber many feet below. They got to work removing dirt and stone. They dug down until they hit the top of the virgin tomb. Finding the ceiling of the chamber reenergized them. Ari cleared a workspace at the bottom of the shaft and began drilling into the limestone cavern using a one-inch diameter drill bit designed for this application. The first borehole, in the middle of the exposed area, hit air at eleven inches, exactly what Ari had expected. He snaked a cable through the hole and fastened it to the tripod-mounted winch. He drilled eight other holes in a three-foot square. Ari instructed Ziva to plug the saw into the generator. With the saw he cut lines in the rock between each of the holes creating a suspended piece of limestone. Activating the winch, he guided the block up through the hole to ground level. Ari swung the object to the side and placed it on the ground.

Ari positioned the tripod back over the opening. He stepped into a seat harness and clipped onto a steel ring attached to the end of the cable. Ziva took control of the winch mechanism. She slowly lowered Ari into the shaft until his feet straddled the three-foot wide space in the tomb's ceiling. Ari could smell a distinct odor coming up from the chamber. An aroma of air filled with micro-particles of death and relic-soaked dust invaded his olfactory system. Without ventilation, the atmosphere in the tomb had become a veritable Petri dish of ancient organic matter from two-thousand-year-old decomposed bodies and artifacts. He paused to imprint the exact fragrance. As he passed from the modern to the ancient world, he wanted to remember this moment with all of his senses.

Life in the first century was not so much different than life in the twenty-first. The city of Sepphoris, known as the "Jewel of Galilee," was a rich Jewish city at the center of regional trade. The absence of toilets, shrink-wrap, and Ambien would have been of little concern to the residents of ancient Sepphoris. They created ways to manage human waste, preserve perishable food, and sleep in accordance with first-century expectations. Like mortals today, people back then didn't know what they didn't know. They lived happy, if not perfect lives, chasing dreams just out of their reach.

Sepphoris was an ancient city on a hill midway between the Mediterranean and Galilean Seas west of the Naphtali Mountains in Northern Palestine. It was a vibrant center of commerce controlled through time by the Assyrians, Babylonians, Persians, and finally the Romans. As a highly synthesized product of various cultures, the people of Sepphoris and the surrounding villages spoke many languages. Aramaic, Greek, Latin, and Hebrew could be heard in the city market and other public places. Musicians played stringed, percussion, and wind instruments introduced by the Greeks and Romans, but which evolved locally to complement indigenous traditions. Lyres, flutes, and drums would have been the trio of choice.

With this incredible diversity came a tolerance for others' religious and cultural beliefs. Pagans and monotheists lived together in peace, accepting the other's beliefs as a personal choice, just like the language and music. The music stopped when the Romans tried to impose taxes on the population in 6 CE.

Such was the scene in ancient Sepphoris during the reign of Herod Antipas who inherited the lands and problems of Galilee and Perea from his father Herod the Great. As part of the Roman Empire, citizens were required to participate in a census for taxation purposes. Their ruler, Herod Antipas, had neither the skill nor the will to execute this mandate, so the Roman's sent the ruthless Publius Sulpicius Quirinius from Syria to do the dirty work. The citizens of the region considered the meaning of the census; the Roman's ruled the kingdom, so they get the taxes. However, for many Jews it duplicated the levies imposed by the religious laws passed down to Moses from God. They already gave tithes of 10 to 20 percent of their hard-earned incomes to the temple and its keeper priests. The Jews would have to cough up even more, a challenging concept.

Enter Judas of Galilee, who rallied his fellow citizens to fight Roman taxation by making an alliance with Zadok, a Jewish Pharisee priest. Together they formed a patriotic group of likeminded citizens called the Zealots. Zadok's participation was important for the success of the movement because, as their priest, he commanded devout Jews to rise up against the Romans. The name Zealot was adopted from a creed embraced by their forefathers that stated, "Be ye zealous for the law and give your lives for the covenant of your fathers."

Most non-Jewish citizens of Galilee accepted the imposition of taxes as a Roman prerogative. Judas and Zadok, believing God to be the only true ruler of the land, founded the first national theocratic movement to fight taxation.

The resistance must have mystified Rome. Emperor Augustus preached religious tolerance before it was popular. The diversity of his far-flung land holdings gave his empire strength. The Romans required payment for the largesse they bestowed upon their subjects in the form of modern currency, security, and construction projects. Aqueduct systems were expensive but necessary for cultural advancement. Lifting heathens out of the sewer was a costly undertaking, and their subjects should pay a fair share of the cost.

As a man of the Torah, Zadok the priest lent credibility to the Zealot's cause. His lineage traced back to the earliest high priests of Israel and directly to Aaron, brother of Moses. His ancestors had protected the Ark of the Covenant for over fifteen hundred years. When Sadducee priests took control of Herod's Temple in Jerusalem Zadok needed little other motivation to throw his hat in the ring with Judas. Zadok needed to take back the Temple.

Zealotry in its most radical form was codified by a group of anarchists called the *Sicarii*, meaning "violent" or "dagger-men." They were a radicalized militia inside the Zealot movement, similar to modern day Hamas, operating as the armed faction of the Palestinian party. The Sicarii attacked Romans and the Jews who collaborated with them. Their Jewish targets were people that acted as tax collectors or administrators for the Romans.

Zadok set up and ran a branch office of the Zealots in Jerusalem while Judas recruited resistors from the margins of society. The Jerusalem Zealots had less interest in political issues and more concern about the preservation of religious traditions. In a grand crescendo of destruction, these radicals took control of Jerusalem and its Temple. They held both for three years. The Roman army eventually fought through the opposition and retook the city, destroying everything except Herod's Temple. Romans would eventually destroy the Temple before the turn of the century.

A group of a thousand Zealots fled the incoming Roman army and made their way to a walled city on a plateau named Masada, located above the Dead Sea. The fort had been captured by the Sicarii from the Romans the previous year. They held the hilltop refuge for over twenty-four months while the Romans attempted to retake their dominion. Finally, the Romans constructed a ramp 375 feet high allowing them to move battering rams to the top of the plateau and into position outside the fortress walls. With some effort, they breached the wall and entered the compound. They arrived to find one thousand dead Jews and the buildings on fire.

Because Judaism forbids suicide, all the men in the compound drew lots to determine the order they would be murdered, leaving only one man to take his own life. Death in this manner was preferable to being captured by the Romans, who would enslave, rape, or kill any survivors. Zealotry had caused the death of many of Israel's most devout Jews, including hundreds of woman and children.

Ari could not contain his enthusiasm for what he discovered in the tomb that night. Ziva heard an excited scream a few minutes before Ari emerged from the vertical shaft.

"You won't believe what's down there," said Ari, climbing out of the hole.

"What is it? I'm dying to know," quivered Ziva.

"The chamber is filled with relics and ossuaries not seen by human eyes for thousands of years. Even I can make out the inscription on one of the limestone boxes." Ari sat on the ground with Ziva, both were covered in sweat and he was shaking noticeably.

"What was the inscription on the box?" demanded Ziva.

Ari paused for a dramatic moment before he said, "We've discovered the remains of Zadok the Zealot and his family. Ziva, do you know what this means?" Ari asked, knowing Ziva was well aware of its significance.

"I need the hacksaw and the dentist's drill." Ari hooked the tools to his belt and Ziva lowered him back down into the chamber. Ari got to work recovering everything he could from the tomb, including Zadok's remains.

Chapter 23

Rachel was at her wits end by the time she reached Trey on the phone. Ari had been missing for two weeks, and everyone she spoke with fed her the same lame story. They all told her, "He's at a population genetics conference in Indonesia."

"Trey, I've been calling his cell phone and e-mailing him for a week with no response. I don't care if he's at the North Pole, he always responds to his little sister. I said it was an emergency in my last message and he should call immediately. So far, I've heard nothing, Trey. What should I do?"

"Try to calm down, Rachel. I'm sure there's a logical explanation. Indonesia is still a third world country and maybe his phone and e-mail don't work. He'll probably turn up soon." Trey tried to direct the conversation toward a solution.

"We've never been out of touch this long in our entire adult lives and certainly not since mother and father died."

She was speaking so fast it was hard for Trey to track everything she was saying.

"I talked to Ziva yesterday. She says she hasn't seen him in two weeks. They had lunch together the day before he supposedly departed for the stupid conference. Trey, where is my brother? I can't lose him. He's all the family I have." Rachel was in tears now, and Trey struggled to find some soothing words. He had to adlib because his personal experience at managing family dynamics did not exist.

Trey's efforts to calm her over the next thirty minutes appeared to work. He agreed to drive up to the Genoshalom Laboratory in Galilee and investigate. He would also check out Ari's house. Rachel gave him ideas on where to find a hide-a-key and the code he usually used for the security keypad. Like it or not, Trey would be sleuthing around in a foreign country, looking for a nut-bag scientist. The thought of Rachel losing her brother triggered a picture of Donny the day they met. Bonding with a sibling was new territory for Trey, but one he intended to develop further. Rachel needed him to find Ari. The search would be good practice for Trey, because he would probably have to go looking for Donny at some point.

Rachel insisted on taking the next plane to Tel Aviv from New York. She would forward Trey her itinerary as soon as she made the arrangements. The prospect of having her with him in Israel gave him a rush of excitement and anticipation.

"I'll meet you at the airport. In the meantime, let me see what I can discover up north. I'll call as soon as I have any news." He could hear that she was still crying. "Try to sneak in a yoga practice before you leave. That always seems to bring you some peace." She agreed and told him thanks before she hung up the phone.

Much of Trey's last three weeks had been spent with his Uncle Omar and cousin Zach. When not visiting with his new relatives, he scoured libraries, the Internet, newspapers, and any public records for information about his father. His visits with the old skirt-chaser Omar usually led him to remember things about Willy he had not shared during the previous visits.

Trey considered himself lucky to have found these relatives. Even if he never located his father, he was grateful Omar and Zach had come into his life. Trey sensed a strong family connection when in Omar's presence. His father's touch was in the air when Omar hugged and kissed him on the cheek as they said good-bye. He loved that feeling, the honest touch of a blood relative, your father's brother. *Brushing cheeks with Omar might be as close to my father as I ever get*, thought Trey.

Trey arranged for a rental car at the hotel, a new Hyundai Elantra. Unfortunately, he would have to drive himself on his search for clues explaining Ari's disappearance. He headed north on the coastal highway out of Tel Aviv toward the port of Haifa. The two-hour drive to Beit Jann ran him straight up the Mediterranean coast and then northeast on a diagonal vector to Upper Galilee and the Genoshalom Laboratory.

Trey tuned the radio to English speaking news and lost himself in thoughts of Rachel's arrival, Uncle Omar, his father, his twin brother, and the craziness of the last few months. A search for answers about his biological family was leading Trey to a deeper understanding of himself. If the tattoo on his ass was a testament to his failings, then his relationship with Rachel and the discovery of lost family pointed to an improving condition. Rather than self-loathing, Trey tried self-loving by facing down his flaws and inadequacies with actions. Rachel would be back in his arms soon. He missed her more than he expected.

"Ari, your sister, Rachel, called me today. She needs to speak with you immediately. I told her you were still in Indonesia but she wouldn't accept the explanation and disrespected me," said Ziva, harboring no fondness for the sister in question.

Ari considered Ziva's statement as he looked up from the table covered with the artifacts they had secreted from the tomb.

"I'll call her when I get a chance. Let's focus on the stone cylinder," growled Ari not wanting to be distracted from the task at hand.

Ari and Ziva had ensconced themselves in the secret, underground laboratory separating, organizing and recording the remains and relics they had hauled out of the tomb. They were able to date the cylinder and certified it to be authentic material from the first century. The writing in three languages, when compared with contemporaneous passages, gave them confidence they had a bona fide article from the time of Jesus.

Ziva had spent the better part of the last three days trying to decipher the message. She was certain that the third line of ancient Hebrew referred to the remains of Jesus and the Aramaic in the second line spoke of his crucifixion. Still trying to translate the Greek characters, her initial translation went something like this:

> The Kingdom of God is overthrown
> His supposed son died on a cross
> Jesus did not ascend, he is with us

Reading the words aloud for the first time caused both of them to shiver at the enormity of the discovery. Could it be that some of the bodily remains on the table or still in the tomb belonged to Jesus? If so, he died and decomposed like a normal man. This supported the Jewish canon that classified Jesus as holy man, not the Messiah. When the Messianic Age arrives, a new "Anointed One" appears and the "end of times" is not far off. The idea that they could prove Jesus never ascended into heaven intoxicated Ari. Jesus was just a normal man who died and decomposed, leaving skeletal remains like everyone else. Ari would definitely keep digging; he required unimpeachable evidence.

"Keep refining the translation. I want to be sure we aren't going down a blind alley in pursuit of the ghost of Jesus. I need facts," Ari said in a clinical way not wanting his emotional enthusiasm to cloud their effort.

"I'll stay on it," replied Ziva.

"Let's start sorting the bones from the ossuary so we can make sure there is only one individual in the box. The inscription says it contains Zadok's remains," stated Ari.

"How many other ossuaries are in the tomb?" asked Ziva.

"I'm not sure," said Ari impatiently. "Maybe another ten or so."

"Do you think one of them contains the bones of Jesus?" queried Ziva, noticeably amazed at where the investigation was leading them.

Chapter 24

Donald "Mad Dog" Murphy didn't stay long in Egypt. He and his make believe wife were escorted through customs with their fake identities by a Fatah agent posing as a Canadian embassy employee.

"Follow me," he instructed. With no checked luggage, the couple walked to the gate for Egypt Air Flight #721 bound for Damascus, Syria. Their unnamed escort handed airline tickets and an envelope to Donny and vanished into the crowd.

Donny and Grace stood in a mass of malodorous, Middle Eastern humanity at the gate. If they thought *eau de Euro* was foul, this stench took the concept of body odor to the next level. The combination of human scents and sandwich cart aromas caused him to breathe through his mouth, avoiding the olfactory pain of actually smelling the putrid funk. Grace covered her face and head in a traditional Arab fashion. Now he understood why all of these women hid their faces. Their husbands reeked like barnyard animals.

They boarded the plane and found their seats in the first class cabin of the Boeing 737 for the two-hour flight. Donny opened the envelope given to him with the tickets at the airport. It was a letter from his contact in Damascus with instructions on his arrival in the Syrian capital. Current events in Syria would not change Donny's mission. Their visas indicated a preferred entry status into Syria as friends of the ruling party. Donny and Grace were to proceed through border control as Canadian tourists on holiday for two weeks. Once through border customs they were to take a taxi to the Damascus Sheraton Hotel. The letter instructed them to wait in their room for a phone call.

Donny's relationship with his Arab associates had developed over many years. Back in Ireland, he had trained numerous Middle Eastern extremists in the art of bomb making and advanced assassination techniques. His reputation preceded him as he made his way to Damascus. He wondered what his new life had in store for him as they disembarked from the airplane and headed to immigration control. The couple held hands like newlyweds on their honeymoon. They sailed through checkpoints, pushed their way past airport peddlers, and hailed a taxi upon departing the main terminal. The Sheraton was about thirty kilometers from the airport, and in Damascus traffic, it took almost an hour for them to arrive at the hotel.

The newlyweds checked in, and a bellhop showed them to their suite on the Gold Club Level. Donny expected a call any minute, but he needed a shower to wash off the travel grime. Exhausted but too excited to sleep, he took a shower after instructing Grace to bring him the phone if it rang.

With the cool water flowing over his head, he thought about all that had happened and what was to come. His Arab brothers arranged for Donny's and his men's departure from Ireland. They had smuggled him to France on a commercial ship delivering heavy machinery to the port of Brest on the Normandy coast. Once in France, a Muslim agent drove him to DeGaulle Airport. Grace met him at the Paris airport for their flight to Cairo. Now he was in a Damascus hotel waiting for the call that would define his future outside of Ireland. He knew returning to Ireland was impossible, at least for a few years, so he had to learn how to live a new life in a strange land.

The phone rang as he exited the shower. Grace brought the cordless handset to him in the bathroom.

"Hello," said Donny.

"Don't say anything, just listen. You will leave the hotel by the main entrance in thirty minutes. A white car with two men in it will pull up in front of the hotel, and you will get in the back seat. Do you understand?"

"Yes," responded Donny. The caller hung up, giving Donny an ear full of dial tone.

"I have to go soon. You stay here and get room service. Don't go outside the hotel until I return. Try to get some sleep. I should be back by tomorrow," Donny commanded. The truth be known, Donny had no clue when he would be back.

Grace was accustomed to Donny's erratic schedule and flighty behavior. She had learned a long time ago not to question him.

"Don't worry. I'll be here waiting for you to get back. And when you do I have a little surprise," Grace said as she pulled a red teddy out of her roller bag. A huge smile came across Donny's face as he considered the implication of the rouge invitation. He removed his towel and began dressing for the meeting with his Arab guardians. He would defer his sexual gratification until later, but he looked forward to having this beautiful Irish woman on her back.

Donny was under no illusion about the transaction taking place. He had rendered useful training services to the Arabs in the years leading up to the recent assassinations. They had reciprocated by getting him and his men out of Ireland and safely hidden. He slipped into the back seat of the white Mercedes and recognized the man in the passenger seat. It was Mustafa, whom he'd met a few years earlier in Ireland.

"How are you, my friend?" Mustafa asked as they pulled away from the hotel.

"I'm fine, Mustafa. How are you?" Donny's response concealed his uneasiness at being driven to an unknown destination.

"Everything is in order. We will arrive in about twenty minutes, and then you will be meeting with the boss and the Committee."

"What Committee?" asked Donny.

"You'll see once we arrive. I brought you some food for the drive. Eat up; you will need your strength." Mustafa handed him the box of food.

The scent of the meal caused Donny to rip into the box with enthusiasm. He unwrapped a falafel sandwich covered with a spicy tahini sauce, which he devoured it in a few healthy bites. A box of juice and some sweet cucumbers completed the meal. With his hunger satiated for the time being, he continued to wonder where they were going and what they had planed. Donny knew he was in Syria to do a job, and the work he knew best was how to terrorize an enemy. Donny assumed his objectives included menacing and tormenting Jews. He always welcomed a new challenge, especially one that might help reverse an illegal occupation. Donny would keep the news of his supposed Jewish heritage to himself.

They arrived at a gated compound on the outskirts of Damascus. Mustafa opened the back door of the Mercedes and Donny stepped out of the car, onto the dirt drive. Mustafa turned and walked toward the front door of a sprawling mansion. Donny followed his friend into the house. A servant led them to a room overlooking a field of Bedouin tents that seemed to stretch to the horizon. Goats, sheep, and camels wandered the open areas between the habitations. Donny could see groups of men sitting in circles smoking from hookahs. Over one hundred tents and at least a thousand people congregated in the area just behind the stately home.

His meditation on the gathering was interrupted by a voice he recognized.

"Mr. Murphy, welcome to my home. It has been too many years since we last met. I trust you are well and Mustafa treated you respectfully on the drive," the man said as he motioned for Donny to take a seat at a long table set for at least ten people.

Fareed al-Husseini was the first Syrian Donny had met in Ireland almost five years ago. He had arranged for the Muslim terrorists to train in Ireland under Donny's guidance. Donny was paid handsomely for the training, and over the years a mutual respect blossomed between the two men. Face to face with Fareed again, but on his turf, Donny sensed that Fareed's plan for him had already been decided. He was anxious to learn the details. Before he could complete that thought, the room began to fill with men in traditional Muslim garb. Fareed greeted each one of them with an embrace and kiss on both cheeks before they took their seats at the table.

"My brothers, I wish to welcome our friend Mr. Donald Murphy to our country. I know I speak for all of us when I thank you for the excellent training you have given to our people. As we suffer under pressure from Israel and the West to conform to their ideals of cultural and political fitness, we must push even harder to exert our God-given right to practice Sharia Law. The outcome of our struggle is not in question, only the method of obtaining this freedom is unknown to us today. We are charged with a responsibility to protect this right given to us directly from Allah and Mr. Murphy has agreed help us." Fareed finished his introduction and took a seat at the head of the table. No one spoke as they all looked at Donny, waiting for a comment from the famous Irish nationalist.

"First, I want to thank all of the esteemed members of the Committee for the support you've shown me and my Irish brothers. I'm here because of my special relationship with Fareed and the trust we have built over the last five years. I offer my services out of respect to him. I intend to do all I can to assist in your fight against the enemies of Palestine. I'm ready to get to work." He sat down and took a sip of tea.

"Thank you, Mr. Murphy. We appreciate your commitment. Your experience in these matters is well documented. We are convening a meeting of our Military Council and invite you to attend immediately after this gathering," Fareed said as he looked to Donny for confirmation, which he gave with a nod of his head.

Donny's thoughts wandered to Trey and the surprising fact of his Jewishness. The irony of the moment did not escape Donny as the half-breed Jew sat with a group of Islam's most radical terrorists, but he was committed to Fareed's cause regardless of his genetic makeup. He hated the Jews and Israel almost as much as he despised the Brits and Britain.

Fareed brought the Military Council to order, and Donny listened intently as each man spoke to a different element of the proposed plan. Their attention to detail surprised Donny a bit. Fareed stood when the last person had completed his presentation.

"Thank you, gentlemen. Mr. Murphy, do you have any questions?" Fareed asked and sat back down to hear Donny's response. The apparent paradox of using an infidel to pursue their religious mission was well understood by Fareed, but he needed Donny. Recently he had instructed a team of his top soldiers to kill a local mullah. The mullah lived through the attack and one of Fareed's men was captured. He knew he needed a professional for a plan this ambitious.

Donny had a clear understanding of what the operation would entail. Learning specifics for the first time, he conceived what skills would be required. His confidence increased as he rose from his seat and said, "What you have presented is very doable, but only with your most skilled marksmen. I am anxious to select these soldiers so we can begin the intense training required to assure victory. Gentlemen, I'm at your service."

Chapter 25

William "Willy" Joseph Cohen was now seventy-one years old and living in a small hamlet outside Lugano, Switzerland. The village of Carona, high on a mountain above the city, was a perfect place for Willy to blend into the surrounding culture. He had moved there two years after his last mission for Mossad. Willy had killed hundreds of Arab extremists over the years, earning him the reputation of Mossad's leading *kidon*. He had escaped death, torture, and incarceration through an incredibly well-developed sense of his surroundings. Willy managed to carry out his missions with minimal support from *sayanim*, Mossad's civilian helpers stationed around the world in support of Israel's clandestine activities. Working as a "lone wolf" got him in hot water numerous times, but each undertaking proved to be such a success they gave him unusual freedom to pursue other targets. The Israeli Prime Minister even granted him a waiver from Mossad's mandatory retirement policy that normally requires agents to leave active service at age fifty-five.

He had decided to take a sabbatical from the assassination business and settled in Switzerland, where he began an in-depth study of the real threats to Israel and the chance for peace in the Middle East. After two years of intense research, he had come to the conclusion that peace was unattainable under the current process being promoted by the United States, Israel, and the few allies remaining at their side. He needed to get back in the game. The time had come to reapply his talents.

Living in Switzerland under the assumed name Joseph Wilfred Adams, his language skills and understanding of the Ticinese people allowed him to blend in without drawing undue attention. He posed as a travel-writer who had found utopia in the mountains of southeastern Switzerland. He made friends with his neighbors, but never built relationships beyond a cordial greeting or nod in a restaurant. He spent hours pouring over reports from Israel and the United States related to the Arab-Israeli conflict. His passion for Israel approached a boiling point as he reviewed articles about failed missions, international censure, and concessions to the Palestinians in the liberal Israeli press.

The crumbling of old guard despots in the Arab world created a fertile environment for Islam's most extreme elements. Tunisia, Egypt, Syria, and Yemen were all in various stages of collapse; the Lebanese Parliament had been literally kidnapped by Hezbollah. The focus of the Arab population was temporarily diverted from Israel onto the leaders of those countries. Before long radical Islam would redirect that anger away from corrupt leaders back onto Israel.

The peace process was a joke. The US government, forever trying to broker a deal between Israel and Palestine, thought that an end to the conflict would resolve a much larger problem between the West and Arab states. The Muslim world's ultimate goal was to force Israel to give away land and money for peace. He saw no end to demands Arab states would place on the negotiations. Not wanting to recognize Israel's right to exist, the Arabs continuously moved the goal line for peace as they pretended to want a resolution. Arabs needed this friction to bind the radical forces within Islam under a common banner for the destruction of the liberal West and the installation of Sharia law. Israel's leaders had lost their way, and someone had to muster the believers in defense of the Jewish homeland.

Willy's plan began to take shape. Those who wanted peace at any cost were pulling the Prime Minister to the left. Willy knew and loved the Prime Minister, but that did not matter when it came to what was best for Israel. If he went any further left, he would have to be removed, either by the electorate or by force. The situation called for a covert military solution. Willy needed to mobilize the best and most trusted operatives he could find. An armed coup was not out of the question. However, he hoped they could find a more peaceful way to wrest control from his friend.

Willy maintained secure lines of communication with a few of his Israeli cohorts, including Isaac "Buji" Stahl, with whom he had trained and worked in North America back in the 1970s. He was Willy's closest friend and confidant. Buji had retired as a Mossad *katsa, similar to a CIA case officer,* and became a private intelligence contractor. As the second in command of Fischer Intelligence until last year, Buji had access to inside information about Israeli defense and espionage operations. Willy needed Buji and his contacts to carry out the mission.

"Buji, it's me," said Willy when his old friend answered the disposable phone. That was the signal for Buji to hang up and call Willy back on another untraceable phone he kept for these communications.

"Where have you been? I have been worried about my dear friend. Are you OK?" asked Buji with a note of concern.

"I am well, but I need to talk with you about the latest screw-ups by our esteemed leaders. What the hell is going on in Pimi's administration?" Willy knew the reference would rile his friend.

"The liberals and their friends in the media have fueled the fires of concession. The cry for peace with the Palestinians has clouded the thinking of our citizens and allies. Everyone is asking for Israel to give up the settlements, release the terrorists, and accept the return of Palestinian refugees as a requirement for continued peace talks. No amount of territory or money is enough for the Palestinians and their supporters. Negotiations are just a stalling tactic designed to get Israel to show weakness so the Arabs can step into the breach and take even more." Buji waited for Willy's response.

"The madness has to stop, Buji. I have a plan I want to discuss with you. Can you meet me in Milan on Thursday?" asked Willy.

"What's your idea, Willy?" Buji answered with a question of his own.

"I can't go into the specifics on the phone, but we need to reassert our might and negotiate from a position of power," answered Willy.

"I couldn't agree more. Also, I've just learned of a meeting between Yussi and a young scientist who is working on some interesting things which could further our effort. I'll give you a full briefing when we meet," Buji said.

He hung up and noticed they had spoken for more than three minutes. He didn't want to give international surveillance systems an opportunity to recognize their call, even if it was on an untraceable phone. Their voiceprints were probably loaded into most communication intercept systems around the world. They needed complete secrecy. Buji would meet Willy in Milan. They would develop a strategy to subvert the failed policy of the Israeli administration.

Willy held the cell phone in his hand for a long time contemplating the plan details that would be required to take his country back from the weakest Jews. Liberal intellectuals and media whores who promoted peace through a give-back of land and assets would pay the price. The remainder of his life would be dedicated to the cause, and he would risk everything in the memory of Eva.

Goran Frankfurter, the CIA's Middle Eastern Director of Intelligence, closely monitored the plan proposed by Ari Kohen to collect DNA from the attendees at the so-called "Conference of Kings" in Egypt. The CIA dispatched an operative to the conference for the purpose of tracking the samples. They were interested in how the specimens would be used and what could be learned from the exercise. He continued the surveillance and reported his findings to the director each day.

Goran determined the DNA samples from twenty-seven of the attendees had been obtained by *sayan*-helpers working undercover at the hotel. The CIA watched as Yussi left his office with the samples for a meeting with Dr. Kohen. He made his way to the meeting place at a nearby mall and waited in the area designated by the scientist. Ziva Wolfson approached Yussi extending her hand and saying, "Dr. Kohen could not be here, so he sent me to collect the samples." Ziva handed Yussi a letter from Ari introducing her as his trusted assistant. It stated that Yussi should give Ziva the package, and she would deliver it to his laboratory.

"This is rather unusual, Ms. Wolfson. I expected Dr. Kohen. I don't know how to take this. I'm upset he's not here." With a stern look he waited for Ziva's response.

"Col. Fischer, I'm sorry you're disappointed. Dr. Kohen would be here, but he had a family emergency. I've been his loyal assistant for over seven years, and these samples will be delivered to the laboratory in Beit Jann and Dr. Kohen this afternoon. I'll personally deliver them and have Dr. Kohen call you once they're in his possession." Ziva crossed her arms and relaxed one shoulder, trying to appear more comfortable than she really was. The "family matter" to which she referred was Ari's unrelenting work in the laboratory on Zadok's remains.

Colonel Yussi "Pussi" Fischer had become soft in his old age, especially when it came to attractive women. "You leave me no choice, Ms. Wolfson. These samples will be useless if they aren't transferred and stored properly. I'm not going to stand on principle and let the fine work of my operatives go to waste," relented Yussi, as he handed over the package and turned to leave.

"Colonel Fischer, wait! Please accept my heartfelt thanks for all you have done in the past and will do in the future to secure our nation. The samples you have assisted us in obtaining could deliver a major blow to the enemy when the results are released." She extended her hand, which he accepted with a lecherous smile. Their hands lingered longer than necessary. They both felt an attraction that went beyond the reason for the meeting. His appeal related to the power he wielded, and hers was the allure of a Sephardic beauty.

Goran's agent in Israel watched the entire transaction and noted the sexual tension between the parties. The account of the meeting included transfer of the samples and the continued observation of Ziva Wolfson as she drove to Upper Galilee. She returned to Tel Aviv that evening with the agent on her tail. The report gave Goran the location of Ziva's apartment in Tel Aviv, information on her work at the IVF clinic, and background on her family, which included the unexplained disappearance of her husband. The CIA would continue to shadow Ziva for the foreseeable future.

Dr. Kohen's plan intrigued Goran. Exposing Arab leaders as having debilitating medical conditions would disrupt leadership structures. Assassinating a few Arab leaders using advanced biological means would eliminate a few top men. But Goran suspected something much bigger playing out in Northern Galilee at the Genoshalom laboratory.

Chapter 26

Rachel's plane from New York was arriving early at the Ben Gurion International Airport outside of Tel Aviv. A strong tailwind had pushed the plane across the Atlantic a full hour ahead of schedule. Trey figured he had thirty minutes to make it to the airport after calculating how long it would take Rachel to disembark the plane, pick up her luggage, and walk to the curb. They agreed he wouldn't come inside the airport, fearing another incident like the one at Belfast International. Instead, they planned to meet outside of baggage claim on the airport's lower level. She called his cell phone after she picked up her bags as she headed to the exit.

Still frantic at the disappearance of her brother Ari, Rachel rushed out of the terminal and into Trey's rental car. As she leaned over the car's center console to kiss him Trey noticed her tear stained cheek, "Are you okay?"

"No, I am so not, Trey. Ari still hasn't returned my calls and e-mails. He recently told me about the suspicious death of one of his colleagues, and I know his work often takes him to the darker side of science. I'm over-the-top freaked out; he never goes away without telling me where he is and when he'll return. Since our parents died, he hasn't been out of touch for more than a week at a time." Her voice cracked, and fatigue was written all over her face.

"When did you sleep last?" he hope to convince her to return to the hotel and rest before they began the search for her brother.

"Not for a few days. I tried every sleeping aid, but they make me groggy without putting me to sleep. Tell me about your trip to Ari's office and house." All business, Rachel was not going to let her lack of sleep interfere with the search for her sibling.

Trey gave her a full report about his trip to Beit Jann. Not that there was much to report. He had been stonewalled by the Genoshalom receptionist, who stated mechanically, "Dr. Kohen is in Indonesia at a population genetics conference and will return to the office next Monday."

Trey asked for the phone number of his hotel, and she refused, saying the information was confidential. She would inform Dr. Kohen of his visit if he called the office. When Trey demanded to meet with Dr. Kohen's assistant, Ziva Wolfson, the receptionist said she was not there and he should leave the building before she called security.

Trey's visit to Ari's house was a little more informative. The doors to the house were all locked, and through the window, he saw that the security system had been activated. Trey also noted Ari's car was in the garage. Wherever he went someone else must have driven him.

"Did you get a hold of Ziva with the numbers I gave you?" Rachel asked with a tinge of hope.

"She isn't calling me back. I've left three messages." Trey replied, knowing it would make Rachel livid.

Rachel's reaction was instantaneous. She blurted out, "That bitch! Where is she? If she knows something about Ari and isn't telling us, I'll personally kick her ass across the Negev Desert."

Her response startled Trey, who had not seen the mixed martial arts side of Rachel's personality. At a loss for words after such a forceful statement, he listened patiently.

"The last time Ari and I spoke, he said Ziva volunteered at a fertility clinic in Tel Aviv. Maybe we can locate her at the clinic since she's not at Genoshalom." Rachel pulled out her iPhone and searched for IVF clinics in the city. She got five results from her search and began calling each one by simply touching the phone number on the screen. The first two produced nothing. The third one she tried was the Babcock In Vitro Fertilization (IVF) Clinic associated with Golda Meir General Hospital on the outskirts of Tel Aviv.

"Hello, I'm calling for Ziva Wolfson. Is she in?"

"One moment please," the receptionist said as she put Rachel on hold. Brahms's piano concerto in D minor played over the phone as she waited for someone to pick up.

"Ziva Wolfson, how may I help you?"

"Ziva, it's Rachel Kohen. I'm looking for my brother. Can you tell me where he is?" Rachel asked as she tried to contain her disdain for the woman on the other end of the line. Rachel suspected that her motives for being with Ari were mostly self-serving. Ziva's husband had disappeared under mysterious circumstances, and Rachel had always cast her as some kind of "Black Widow" who preyed on men. Bottom line, she did not trust this bitch.

Ziva, noticeably shocked and flustered by the call, responded, "No, I…I don't have a clue where your brother is. I thought he was in Indonesia at a conference. Is something wrong, Rachel?"

"Yeah, what's wrong is you're lying to me, and everyone at the company is telling me the same bullshit lie you just told me. Now come clean with me, Ziva, please. Where is Ari?"

"If I speak with him before you do, I'll tell him you're anxious for him to call. What's your number?" Ziva's patronizing tone confirmed Rachel's intuition. Ziva knew where Ari was and was angling to hang up.

"He has my fucking number. Now tell me where he is or I will come over to that clinic for frigid women and we can settle this in person." The words were just out of Rachel's mouth when she heard a click on the line followed by dead air. Ziva hung up without responding to her threat, which infuriated Rachel.

Trey and Rachel sat silently in the car as he continued to drive toward his hotel. He did not hear Ziva's side of the conversation, but it didn't take a genius to figure out it had not gone well. He tried to lighten the mood by saying, "I guess Ziva's going to rush right out and find Ari for you."

Just then Rachel's phone rang. The caller ID lit up with her brother's number. She answered, "Ari, where the hell are you? I've been calling and e-mailing you for almost two weeks!"

"Hello, Rachel. I'm fine, a little buried in my work. Where are you?"

"I'm in Israel. I flew here when you didn't answer my calls and e-mails. I thought something terrible had happened to you. They said you were away at a conference. Where have you been?" Rachel was noticeably relieved now that she had heard Ari's voice.

"Rachel you overreacted. I can't believe you've flown all the way here because I failed to return a few calls. You worry about me too much," said Ari who was more than a little surprised by his sister's behavior.

"Excuse my concern. Your work is controversial, you live in a war zone, and someone died at your dig site recently. You don't return my calls and e-mails for two weeks. Call me reactionary, but you're all I've got. Where the hell have you been? Spill it!" Rachel was letting him have it.

"I have an important deadline on a project I've been working on for over a year. I made up the conference trip to buy some time in the laboratory. Sorry to alarm you, but I'm fine." This was little consolation for the stress endured by Rachel over last two weeks.

"I'm your sister, Ari. Don't do that again. I worry about you so much," she said, beginning to relax after going through a living hell. "When can I see you, Ari?"

"I'll be wrapping up the project tonight and plan to be in Tel Aviv for a presentation tomorrow. Let's meet tomorrow morning. Where are you staying?"

"I don't know. Here's Trey. He can tell you where to meet us." Rachel handed her phone to Trey. He gave Ari the hotel name and his cell phone number. They agreed to meet in the lobby of the hotel at nine o'clock the next morning.

Trey continued the drive to the hotel where he planned to have some time alone and an opportunity to catch up. Trey had so much to share with Rachel about the search for his father and his new relatives, Omar and Zach. His feelings for her had increased in her absence. Trey's relationship with Rachel was feeling good in all the right spots. The car gained speed as Trey considered an opportunity for afternoon sex.

Ari hung up his cell phone and smiled with the realization God's plan for him included his sister. Why else would Rachel be in Israel if not to assist Ari? God spoke to Ari through the actions of others.

The DNA gathered from the "Conference of Kings" was exceptional. As soon as Ari got his hands on the samples, he set aside his work on Zadok's remains. He worked night and day to analyze the genetic material from these self-proclaimed kings. Ari had instructed the colonel to have his *sayan*-helpers focus on the bathrooms of the hotel guests; there they would find the ripest ground from which to harvest useable DNA. He suggested they collect hair from a brush or drain screen, discarded tissue, a Q-Tip, or even fecal matter from inside the toilet bowl, any of which would provide good samples. He received a large brown envelope containing twenty-seven sealed and labeled pouches.

The bags contained a wide range of items with adequate human DNA for testing. One bag had a used condom with ejaculate material in the tip. The next had a cigar with a well-chewed butt, and another consisted of a ball of hair with the follicles intact. Ari was amazed how these items let him peer into the world of his enemies on a very superficial level and at the same time explore the very nature of their being. A molecular view of the samples would uncover environmental conditions, while a study of the DNA would unearth any genetic abnormalities.

Colonel Fischer had been unimpressed when Ari told him the results could expose high-ranking Arab leaders as having illnesses. Ari had secured the colonel's agreement to collect the samples based upon the promise that he could deliver a biological weapon capable of silently killing an individual without collateral deaths. Ari paused to reflect on the elegant brilliance of DNA science and the role his personal genius played in its application.

The secrets Ari first uncovered were contained within human genes, locked inside chromosomes. Genes make up about two percent of the human genome and are responsible for the manufacture of proteins. Protein chemistry and behavior are programmed by genes in the host organism to control cellular activity. These events define how we combat disease, digest food, grow tissue, and a multitude of other bodily functions. Behind the facade of population genetics, Ari had been amassing DNA specimens of various ethnic groups for years. The public and his commercial partners believed he was trying to further man's knowledge of human migration and ancient ancestry as he collected samples for another purpose.

Ari defined and sequestered a number of genes persistently present in Arabs and not in Jews. He reprogrammed those genes to produce proteins that disrupted normal cellular activity with lethal results to the host. Ari nicknamed this militant manipulation the 'mean gene.' He took each sample Colonel Fischer procured and married it with a mean gene through a unique process he developed while at MIT. The result was a killer gene that would eliminate only the person who had contributed the DNA sample.

Ari needed to decide whom to infect and what method he would use to deliver the deadly dosages. Ari knew he could get the colonel excited if he selected the right Arab leaders to eliminate first. Colonel Fischer had the military experience and undercover resources needed to assure delivery to the target. Ari's meeting with the colonel in two days would confirm Fischer's interest in his preliminary plan. He would need every minute in the meantime to select the prey and weaponize the killer gene.

Killing an Arab leader here and there was mere child's play compared to what Ari had planned next. He was building a bio-weapon that would wipe Israel's Arab neighbors off the map and leave all others unharmed. Ethnic cleansing was required to clear the land of the Islamic vermin in preparation for the construction of the Third Temple in Jerusalem. Muslims worldwide would regret building their mosque directly on top of the ruins of the Second Temple in 690 CE. Ari considered this the ultimate insult to his religion, and he was ready to deliver an eviction notice some 1300 years later. Ari longed for the day when he would witness Arabs falling face down in camel dung and burkas blowing in the wind tethered only by the weight of dead Arab women. Exacting revenge for ancient acts of disrespect was preparation for Ari's ascension.

Chapter 27

Willy was in the best physical shape of his life. Daily runs and bike rides through the mountains of southeastern Switzerland gave him legs of twisted steel and the cardiac fitness of a mountain goat. He balanced his workout program with a diet of fresh fruits and vegetables, protein shakes, whole grain breads, and fish. His resting heart rate, 49 BPM, placed him in a class with elite athletes of any age. His high metabolism translated into a body type that would be the envy of any thirty-year-old. Quite simply, Willy was a physical specimen to behold.

Willy arranged the meeting with Buji to coincide with a UEFA League football match between Inter Milan and Liverpool. Dressed in the royal blue and black home colors of the local team, Willy made his way from Lugano to Milan. They had agreed to meet at a pub not far from the stadium, a favorite watering hole for fans without tickets to the game. Looking and speaking the part, Willy found a seat and ordered two pints and some pastries. The beer still had a frothy head when Buji came walking up dressed in a red Liverpool jersey. Always one to play his part, Buji had assumed the identity of a visiting fan. They greeted with a kiss and a bear hug.

"You look younger today than when we last met, and I'm afraid the years haven't treated me as kindly," Buji said patting his considerable gut. "Don't mind if I do," as he grabbed a pastry from the plate.

"Nice to see you, it's been too long. How's your family?"

"Crazy as ever. My son is convinced money grows on trees and higher education means trying to get as high as you can while occasionally attending class. He's in year six of a three-year graduate program for computer science." Buji jammed the pastry into his mouth. He chewed for a few seconds and continued with a mouthful monologue. "My daughter married a Gentile. She moved to Utah, converted to the Mormon faith, and is producing grandchildren I will likely never see. My wife died of grief just last year, and the gout flares up about once a month. Other than that, I'm just fine."

Buji was smiling, realizing his old friend understood. All of these things meant far less to Buji than the state of Israeli affairs. He could get over the loss of his wife, children, and grandchildren. However, Buji would not survive the loss of his cherished Israel.

"I'm ready to come out of retirement, Buji. I'm afraid for our country. The current administration doesn't have the courage to do what's necessary to secure Israel. We've got to take charge of the situation. Have you spoken with Yussi?"

Willy and Yussi had been members of the same Israeli Air Force unit, having been conscripted in the same month. The two men had become fast friends, sharing a passion for the defense of their fragile country. Yussi flew F-16 jet fighters into battle against many regional foes, gaining recognition from his superiors for missions over Syria. Willy made a name for himself in the area of combat planning. His work coordinating the ground, air, and sea activities of the military had become stuff of legend. Willy had become an expert at calculating the size and capabilities of enemy troops; skills he parlayed into a career as a serial observer of his prey's actions and weaknesses. Yussi continued military service until the founding of Fischer Intelligence in 1991. The company assisted the Israeli government with enemy surveillance throughout the region.

Willy had worked with Buji in the early days of his time as a Mossad *kidon.* He had remained in contact with Yussi and Buji through couriers, encrypted phone calls and e-mails until his sabbatical began a couple of years ago. Willy hoped the three men would work together again. Someone needed to assure Israel's future.

Israelis had lost their will to fight for God's gift to the Jews. Their morale suffered because of repeated suicide bombings and the senseless killing of women and children by Islamic terrorists. The once vaunted Israeli Defense Forces (IDF) and Mossad stepped on their dicks with regularity, and the Israeli citizenry openly criticized their actions. No one used to speak out against IDF and Mossad, but today stories of their mishaps ran on the front pages.

"Yussi's with us, Willy. We spoke yesterday. All of his contacts and manpower will be at our disposal, and his relationship with the Prime Minister will give us access to the top."

Buji's voice confirmed how comfortable he felt with Willy. It had been almost three years since their last visit, but these two men did not miss a beat. They jumped right into the issues of the day. Willy and Buji had no secrets from one another. Buji's contacts inside Mossad gave him weekly briefings on everything from a nuclear Iran to Hamas's continued shelling of Israel.

Buji laid it all out for Willy. "The entire Zionist movement is in jeopardy. The Prime Minister tacitly understands the situation but doesn't have the balls to stand up to the liberals and peaceniks. He's at risk of losing the next election, and if he goes, we'll be fighting ourselves as well as the Arabs."

Thinking about taking up arms against other Israelis aggravated Willy even more. *Senseless,* he thought, as he spit out, "That's not going to happen. The three of us need to get together, soon. Can you arrange a meeting in Cyprus for next week?"

"I'll do my best. Yussi is working on some interesting things having to do with genetics. I think you'll be interested in what he says about a 'New War' against radical Islam, specifically our crazy-ass neighbors." Buji, gaining enthusiasm thinking about working with Willy again, queried, "I've missed you, my friend. How have you been?"

"My life's been solitary but rewarding. But I miss the fight, Buji. Being on the shelf for two years has been difficult. I often think of

Eva and the promise I made to her dead body." Willy's eyes started to mist as he recalled the pledge he made to his beautiful wife.

A *sayan* working at the university had positively identified Trey as the user on the library computer who tried to access information on William Joseph Cohen. Mossad's Collection Department then decided to begin following Trey. The collections operative passed the file to his boss Jamie Sachs, who had enlisted a local *katsa* case officer named Simon Adler to provide surveillance on the ground. Adler, a Mossad veteran who handled sensitive matters for the directorate, had followed Trey since his search at the university. Adler had also become interested in his connection with Rachel Kohen. Photographs of the couple had been taken when she arrived in Israel and promptly run through Mossad's facial recognition software. Trey's image matched an Irish terrorist who escaped authorities after orchestrating three assassinations in Ireland. He was believed to be in hiding somewhere in the Middle East. Simon decided to enlist the aid of the Israeli Police to question Trey so as not to blow Mossad's cover should this match prove to be an error.

Trey and Rachel had just finished breakfast in the hotel restaurant when a man in uniform approached their table. He identified himself as Inspector Rafael Bronner from the Israeli Police Department who wanted to ask them a few questions. He requested they settle their bill and meet him in the lobby. Trey was alarmed by the proposal but went along, not wanting to cause a ruckus.

"Mr. Cowens, what is your business in Israel?" asked the man in uniform.

"I came to investigate my Jewish heritage. I'm trying to locate my father, whom I believe used to work for the police or some other division of the Israeli government," Trey said, avoiding mention of his father's connection to Mossad.

"Have you had any luck in your search?" asked the officer.

"In fact I've located an uncle and cousin. I'm still hopeful I'll find my father." Trey became uncomfortable with the line of questioning.

"Ms. Kohen, what brings you to Israel?" asking another open-ended question.

"It's Dr. Kohen and I'm here to assist Trey in his search," responded Rachel, short and cold with the officer.

"Do you have immediate family in Israel, Dr. Kohen?" Inspector Bronner inquired.

"Yes, my brother moved to Israel not long ago. He's the only family member who's here." She didn't like the questions any more than Trey.

Trey sensed her unease and broke into the conversation, "Look here, Officer, I'm not sure what this is all about, but we're doing nothing illegal, so I don't know why you're even talking to us. I think this interview is over."

Trey was concerned this second confrontation with authorities since leaving New York would give Rachel the wrong impression about his relationship with the law.

"Mr. Cowens, this is just a polite visit from the local police. It's not unusual for us to speak with foreigners about their reasons for being in Israel. We are under constant attack from our enemies, who use unlikely operatives, such as you, to undermine our security. We're only interested in why you're here and when you plan to leave." Bronner looked at him with an intensity Trey had rarely experienced; this policeman meant business.

"All right, Officer. I'm well aware Israel has special security considerations, but we're certainly no threat to your country. We're just trying to find a relative and visit some other family," Trey said with every effort to conceal his anger.

"May I please see your passports?" Bronner asked with authority.

Trey and Rachel both offered the little blue booklets evidencing their American citizenship. Bronner thumbed through the documents paying special attention to immigration stamps indicating the countries they visited.

"Mr. Cowens, why did you visit Ireland?" Bronner bore down on the Irish connection that brought him to the hotel in the first place.

"I'm on a leave of absence from my business and using part of the time to research family genealogy. My mother's family is from Ireland, so I began my search for relatives there." What did his stay in Ireland have to do with anything in Israel?

"And you Ms. Kohen, what took you to Ireland?" The questions kept coming, and Rachel was a visibly taken aback.

"Again officer, it's Dr. Kohen, and Trey invited me to visit him there," Rachel said with some hesitance.

Turning to Trey, the inspector asked, "Did you find any Irish relatives?"

"Only dead ones, but I'm still hopeful I'll find some alive," Trey said with a note of sarcasm.

Inspector Bronner handed the passports back to the couple saying, "I'm sorry to have bothered you both. I hope your stay in Israel is a pleasant one and that you find the information you're looking for. Let us know if we can assist in any way." He handed Trey a card with his name and contact information. He bid them good-bye, leaving Trey and Rachel standing in the lobby wondering what the hell had just happened.

What's the deal with Trey and the authorities? Rachel asked herself worried that his brushes with law enforcement had become a trend. What she didn't know about Trey started to alarm her as much as what she already knew.

The entire conversation between Bronner and the two Americans was transmitted to Simon Adler by a concealed microphone in the tip of the inspector's pen. Listening to the questioning of Trey and Rachel, Adler surmised there was more to their visit than they had disclosed. The hit on the facial recognition software indicated 100 percent that the subject was an Irish terrorist, but he spoke American English with no Irish accent and had a good cover story. A phony passport and clever linguistic training would not fool Adler. He believed the supposed American was hiding something, and he would find out what. If Cowens was the man British authorities were after, his contacts with known Arab extremists made him a definite risk to Israel's security. Adler would continue to follow the couple until he could corroborate their story or uncover the true reason for their presence in Israel.

The parallels between the situation in Ireland and Palestine did not escape Fareed and the Committee of Ten. They shared a similar history of occupation and limited human rights. Donny needed Fareed to secure his freedom from the British authorities, who were fast on his trail after the shootings in Ireland. Having delivered on his promise to get Donny and his men out of Ireland, it was time for payback. Fareed was counting on Donny to execute a plan, similar to the Irish action, against targets to be identified shortly. As an added inspiration, he would receive one million Euros for each kill. The cash assured Donny a comfortable retirement and a new life with Grace in some exotic location without a British extradition treaty.

Donny was busy trying to identify marksmen from among Fareed's soldiers who had the skill to carry out assassinations at a great distance. The quality of the firearms provided by Fareed surprised him, especially the .50 caliber M107 long-range sniper rifles fitted with advanced electro-optics. An experienced marksman could hit a nickel at a thousand yards and a Krugerrand at two thousand yards. Donny needed to identify the top shooters and begin an intense training program that would uncover the best of the best. He wished he had his Irish team, but it was too risky to bring them together so soon after the events in Ireland. Fareed had high expectations for his guest, and the pressure was on Donny to perform. He was well aware that his own life hung in the balance.

Donny selected five men who exhibited considerable shooting skills. Among them was Fareed's twenty-year-old nephew, Abdul Habib al-Husseini, who had dedicated his life to the destruction of Israel. He went to school at Damascus's Al-Adiliyah Madrasa where, beginning at age six, they indoctrinated him in the ways of Islam. Schooled in Wahhabism and strict Sharia law, Abdul had been on his way to becoming an *imam,* a spiritual leader in the mosque. Instead he had decided to become a soldier in the name of Allah. By the time he turned twenty, Abdul was the best shot among Fareed's men and likely the best in all of Syria.

Donny summoned the five recruits to the shooting range, a fair hike from the main camp. Each candidate had a M107 loaded with practice rounds. Coming to the firing line one at a time, each candidate took five shots from the three positions demonstrated by Donny, standing, lying on their stomachs, and from their knees. Donny did not need to give any remedial instruction to this group; they were all good shots.

Abdul was in a class by himself. Of the fifteen targets, he missed only one by a whisker. Between the other four recruits, two rose to the top, and Donny had his three shooters. He gathered the three together for some intense training sessions that included distractions, conflicting orders, and many other techniques that would prepare them for what they might face in the field. One fact of Middle Eastern life was the almost cookie-cutter days of heat and blue sky. In Ireland his men often trained in the rain, wind, and at night to replicate the most extreme shooting conditions. It still got dark at night in Syria, but rain was unlikely, so Donny settled for a sand storm. It was the same principle.

The identity of the targets would be disclosed soon, and then the real planning for the mission began. In the meantime, he put the *Three Musketeers* through exhausting rounds of physical and mental training. Taking nothing for granted, he pushed them to the limit and beyond.

Chapter 28

Rachel's mood had lifted after speaking with her brother and had improved even more after their *afternoon-delight*. Trey and Rachel were basking in the reverie of that freshly fucked feeling while enjoying Champagne and oysters at a local eatery. Trey wanted this moment to last forever. His phone rang; it was Zach.

"Omar's had a turn for the worse. He's asking for you to come right away. Trey, I think he's dying. Come quickly, there's not much time," implored Zach in a shaky voice.

The glow of the prior moment evaporated and all Trey could now think about was his dying uncle, an uncle he had just met, an uncle he looked forward to knowing better. They hastily paid their bill and grabbed a taxi.

They arrived at the retirement center in record time. Trey paid the driver, and they rushed through the front door to the reception area where Zach waited.

"How is he?" asked Trey.

"Not well. The doctors think he had a stroke sometime during the night. His whole left side is paralyzed, and his mind is working at a slower pace. Last week they discovered an aneurism above the brain stem. It may have burst, and his brain could be flooding with blood…. It…it doesn't look good at all." Zach dried his eyes as he led the couple to Omar's room.

Trey was shocked by the condition of the patient. Omar had lost all of the vibrant color from his face, and a deathlike stillness pervaded the entire room. Trey touched his uncle's liver-spotted, purple-veined hand, alerting him to his presence. Omar's right eye opened slowly while his left struggled to free itself from the effects of the stroke.

"Trey, you came. I'm not going to be here much longer, and there's something I need to tell you before I go. Zach, get me my box." Omar was still in charge even though he could barely raise his head from the pillow. Zach went to the closet and brought a metal lockbox to the side of the bed. Omar ordered him to open it. Searching through the box with his only good hand, Omar pulled out an envelope with the word "Willy" written on the front. Speaking in a halting cadence, barely audible, Omar told Trey to open the envelope and read it aloud.

> *Dear Trey,*
>
> *I have not been totally truthful with you about your father. I have known how to reach him for years, but I resisted because of his entreaties for me to stay away for fear of implicating me in his actions. The true love of my brother is shown by how he protects his family. Your father is an exceptional man who deserves to meet his son, so I am making this gift to you as one of my last acts on earth. If you are reading this, I am close to death. I warn you that this information could expose you to risks you never imagined, and I encourage you to take all necessary precautions.*
>
> *One man knows how to locate him. His name is Isaac Stahl, also known as Buji. He and your father are brothers in arms. Buji and I have spoken many times over the years about your father. William was a great leader in the cause of Israel's security and could have become Prime Minister if he had chosen. But it was not to be, and we all live with the consequences of our decisions.*
>
> *Buji Stahl can be found at the Hebrew University where he teaches a class on "Ancient Warfare in Classical*

Literature." Go to the University at ten in the morning when he is in his office meeting with students. Tell him you are my nephew. Buji will recognize your resemblance to your father. He will get word to him about your search. Good luck, and tell my brother I love him.

In the arms of God, I await the call to an eternal life free of pain and suffering.

God Bless You,
Omar

Trey finished reading the letter and looked up at his uncle. The heart and blood pressure monitors started to squeal and ding. He was not breathing. A nurse was immediately at Omar's bedside. She called for a doctor and instructed Trey and Rachel to leave the room. Zach stayed with his father while the other two stood in the hallway outside the closed door. They could hear the doctor and nurse trying to revive the old man, but to no avail. When they left the room almost thirty minutes later they had the look of death on their faces. Zach followed them out with swollen eyes.

"He's gone," Zach muttered.

The three came together in an embrace that lasted for quite awhile. Zach broke loose and said, "I need to call the family and begin preparations for his funeral. Thank you both for coming. It means a lot to me you are here and I didn't have to go through this alone. Now that Omar's gone, I want to help you find your father in any way I can."

"Don't worry about me; your other responsibilities are far more important right now. Rachel and I are here for you. How can we help?" Zach's pain was palpable. Trey looked at Rachel with the sudden recognition that this might be the first time he'd experienced honest empathy. Rachel responded with a shrink-like wink conveying her understanding.

Zach told them about the prearrangements for the calling, funeral, reception, and the obituary Omar had written himself. Omar gave instructions to Zach almost a year before when it became clear he would not live much longer. He had directed

Zach to call family and friends from the list he had carefully constructed.

"Buji Stahl's name is on the list of people I'm supposed to call. Will you tell him Omar's died when you visit him at the University? I assume you'll be going tomorrow. Informing Buji would help me and might get him to open up about Uncle William."

"Thanks, that's a great idea." With one more hug and a cousin-like kiss on each cheek, Trey and Rachel departed, leaving Zach alone with his deceased father.

Once outside the rest home, Rachel spoke, "Trey, I'm so sorry about Omar. It must be difficult to say good-bye to a new uncle, but you were lucky to have him in your life, if only for a short while."

They rode in silence back to the hotel. Zach had said he would call with details on the reception and funeral. Jewish tradition dictates that the deceased be buried as quickly as possible, within 24 hours if practical. There are exceptions when family members must travel long distances to participate in the mourning. In Omar's case, Zach was his only child and Omar's wife had died some years ago. Omar's only brother had not been seen or heard from in many years. Yet the family still held out hope Willy would learn of Omar's passing and return, so they would delay the funeral for a few days. His father needed to know that his only brother had died. Trey would be at Professor Stahl's university office before he arrived the next morning.

Rachel rolled over in bed at four o'clock in the morning to discover she was sleeping alone. She looked for Trey in the bathroom, not there. Throwing on her hotel-issue robe, she called his cell phone and got voice mail.

"Trey, where are you? It's four o'clock and you are not in the room. Call me," she commanded before hanging up.

She convinced herself he couldn't sleep and had snuck down to the lobby for an early morning coffee; he would soon return.

She imagined him coming to the hotel room door balancing two cups of steaming, hot coffee as he quietly slid the card-key into the door. That myth was debunked after thirty minutes when no one tried to reenter the room. She tried to persuade herself he went for a run to relieve the stress of losing his uncle. But then thought, *How stupid, no one runs in downtown Tel Aviv before sunrise.*

Trey had lain awake in bed waiting for Rachel to fall asleep before he snuck out of the hotel room. Losing Omar had brought back all the feelings of abandonment he had tried to overcome. He had connected with his biological uncle, and now he was gone. The unthinkable trauma of being separated from his parents at birth came crashing down on him in one giant eruption of molten-hot emotion. The comfort of Rachel's companionship vanished, replaced by the fear of her certain abandonment, just like his parents and Omar. This called everything into question. Trey needed to anesthetize the pain.

"I'll have a double Crown Royal on the rocks," said Trey to the bartender at Molly Bloom's Irish Pub, located a few blocks from the hotel. Earlier in the day he noted the pub's hours of operation were two o'clock in the afternoon until "late." In Irish pub parlance: the bar is open until the last patron is safely placed in a taxi.

"What brings you to Israel, mate?" asked the convivial barkeep.

"Family," Trey said shortly, waiting for the whiskey to do its job.

"I'm from Dublin. I've lived all over the world, most recently in Australia, but Ireland is home. Ever been to Ireland?" asked the barman.

"Yes. It's a lovely place," responded Trey, beginning to feel the effects of his cocktail.

"John over there is from Belfast. We don't see eye to eye on anything except Guinness stout," the alcohol reference got a chuckle out of Trey.

The gentleman in question, John, sat a few stools away from Trey and overheard the bartenders comment.

"Cram it Kieran, he doesn't need his head filled with all of your malarkey. Give him another drink on me and shut up about politics for once." John slid his pint down the bar and took the stool next to Trey.

"John Daley's my name," the big guy said as he extended his hand to Trey.

"Trey Cowens, pleased to meet you," Trey responded as he returned the firm handshake.

"I overheard you're in Israel to visit family. How's it going so far?" asked his stool mate.

"Not so good right now. My uncle died yesterday," said Trey despondently.

"I'm sorry for your loss," John said in a subdued, predawn voice.

The two men continued to talk for the next hour. The conversation ranged from Trey's experiences in Ireland to John's work in Australia. Trey recounted his success at locating a biological uncle two weeks ago who died suddenly the day before. Trey began to warm up to the gentle giant.

"How about a nightcap?" asked John.

"Isn't that what we're having now?"

"I know a place close by where we might even run into some pretty women," John said with a glint in his eye.

Trey's phone rang. The caller ID displayed Rachel's number. He considered answering but decided against it. He didn't want to diminish his buzz or interrupt the good time he was having with his new friends.

It had happened again; he was missing without an explanation. *Déjà' fucking vu,* thought Rachel as she opened her suitcase and began to pack. Then she heard Trey's multiple attempts to slide the keycard into the door. He eventually gained entry in spite of his highly inebriated state.

"Good morning," said Trey in a drunken cadence, trying to keep his balance by leaning against the hallway wall.

Rachel didn't say a word as she continued to throw her clothes into the suitcase. Her lips pursed tightly, her eyes narrow slits and her chin wrinkled to a point from the stress of the last hours.

"What's going on? Why are you packing?" asked Trey finding his way to the corner of the bed.

A stone-cold stare was accompanied by complete silence. Rachel was a woman on a mission to get the hell out of the hotel and away from Trey. She had decided to go Beit Jann to be with Ari.

"Rachel, please don't go. I just needed to let off a little steam. I went out to have a few drinks at a bar around the corner," said Trey, beginning to sober up.

She broke her silence by saying, "Trey, I get that, but it must have occurred to you I would be worried if I woke up and you were gone." Rachel thought about her father and Ari, and their famous vanishing acts. "I thought you would be more considerate about my feelings since my brother caused me such anxiety when he disappeared. I'm worried about your drinking but I'm more concerned about your insensitivity to what I need. I'm going stay with Ari in Galilee for a few days. Now if you'll excuse me..."

Rachel turned toward the bathroom to collect her toiletries. As she brushed by Trey, he grabbed her robe causing it to open, exposing her naked body. She attempted to close the robe but Trey did not let go. He pulled her on top of him as she struggled to free herself. He outweighed her by more than fifty pounds, and in his half drunken state, he rolled Rachel over pinning her to the mattress.

"At least let me explain Rachel. I'm so in love with you I can't stand the thought of losing you. Omar's death was a brutal reminder of my lost childhood. I know it's no excuse for leaving you to worry about where I am, but my love for you is real," Trey said, looking at Rachel's turned away face.

She had stopped struggling, but she refused to look Trey in the eyes as she said, "Get off me right now, you're hurting me."

Trey released her arms and was immediately greeted by a firm slap in the face. He was stunned Rachel had struck him, but what did he expect after wrestling her to the bed like a cheap whore?

"Please, Rachel I'm sorry, I need you, it won't happen again," said Trey refusing to let the blow to his face affect his mission to keep her in the room.

Her naked body pressed against his street clothes. She began to feel the warmth of his body through the fabric. Her anger abated a little, but her concerns still ran high. She could understand the trauma of losing an uncle, especially one he had only known briefly. She reminded herself that a nanny, an alcoholic grandmother, and a grandfather with dementia raised him; his early childhood experiences would scar the most stable of constitutions.

"Why, Trey? Why did you go...without telling me?" she asked with an emotional stutter.

"My mind was racing and I couldn't get to sleep. You were out like a light and I didn't want to bother you. I went for a walk to clear my head," said Trey knowing that this was only a half-truth. He had already decided to go to the pub as he entered the elevator earlier that day, having noticed the hours of operation.

"But you came back drunk. What's that all about?" asked Rachel, mixing her roles as lover and shrink.

"I was walking by an Irish pub and before I knew it I was seated at the bar. I met a couple of Irish fellows who bought me a few drinks. The next thing I knew the clock struck half past five," Trey tried to minimize his alcohol consumption, making himself seem less a drunk and more a mourning nephew.

"At least you don't smell like cheap perfume and have lipstick on your collar. I guess I should be grateful," responded Rachel giving into his effort to keep her in the room. "You better shape up, mister, because I'm not going to stand for you leaving me like that again. You have a big day ahead and need to be thinking clearly."

They lay in bed together for another hour. Trey was pleased he had successfully eradicated the smell of the other woman. The hairspray had removed the lipstick from his collar. He was pretty sure he did not have any new tattoos. A remorseful relief settled over Trey as he reflected on his congenitally bad behavior.

Chapter 29

The CIA's new Director of Intelligence, Mark Manning, called Goran Frankfurter into his office. Manning had been appointed the month before and was conducting preliminary meetings with all the regional intelligence directors to get up to speed. Goran's responsibility for the Middle East file made him a key player on the intelligence team. The meeting began well enough with Manning complimenting Goran on his work to set up the Company under an assumed corporate name in Upper Galilee. The building Goran rented housed a key CIA listening post that intercepted Syrian and Hezbollah communications from Southern Lebanon.

Manning's reputation had preceded him. He was a Yale graduate, his father a close friend to the U.S. Vice-President. Manning had never spent a day in the field as an intelligence officer or in any branch of the military for that matter. More than one seasoned agent had made negative comments about the new director in front of Goran, but he filed away the criticisms and kept his opinions to himself. Fifteen minutes into the meeting, Manning launched into a tirade about Goran's favoritism toward Israel.

"Goran, I read your most recent report on Israel's settlement activities. In my years as a public servant, I don't think I've read a more biased or slanted report. Your conspicuous favoritism toward Israel is troubling. You have to stop sweeping Israeli screw-ups under the carpet. As you know, the Vice President was gravely embarrassed on his last trip to Jerusalem. Don't let that happen again," Manning said firmly as he leaned back in his oversized chair.

Goran took the criticism by saying he would try to be more objective in his reporting on Israel. He tried to impress his new boss with his knowledge of the current situations in North Africa and the Middle East. Revolutionary activity had heated up in his region of responsibility ever since the collapse of the Tunisian regime, the ouster of the Egyptian president, and the uprisings in Syria and Yemen. Goran reviewed each theater of conflict with his boss. Goran had remarkable command of the details as he named the rebel groups and the insurgent leaders the CIA was supporting. Switching to other matters, he gave his boss a briefing on the lunch meeting between Dr. Kohen and Colonel Fischer.

"Is Dr. Kohen legitimate? What's his profile?" asked Manning.

Goran rattled off his credentials, "Born in Brooklyn, Rabbinical School in Tel Aviv, PhD from MIT in genetics, owner of a New York-based population genetics company with a branch office and laboratory in Upper Galilee."

"That's a respectable résumé, but I'm still skeptical. Our scientists have tried for years to develop a selective biological weapon. The best we've done is to limit the kill radius to one kilometer," Manning said authoritatively.

"I agree with your cynicism, but if he is able to deliver, we need to be in a position to take control of both Dr. Kohen and the weapon. We can't let technology like this circulate freely in the region. I suggest full-time surveillance of both Kohen and Fischer."

Manning instructed Goran to go to Israel. Goran would work with the CIA liaison at Mossad, Jamie Sachs, to coordinate the observation of Dr. Kohen and Colonel Fischer. He would continue to oversee the CIA's covert support of the region's prodemocracy movements while in Israel.

Five years prior to that meeting while on vacation in England, Goran had attended a cocktail party arranged by friends of Asma al-Assad, the first lady of Syria and a Briton by birth. That evening, Goran was approached by Rahman al-Sayad about working with the Syrian Air Force Intelligence Directorate called Idarat-al-Mukhabarat al-Jawiyya (IMJ) as an undercover agent. The directness of the overture shocked Goran. They had known each other for less than thirty minutes when Rahman asked him into the study for a private conversation where the financial terms of a relationship were discussed. The two men agreed to meet the next day, giving Goran time to think about the offer. As he departed the building, his mind was already made up. He had been passed over for promotions at the CIA one too many times. Goran would become a double agent for Syria. All he had to do was figure out where to deposit the money.

Goran purposely slanted his reports to Manning in favor of the Jews. Amongst his coworkers, he was openly pro-Israel. These tactics helped to disguise his motives as a Syrian operative and it delighted Goran that Manning had swallowed the bait.

His mission for the Syrian government was to expose undercover CIA agents and to inform the IMJ about covert operations affecting Syria and their allies. Over the last five years, Goran had passed significant amounts of secret intelligence to Syria about the United States and their military operations in the Middle East. The information Goran had collected was compiled in an encrypted format and transmitted to Syrian Intelligence embedded in telecommunications data or HTML code of random websites. Billions of bytes of data transmitted daily through the world's vast network of satellites provided a perfect cover.

Goran had successfully notified the Syrian government about the imminent attack on Iraq in 2003. In addition to information on America's efforts in the region, Goran had access to "fair warning" communications from the Israeli government informing the CIA about actions against enemy targets. He had communicated particulars of an October 2003 attack on a Palestinian training camp twelve hours before the first bomb landed. He also told Syria about Israel's plan to blowup a nuclear site in northern Syria on September 5, 2007, a full day in advance of the attack. Syria credited Goran with saving hundreds of lives.

The Syrian intelligence community celebrated Goran's work anonymously, as did the office of the Syrian president. Goran didn't give a shit about notoriety as long as the money kept getting wired into his Swiss bank account every month. He headed to Israel as the CIA's Director of Middle East Intelligence. Goran would coordinate his activities with Mossad as instructed by Manning. Once inside the head of the beast, he could inflict major damage on Israel and show that asshole Manning who was really in charge.

Chapter 30

Donny woke up with one of Fareed's men staring down at him. He wiped the sleep from his eyes and looked up from the carpeted floor of his Bedouin tent. Usama Jabbar al-Husseini, Fareed's son, the most junior member of the Committee of Ten, had come to wake him. At twenty-seven years of age, Usama had been educated at the Islamic seminary in Iran called Hawzah-e Ilmiyyah. Having been indoctrinated by Koranic imams, he knew the protocols for being a true Jew hater. His appointment to the Committee came after his return to Damascus and the realization that his computer skills could further the Committee's objectives. Usama's technical wizardry was evidenced by the new website his father, Fareed, anxiously displayed for Donny upon his arrival. Donny wondered why he was being roused at this hour.

"My father wishes to see you immediately. Please hurry, it's important," Usama said. He turned away from the tent opening and walked toward the main house with his white robes reflecting a crimson sunrise.

Donny checked his watch. It was 6:05. Notoriously late sleepers, Arabs rarely got started before ten. Rolling off his desert bedroll, Donny put his street clothes on under the floor length garment he had been given upon his arrival. The white Islamic *galabiyya* allowed Donny to circulate throughout the community without sticking out like a buzzard in a flamingo pond.

When he had last spoken with Grace, she was at the hotel waiting for his return. What he thought would be a twenty-four-hour stay had turned into a week with no end in sight. Grace busied herself with trips to historical hotspots and shopping bazaars. She seemed to be enjoying her time in the luxury hotel. They had agreed to talk the next day, when Donny hoped to have a better idea of when he would be leaving the compound.

He exited the three-sided, grey-and-white-striped tent and headed to the main house a hundred yards away. The morning desert retained the chill of the night air. The sun's rays began to dispense the heat that would soon cause the sand to burn unprotected feet. Donny's senses were taking it all in as he walked up the steps to the main entrance. The door opened on cue. An alert attendant escorted him to a room in the back of the mansion.

The room was decorated just like the interior of a luxury tent, complete with sheets of linen strung from the rafters and intricately woven rugs lining the walls. The cushions on the floor were arranged in a circle; a tray of tea and pastries had been placed in the middle. Two hooded figures sat on the floor with their backs to Donny. Fareed stood up as he entered the room. Donny recognized Usama from the robes he wore, but not the other person. Fareed greeted Donny and directed him to sit facing the other two people.

Donny sat down, looked up at the mystery guest and immediately said, "Grace, what are you doing here?" He noticed the fear written on her face, confirming she had not come voluntarily.

Fareed interceded, "The woman was brought here for her own safety. Rebel forces in Damascus are closing in on the foreign embassies and hotels. She will be out of harm's way and well cared for while you execute the Committee's plan. Don't worry about her. Once you've completed the mission, you and the woman will be free to go into hiding. We've arranged for both of you to travel to a safe house in Turkey where you'll find it easier to reenter the western world under new identities."

Donny got up to go to Grace, but Fareed restrained him with a strong hand on his shoulder. "She'll be going now. You won't have any contact with her until you're job is done."

An attendant led Grace out of the room. She didn't utter a word, but her eyes communicated a terror that tormented Donny. "You can't hold her here against her will. Why have you done this, Fareed? I thought we had a deal, and now you kidnap my girlfriend? What the hell is this all about?" Donny was apoplectic. His temper almost got the best of him as Fareed listened politely, realizing the explosion would soon subside and Muslim reason would prevail.

"We've no intention of hurting the woman. Now it's time for you to focus on the mission. The sooner we complete the preparations, the quicker you and she will be free to leave." Fareed inferred Grace could not leave at this moment, a feeling confirmed by Usama's steely-eyes.

"Now I understand how this is going down. You hold my girl hostage until I complete the assignment. I'm okay with that, but you will seriously regret it if I find out she's been harmed or mistreated in any way." Donny wanted to say, "*I'll blow your camel-humping asses to eternity,*" but thought better of it. Fareed, unfazed by the verbal threat, had already instructed Usama to kill the Irish infidel once the mission was complete. Fareed would deal with Grace personally, and he looked forward to spending time with the beautiful Irish redhead.

"We've established the targets for your mission," said Fareed, presenting Donny with a profile on each marked man. "A Hezbollah surveillance team is providing us with information on their daily habits and vulnerabilities. They have identified recurring situations when the targets are most susceptible to attack. These are merely recommendations; the final decisions are yours to make." Fareed left the room without waiting for Donny's response, leaving Usama to answer his questions.

They both knew the events of the next few days would define each of their lives. For Usama, it meant commanding his first mission under close guidance of his father and the Committee. He needed to prove himself as an Islamic warrior. For Donny, the urgency of his task ratcheted up with Grace's abduction. Donny needed to clear his mind and focus on implementing the plan.

"I'm sorry you're upset about Ms. Kinney. She's a lovely woman who needs to be protected while you finish the job we hired you to do." Usama spoke calmly as he tried to convince Donny to think of the big picture and the job at hand.

"Abdul and the two other marksmen are ready. All I need is more time to study the Hezbollah surveillance information," Donny said in a clinically businesslike fashion.

"While you do that, I'll round up your three men for some final training," Usama offered, hoping a call to work would calm Donny.

"Take them to the shooting range. Focus on distances between six hundred and one thousand meters. Practice head and neck shots," Donny said firmly.

He tried to get Grace out of his mind but the fear in her eyes tore at Donny's heart. Why had he involved her all of this? She was an innocent woman whom he loved deeply. He had entangled her in a scheme to kill three people for money and now she was a prisoner. Upset with himself, he grabbed the Hezbollah file and headed for his tent.

Samir al-Khalidi watched as Donny returned to his abode. Samir had a view of all the tent openings from a guest room on the second floor of the main house. He was a member of the Committee of Ten and a lifelong friend of Fareed's. Samir was in charge of security for the group, an advantageous position for the undercover Mossad agent.

Samir al-Khalidi and Fareed al-Husseini were descendents of prominent Arab families exiled from Jerusalem to Damascus in the early part of the twentieth century. Both the al-Khalidi and the al-Husseini families traced their lineage back to the Prophet Mohammed. Samir's great-grandfather had been mayor of Jerusalem while Fareed's relatives succeeded as Palestinian merchants and land barons. The families settled in a Damascus neighborhood and the two boys were born the same day in 1962. It was customary for neighbors in Jerusalem to have their children breast fed by both mothers if they shared the same birthday. This created lactose tolerant foster families. The al-Khalidis and the al-Husseinis shared everything during their exile in Syria, including stories about old Jerusalem, recounting the history from Mohammed to the Ottomans, the British, and finally the Jews.

Fareed and Samir were expected to be best friends, a fact resented by Samir since his early teenage years. Samir was book smart, while Fareed was a social creature. Fareed used Samir to complete his schoolwork while excluding him from activities with the popular children in the neighborhood. The scars of those years grew in adulthood. Samir wanted revenge for Fareed's thoughtless acts and continued ignorance of the damage he caused.

He finally turned against his Palestinian "foster" brother when Fareed began to recruit women as suicide bombers. To Samir, his three daughters were angels on earth. He never produced a son, which relieved him of the responsibly of training a young warrior for Islam. Samir hated Fareed, his son Usama, and his nephew Abdul. They represented the worst radical Islam had to offer—intolerance and brutality in the name of Allah. He had done his best to obstruct their plans over the years.

As an agent for Mossad, Samir sat at the heart of Arab terrorism machine and was preparing for his last act as an operative for the State of Israel. He had already communicated the identities of the targets to his Israeli handler. Samir would leave the country with his family after the upcoming mission was launched.

Over the last ten years he had forewarned Israel about Hezbollah raids on Shiloh. He relayed the location of underground tunnels near the border with Lebanon and the coordinates of missile launchers aimed at Israeli settlements in the Golan Heights. Samir's work over the years had saved innumerable Jewish lives, and that counted for a lot as he envisioned his career with Mossad coming to an end. He would live out his years under an assumed name in a foreign land or be exposed as a traitor. Either way, he was ready to get on with his life or afterlife.

Samir transmitted a picture of Donny directly to Jamie Sachs at Mossad. Sachs immediately recognized the resemblance to the American who had been questioned by Israeli Police the day before. How could this man be in two places at once? Then it occurred to him, the men could be related and might even be twins. He decided to share this revelation with Simon Adler, Mossad *katsa,* during their daily briefing, and with the newly arrived CIA agent Goran Frankfurter.

"Gentlemen we have a real fiasco on our hands. The Committee of Ten in Syria is planning the assassination of three leading Middle East peace proponents. The targets are the Israeli Prime Minister, the lead peace negotiator from the United States, and the head of Fatah. To make things even more complicated, the Syrians have hired an Irish nationalist named Donald Murphy to coordinate the assassinations. Mr. Murphy was recruited after he allegedly orchestrated the execution of three leaders of the Northern Ireland peace process. And if that's not weird enough, Donald Murphy is the spitting image of a young man we questioned in Tel Aviv yesterday about his search for his biological father. The missing father turns out to be a former Mossad *kidon* named William Joseph Cohen."

Both men sat with shocked expressions on their faces. They needed a scorecard to keep track of all they had just heard. Adler spoke first. "I assume the information on the planned attack came from our man on the Committee."

Goran wondered who "our man" was; they never used any names, even within the department. Samir's identity was known only to Jamie Sachs, the head of Mossad, and the Prime Minister.

"Yes. He'll send along more information once it becomes available. We only have an outline of their plan, but no real specifics. I have a team working with the PM's office to prepare a strategy to prevent the attacks. I want you two to focus on Colonel Fischer and his plans for the DNA they collected from the

Summit of Kings." Sachs completed his comments in a sarcastic tone confirming his disdain for the ridiculous name of the Arab gathering.

Goran chimed in, saying, "Director, shouldn't we pick up this guy who resembles the Irish assassin just to be sure he isn't involved? He could have information on the attack."

"No, not now. Leave him to me. He's being followed closely by one of our *sayan*-helpers. I need you to get to the bottom of this DNA thing and Colonel Fischer's relationship with the doctor. If this genie gets out of the bottle, we're all screwed." Sachs rose and left the room without offering any additional guidance.

Simon and Goran sat for a while without talking. Simon finally broke the silence. "Let's check in with the Collections Department about the latest communications involving Colonel Fischer. I'll get you up to speed on what we've learned since our last briefing. First, how about some lunch?"

"That would be great. Let me check the overnight traffic on my tasking list. It's early morning in Washington, but like Mossad, the CIA never sleeps, and I need to get caught up before we launch into our afternoon. I'll just go back to my hotel to get some things I forgot this morning and meet you for lunch in the hotel lobby. Does that work for you?" Anxious to get out of Mossad headquarters, Goran needed to connect with his Syrian handler.

"Let's meet at your hotel in an hour," answered Adler.

"Works for me, see you then." Goran left Adler sitting in the conference room fingering his smart phone trying to access voice mail.

Rushing back to the hotel, Goran went directly to the Business Center right off the main lobby. He logged onto a public computer and navigated to an anonymous e-mail account created to communicate with his Syrian handler. The message would be placed in the trash of the shared e-mail account so they could access the information without Goran having to transmit anything over the Internet.

Goran's e-mail explained that Mossad had received information about the Committee's activities from an unknown source within the group. He added the names of the intended assassination targets to prove his point. Goran felt uncharacteristically panicked by the course of events since his arrival in Israel.

Chapter 31

It was the third week of September in 1908, a few days before the Jewish holiday of Rosh Hashanah. With the sighting of the new moon, the Islamic month of fasting, Ramadan, had just ended. Feasting and dancing were underway in Jerusalem with everyone dressed in their finest attire. The city crawled with visitors wanting to be close to the seats of spiritual power during one of the high holidays for both Jews and Muslims. With hostilities temporarily suspended, both ethnic groups tried to focus on the historical and devotional aspects of their religions rather than the current events driving them apart.

The scent of ground spices and fresh produce filled the air as Ruhi al-Khalidi walked through the market. The stands overflowed with fruits and vegetables, displaying shiny red pomegranates, over-sized green grapes, royal purple eggplants and dark brown dates. His destination was the Vagabond Café, near the Jaffa Gate in the Old City, and a meeting with his dear friend Kamil al-Husseini.

Once inside the café, Ruhi found a seat in the back next to a table of old men playing backgammon. Smoke from *arghilehs*, Arab water pipes, hung in a cloud releasing a hint of tobacco infused with fresh fruit. After ordering a Turkish coffee, Ruhi busied himself reading a newspaper. Kamil was late as usual, a fact of his busy life as a journalist.

Coming in the door with an arm full of papers and books, Kamil made his way to Ruhi's table. "Hello my friend, sorry I'm late, but we just received word that the youth movement in Syria is gaining momentum. The government is talking about lifting the twenty year old emergency order and reinstating the constitution," reported Kamil still out of breath from his hurried walk to the café.

"That's great news, Kamil. The Syrian officials have filled their pockets through the sweat of common citizens for too long. Do you think the rebels can force the president and his security thugs to relinquish even an ounce of power?" Ruhi asked, delighted at the news but still skeptical.

"It remains to be seen, but my sources confirm that discussions are underway with the rebels. Smaller demonstrations are springing up in towns and villages not far from the capital. It's just a matter of time before they organize into a coherent revolutionary movement," responded Kamil.

Kamil was a lawyer and journalist who had written extensively about the corrupt ruling classes infecting communities in the region. He had become a spokesman for the Arab street by risking his life to report the contemptible behavior of their leaders in the Middle East and North Africa.

"I am afraid the Islamists will commandeer the revolutionary movement and we will be driven into the medieval arms of strict Sharia Law," said Kamil. His well-informed views and considerable education made him both a student and a professor of current events.

"But more importantly Kamil, we need to talk about what the Jews are doing in Palestine," said Ruhi, visibly perturbed. "They have managed to purchase almost one-half of the arable land in our country. If this continues, we will sell all of our precious territory to the Jews and become serfs in a Zionist land."

"I know, the chaos in Constantinople with the overthrow of the sultan and the ascension of the Young Turks has created a perfect cover for the Jews to continue their land acquisition strategy unabated," responded Kamil, well aware that the Jews would take advantage of the political turmoil for there own benefit.

"Hebrew-only schools are popping up all around the country. They are siphoning and redirecting water away from Arab lands to their settlements. The Jews even issued a stamp with a portrait of Josef Gertl," said Ruhi with disgust.

Based on their firsthand observations and analysis, the Jews were more organized than the Arabs. They had both visited Jewish settlements, had seen their houses with bright red roofs, and had walked the clean, tree-lined streets. If the two men were going to halt the encroachment of the Jews on more of their cherished earth they had to act quickly and decisively.

"Our families have governed Jerusalem for over one hundred years, Ruhi. We have to fight for what's ours, or risk losing everything to the interloping Jews. In the past we only had to fight the Christians, Greeks, and Armenians for control of Jerusalem. Our families held the keys to the Church of the Holy Sepulchre and could influence their behavior, but with the Jews arriving in growing numbers we have no such leverage," Kamil was ready for the fight with both words and actions.

Ruhi al-Khalidi and Kamil al-Husseini agreed that day in 1908 to fight the Zionist movement with all the energy and people they could mobilize. They formed the *Society for Arab Revival*, creating a new cultural voice for Arabs in Ottoman Palestine. Jerusalem became the capital of the Arab movement that sought to regain ownership of Palestine. Jews and Arabs were blood brothers, having evolved from the same prehistoric milieu, but hatred for one another grew daily without regard for their shared DNA.

The Balfour Declaration

Foreign Office
November 2nd, 1917

Dear Lord Rothschild,

I have much pleasure in conveying to you, on behalf
of His Majesty's Government, the following declaration
of sympathy with the Jewish Zionist aspirations which has
been submitted to, and approved by the Cabinet.

"His Majesty's government view with favour the establishment in Palestine of a national home for the Jewish
people, and will use their best endeavours to facilitate the
achievement of this object, it being clearly understood that
nothing shall be done which may prejudice the civil and
religious rights of existing non-Jewish communities in Palestine, or the rights and political status enjoyed by Jews in
any other country."

I should be grateful if you would bring this declaration
to the knowledge of the Zionist Federation.

Yours Sincerely,

Arthur James Balfour

On December 10, 1917, both the al-Khalidi and al-Husseini families fled to Damascus during the Battle of Jerusalem. World War I
had found its way to their doorstep. They left the city of their birth
to continue the fight for an Arab Palestine from abroad. The British had invaded Jerusalem on November 17, 1917 on the pretense

they were securing remote territories within the Ottoman Empire to limit armed rebellion. On the heels of the Balfour Declaration, the assault felt more like a purging of the Arabs so the Jews could take over Palestine.

The timing of the Balfour correspondence and the breeching of the Jerusalem gates was no coincidence. The Brits were skilled colonizers and careful not to contravene international law. The *King James Bible* was their rulebook, and by their reading, the Jews belonged in Palestine. This interpretation let the British off the infamous *moral hook,* allowing them to make amends for the historical anti-Semitism of the Crusades, Martin Luther and the Russian Pogroms all in one sweeping enterprise. It did not matter that, in the process of giving Palestine to the Jews, they broke every law of nature and mankind.

Sadly, Ruhi and Kamil never made it back to Jerusalem, but they inculcated their children with the belief they would return victorious to the land of their fathers. A free and independent Palestine had been left to their heirs who were still in Syria well into the twenty-first century. Samir al-Khalidi and Fareed al-Husseini hungered for the day they would return to Jerusalem as their grandfathers predicted; even though they had chosen separate paths, they were committed to the journey.

Chapter 32

Rachel fell asleep after a lengthy discussion of Trey's disappearance and her own fears of abandonment. She calmed down once Trey explained how he was feeling at the loss of his father's only brother. Still unable to sleep, Trey lay awake with thoughts of his father, Omar and Rachel whirling in his head. After showering and shaking off the effects of his alcohol debauched early morning, Trey left the hotel at around eight o'clock for a trip back to Jerusalem and an unannounced meeting with Professor Stahl at the Hebrew University.

Although his office hours began at ten a.m., Trey hoped Professor Stahl would arrive early. He had located Stahl's office from the university's online directory the night before. Trey entered a three-story concrete building and found his way to the second floor and room 209. He approached the open door and heard a man's voice speaking on the phone. Trey waited in the hall for Buji to hang up. Eavesdropping on the conversation, he listened for anything that might give him insight into the professor. After he hung up the phone and the room fell silent, Trey summoned the courage to knock and Buji looked up.

"Student office hours begin at ten o'clock, son. Come back in about thirty minutes," Buji said, returning to the open book on his desk.

"I'm not a student, professor. I'm here on a personal matter. May I come in?" Trey's eyes softened, realizing the unusual nature of his statement.

Buji analyzed the threat level posed by the visitor and determined it would be all right. "This is most unusual young man. I'm preparing to meet with students shortly, but come in and take a seat. We can speak for a few minutes."

"Professor Stahl, my name is Trey Cowens, and I'm here on advice from Omar Cohen, my uncle, to find out if you can help me locate my father. His name is William Joseph Cohen," Trey said hopefully.

Stahl stared at the man standing before him without giving anything away.

Trey continued in a controlled manner. "I understand you and my father are close friends. Omar told me you could help me find him." Trey fought back his emotions.

Buji's eyes never left Trey's as he leaned back in his roller chair. He let Trey's query sink in, allowing the silence to continue for an uncomfortable moment and then he spoke, "How is old Omar?"

"Dead," said Trey.

"What? Omar died? When? How did it happen?" bolting upright in his chair, Buji appeared surprised and upset.

"He passed away yesterday at an assisted living center in Tel Aviv," Trey responded. "He'd been ill for the last year. They think it was a combination of things, but he went peacefully with his son at his bedside."

"I'm sorry for your loss, Mr. Cowens." The professor was moved by the news of Omar's passing.

"He was the only living connection I had to my father's whereabouts. He was near death when he told me about your close relationship with my father." Trey watched Buji for any sign he could help.

Buji, shocked by the news of Omar's death, had planned to visit him next Sunday. He had enjoyed many Sundays with his old friend Omar playing cribbage and reliving sexual exploits, some real and some fantasy. Now he was gone.

"How did you come to learn you were related to Omar if you never knew your father?" Buji needed more information about Trey's search before talking to Willy.

"I've been doing research on my family for several months. I traced my mother's side of the family back to Ireland through a combination of traditional genealogy and a DNA test. I submitted my paternal DNA results to a website designed to uncover matches with people with the same DNA. That's how I met Omar's son Zach, who also participated in the program." Trey paused to make sure the professor understood his explanation.

Buji seemed to be engaged, so Trey continued, "Purely by chance, I found someone who matched my father's DNA here in Israel, and then I contacted Zach. I met Omar at the assisted living center. Uncle Omar told me that my father worked for the Israeli intelligence service and he was probably living undercover in a foreign country." Trey stopped, allowing his story to sink in with his reluctant host.

Buji's mental hard drive worked on three levels. He was sorry about Omar's death, he had enough information to inform Willy of his alleged son's search, and this would be a distraction to the plans he and Willy were developing with Yussi. Selfishly, he wanted this man to get lost and come back another day. He suspected that would be unlikely based on the intensity of Trey's demeanor.

"I haven't been in touch with Willy for years. I don't have a clue about how to contact him. If what Omar says is true, then he's probably living under an assumed name in a faraway place. That's what old spooks do. They become chefs and gardeners in South Africa or Canada," Buji said with a wry smile.

Trey glared at Buji with contempt.

"With all due respect, sir, don't bullshit me. Omar told me how to reach you on his deathbed. According to him, you are the only person who can help me," Trey said hoping to inspire a reaction.

Buji sat completely still without any expression.

Trey continued, "As a man of honor, I'm sure you understand your obligation under these circumstances. So let's cut to the chase, and you can begin telling me the truth about my father."

The professor calculated a response to Trey's demand for action and said, "I recognize your frustration. Let me do some checking with my contacts in the intelligence community. If you'll excuse me, there are students waiting for me outside in the hall."

Trey stood up and gently closed the door. He turned, placed both fists on Buji's desk, and leaned forward. "I don't give a fuck about your students. I'm not leaving here until you tell me something I can go on."

This was Willy incarnate. Aside from the physical resemblance, Trey's fiery outburst even sounded like his old buddy Willy. Trey Cowens was Willy Cohen's son.

"Trey, I can't do anything right now. I have appointments with my students over the next three hours. I'll make some calls this afternoon, and see where it goes from there. Understand I can't materialize information about a missing person out of thin air. If the calls I make don't uncover anything helpful there's not much else I can do." Buji began to accept the fact Trey wasn't going away empty handed so he offered hope in the form of a closing comment.

"I knew your father very well, as Omar said, 'like a brother.' In my heart I would love to help an estranged son find his lost father, especially someone I was so close to. However, my last contact with Willy was ten years ago," said Buji, preparing Trey for failure if Willy did not want to be found.

"I'll take anything you can find out professor. I'm out of options," Trey responded, revealing his desperation.

Buji started to feel sorry for the young man as he volunteered, "Your father was one of the best Mossad agents of all time. If he's still active, then it will be difficult to find him. If he's retired, he will have started a new life in a place where he can hide in plain sight. I don't know what he is doing or where he is, but I will try to find out." As Buji concluded his remarks he stood up and extended his hand across the desk to his guest.

Trey shook his hand firmly and hung on as the professor tried to pull it back. With Buji's sweaty hand in his, Trey said, "I appreciate your efforts to protect my father, but as his son, I have a right to know him. I reckon you've not been totally honest with me today. But that's fine, because I came barging in here unannounced on a mission. My expectations were probably too lofty, but I'm still hopeful you'll recognize the justice in helping me." Trey released Buji's hand and left.

Buji was moved by Trey's emotional intensity, but grateful he was leaving. The professor would tell Willy about Trey; he didn't know how, when, or where.

Students lined the hall, queued up for their fifteen minutes with Professor Stahl. They looked down at the floor or busied themselves with cell phones as Trey walked past. Parts of their conversation must have been heard through the office door. Certainly his profanity-laced outburst had been audible. Trey did not care; he had a father to find, a girlfriend to support, a blood cousin to know, and a twin brother to…God only knew what.

Once his office hours concluded, Buji walked home for lunch. He used the opportunity to write an e-mail to Willy that he left in the 'Drafts' folder on their shared e-mail account. Buji instructed Willy to call the disposable phone as soon as possible. Willy must be told about Omar's death, and Buji was the only one to do it. Willy would likely insist on returning to Israel for his brother's funeral, not what Buji would advise, but hardly something he would deny a mourning brother. Buji wouldn't divulge any information about Trey at this time. Telling a man about his unknown son wasn't information you shared in an e-mail or over the phone.

Buji grabbed his cell phones and exited the apartment for a meeting with Colonel Fischer. The get together was planned to continue discussions about Yussi's work with the American scientist Ari Kohen. Buji would tell Yussi about Omar's death but not say anything regarding Trey.

On Buji's way to meet Yussi, the framework of a plan took shape in his mind. The addition of Dr. Kohen to the team gave the warriors new resources in the fight for a secure Jewish state. Buji, Yussi, and Willy could prosecute a silent war against the enemies of Israel. Buji had been informed that the DNA collected at the Conference of Kings could be used to formulate rounds of genetic ammunition capable of striking human targets without detection or unintended deaths. If true, these men had a tool only dreamed of by the Israeli military: a way to eliminate evil Arab leaders without killing innocent people.

Chapter 33

Rachel's arrival in Israel gave Ari's plans a boost. He needed a female with the correct genetic makeup, someone he trusted. Her presence could actually be a positive development if he could convince her to participate. Ari would give her enough information about his work and spin it in such a way that she would be obliged to help him. The family card always worked with Rachel. He convinced himself she would agree once she realized how vitally important it was to her brother.

Rachel sat at a Tel Aviv cafe waiting for Ari. Late as usual, it crossed her mind he might not show, but then she spotted him crossing the street, heading directly for the front door. Seated behind the cafe window, Rachel saw him, but he couldn't see her. He stopped walking before entering the café. With his cell phone pasted to his ear, he listened intently to the person on the other end. All of a sudden he began to scream into the phone. His face reddened as the intensity of the communication increased. He abruptly terminated the call, composed himself, and entered the café.

Ari located his sister sitting next to the window. He smiled as he approached her table, hoping she hadn't witnessed his outburst. Rachel rose to greet her brother who immediately swallowed her in a big bear hug and gave her kisses on both cheeks. As they broke their embrace, he noticed she was crying. "Why are you crying?"

"I don't know. I guess I'm emotional because I thought you were in trouble or something. Why didn't you return my calls and e-mails?" Rachel asked, wiping her eyes.

"I'm sorry, but I've been buried in my work. I instructed the staff to hold all calls without thinking you might be trying to reach me. My e-mails have been piling up for weeks," Ari summarized, not sure how much information to share with his sister right now.

"What's so important that you could ignore my frantic communications, Ari? I'm a wreck and have been for two weeks. I thought you were either dead or missing." Rachel tried to contain her anger, realizing her genius brother was often consumed by the science and his work in the laboratory. His intense focus on his job was one of his strengths, but like their father, also one of his weaknesses.

"I'll tell you what I'm doing, but let's order some breakfast first. I haven't eaten in a day or two, and I'm famished."

It concerned Rachel that her brother was getting too skinny. She needed to fatten him up. "You're too thin, Ari. You've got to eat more. Your work is important, but not if it kills you. Let's get some food in you, and then we can talk."

Rachel hailed the waitress and placed an order for both of them: lox, bagels, eggs, and potatoes for Ari and yogurt, fruit, and granola for her, juice for both. Once she ordered, Rachel turned to her brother with inquiring eyes as if to say, *Okay, now tell me what you're up to.*

Without hesitation Ari began, "My work with population genetics is what brought me to Israel. We've had amazing success in identifying indigenous groups and migration patterns. My work with the Israeli Antiquities Authority took me in a new direction. If we add genetic science to the work of paleoanthropologists, which is the study of human evolution through bones and footprints, we can peer further into the life and culture of prehistoric people. Paleogenetic data harvested from these skeletons has expanded our understanding of how they lived, migrated, and died. Rather than working exclusively with modern human DNA, we widened our database to include ancient DNA. This allows us to analyze the genome and the mutations of human DNA over a longer timeline than we ever thought possible."

Rachel gaped at her brother as he talked. Lost in his passion for the science, he was completely oblivious to how much he scared her when he could not be reached. Hearing him speak about his new discoveries increased her concerns.

"Listen, Ari, I have you, and you have me. That's it. When you go missing like you have for the last two weeks, I get scared that I've lost you. However ridiculous that sounds, I thought you were dead. Please promise me you'll never leave again without telling me where the hell you are. I'm your sister and I can keep your secrets. Keep me informed. Okay?" Rachel's eyes had dried, and she demanded an affirmative response with an icy look.

"Fine, Rachel, but don't you think you overreacted a little?" asked Ari. Not expecting an answer, he went on, "I got wrapped up in the laboratory because that's what scientists do sometimes, especially when they're having major breakthroughs, daily. We've recovered DNA from some of the most remarkable Jews in history. The findings will give us a provenance on this land that is indisputable."

Ari's commitment to the science was steadfast. Rachel had no choice but to soften her protestations and accept her brother as the gifted, mad scientist she loved. Ari attacked his breakfast like a starving animal while Rachel watched with maternal delight. Wiping the crumbs from his face and the cream cheese from his fingers, Ari looked at his sister. She met his gaze and smiled, realizing the unshakable love she had for him.

"As we delve into the genetic material of our forefathers we also see a future for Israel."

"You see the future of Israel in DNA?" asked Rachel.

"Yes, with ancient DNA we can rebuild Israel in the likeness of our ancestors. I'll show you what I mean when you come visit me at my lab up north," Ari stopped there for fear of scaring his sister with too much information on his plans.

Changing the subject, Ari asked, "What are you and Trey doing?"

"Trey is here on a search for his father. While I'm around, I'll give him all the help I can," Rachel said, checking Ari's interest level. Ari appeared genuinely engaged, so she went on. "Right now, he's at the Hebrew University meeting with a family friend. He found his father's brother, but he was very sick when he arrived and died just yesterday. Before he passed away, he shared some information with Trey about his father. I'm meeting him back at the hotel after breakfast to find out what's next."

"Let me know if I can help," responded Ari, anxious for the breakfast to end and to return to the lab, his sanctuary. "I'll call your cell phone tomorrow."

Rachel needed to punctuate the breakfast with a motherly comment. "I guess I'll never understand exactly what you do. What I do know is you will be severely punished if you ever disappear again. Understood?"

"Got it. We'll speak again tomorrow," Ari replied in a brotherly voice.

Rachel and Ari shared a departing hug. She returned to her seat as Ari made his way onto the street. Watching as she had before, she noticed he was back on the phone. The anger returned to his face, and she wondered what was really up with her brother.

Trey left his meeting with Buji and returned to the hotel to meet Rachel after her breakfast. She arrived at the room all smiles and proceeded to recount her rendezvous with Ari. Trey listened intently wanting to respect her need to tell him everything, as lovers do. After she finished her monologue, she asked about Trey's morning.

"I had an interesting meeting with Professor Stahl. I'm not sure if he can help me find my father, but he said he would call me later today after he has a chance to touch base with a few mutual friends. He knows things he didn't share. I think I'll find him, Rachel. It was meant to be."

"Wonderful news, darling," Rachel cooed with the skill of a trained thespian. She was having severe doubts about her relationship with Trey; literally waiting for the other shoe to drop. Her thoughts were with Ari, consumed by an overriding need to be his sister and protector.

Chapter 34

An e-mail was waiting for Willy when he arrived at his Cyprus hotel. The message said Omar had passed away and the funeral would take place in a few days. Condolences from Buji concluded the communication. Willy knew Omar was in an assisted living center but had no idea he had been so close to death. Buji's e-mail didn't indicate how Omar died; only that he had passed the day before.

Willy became remorseful as he thought about his mother, father, Eva, and now his brother, who were all gone. He had squandered the time with his family in pursuit of loftier goals, and now those goals didn't seem so worthy. He reflected on the enemies of the state he had killed and where that had gotten his beloved country. Israel was still vilified by the West when it suited their purposes and attacked by their Arab foes as a fulfillment of their mandate to rid Palestine of all Jews. In fact, the situation was more grave and tenuous today than when he had started his career as a *kidon* in 1973.

The newest proposal by the United States dictated Israel return to the 1967 borders and give up land in the West Bank before sitting down at the negotiating table. According to the United States, the issue of Jerusalem and the repatriation of Arab refugees would be deferred until issues related to territory and security could be resolved.

Screw the Americans and their duplicitous policy of propping up Arab tyrants under the guise of a "war on terror" while all along coveting Arab oil to keep their economy running. With friends like that, who needs ene-mies? Willy's dander was up and he chomped at the bit to mix it up with the Palestinians, the Israeli leadership, and the Americans if necessary.

Willy had paid the price for his current existence as the pre-mier *kidon* of all time. What else did he have to lose? Not a god-damn thing, so he might as well finish what he started. He needed to contact Buji with a change of plans. He was coming to Israel to attend his brother's funeral, undercover as a friend of the family. He would pay respects to his only sibling at the funeral, and after-wards, he would launch a new attack on the enemies of Israel. If death came as a result of those efforts, then he would gladly take the eternal rest.

Willy found an Internet cafe near his Cyprus hotel. He logged onto the e-mail account he shared with Buji and typed a letter to his old friend:

> *I am coming to Israel for Omar's funeral. I know this will be risky because I am still a hunted man, but I must be there for him. No need for you to come to Cyprus, unless you are planning a holiday. I have booked a ferry from Cyprus to Haifa for tomorrow. The hydrofoil will arrive at seven-thirty a.m. Meet me at the port and arrange for me to stay at one of Yussi's safe houses. We need to sit with Yussi as soon as possible to discuss our plan of action. Look for me in traditional Hasidic dress. Shalom.*

No response from Buji was necessary. Willy knew his old friend would act on the request and be there when he arrived. Willy couldn't contact Omar's son Zach directly, so he would have to see him at the calling. Buji would have the schedule of the funeral ser-vices when he arrived. It had been too long since he had enjoyed the smells and sights of his homeland.

Buji accessed the shared e-mail account to find a message from Willy in the "drafts" folder. Yussi and Buji would pick him up at the port and transport him to a safe house on the outskirts of Tel Aviv.

A plan to permanently change the dynamics of the conflict with Dr. Kohen's new science would be the under consideration. Buji felt a rush of excitement as he considered the significance of the three of them being back together again. He always did his best work when teamed with these men.

Yussi's follow up meeting with Dr. Kohen turned out to be more than he expected. Ari's work on the bio-bullet had been reviewed. It would take a few more days to complete the gene isolation work necessary for the person-specific viruses. Ari's eloquence captivated Yussi as he described how the virally enhanced munitions would change the course of the conflict by surgically destroying the enemy's command structure.

The young scientist also worked feverishly to uncover terminal and embarrassing diseases among the attendees at the Summit of Kings. Yussi was ignorant of these conditions, but when Ari explained them in laymen terms, he began to understand the power of the diagnoses. Ari had come up with some incredibly damning afflictions, including: bipolar disorder (characterized by wide mood swings), Klinefelter's syndrome (the presence of an extra X chromosome that causes increased breast tissue and small testicles), *Hirsutism* (uncontrolled hair growth all over the body), *Pseudohermaphroditism* (both female and male genitalia are present), to name a few. All of the inbreeding done by his camel jockey neighbors had evidently increased the incidence of genetically inherited diseases. Added to this list were two attendees who tested positive for AIDS, not inherited but just as damaging. Yussi would wait until his meeting with Willy and Buji to decide how the medical information and the viruses could be used in the most destructive way.

Chapter 35

Dressed in traditional Arab garb, Donny left Syria for Southern Lebanon. His thoughts were with Grace, now a prisoner in Syria, and the fact that her life depended on the outcome of the mission. It reminded Donny what was at stake and he had better not screw this up, or she would undoubtedly pay the ultimate price. Muslim women were second-class citizens within their own culture, and he imagined Catholic women ranked just above Jewish females, which was marginally better than donkey shit. Donny would succeed for the money and their future together.

Usama, Donny, the three shooters, and Hezbollah escorts crossed into Lebanon under the cover of night. They cleared the border with ease, no identification required. The border guards had been bribed by Donny's Hezbollah security detail. Free passage into Lebanon from Syria was a given if you were with Hezbollah.

The brave Hezbollah fighters fought the Israelis in 2000 and again in 2006, causing the Jews to flee from Southern Lebanon. In the minds of many Lebanese, the courage of Hezbollah had thwarted the Israeli invaders and caused their retreat. As the only armed deterrent to further Israeli aggression, Lebanon granted Hezbollah guardian rights over the border area with Israel. Shia citizens in the south revered them while they were reviled by Christian and Druze politicians in the north. Nevertheless, they controlled the southern territories with a combination of military strength and social services. Home loans, hospitals, Muslim schools, and drinking water were all provided through the good graces of Hezbollah and their Iranian benefactors. The group had also made inroads in parliament. They recently became Lebanon's majority party, stifling the sitting Prime Minister's efforts to limit their powers. The Syrians and Donny were afforded free passage through the southern territories by Hezbollah's grateful Muslim followers.

The long, dusty drive through the battlefields of Southern Lebanon delivered Donny and the men to a seaside safe house just north of the Mediterranean port city of Naqoura. They were greeted by three Hezbollah elders who had arranged the accommodations and sourced the equipment for the mission. Donny drank tea with their hosts, relying on Usama to interpret the conversation and their questions about the operation for him. Their professionalism and attention to detail encouraged Donny. It harkened back to the day when the IRA had a potent paramilitary force with committed leaders and competent soldiers. Today, a gun-shy population that wanted the bloodshed to stop forced the fractured movement into seclusion. Donny knew that blood must spill for Ireland to be united. He saw that he could learn many things from his Arab collaborators.

A small garage attached to the house contained all of the equipment and supplies they would need to complete the planned incursion. An ultra-modern inflatable boat commanded the center of the garage floor. The skin of the boat was made of sound-absorbent material designed to frustrate tracking by radar. The motor was a small turbine tuned to mimic the white noise normally filtered out by acoustic listening devices. The combination of technologies created a high-speed, stealth watercraft capable of carrying six passengers to a drop off point at sea. Rebreather units, rather than traditional scuba gear, would be used to reduce detection risk once they entered the water. This closed circuit underwater system actually scrubbed the CO_2 from the divers' exhaled air and allowed it to be reused in combination with a helium and oxygen mixture, thereby eliminating surface bubbles. Their fire-arms, sealed in waterproof cases, floated just behind the men. They each carried a bomb detection instrument to warn them of marine incendiary devices that were often used by the Israelis to protect their seaports.

The quality and quantity of the equipment astonished Donny. The Iranian backers of Hezbollah demonstrated they would spare no cost to bring down Israel and were more than willing to try anything to wipe out the Jews. Donny began to see his Hezbollah partners as thoughtful, kind men who believed in their cause. The reverence shown to them by the local population indicated a deep trust and hope that these missions would further Islam's reach. The only hope of a return to normalcy had been vested in the work of Hezbollah. As a proxy for Iran in the region they had the resources to do the job.

Donny was an expert scuba diver, trained and employed as an underwater welder for the Irish Petroleum Corporation on North Sea oilrigs back in his early twenties. He hadn't participated in any sub-aquatic pursuits for many years, but he was fit and ready for this mission. The scuba training his men went through in Syria pre-pared them for the dive they would take the following morning.

The plan was to come ashore just north of Haifa where they would be met by three cars driven by Syrian operatives. These driv-ers were fully integrated into the population of Northern Israel, planted there by the Syrian Security Directorate. They took on the identity of secular Palestinian citizens, and they worked for Israeli employers without fear of detection. Like many Palestinians in Israel, they maintained peaceful relations with their Israeli neigh-bors and bosses, not wanting to jeopardize their family's security. Still hopeful for a resolution to the conflict, they waited and worked without drawing attention to themselves. But when the time came to spring into action, they threw off the garb of the amiable Pales-tinian and became an instrument for the destruction of Israel.

Donny gathered his men for a final briefing before bed. He asked for questions, and no one spoke, so Donny concluded the meeting by saying, "We have a great opportunity before us. The success of the mission depends on each of you focusing on your part of the plan to the exclusion of any other thoughts. The combination of your efforts will result in maximum harm being inflicted on the enemy. Now go get some sleep. You will be awakened one hour before we leave."

Donny finished and Usama offered these additional words, "Allah is great, there is none worthy of worship other than Allah. Glory be to Allah and to those who serve him. Mohammed was his servant on earth and it was Allah's blessing on his Holy Warrior Mohammed that defeated the Jews. So fight in the way of Allah against those that battle against us; for we face one of two happy endings: the death of our persecutors or martyrdom."

Samir al-Khalidi, the Mossad undercover agent, was troubled by the lack of specifics on the planned attack. Aware the men went through scuba training but not privy to any specifics, he considered their options. Having communicated with his Mossad handler, all Samir could do was wait. He was feeling uneasy when Fareed al-Husseini knocked on his bedroom door and asked to come in for a talk around midnight.

"Samir, you know you are my dearest friend. We have been through much together, and now we are on the brink of delivering a devastating blow to our enemy." Fareed stood staring down at Samir who was seated on the bed, trying to maintain his composure while thinking, *I'm so close to getting even with this bastard, be calm, don't mess it up now.*

"But all is not at peace within the camp. I've learned that one of the Committee members is working for the Israelis. You are the head of our security. How could this happen, Samir? I need you to find out who it is," Fareed paused, letting the allegation hang in the air.

"Are you sure, Fareed? It's not possible one of our brothers on the Committee works for Israel," said Samir, doing his best to appear surprised.

"I assure you, it is true. I received the information from a very reliable source. Tomorrow we will convene a meeting of the Committee to discuss a new plan to attack the Jews on their southern border. I want you to help me smoke out the traitor and exterminate this rat," Fareed bid Samir goodnight with kisses on both cheeks and a longer than normal embrace. *The true rodent in this scenario is you Fareed,* thought Samir as their hug ended.

Samir was left alone, reeling in a fit of doubt and fear about his future as a Mossad agent. He would have to implicate someone on the Committee in order to protect himself and preserve his cover. Samir's choices had delivered him to this untenable moment. Had he chosen the right path? Would his family ever forgive him? These thoughts and a sense of impending doom settled over him, as he lay motionless, preparing for a sleepless night.

Chapter 36

Ali Hassan al-Husseini, code name Abu Hassan, fled Beirut in 1972 just after the events in Munich. He was Chief of Operations for Black September, the ultra radical arm of the PLO, and Fareed al-Husseini's father. The plan to abduct the Israeli athletes from Munich's Olympic Village was his brainchild. The objective was to ransom them for members of the PLO held in Israeli jails or to execute the hostages for crimes against Palestine. Their exact fate did not concern him; he just loved to kill Israelis, like father like son.

Abu Hassan arrived in Paris from Lebanon where he received a new identity and facial reconstruction. As a teenager, he had studied at the finest schools in France. His knowledge of its culture and language was impeccable. The support system provided by French-based Fatah operatives shuttled him between cosmetic surgery sessions and a different safe house each night. The investigation into the events in Munich had certified his status as the mastermind of the plot and had made him the target of a vigorous Israeli manhunt. Daily briefings by the head Fatah operative in France about efforts to locate him eventually confirmed that Israel's dragnet would capture him soon.

Facial surgery remade his appearance, and by adding a few extra pounds to his slender frame, he became Rayan Hariri, first generation French citizen whose parents emigrated from Lebanon in 1936. With his back-story intact, and his appearance radically changed, the time came for him to leave France for a new life in a different country. He boarded a train and made his way south through Spain to the port of Tarifa, where he embarked on a ferry for the one-hour cruise to Tangier, Morocco. Mr. Hariri was elated to be back on Arab soil. His French citizenship and Lebanese name made the trip through passport control just a formality, because Morocco loved Arab tourists. He cleared customs and was met by a Fatah operative who shuttled him out of the crime-ridden city of Tangier onto a coastal highway that would take them to Casablanca.

The 300-kilometer trip provided panoramic views of the Atlantic Ocean as they sped by rickety old trucks filled to the brim with produce and livestock. Rayan Hariri contemplated his new life with enthusiasm as he meditated on the windswept, deep blue ocean and the setting sun. When they finally arrived in Casablanca, it was approaching midnight, and the party was just getting started at the Hyatt Regency's Black House Discotheque. He dispatched his driver with a curt thank you and hurriedly checked into the hotel under his new identity. He went directly to the disco.

As a secular Arab, Rayan had no aversion to imbibing in alcohol or having sex with non-Muslim women. In fact, he preferred chatty blonde American coeds and had enjoyed the company of quite a few during his studies in the United States as a graduate engineering student. At Georgia Tech, he was introduced to the clan of Southern Belles whose conservative tastes in public gave way to wild sex parties in private, the likes of which he had never experienced with Muslim women.

Rayan ached for some action as he entered the disco and took a seat in the shadow of a back booth. He would survey the crowd before forming a scheme to get laid tonight. A waiter came to take his drink order. He requested a bottle of Cristal Champagne in perfect Moroccan Arabic. He planned to leave it unopened on ice until he found his mark. A baited hook in the form of a chilled bottle of the bubbly was Rayan's calling card. He also ordered a Johnny Walker Black for the courage needed to approach the prettiest lady in the room.

Rayan drank the scotch in a couple of big swigs, and the waiter appeared with another right on cue. One more drink should do the job. He lifted the second tumbler from the table and made his way to the edge of the dance floor for a closer inspection of the crowd that had grown to fill the available space. Donna Summer's "Love to Love You Baby" played loudly, the bass line reverberating in his diaphragm.

Each dancer demonstrated a rhythmic Kama Sutra. Men dancing with ladies invariably reverted to poses that simulated copulating farm animals. Women danced with other females, some in pairs, and others in larger groups. Female couples preferred to take turns positioning their heads over their partner's erogenous zones and doing either an air lick or, if drunk enough, a full-on face plant to mimic a sex act. Their expressions conveyed feelings of erotic pleasure akin to the facial contortions after an orgasm.

The crowd was an international mix, at least half Muslim, who enjoyed the guilty pleasures of alcohol and uncovered women behind the walls of the western-owned establishment. Many of the Arab patrons were so intoxicated they could not manage a normal dance step. They shuffled back and forth supported by a more sober partner or friend.

Rayan made his way around the dance floor without drawing attention to himself. He completed the circuit and returned to his booth with a plan to approach two women, one blonde and one brunette. The two attractive women left the dance floor as the song ended. They went to the corner of the long bar where their drinks sat under cocktail napkins. Watching their every move, he observed the blonde remove her high heels and rub her feet.

Opportunity, he thought.

Rayan hailed the waiter and asked him to extend an invitation to the two lovelies at the bar on the pretense they needed to rest their feet. Women did not get booths at nightclubs; they looked for single men who did. A booth required a minimum purchase of booze and sometimes food. As the waiter explained the invitation from the man in the booth, one of the girls looked directly at Rayan with a smile. That was his cue to slide out and personally welcome them to his padded lair.

The blonde scooted to the middle of the semicircle and the brunette slid in right next to her. Rayan sat to their left. Quickly sizing them up as Americans, he said in his best American English, "Good morning, ladies, my name is Rayan. May I interest you in some champagne?"

They glanced at each other, weighing the significance of the offer and agreed to accept after some unintelligible girl-speak. "Sure, but just one glass, Mr. Rayan. We have an early flight in the morning. This is Melanie, and my name is Lori," said the perky blonde.

Tilting each glass to limit the bubbly foam, Rayan expertly poured two flutes of champagne while asking, "Where are you ladies from, and what brings you to the land of Bogart and Bergman?"

"Ah...do you mean Morocco?" asked Lori, confused by the movie reference.

Melanie, the smarter of the two, spoke next, "We're graduate students from the University of Vermont in Burlington. We've just completed a trek through the Atlas Mountains and visits to the main archeological sites in the area."

Then ditzy Lori added, "We study anthropology."

The three of them talked about the Americans' experiences in the mountains and their impressions of Morocco. Rayan told them he was from a Lebanese merchant family with business interests in Morocco. The young ladies nursed their first glasses of champagne and seemed to be enjoying the conversation with their exotic host. He sensed they were contemplating another glass. He reached for Lori's flute, but she covered with her left hand.

"We have to go, but thank you for the drink and chat, Rayan. We really enjoyed meeting you." With a sexy wink from Melanie, the two ladies slid out the opposite side of the booth and vanished through the exit into the lobby.

Filling his glass, Rayan Hariri took a deep breath and let out an audible sigh as he surveyed his remaining options on the dance floor. His balls were swollen from not having had sex in two weeks, the titillation of the encounter with the UVM girls caused his junk to overreact; he was a borderline predator. Unless he found someone soon he would have to return to his room for a date with the hotel porn channel, which he considered marginally better than raping someone in the stairwell.

A shadow appeared on the table, and Rayan, in character, peered up meekly to see what was casting it. A person stood in front of the spotlight that illuminated the booth. Judging by the shape of the silhouette, it was a woman. He rose from his seat to get a better look. As he extended his hand, the form spoke.

"I'm from the club's champagne police, and any bubbly not consumed by three a.m. must be confiscated. It's two-fifty now, so you've got some work to do in the next ten minutes."

"Well then, please join me in a Herculean effort to polish off this bottle of Cristal by three o'clock." He concealed his surprise at her clever approach as he continued a virtuoso imitation of Rayan Hariri, debonair European playboy and successful businessman. He introduced himself and waited for her reply as she slid into his refuge. He got the distinct impression he was now the hunted as she introduced herself.

"Ana Rodriquez, pleased to meet you, Rayan. What are you doing in Casablanca?"

"Drinking champagne and drowning my sorrows," he offered with a wry smile as her face appeared from the shadows. She was a black-haired beauty he recognized as pure Castilian by her extended sideburns and dark arm hair. He loved blondes, but the thought of bedding this Spanish señorita began to consume him as he waited for a response to his theatrics.

"Awe, poor baby. Let's see what I can do to help. How about we get another bottle of champagne, a bowl of strawberries, some whipped cream, and head back to your room?"

Her knowing gaze made his smile seem like it came from a pimpled-faced teenager. She lured Rayan with an unsung siren's tune and come-fuck-me eyes as they made their way onto the elevator. He led her to his room, shut the door, and transformed into the cynical terrorist. He had not become a leader in the Palestinian movement by ignoring uninvited entreaties from women or men. He played the drunken businessman to get her to his room. He needed to confirm her true identity before he killed her or fucked her brains out. Either way it would be an enjoyable end to a long and tiring day.

After shutting and locking the door, Rayan turned to his new friend and said firmly, "Give me your purse."

"No need to get tough with me, Rayan. I'm just looking for a good time." She handed him the purse which he emptied on the bed. No guns, knives, or pills. That was a good sign.

"Take off your clothes," he commanded.

"A girl likes a little foreplay before she gives herself to a man, but I'll play along if it makes you happy," she said as she motioned for him to help her unzip the back of her dress. She slipped her shoulders from the armholes, and let the garment fall to the ground, exposing her well-sculpted body clad only in a sheer bra and skimpy panties. Ana stood in the fully lit bedroom with the confidence of an underwear model, never showing any sign of fear or embarrassment.

She didn't have any weapons. His eyes softened as he approached her and said, "I live a complicated life, and unfortunately many people want to harm me. I'm sorry my beauty. Now we can relax and enjoy each other's company."

"I rather liked the Gestapo act. It turned me on." Ana put her arms around Rayan's neck, hoisted her thighs onto his hips, and locked her legs behind his waist. With her breasts snuggled under his chin he turned their conjoined bodies toward the bed and dropped her on the mattress. He was on her like a wildebeest in heat.

Ana Rodriquez departed Rayan Hariri's room, leaving him snoring in the king-sized bed they shared for over two hours. She took him to sexual places he had never been. She left him in a pile of satisfied human flesh, but not before removing a tiny tracking device from her barrette and sliding it into a stitched seam of his briefcase. The micro-device was a new breed of surveillance technology made possible by the presence of geosynchronous satellites in space above the Northern Atlantic. Satellite communications moved from a U.S. Defense Department controlled activity into the private sector in the early1970s. Mossad was in the game through numerous shell companies whose bandwidth agreements with major satellite owners generated their global surveillance network. They now had the ability to track a subject to within three feet anywhere on the planet.

Mossad had followed Abu Hassan from the time the Arab extremist left Beirut. The Israelis waited patiently for an opportunity to prey on his weakness for alcohol and female companionship. He had been passed from one Mossad operative to the next until he departed Paris with his new identity. Ana Rodriquez first spotted him at the train station in Tarifa, Morocco. She had been alerted to his destination by another *sayan* helper who rode with Abu Hassan from Paris.

Ana had executed her part of the plan with incredible skill and courage. Abu Hassan would be electronically tracked wherever he went. She wanted to kill him, but she deferred realizing once it was Abu Hassan's time to die, he would have hopefully led Mossad to numerous other scumbag terrorists. With her mission successfully completed, Ana left that morning in 1973 before the sun broke over the coastal desert.

Chapter 37

Fareed al-Husseini expected an update from Syrian intelligence on the status of the traitor in his ranks, but the call to his contact had not been returned. He couldn't wait any longer to uncover the person responsible for compromising their activities, so he came up with a plan of his own. He would share separate facets of a fake operation with each of the Committee members privately over the course of the next twenty-four hours. They would be told one unique element known only to that individual. They would be told not to disclose the "classified" information to the others, making them feel important. His suspicions would be confirmed when the false detail was repeated back to him through Syrian intelligence from their Mossad informant. Sadly, unknown to Fareed, the real target of his investigation was his close childhood friend, Samir.

Information on the planned attack provided by Samir al-Khalidi caused alarm at Mossad Headquarters. Jamie Sachs, Director of Collections, and Simon Adler, *katsa* and informant handler, along with the CIA's Goran Frankfurter sat in a meeting room trying to make sense of the encrypted messages. Three communications had been transmitted by the spy to Simon Adler the previous day.

Director Sachs began the meeting by saying, "Gentlemen, we have a real situation on our hands. Based on today's information, there are planned attacks on at least three Israeli targets. The information leads us to believe they crossed into Lebanon from Syria at the Masnaa border just northwest of Damascus and headed southwest. Our undercover agent at the border could not verify their exact destination due to the presence of a Hezbollah security detail who did all the talking. We are also aware that the attackers went through extensive underwater training."

"It's most likely that they will attempt to enter Israel via the Mediterranean," offered Simon Adler, trying to make sense of the information. "I suppose it could be anywhere along our shoreline, but most likely in the area of Haifa because of its proximity to Lebanon."

"We are assuming they will launch the assault from Lebanon; unfortunately this is only a guess at this time. In the past they've purposely put out misleading intelligence to distract us." Sachs pontificated, displaying his command of history and deception.

Sachs went on, "Remember the film crew that arrived on a boat from Turkey? Under the banner of Turkish-Israeli cooperation, the filming of a movie was agreed by the Prime Minister and approved by the Director of Mossad and IDF Commanders. A thorough search of each container, much protested by the Turkish government and the more liberal Israelis, uncovered firearms and incendiary devices. Hezbollah had infiltrated the Turkish film industry and planned on attacking Israelis using a friendly foreign government as cover. I don't put anything past these bastards."

They agreed Adler would try to get more information from his source inside the Committee. Sachs would brief both his Mossad boss and the Commander of the Israeli Navy. The two organizations would work together to define the potential routes for the sea assault. All incoming vessels would be searched extra hard and shoreline surveillance increased by adding more soldiers to radar, sonar, and heat detection duty.

Sachs wanted an update on Colonel Fischer, the DNA, and Dr. Kohen before he turned his full attention to the upcoming attacks.

"How's it going with the DNA project and our old friend 'Pussi' Fischer?" Sachs' disdain for the colonel was common knowledge within the intelligence community. He wanted the fat Israeli to keep his nose out of Mossad business. Sachs had been frustrated more than once by Fischer's involvement in Mossad affairs only to have the Prime Minister's office intervene on the colonel's behalf.

"The samples were successfully taken from the conference and delivered to one of Dr. Kohen's employees. We have an operative in Upper Galilee monitoring Dr. Kohen's movements. We should have more to report by tomorrow after our agent checks in," Adler responded, adding little to what Sachs already knew.

Sachs' stepped closer to his men, temporarily invading their personal space and said, "Don't let Dr. Kohen out of our sight. I need to know exactly what they plan to do with the DNA before they do it. Do you understand?" He was reminding the men who was in charge.

The meeting was pronounced over when Sachs and Adler left the room, dispatched to their various duties, leaving Goran alone with thoughts about what to do next. He needed to communicate with his Syrian intelligence contact and tell him the Israelis were preparing to intercept the Committee's assault team.

The Israelis had an agent in deep cover with the Syrian Committee of Ten who passed information to Mossad. In turn, Goran confirmed Mossad's receipt of that intelligence, exposing a mole, while relaying Israel's plan to frustrate the incursion. A Syrian operative communicated Goran's reports to Fareed, who was now trying to uncover the traitor in his ranks. Goran left the building shaking his head at the complexity of this undertaking. He needed a break and would return to the Mossad office after lunch.

Since his arrival in Israel, Goran had been followed by a Mossad *sayan* helper. Israel maintained a healthy cynicism about the CIA's intentions in the Middle East and went to exceptional lengths to monitor all their activities in the region. The *sayan* noted the oddities of Goran's work habits, especially the business of using a public computer. The CIA generally restricted communication with

Langley to company-issued, encrypted laptop computers. Maybe he was communicating with his gay lover.

Goran sensed he was being tailed as he left the office and continued to feel uneasy as he entered the hotel. He went straight to his room, which he was certain had been bugged. As the world closed in around him, Goran surmised his undercover work with Syria was coming to an end. He committed himself to redoubling his efforts over the coming days and obtaining a mother lode of intelligence. Rather than sending his findings piecemeal, he would aggregate the data and give them one last information dump. He would focus on uncovering the identity of the informant in Syria, thereby earning brownie points as he faced the prospect of a solitary retirement. At least he would have enough cash to attract any woman he wanted. He went to the mirror and gave himself a good mental talking to, not wanting to speak out in the bug-infested room.

The incriminating discoveries of the "Summit of Kings" DNA samples would be made public in the next few days. The tests uncovered numerous diseases among the Arab hierarchy. Ari trusted Yussi and his team would use the findings in the most ruinous way possible against the enemies of Israel.

Ari's plan to create a bio-weapon proceeded on schedule with the isolation of specific "mean genes" that could be programmed to attack their human hosts without leaving any forensic traces. These vagrant genes would be held in abeyance, awaiting Colonel Fischer's decision on when to deliver the lethal dosages.

Ari and Ziva's successful raid on the first century tomb provided the inspiration for the next phase of Ari's plan. The ossuary contained only the remains of Zadok the Pharisee who founded the Zealot movement, a fact confirmed by the inscription on the box. As one of the supreme patriots of his day, along with Judas of Galilee, Zadok had resisted Roman rule and their system of taxation. His remains included two incisors. It was from these teeth that Ari harvested sufficient DNA to reincarnate the great Zealot.

With Ziva's help, he was well on his way to cloning this extraordinary religious figure. The first step was the enucleation of ovum, the process of removing the nucleus from unfertilized human eggs. This left the remaining cell free of DNA and all other genetic material. Having enucleated fifteen of Ziva's eggs, he introduced Zadok's DNA into the blank eggs in a procedure known as "somatic nuclear replacement." He applied an electric current to stimulate the development of the genetically enriched eggs. These electrified eggs were placed in a laboratory-controlled medium that simulated a female oviduct, the normal staging area for fertilized eggs in a woman's body. The fertilized eggs began to divide. Within three days six cells were visible, transforming the eggs into embryos. Two of the healthiest zygotes would be surgically implanted into the uterus of a surrogate mother where they would continue to develop until birth. If both scientifically fertilized eggs made it nine months, the result would be twin Zadoks.

Ziva was excited about carrying the radicalized cells to term. Bound to one another by the murder of Ziva's abusive husband, she had hitched her horse to Ari's wagon. It did not occur to her that Ari might select another womb. She had been his faithful servant in the workplace and in the bedroom. She deserved to be recognized as the high priestess in the new temple. Being the mother of the Zadok child would assure her rightful place at Ari's side, forever.

Chapter 38

The ferry from Limassol, Cyprus, to Haifa, Israel, departed about thirty minutes late due to the usual, last minute bustle of passengers cutting in line and shoving their way to the front of the queue. No one wanted to wait their turn, so everyone had to wait longer while security officers scolded the cutters. Willy had anticipated the chaos on the landing and purchased a more expensive ticket. He was permitted to board the ferry by the forward gangway and sit on the business class deck with a view of the water over the bow. Willy's watch read nine p.m. as he prepared for the more than ten-hour crossing to his homeland.

No longer the travel writer Joseph Adams, the identity he used to enter Cyprus, Willy assumed the identity of ultra-Orthodox Jew Saul Berkowitz, son of a Ukrainian who immigrated to Israel in 1947. In the dress of a traditional Ukrainian Belzer Hasidim, he wore a long black *rekel* (coat) made of silk, a black *gartel* (tasseled belt), and a white shirt with black pants and shoes. Willy sported a full Hasidic beard with *payats*, long curled sideburns, and a traditional fedora. His many years as a *kidon* had taught him all the tricks of the trade when it came to masquerading as an Orthodox Jew or a radical Islamist.

Over time he had accumulated a handful of passports enabling him to move freely between countries and cultures. Mossad seemed to have an endless supply of passports for the forging. Shoe lifts made him two inches taller. Minor surgery to his face and eyes allowed him to dupe facial recognition systems. His mastery of eight languages and ability to transform his appearance combined with these multiple identities made him undetectable to immigration and customs authorities around the world.

Willy sat quietly on the right hand side of the forward deck reading the Torah while holding the tassels on his belt. A black satchel resembling an oversized doctor's bag contained everything he would need to reinforce his new identity, plus a few things for his personal entertainment. One of these was a specially programmed Apple iPad which doubled as a military and police scanner. Military frequencies were closely guarded secrets. Willy's pirated copy of the famous PROMIS program gave him access to frequency settings and de-encryption codes for all broadcasts. He had been an active PROMIS user for over twenty years. He had obtained a copy of the program directly from Mossad.

The United States, United Kingdom, Greece, Turkey, NATO, and other countries with a military presence in the region were actively conversing as the sun set on the three-hundred-foot ferry. Willy fell asleep clutching the black bag in his lap with his fedora tipped over his eyes and an iPad ear bud crammed into one ear.

Willy woke to the sound of gunshots. He bolted up in his seat, thinking it must have been a dream, a *kidon* flashback. Recognizing the alarm on the faces of the other passengers, he realized the gunfire was real. He surveyed the sea and noticed a group of boats off the bow at about two o'clock on the dial. He tapped the auto-scan function on the tablet, looking for the strongest signal. The Israel Defense Forces Naval Unit broadcasted a hectic communication explaining the capture of a small inflatable watercraft that had entered Israeli waters from the north. He continued to hear gunshots from both the iPad's ear bud and on the water at a distance of about a kilometer. He removed binoculars from the black bag and focused on the small flotilla as the morning sun lit up the surprise proceedings.

Donny and his men were taken out to sea on a fishing boat four hours before sunrise. The inflatable had been lowered into the water about fourteen kilometers from the Israeli shore. The men, already in wetsuits with rebreathers on their backs, boarded the watercraft with their firearms. Pushing away from the fishing boat, they made their way further out to sea before turning toward Israel on a vector that would deliver them just north of Haifa. Traveling at top speed they arrived in total darkness at a preprogrammed GPS coordinate where they shut down the engine.

Donny's men chatted nervously as the boat came to a stop. "Quiet! No more talking," Donny demanded.

With lights on the Israeli shoreline visible, Donny ordered his men into the water. Suddenly, a halogen spotlight invaded their darkened space. An Israeli patrol boat had snuck up on them using a silent turbine engine of their own.

"Raise your hands and stay where you are," called out the Israeli captain in English.

"Get in the water now," shouted Donny knowing the sea was the only place they had a chance of escape. He pulled out his handgun and attempted to shoot out the searchlight. He missed.

Before exiting the boat, the head of the man seated next to Donny exploded like a ripe watermelon spewing blood and skull fragments all over him. Another shot missed him but hit the man on his other side in the chest causing him to fall lifelessly into the water. Unharmed, Donny fell backwards into the water and attempted to swim down out of range of the sailor's bullets. He was twenty feet below the surface when he came face to face with a large shark. The fish brushed by Donny on the way to investigate the smell of blood from his dead companions. Another shark appeared, then another, attracted by the blood and the intense white light from the patrol boat.

How could I have miscalculated so terribly? The Jews must have known we were coming. Now I have to choose death by shark or by Jew, Donny frantically thought as he decided to resurface and surrender.

Donny popped out of the water with his hands raised shouting, "Help me! I surrender. Get me away from these sharks."

A large dorsal fin appeared next to Donny as he pleaded to be saved. All of his men, now dead, floated in clouds of blood not far from where he treaded water. Luckily the sharks were more interested in them than they were in Donny, but he knew his time would come unless he got in that boat. Fear choked off his words as he tried to cry out for rescue. Donny was fish food if he didn't get out of the water soon.

"Shoot them," screamed the Israeli commander in Hebrew. Willy heard every word being broadcast. Shots continued to ring out. "Don't let them eat the bodies," was the next directive from the commander. "Those are white sharks, men; you have to shoot them in the eyes. Do it now, fire! Save the bodies or we will have a lot of explaining to do."

"One of them is still alive commander," shouted a sailor.

"Get him onboard before the beasts take him. Hurry. We need this man breathing," yelled the commander.

"Got him sir, he's coming up over the stern," came the reply.

The sailors lifted Donny onto the boat and immediately stripped him of his wetsuit to check for firearms. He lay naked on the wet deck with numerous guns pointed at him while the commander made his way from the bridge. "Who are you?" he asked, this time in Arabic, as he looked down on the terrified and exhausted man. No response, so he tried in French, still no answer. In a last attempt to communicate with the prisoner he asked in English, "Who are you, and what are you doing in Israeli waters?"

Donny looked up and said, "Fuck you, Captain Jew-boy," in a heavy Irish accent.

Willy caught the entire exchange through the commander's microphone while gunshots continued to ring out over the otherwise calm waters. The sailors retrieved the three remaining bodies from the sea. One of the men had been bitten in half by the white leviathan, as witnessed by a transmission from the gunwales of the boat.

"Sir, we only have the top half of this man," cried a crewmember, sickened by the sight.

So with two and a half dead bodies and one lone survivor onboard the shooting finally stopped. Willy estimated that over one hundred rounds had been fired during his monitoring of the transmission. He listened intently as the naval commander called in a summary report to headquarters.

"We came upon an inflatable watercraft with four men at zero six-thirty hours in Israeli waters. We received gunfire from the water and my men commenced firing in accordance with naval engagement protocols. At zero six-forty hours I called for the shooting to cease. Upon further inspection, we discovered one of the offenders still alive and swimming toward our boat. We retrieved and searched him before taking him to the brig. The three remaining occupants of the offending craft are dead and onboard. One of them was bitten in half by a white shark. We could only retrieve the top half of his severed body. All three dead men appear to be of Arab descent. The surviving prisoner is possibly British."

The commander continued with a description of the watercraft and the occupants. "The inflatable boat was powered by a whisper-sync turbine motor. Each passenger wore a wetsuit and had rebreathing units on their backs. Three waterproof suitcases contained M107 sniper rifles with long range scopes and ten rounds of ammunition."

The transmission from the boat ended and Naval Headquarters switched their response to a random series of military frequencies so people like Willy could not listen to the entire dialogue. He had heard enough anyway. Willy thought about how crazy things had gotten since Arafat turned down the Wye River Peace Accord. It had been more than ten years and the two sides seemed further than ever from a resolution to the problem of Palestinian sovereignty.

Thank goodness for large favors. Arafat's decision to walk out at Wye River gave Israel the political cover to keep all of its hard won land. *The Islamists can have Gaza; it's the butthole of humanity anyway*, Willy thought. *But don't take any part of the Golan Heights, the West Bank, or East Jerusalem.*

Israel needed all of this land to assure its security. The Jews had an obligation to hold the line, even if it infuriated every Arab in the world. And now, of all times, the United States had turned its back on Israel? The U.S. president had caved under pressure from liberal progressives and their anti-Semitic agenda. Accusations of human rights abuses by Israel had become an epidemic on talk radio. Sympathy for the Palestinian cause increased even as the suicide bombs kept coming. This was crazy but a fact of life, and one Willy would deal with one Palestinian at a time if necessary. He would pay respects to his only brother as he was laid to rest and then continue the fight with Omar's heavenly blessing.

Chapter 39

Trey was completely oblivious to the magnificent military heroics of his uncle Omar. His death caused an outpouring of support from high-ranking military officials and politicians alike. A rumor even had the Prime Minister coming to the funeral. As Trey listened to the stream of mourners, he began to understand his dead uncle's incredible bravery and big heart.

Rachel amazed everyone. Her command of Hebrew and Yiddish made her an immediate darling of the event. Trey fell deeper in love by the hour. He observed her negotiate discounts on flowers, arrange what dishes friends brought to the *Shiva*, and turn away gawkers who wanted to pay final respects to Omar just to say they had done so.

Shiva is a Jewish custom where family members of the departed stay home and receive friends, neighbors, and relatives with food and accept condolences. The immediate family can't cook, go out, work, read, or do anything that distracts them from the deceased. As Omar's only child, Zach became the focus of the lamentation. He received mourners while sitting on a stool dressed in black clothes. Each person kissed him on the brow, cheek, or lips depending on the closeness of their relationship. Meanwhile, Zach's wife sat dutifully beside him as their children took turns sitting on a third stool in support of their dad.

"Rachel, this is an incredible turnout. I can't believe the things I've learned about my uncle. He was a famous Israeli." Trey noticed Rachel staring at a man entering the room.

"Excuse me," she said as she walked away and approached the guy now standing in line to greet the family. Trey paid keen attention to their interaction, especially her friend who sprouted a large smile upon recognizing Rachel. They exchanged friendship kisses and hugged longer than Trey thought necessary. After speaking with the gentleman for a few moments, Rachel returned to Trey's side behind the mourning couple.

Unable to contain his curiosity Trey asked, "Who's the fellow?"

"Oh, just someone I used to know," Rachel said, adding intrigue to the encounter.

"Used to know? Looks like you still know each other pretty well. Is he an old boyfriend?" He hoped the answer would be negative.

"Yes. Why are you jealous?" Rachel jousted back with a hint of sarcasm.

"In fact…I am. I'm a little surprised at my reaction, but to be honest I think what I'm feeling is jealousy. Should I be?" Trey had sick puppy eyes.

"No, not in the least. It was many years ago when I worked on a kibbutz in Beersheba. He's now happily married with three children. I'm joyfully single with no kids and have an amazing boyfriend who might one day give me a son or daughter." Her eyes were fixed on Trey's with the intensity of a woman who knew what she wanted.

The sexual tension was becoming noticeable to the people around them, even the handsome schmuck from the kibbutz who stared straight at them as if to say to Trey, *I had her before you.*

Ripping kibbutz-man's throat out was not an option, so Trey had to settle for a laser-like look that communicated: *I understand you had her first, but now she's mine. And judging by the shape of the bleached-blond, midget whale you married, I got the better end of the deal.*

Yussi and Buji sat in a Mercedes G-Class SUV retrofitted with bulletproof glass, armor grade side panels, Kevlar tires, and a bomb plate protecting the undercarriage of the vehicle. Fischer Scientific purchased two of these 250,000-Euro vehicles after death threats against its employees resulted in the kidnapping and murder of Yussi's CFO. Hamas took credit for the murder, which culminated in the slain man being left naked on the side of the road near an Israeli-West Bank checkpoint.

They waited for Willy to come out of the Haifa Ferry Terminal. Yussi would be with him for the first time in over thirty years, and he was a little nervous. He went to get copies of today's papers from the newsstand outside the terminal. He returned with editions of *Haaretz*, the *Jerusalem Post*, and the *International Herald Tribune*. What they read shocked them both and infuriated Yussi.

The *Haaretz* headline read: "Saudi King Has Advanced AIDS—Disclosure Sparks Competition for Crown."

The *Jerusalem Post* headline proclaimed: "HIV/AIDS Infects Saudi Kingdom as Disclosure of King's Disease Starts Succession Fight."

The *New York Times* headline reported: "King Fights AIDS as Princes Fight for Crown."

The articles reported the information came from an unnamed source who had also provided test results that confirmed the diagnosis. There was no proof to tie the test results to the Saudi King, but calls made to the Kingdom's press liaison two days ago had not been returned. The news reports claimed the King checked into the Saudi Royal Hospital hours after the story originally broke. A royal family spokesperson gave the official reason for the king's hospitalization as "suffering from exhaustion and work-related stress." Close inspection of recent photos of the seventy-three-year-old potentate revealed skin lesions and weight loss, signs of someone suffering from advanced AIDS.

The Saudi Royal families' sexual exploits had been fodder for gossip columnists for years, but the King's private life had been strategically shrouded in secrecy. With four wives and twenty-two children, the King had always appeared to be an exception to the philandering reputation of his heirs and other Muslim leaders. Exposing the King as having AIDS, which he likely contracted while shunning his own laws, showed the duplicity commonly found in Muslim nations, where leaders are exempt from the laws they so ruthlessly enforce.

The crown prince, dubbed as the Party Prince by British tabloids, took after his other Muslim chums. Dalliances with attractive European models and actresses caused many to doubt the crown prince's fitness to lead. According to Saudi insiders, he would never be the protector of Islam's two holiest sites. The battle to replace the king was on, and the stakes were high.

Yussi was irate. He could not believe that punk scientist had released the information without his approval. Yussi and Ari had agreed to "wait for the right time" to transmit evidence of the king's condition, but instead Kohen had acted independently. The Prime Minister would be outraged if he found out about Yussi's involvement. Someone would pay dearly for this lapse, and Yussi hoped it wouldn't be him. His contracts with the Israeli government totaled over one hundred million Euros annually, and he truly valued his continued heartbeat.

"I had a deal with Kohen. He promised me he'd withhold the results until I gave the go ahead to release them. Now it's plastered all over the fucking papers." Yussi's anger turned his face beet red.

"Don't have a stroke. What are you so worried about? This is good for us. Confusion among the Saudi's distracts the focus from Israel. Plus, I think it shows he's got chutzpah and it's timely for us. He's now proven himself to be a rogue scientist, and he'll become an excellent scapegoat when needed. Are there any more diagnoses from the samples at the conference?" Buji, always the voice of reason, attempted to get his fat friend focused on fighting Arabs not a Jewish geneticist.

"You wouldn't believe it if I told you. I can tell you it's big. I'm just irritated we lost control of the news cycle. It could've been managed so much better."

Willy disembarked the ferry with the electronics stashed in his black bag. A Jew reentering Israel only had to answer a few questions about his trip and disclose any items acquired abroad. A quick check of his bag and a walk through a total body scanner completed the entry screening. The ferry terminal was much easier to negotiate than the airport when it came to security, no facial recognition, no fingerprints, and rarely secondary interviews.

Willy exited immigration control. Assuming the gait of a deeply religious Hasidic Jew, he slowly made his way out of the terminal. He was looking for Buji's car when a black Mercedes SUV came roaring up and stopped in front of him. The door opened, and Willy got into the back seat. There sat his old friend Yussi, whose smiling face filled Willy's view. It was as if they had never been apart, as Willy said, "Yussi, you have gained a lot of weight. Your mistresses must be fattening you up in hopes you will croak and leave them the apartments you so kindly provide for them."

"I'll have you know, all my mistresses appreciate a man of my stature, knowing my wife worries less because she can't imagine anyone being attracted to my fat ass. A woman's ability to see the truth diminishes proportionate to the amount of one's money and power. In fact, the other day one of my girlfriends mistook me for Brad Pitt." All three of them laughed as Yussi rearranged his girth in his plush leather seat.

"Have you heard anything about an incident at sea this morning?" asked Willy, referring to the shooting he witnessed.

Neither one of them had been briefed on the IDF Naval action. Reports of the clash came in after the early news had been gathered and had not yet been reported on radio or TV. Willy told them what he had heard on the radio transmissions, finishing with the body count, the sharks, and the lone survivor.

"Oh, wonderful," said Buji sarcastically, from the driver's seat. "We enraged the Turks by turning their flotilla to Gaza into a bloody massacre and now we shoot up a bunch of Arabs invading us from the sea."

"Four men in a raft hardly constitutes an invasion," quipped Willy.

Switching gears, Buji said, "You probably haven't heard that the Saudi King has AIDS. His heirs are fighting it out to determine

who will be the next king. Things should get interesting during
the next few weeks."

"How does the King of Saudi Arabia get AIDS?" asked Willy,
who immediately realized the rhetorical foolishness of the question.

"By screwing dirty whores," was Buji's immediate response.

"So I guess Yussi doesn't have a corner on the market for dirty
whores after all." Willy laughed, causing all of them to break up
again.

These three men, who had forged their relationship in the
intense heat of battle, remained the closest of friends even as time
and distance had kept them apart.

Buji had so much to tell Willy, but that information was best
left to a private conversation. They were on their way to one of
the safe houses maintained by Fischer Scientific as a surrogate for
Mossad. When not in use by the intelligence service, these locations hosted Fischer Scientific's out of town clients and all night
sex parties thrown by Yussi and his perverted friends.

After traveling for just under an hour, Buji pulled up in front
of a Tel Aviv high-rise and got out of the driver's seat. He opened
the back door for Willy and handed the car keys to Yussi saying,
"I'll get Willy settled here. You take the truck, go home, and dress
for Omar's calling."

Buji led Willy into the building and up the elevator to the
twenty-second floor. They entered the condominium that had a
view of the sea and downtown Tel Aviv. Buji directed Willy to the
master suite, where he removed his clothing and took a shower.
The water ran over his head as he thought about being back in
Israel for the first time in years. And, of course, he also thought of
Eva. He shook the water and those thoughts from his head while
he toweled off, put on some boxers, and walked back into the living room where Buji waited patiently. Life was about to get a whole
lot more confusing for Willy.

"Willy, sit down. I have something important to tell you." Buji's
eyes took on a grave look.

"What's wrong, Buji? You look like your dog just died."

"No, my dog is alive and well. So is someone you need to meet. Yesterday a young man came to my office at the university. He's an American fellow who said he was Omar's nephew."

Buji paused, knowing that Willy would eventually make the connection.

"What are you talking about, Buji? I'm the only brother or sister Omar ever had, and I don't have any children."

"I don't have a lot to go on except Omar's word, but I believe this man is your son. I spent over thirty minutes with him, and if he is not your offspring, then you have a clone out there knocking up women." Buji noticed Willy's demeanor soften.

"Where is he?" asked Willy, trying to conceive how and when he could have fathered a child.

"He and his girlfriend are assisting your nephew Zach with the Shiva and funeral preparations. He'll be at the calling this afternoon. To make things even more bizarre, his girlfriend is sister to the geneticist, Dr. Ari Kohen, who uncovered the Saudi King's condition. Small world, eh?"

And getting smaller by the second, thought Willy. He began to feel the weight of the disclosure pounding on his brain. Even for a person with extraordinary stress tolerance, the appearance of an adult son out of the blue was a colossal bombshell. Willy was never a philanderer, but he had his share of action between the sheets. Then he wondered if Mary had been pregnant when he left but never told him. If so, he calculated his son to be almost forty years old.

Buji's phone rang; it was Yussi calling from the street. Willy finished dressing in his Hasidic costume and left the condo. Buji had purposely kept Yussi in the dark about Trey out of respect to Willy who needed to handle this without interference from his friends, unless called on.

Yussi greeted them with some new information. "I received an update on the Navy's operation this morning. Just like you said Willy, all of the intruders are dead except one man who is not Arab. My contacts at the IDF are saying he's not talking to anyone, but they think he's Irish."

"Any mention of sharks and one of the men being bitten in half?" asked Willy.

"No, nothing like that but I'm sure it will all come out. It always does. You know they record all of these actions on video and the radio transmissions are saved for review by the IDF's internal investigators. We've gotten very skilled at anticipating public outcries whenever we spill the blood of our enemies. Guilty until proven innocent."

The liberal media would find a way to make the Israeli Navy the bad guys in this deal, and Willy knew it. What about the Irishman they fished out of the ocean? That was outlandish, but new actors entered the fight every day. He guessed this man was a mercenary who ran out of things to fight for in Ireland.

Willy, Buji, and Yussi arrived at the home of Zach and Milcah Cohen. Cars lined the street and filled the driveway. Yussi parked the black SUV in a space at the end of the driveway, blocking all of the cars in their spots. Power parking was one of his skills, and he could care less whom he inconvenienced by his actions. His license plates and window stickers gave him a free pass wherever he chose to park. Besides, they would not be staying long.

Willy, as Saul Berkowitz, along with Yussi and Buji went into the home. Willy was sweating bullets under his black garments. He entered the living room looking for Zach and any sign of the young man who visited Buji. Zach rose from his stool to greet the two dignitaries and their Hasidic friend.

"Buji, Yussi, thank you for coming. My father loved you both and often talked about your friendship. I'm honored you've taken the time to pay your respects today," Zach said as he escorted them to the sunroom where a smorgasbord of food was laid out.

Before they began to fill their plates, Buji turned to Willy and introduced him as an old friend of Omar's. "Zach I'd like you to meet Saul Berkowitz. He knew your father from the university and they trained together during their first year of military service."

"Thank you for coming, Mr. Berkowitz. I don't recall my father speaking about you, but he had so many friends whom I am just now meeting." Willy extended his hand and gave Zach a limp

Hasidic shake, common among staunch religious types and part of the act he played to perfection.

Willy studied everyone in the house but he couldn't pick out a man who fit Buji's description. He asked Buji in a whisper, "Is he here. Do you see him?"

A simple shake of Buji's head indicated Trey was not in the house. Willy would wait until the funeral to lay eyes on the man who claimed to be his son. What a bizarre chain of events. But what did Willy expect, having led such an unorthodox life? His choices had led him to this point, and with choices came consequences. Nonetheless, he never imagined they included fathering a son who four decades later would be looking for him.

Chapter 40

Ari's decision to release information about the Saudi King's illness without approval from Fischer was precipitated by his fear that the King's condition would be leaked through another source. Ari wanted to control the message for maximum impact. Further review of the King's AIDS test revealed that his condition was entering a very aggressive stage. His antibodies were compromised, making survival impossible. Ari needed to rush to print before the Saudi PR machine buried the true nature of the King's ailment.

Anonymously, Ari had sent the blockbuster report to Robert Maximilian. He was the owner of the British tabloid *Sun-Star* and thought by many to be a Mossad *sayan*, civilian helper. Ari prepared a narrative to accompany the test results. He also promised other medical conditions, of a more shocking nature, would be forthcoming, and if Maximilian printed the story, he would get an exclusive on those findings. But the real hook, a before-and-after picture of the King, comparing a photo from five years ago to one taken just the week before revealed a shocking change. He clearly had the hollow-man, death look of someone suffering from advanced AIDS. This, along with some suspicious skin lesions on the King's face, authenticated Ari's case, and the story ran.

The chain of events following the release of the information was textbook perfect. The silence of the Saudi PR apparatus confirmed the veracity of the report, and most major newspapers picked up the story the following day. The *International Herald Tribune*, the *Jerusalem Post*, and the *Guardian* all ran the blockbuster story on their front pages. Ari thought, *It could not have gone any better, although, Yussi will certainly be pissed.*

The fruits of Ari's scientific brilliance were ready to come out of the laboratory. He planned to shock and awe Yussi with the details of his scheme and urge him to act promptly, because the Israeli Prime Minister was being forced to initiate direct talks with the Palestinians. The PM offered to freeze settlement construction and return to the 1967 borders for a promise from the Arabs to negotiate in good faith. These concessions would have been inconceivable just one year ago. Talk of establishing East Jerusalem as the capital of Palestine was the last straw for Ari. The Arabs had already appropriated the entire Temple Mount; they would get no more land in Jerusalem.

Word of Donny's capture and the death of the other three men reached the Committee of Ten. It was devastating news, not so much for the loss of life but for the capture of the Irishman who would certainly tell the Jews everything about the Committee. Even the loss of Fareed's nephew, Abdul, did not seem to have a negative effect on the group. The value of human life in radical Islam had been reduced to a spiritual currency for the cause of expelling the Jews.

An emergency meeting of the Committee convened with Fareed expressing concern about the failed mission. He praised Allah for taking his nephew and the other men to paradise. They decided to take no further action on the matter except to prepare for the predictable Israeli response. Hezbollah would ultimately take credit for the attempted incursion, and life would go on.

Fareed had given details about a fictitious operation to each member of the Committee in private over the course of the previous twenty-four hours. He told Samir of a plan to blow-up a specific checkpoint at rush hour along the Israeli border by a female suicide bomber dressed in a light blue burka. The entry, moderately popular with Arabs, was used mostly by Israeli's from West Bank settlements passing into Israel proper.

The border crossing appeared a logical target to Samir. The operation would kill a lot of Israelis if the Committee's plan worked. He had to get this information to his Mossad handler immediately. After meeting with Fareed, he went to his second floor room and retrieved the disposable phone he used to call in his reports. He placed the call and relayed the information on the checkpoint target. Hanging up after ninety seconds, he stashed the cell phone in his dirty laundry. Samir returned to the first floor for lunch, confident his cover was intact.

Jamie Sachs had just hung up with Samir when Goran knocked on his open office door.

"Did you hear about the Saudi King? He has AIDS," Goran said with a smile, hoping this tidbit would elevate him in the eyes of the Mossad boss.

Sachs had read the news reports and was not impressed. "Yes, I'm aware of the reports. One dies and another rises up to take his place. The scandal will go to hell with the King. The names change, but the culture remains the same as their governments continue breeding Jew-hating bastards."

Sachs went on without interruption, "I just received word from our man in Syria. Hezbollah is preparing to bomb a checkpoint on our southeastern border tomorrow. I am sending Agent Adler to the border crossing to brief immigration control."

"Adler and I reviewed the updated files on Colonel Fischer, Dr. Kohen, and the DNA samples last night. They are closer to activating an operational plan then we thought." Goran was itching to communicate with the Syrians about what the Jews knew of the upcoming border action.

"We need to know exactly what they are planning before they pull the trigger. Go to Beit Jann and continue surveillance of Dr. Kohen. Don't let him out of your sight," Sachs ordered, distracted by the Syrian situation.

Goran returned to his hotel room to pack an overnight bag. His trip to Upper Galilee would require at least a three-night stay. Before leaving the hotel, he went to the Business Center to e-mail his Syrian contact the details of what Mossad knew of the planned bombing at the checkpoint. He completed the e-mail, placed it in the trash, and logged off.

A keyboard monitor had been placed on the computer after a Mossad tail witnessed Goran's previous activities in the Business Center. Every keystroke was recorded and transmitted to a collections agent who relayed the information to Director Sachs within minutes. Goran departed the hotel knowing nothing of his imminent capture.

A call from Syrian Intelligence to Fareed came early the next morning. Their mole within Mossad parroted back the information he had given only to Samir. Fareed's heart broke upon hearing the news his dearest friend was a traitor to Allah and the Palestinian cause.

How could it be Samir? Haven't I always treated him like a brother? He was suckled at my mother's breast as I was by his and now I must kill him. This is a tragedy beyond comparison, knowing you must take the life of a man you love so dearly. Yet Allah demands it.

Fareed's tearful realization transformed into a resolve that the consequences must be fierce and in earshot of the entire camp. Samir would be an example of what happens to those who betray their Muslim brothers and the ideals of Islam. Fareed continued to cry as he contemplated the loss of his dearest childhood friend, but Islamic culture demanded that torture be painful, bloody, extended, and loud.

Chapter 41

Omar's service at the synagogue included eulogies by former military colleagues and political leaders. Trey was overwhelmed by the accolades bestowed upon his uncle in the short speeches. They recounted the bravery of a man Trey only knew as a serious, yet fun-loving, sex-crazed septuagenarian he had met just weeks before. Omar was among a handful of Israeli folklore heroes whose courageous acts on the battlefield helped assure victory against all of Israel's Arab neighbors in the 1967 Six-Day War. His Medal of Valor hung conspicuously behind the coffin during the service as cabinet ministers and high-ranking military types spoke in recognition of his greatness and contributions to Israel. Each person had a different memory of Omar—his courage in battle and his love of family.

As Zach tearfully concluded what the entire gathering thought was Omar's final eulogy, Trey discerned an unusual rumbling out of the congregation's sight. The noise, a combination of whispers, foot scuffling, and metal on metal, increased as a detail of dark suited security officers entered the area of the coffin and surrounded the pulpit. Looking like a scene from "Men in Black," the unit stood in perfect formation with hands at their sides, eyes fixed on the crowd and ear buds clearly visible. Bulges in their suit coats announced that these men were vested up and armed.

A few tense moments passed as a deathly silence fell upon the gathering. What followed was an incredible statement about the notoriety of this man, Trey's uncle. The Prime Minister of Israel entered the synagogue and took his position in front of Omar. The entire hall let out a collective gasp when they realized who stood at the dais in testament to the life of Lieutenant Colonel Cohen.

"Ladies and gentlemen, we gather here today in recognition of an extraordinary Israeli patriot. But more than that, he was my dear friend. While we disagreed about military policy in later years, Lieutenant Colonel Omar Levi Cohen always had the best interest of Israel in his heart. I have witnessed bravery on the battlefield on many occasions, but I have never seen a man risk his life for such humane and selfless reasons over and over like Omar Cohen. There are too many examples of his sacrifices to recount in a short eulogy, so I want to share one story that has shaped my view of the world to this day.

"The 1967 Six-Day War was fought in the trenches of the Golan Heights and Sinai. Lieutenant Colonel Cohen was in charge of a battalion pushing into the Sinai Peninsula on the first day of the war. Retreating Egyptian soldiers stumbled over each other to get out of the way of the superior firepower of Israel's surge. Israeli Air Force jets peppered the sand behind the retreating soldiers with considerable accuracy. Ultimately the push west took our soldiers right to the edge of the Red Sea and the Suez Canal. Many civilians were caught in the military action, believing the Egyptian military would certainly defend their homeland. Omar's actions that day demonstrate the compassion and kindness of this man we have before us.

"His battalion fired rockets and guided missiles over the heads of the trapped civilians onto targets along the coast of the Red Sea. Omar assembled a team of his best men to leave the safety of their tanks and go out to save the remaining Egyptian citizens, stuck in the crossfire. As enemy rounds rained down on Omar and his men, they ran toward the civilians huddling in small groups, just east of the seashore. Women, children, and elderly men all prayed in unison for Allah to save them as Omar miraculously appeared.

He instructed his men to holster their weapons and gather the women and children first. Carrying those who could not walk or keep up, he led the refugees back to the relative safety of the tanks and support vehicles.

Six more times he ventured into harm's way to rescue every remaining man, woman, and child. The efforts of he and his men saved one hundred Egyptian children, seventy-five women, and fifty old men from certain death. In this single moment of compassion, Omar defined what is best about Israel. He risked his life to save those who, through no fault of their own, found themselves in harm's way. He showed me that the women and children of soldiers and enemy combatants don't choose to fight but are often caught up in the tragedy of war. So rather than making them pay the ultimate price, he risked his life to do the right thing.

"Today Israel is a stronger and more compassionate country, a true democracy where the love of fellow humans must supersede acts of violence whenever possible. Thank you, Omar, for your legacy of tolerance, kindness, compassion, and charity. Israel would do well to follow your lead and find a way to bridge the ideological gaps in the world today by reaching out and saving those who can't protect themselves. Thank you for your service, but mostly for reminding us that the children didn't choose to wage war."

Loud sobs were clearly audible in the sanctum as the speech concluded. Trey's eyes began to react, and Rachel was in a full-on waterfall staring straight ahead at the leader of Israel. Pimi's eulogy was an epic speech by a man under extreme pressure from the far right for being too conciliatory to the Palestinians. The tribute to Omar would provoke more calls for his resignation. Today he didn't worry about reelection; he was honoring a friend and patriot. Tomorrow he would deal with the fallout.

Omar's coffin was draped with the Israeli flag before it left the synagogue on a colorfully decorated buckboard drawn by two beautiful black stallions. The funeral procession trotted along the street to the entrance of Kiryal Shaul Cemetery with over a hundred mourners walking in tow. The hearse-carriage came to a stop in front of Omar's gravesite. The military pallbearers carried the coffin to a platform positioned next to the grave. Trey stood with the family scanning the crowd for Buji Stahl. He spotted him standing with a fat Israeli in a business suit and a Hasidic Jew. Trey intuited the presence of his father. An elbow from Rachel confirmed his fear and elation as he studied the black-clad figure next to Buji.

The rabbi concluded his part of the graveside ceremony by shoveling three loads of dirt onto the coffin which was already lowered into the hole. He stuck the shovel in a pile of grave dirt, walked away and the next mourner took the handle repeating the gesture. Each member of the crowd took his or her turn until it was time for the family to say good-bye. Rachel and Trey held the shovel together. They dropped three loads of dirt into the grave and returned the shovel to the mound. Then the cloaked mystery Jew scooped his first offering, but before releasing the soil into the grave he paused to whisper a few words intended for the deceased. Rachel was close enough to catch the word "*ahch*" spoken in Hebrew. He was talking to his brother.

Chapter 42

Goran's arrest went badly. They picked him up four blocks from the hotel as he made his way to the car park. Three Mossad agents surrounded him on the sidewalk and pushed him into an alley, not wanting to draw attention from passing cars or pedestrians. Goran started to scream, "Help, somebody help me." The lead agent flashed his badge and pressed Goran's face against the building while another frisked him and applied handcuffs, cinching them as tightly as possible for maximum effect.

"You don't have the right to remain silent, and anything you say will be deemed a lie until we begin the real interrogation. Said interrogation could include but is not limited to sleep deprava-tion, water boarding, electric shock, removal of nails, and many other techniques that have been refined over the years. Once you have told us everything you know, we will turn you over to the U.S. authorities, who will begin the process all over again, albeit in a more genteel fashion. Do you understand your rights?"

This sarcastic rendition of Miranda gave the sanctimonious agent visible satisfaction. Weakness shown by the United States in recent years when it came to dealing with terrorists was a topic of keen interest within the Israeli intelligence community. America continually demonstrated absolute ignorance of and lack of com-mitment to the so-called "War on Terror", which they now referred to as "Overseas Contingency Operations," or "Responses to non-

National, Asymmetrical Threats." Many bad players found their way to the North American mainland as a result of U.S. impotence abroad. Israel had other ways of dealing with these dangers, and they would not let the United States or anyone else dictate how to run their war.

They took Donny to the Haifa Naval base. He was held in solitary confinement as an enemy combatant awaiting the arrival of Mossad interrogators. Once they arrived, Donny demanded the interrogation be conducted in his native tongue, Gaelic, by repeating, "*Amhain i an naisiunta de teanga de Eire,*" (Only in the national language of Ireland.) Donny's refusal to switch to English was the remaining hope he had of keeping information on the Committee of Ten secret. Under the Geneva Convention, "enemy combatants" had rights exceeding the terrorists who sent him on the mission, who in this case were sitting safely in Syria. Speaking Gaelic was a temporary distraction for the Israelis. Donny would eventually talk, but they would try it his way first.

Israel's diplomatic relationship with Ireland was in the toilet. The Israeli's had recently carried out the assassination of a senior Hamas military leader in Dubai. The Mossad agents who conducted the execution had used forged Irish and British passports. Ireland was outraged and had reacted swiftly by expelling three Israeli staff members from the Israeli embassy in Dublin.

Israel had the UK's most-wanted man in custody. The Israeli interrogators were in no rush to inform the British authorities about Donald Murphy. The Brits would find out soon enough. Handing Donny over was a delicate matter. The Israelis needed to extract as much information as possible from Murphy without interference from their weak-stomached counterparts at the UK Intelligence Service. Once Donny spilled his guts and the interview concluded, they would turn him over to the Arab-loving Brits.

Many people in Ireland considered Donny a hero for delaying Northern Ireland's permanent handover to the British. The crosscurrents of public opinion and diplomatic necessity created a conundrum for Israeli authorities, but first they needed to find someone who spoke Gaelic.

Fareed asked Samir to meet him in the tent where the Committee normally socialized. Samir thought he would be joining his old friend for a brotherly conversation over a cup of tea and a relaxing smoke from a hookah. As soon as Samir entered the enclosure he knew something was amiss. All of the cushions, hookahs, rugs, and trays had been removed. A single chair sat in the middle of the sandy floor surrounded by every torture device available at the camp. Thumbscrews, a rack, Tasers, and cattle prods were standard, but Fareed had added some medieval looking contraptions for the occasion. Among the more esoteric torture devices were "crocodile shearers." This device looked like a metal tube with handgrips. Opening the handles separated the tube revealing razor sharp teeth. When heated and closed around a man's penis it caused either mutilation or amputation of the organ depending on the operator's intent. Samir worried, *This can only mean one thing; the traitor has been discovered.*

Fareed entered the tent accompanied by three large men. One of the bruisers stayed at the tent's exit while Fareed and the other two made their way to Samir who had a puzzled look on his face.

"What's this all about, my brother? Have you caught the traitor?" Samir asked nervously.

"Yes, my brother, we have." Fareed looked at the two men, who then escorted Samir to the lone chair. They bound his arms behind his back and stood at attention on either side, awaiting further instructions.

"What's going on, Fareed? Why are you doing this?" asked Samir, aware his work with Mossad was no longer a secret.

"You betrayed Islam and Palestine, Samir, and now you must pay the price." Fareed tried to contain his emotions as he thought about what must come next.

"You're wrong, Fareed. I am not the traitor," Samir lied with the desperation of a man sentenced to death.

Fareed produced a single sheet of paper from Syrian intelligence that described information on the phony mission he had shared only with Samir. As Samir read the report from Fareed's outstretched hand he realized it was over. With hope of maintaining his innocence melting away, Samir's demeanor changed from a conscientious denier to an overt hater.

"Fareed, you are the one who betrays Islam. Peaceful Muslims everywhere are being harmed by your extremist views and actions. Good Arabs all over the world pay the price daily for your deeds by being ostracized from modern society." Fareed slapped Samir across the face at the suggestion that somehow Fareed and the Council of Ten were the problem.

Unfazed by the blow, Samir went on, "You deny your people the opportunity to succeed in the real world so you can satisfy your own sick ambitions." Samir's eyes locked onto Fareed's. Blood trickled from the corner of his mouth as the two thugs stood silently over the chair awaiting instructions.

The hatred can be clearly seen in his eyes, thought Fareed. *How could this happen? I've loved Samir since childhood and today I must end his life. Oh Allah, give me the strength to do what I must. Jerusalem awaited our joyous return as brothers in arms, but we are brothers no more.*

"Fuck you, Fareed!" shouted Samir. His anger had increased to a boiling point. One of the two men jammed a headscarf into Samir's mouth to stop his tirade. Samir bit the finger of his captor, causing the back of the man's free hand to land another ferocious blow on the side of Samir's head.

Momentarily dazed, Samir regained his senses long enough to calculate what would come next. Terror raged through his body. Samir's bladder let go and a pool of yellow liquid formed in his seat. The torturers lifted the soiled Samir, still tied to the chair, and placed him directly in front of the crocodile shearers.

"I will tell you everything. Please don't do this. I will tell the truth, I promise. I know the identity of other Israeli agents in our ranks. Let me go, and I can lead you to them." Another lie.

Samir had nothing to bargain with except falsehoods. The case was closed, Fareed had adjudged him guilty, and whatever Samir said would not change his sentence.

The crocodile shearers were placed in the fire. As the metal shearers began to glow white hot, an attendant ripped open Samir's outer garment exposing his genitalia.

Samir now understood that no interrogation would be forthcoming.

CIA Director of Intelligence Mark Manning picked up the "Israeli Hotline", an encrypted phone line securely linking Langley with Mossad Headquarters.

"Mark Manning," was his greeting to the caller he knew to be the Deputy Director of Mossad, Jamie Sachs.

"Mark, Jamie here. Look, we have a big problem. Your man Frankfurter works for Syrian intelligence. You should get over here ASAP before my people do something stupid. My field agents are really upset that the identities of undercover operatives have been compromised."

"I'll arrange a plane and be there in the morning. Where is Frankfurter now?" asked Manning, horrified at the news.

"We transferred him to Ofer Military Base where there is a maximum security prison and specially trained interrogators. I'm not sure how long I can delay questioning. We're losing time as we speak, but out of respect to our relationship, I wanted to alert you to the situation. Please come quickly." Sachs emphasized the "quickly" part. His men were chomping at the bit to get their hands on this turncoat.

"I'll be there as soon as I can, tomorrow morning at the latest," responded the irate director.

He instructed his assistant to contact CIA Flight Command who alerted the pilots to begin fueling the agency's Gulfstream G550 for a trip to Israel. The specially adapted version of the Gulfstream V was capable of flying non-stop to Israel in ten hours or less, depending on the winds at altitude. He would be at the Ofer Military Base first thing in the morning. If the interrogators didn't kill that two-faced bastard, he thought he might do it himself.

Chapter 43

Trey and Rachel followed the man whom they thought was Trey's father back to the parking lot at the synagogue. The long procession of people leaving the cemetery included many Hasidic Jews in their full-length *bekishes* and black fedoras. Trey and Rachel tried to keep up with a man only to find he was the wrong person once they reached the cars.

Willy sensed Trey and Rachel following him after clearing the cemetery gates. He quietly slipped out of the crowd. He did not want to be confronted by his supposed son at Omar's funeral. Even though he trusted Buji's judgment, Willy was skeptical the young man was his offspring.

Yussi, Buji, and Willy had a meeting scheduled with Dr. Kohen. Yussi was still peeved at Ari about the Saudi King and the premature release of his medical condition to the media. He arranged for the meeting at his mistresses' condominium. Each day one of Fischer Scientific's surveillance teams swept the condominium for listening devices. The property had been cleared just an hour before, after the cleaning lady completed her daily chores.

Ziva delivered Ari to the front door of the building and parked the Mercedes in a visitor's space. Ari entered and went directly to the twenty-second floor where the men waited. Once inside, Yussi introduced Ari to Willy. All four men were in the same room for the first time, and the power of the assembly was palpable. Each man was a formidable defender of Israel in his own right, their methods different, but the goals the same. Together, they represented a force for change rarely amassed in one place; all four appreciated the responsibility they had for the fate of their country.

"Dr. Kohen, why did you release the information about the King?" asked Yussi with a fierceness contradicting the cordial introduction just moments before.

"I had no choice. The King's health deteriorated faster than anticipated. In a matter of days, the Saudis would have hospitalized him with a diagnosis of a heart ailment or something less incriminating. At least his true condition is on the record and the Saudi's are reacting to the news reports rather than making them." Ari concluded the statement with a stare just as icy as the one he received from Yussi. He had righteously killed the diamond Jew in New York, and the same fate might befall this fat fuck if he didn't back off.

Willy intervened, breaking the tension, "What other diseases have you discovered, Doctor?"

"The tests uncovered a few other pathologies and genetic conditions. I think its best the Saudi disclosure runs its course before we introduce any more." Ari did not want to unveil additional diagnoses at this time.

"Doctor, there seems to be a disconnect. If we are going to work together, we require full disclosure, no secrets." Willy paused and then asked forcefully, "What are the other medical conditions?"

"I can't go into that right now because there are more important things to discuss," Ari stated, angling to move on to the next topic.

Willy did not let go. "Look here, you little shit. I've known scientists like you who think they are God's gift to Israel. You will answer our questions and we will decide what's important."

"I'm sorry if you think I'm being evasive, but I thought you might be more interested in information on the ethnically targeted bioweapon I've developed," Ari countered with a hint of sarcasm hoping the conversation would turn to the bio-bullet.

"You're building what?" Willy had already forgotten about the illnesses.

Yussi interrupted and said, "Dr. Kohen is attempting to construct a weapon which can be programmed to kill specific individuals based on their genetic makeup."

"How the hell can you do that without killing everyone else?" Buji asked, knowing the limitations of past Israeli attempts to engineer a similar weapon.

"I've discovered genetic correlations specific to individuals," answered Ari. "For example, these might be mutations uniquely found in a child and not in the parent. Most genetic material is passed unchanged from one generation to the next, but about fifteen percent of our genes can 'jump' from one part of our DNA strand to another. Most of these jumping genes, which are known as 'transposons,' reinsert themselves into a new stretch of DNA and just sit there. However, a small portion of these relocated genes can be switched on by signals from other genes causing the production of malicious proteins." Ari paused to let the men digest the information.

"I admit I was skeptical when I first heard about Dr. Kohen's work. Subsequently, I learned from knowledgeable third parties that what he says is possible, but has never been done successfully," Yussi interjected in support of Ari's introduction.

The men looked silently at Ari indicating he should continue with his presentation.

"These signature mutations are key to attacking an individual with a targeted bioweapon. Genes are protein factories. Protein regulates proper human physiology by instructing the organs to function in specific ways. In turn, genes infected with a virus can be designed to produce malicious protein that only harms the intended subject. This will enable us to infect the surrounding environment of the targeted individual without fear of collateral damage." Ari punctuated the last phrase, leaned back in his chair and folded his arms across his chest. He maintained a serious demeanor as he waited for questions and comments. The other three men sat in disbelief trying to sort through all of the scientific gobbledygook they had just heard.

"Let me get this straight. You're able to specify targets based on their DNA and kill only that person using some kind of bio-weapon," Buji said incredulously.

"Yes," was Ari's curt response.

Willy became very interested. To his knowledge, all attempts to construct a genetic bioweapon had failed because the death radius too large.

"Are you saying you can deliver this dosage, or material using water or air without killing everyone who's exposed?" asked Willy.

"Yes, close relatives might get flu-like symptoms, but they'll recover in twenty-four hours. The marked man will die within a few days. Three days is the minimum time required for the malicious protein producing agent to replicate itself in the DNA and kill the quarry," responded Ari with the pride in his discovery evident on his face.

"Have you been able to isolate genes from the Conference of King's samples?" Willy became commander of the questioning.

"I have three subjects already, and I'm working on four more." Ari waited for the question he knew would come next.

"Who are they?" asked Willy

"The President of Iran, the President of Syria, and the Chairman of the Hamas Political Bureau," he slowly enunciated the titles of their prey. Ari selected these samples to work on first, knowing they would inspire his Israeli coconspirators.

"So you're saying we can eliminate these terrorists without a traditional bullet or bomb?" Willy remained hot on this trail and unlikely to get distracted once he learned the identity of the initial targets.

"Correct," responded Ari. "Delivery of the lethal dose in the proximity of the intended target will infect only that person."

"Doctor, you'll forgive me if I'm unconvinced, but to my knowledge no one has succeeded in doing this before. What is the margin of error in your professional opinion?" asked Yussi, concerned about what might go wrong.

"The main risk is that the person delivering the dosage will be caught with the material before releasing it," Ari responded, faking concern about the human rather than scientific elements of the plan.

"You let us worry about the delivery. Tell me, how can you be sure your genetic formula won't have any adverse effects? Could this material infect the environment in any other way?" Fischer Scientific had a lot on the line if the mission failed and the Israeli government discovered Yussi's involvement.

"The compound is benign to everyone except the individual for whom it was formulated. Human DNA doesn't enter the genome of nonhumans, therefore infecting something or someone besides the target is not a risk," Ari said, not backing down and refusing to show any sign of weakness.

"What about the Palestinian president?" asked Willy, looking to rid the region of his nemesis. As the head of the PLO, he had inherited the responsibility for Eva's murder.

"Next on my list, sir," Ari responded respectfully.

"Good, now if you'll excuse us, Dr. Kohen, we need to discuss many things before we agree to your proposal. We'll be in touch with our decision," Yussi said as he rose from his chair.

Ari stood up and said, "Gentlemen, thank you for your time today. DNA science presents us with unique alternatives to traditional warfare. I hope you will embrace these advancements for the benefit of Israel." Ari shook hands with the three men and exited the condo.

Yussi, Buji, and Willy discussed the shit-storm they could create if Kohen's weapon did what he said. They considered the fallout from assassinating Arab leaders and the effect on Israel. Removing these despots would further empower the oppressed citizens of those countries. As the secret police and military struggled to contain the fallout from democracy movements sweeping their countries, the death of their leaders would throw them into tailspins.

The response to quell internal uprisings would take the focus off Israel and create openings easily exploited by the Jews.

If death came as Ari claimed, silently and slowly over a period of days, the Arabs would point fingers at one another. Sunnis would blame Shiites and vice versa. Israel could add fuel to the fire by planting evidence of tribal involvement at the time of the assassinations. Arabs would be fighting Arabs. The Muslim world would be too concerned about their internal leadership structures to worry about Israel for a period of time; maybe enough time for Israel to also neuter Hamas and decapitate a weakened Hezbollah.

Eventually, Israel would be implicated in the murders by Muslim media whores who made up stories about Zionist plots. Whenever an Arab gets shot or a Christian blown up, conspiracy theorists find a way to blame the Jews. Until recently, Arab claims of Zionist terrorism had been ignored by the West as biased and lacking evidence. Israel's staunchest allies were now referring to the "occupation" and "human rights violations" when speaking of displaced Palestinians and dead Arabs. Israel would claim its innocence or be silent on the matter.

"What should we do?" asked Buji who had been quiet during most of the back and forth.

"I think we have to go with Kohen and believe in the science," said Willy. "If he doesn't do this with us, then he will find someone else, or he will go it alone. We need to control this thing and keep an eye on this scientist."

"I don't know," responded Yussi, still mulling over the consequences if the plan failed.

"Yussi, Israel is surrounded by countries refusing to recognize its right to exist. Everyday their cause is emboldened by claims of Israeli occupation and racism. Hezbollah controls the Lebanese Parliament. Our treaty with Egypt is under review by a new military government and Iran is butt-fucking Turkey using its gold reserves as a lubricant. The old paradigms won't work anymore. This new science can redefine warfare, and we need to be in control of how and when the technology is used," Willy professed, hoping to seal the deal.

"I agree with Willy," said Buji. "If nothing else, we will get a chance to kill some of the top Arab goat-fuckers."

The three patriots discussed these and other scenarios. The plan to infiltrate their enemy's inner sanctum and kill the three leaders would be finalized over the next couple of days. As the other two men continued talking, Willy was thinking, *Who should I kill first?*

"Willy, what are you smiling about?" asked Buji.

"Oh...nothing."

"I'll contact Dr. Kohen and arrange another meeting. He will need to be monitored closely in the near term and eliminated once the mission is completed. We don't want any lose ends implicating us down the road," Yussi concluded with the steely glare of a man who had an unyieldingly loyalty to his own self-preservation.

Back at Zach's house, Rachel and Trey waited patiently for Willy to arrive. Day turned to night, and he never appeared.

Trey started getting anxious, and Rachel tried her best to redirect his emotions. "You should focus on mourning Omar and supporting your cousin Zach. Your father will show up because he is duty bound. He will be here; I know it."

Trey realized she was right. He had made it thirty-seven years without a father. He could wait a few more hours. Rachel left to help Milcah with the food, and Trey went to sit with Zach, who perched on a stool in the middle of the living room.

"Zach, what a lovely service. Omar was an incredible man," he said, placing his hand on Zach's shoulder.

Zach considered Trey with tired eyes. "Thanks for being here with me and the family. Omar was very fond of you. He always anticipated your visits with such delight."

"Me too. Omar could be very entertaining. The stories about his childhood and my father might be as close as I ever come to knowing where I came from."

"Omar predicted his brother would return when he died and give you an opportunity to meet. He made me promise to do whatever was necessary to make that happen. This was his last wish and one I intend to honor." Zach inventoried the room hoping to see his uncle.

"I think we saw him at the cemetery. Rachel overheard him speaking into Omar's grave during the covering ceremony. We followed him after the service but lost him in the crowd. Thank you for your offer of help. I know you have more important things on your mind right now." With tears pooling in his eyes, Trey said, "I may never meet my father, but at least I've had the reward of meeting yours. I already miss that old curmudgeon."

Trey's concern for Zach's well-being was deeply felt. He used to think compassion was an emotion only experienced by new mothers and Buddhists. His expression of empathy gave Trey the sensation of belonging, being part of a real family, complete with all of the risks of emotional attachment.

Yussi received a call from one of his contacts at Mossad as the men left the condo. Mossad interrogators had run out of options and sought anyone fluent in Gaelic. They called Yussi, as a last resort, hoping someone at Fischer Scientific spoke the native tongue of Ireland.

"No one in my company speaks Gaelic," said Yussi loud enough for his two mates to hear.

"I do," Willy offered. He had learned the language from an Irish farmhand during summers in England. It was a proud language, charged with feeling and emotion. Willy still listened to Gaelic recordings and read the poetry to remind him of his days in the British Isles. He might be a little rusty, but with a few sentences under his belt he knew it would all come back.

"Wait, I think I have someone who can help," said Yussi, barely catching the caller before he hung up. He explained that one of his associates recently arrived in the country and spoke Gaelic. "We're in Tel Aviv and on the way. Give us about ninety minutes," Yussi concluded and hung up the phone.

Yussi informed the men of the plan while they walked to the parking garage to get into the SUV. They headed back to Haifa for an interview with the sole survivor of yesterday's boat incident. Willy was to conduct the interrogation under the direction of both Mossad and the IDF. Buji and Yussi would observe the proceedings from behind a one-way mirror in an adjoining room. Buji drove out of the lot and accelerated northwest out of town.

Chapter 44

The entire Mossad team was at Ofer Military Base in the Negev desert waiting for the CIA jet to land. They had placed Goran Frankfurter in a holding cell at the base. The Israeli agents were outraged and disgusted the CIA had compromised Israeli intelligence. They had enough to worry about from their own defectors and Arab-lovers without having to waste time questioning an American agent turned traitor. The Israelis suspected Goran had valuable knowledge on Syria's spying. The men filed away their grievances and focused on the upcoming interrogation.

"Sir, the Americans just landed. Shall I escort them into the building?" said the duty officer over the intercom.

"Yes, bring them into the reception area by the commander's office," said a frustrated Sachs.

Jamie Sachs looked forward to the meeting with this fuck-wad, the new CIA Director. The last meeting, prior to Manning's elevation to director, had not gone well. Manning had insisted Mossad's actions were getting reckless. He demanded any plans to attack common enemies be cleared through the CIA first. Manning had recited a list of Mossad's recent screw-ups and their effect on international relationships. Manning took advantage of a perceived weakness within Mossad to exert greater authority. Sachs had exploded at the suggestion and left the meeting in a huff. That encounter was the last time Sachs had been the same room with Manning, the U.S. country-clubbing spymaster.

Today the tables were turned. Mossad had done their job to perfection and the CIA had their tit in the wringer. Manning entered the reception area with two goons spiffed out in U.S. military garb at his side. The two principals exchanged an awkward greeting. Manning got right down to business. "I'm ready for you to bring the prisoner in so we may begin the interrogation."

"Not so fast, Manning," Sachs barked, interrupting the presumptuous prick from the CIA. "He's *our* prisoner, and it will be *our* interrogation. When we're finished, there will be plenty of time for you to question him, but for now you get to sit and watch. I called you out of respect for our countries' relationship, not for you to take over my investigation."

Resigned to Sachs' home-field advantage, Manning and his team sulked into a room adjoined to the grilling area by a one-way mirror. Goran entered the interrogation room in shackles. Two Israeli interrogators accompanied the prisoner; one sat directly across from him and the other moved about within the defectors peripheral vision. It was a standard ploy designed to intimidate the subject and keep him off guard. One man would ask a question, and before Goran could answer, the other would forcefully demand the truth. This went on for about thirty minutes as the cross-questioning softened up the treasonous scumbag.

Goran had no idea Manning and his team were watching when he blurted out, "I want a deal."

"You're not in any position to ask for a deal, Mr. Frankfurter. Answer our questions, and then we will determine what can be done to make life easier for you. Right now you are just a traitor. So tell me, who is your primary contact at Syrian intelligence?" probed the Mossad agent.

Goran tried to avoid giving up anything about his Syrian handler by saying, "I want a lawyer; you can't question me without legal counsel."

"You forfeited your right to legal counsel when you entered Israel. You are subject to the security laws of our country. I suggest you tell us everything right now or we will resort to other methods of extracting the information." The reference to torture was clear, and it got Goran's attention.

"I'm willing to become a double agent," Goran gushed. He begged for a resolution that would save his life and appease his captors.

The Israelis listened intently as Goran continued his plea. "I'll do whatever you want; I know names, places, and operations."

"Why should we trust you, Frankfurter?" demanded the seated interrogator.

"I became a Syrian spy for the money and to get back at the CIA. I'm a Jew by birth. My loyalty was never with the Syrians, just to the cash." Goran tried to position himself as a CIA-hater, Jewish sympathizer, but he was just a duplicitous schmuck.

"We find that hard to believe based on the information you sent to Syrian intelligence from the hotel business center. Only you and your Syrian friends know the exact damage you've caused. What makes you think becoming a double agent would work anyway?" asked the Israeli who was standing behind Goran.

"No one outside Mossad and the CIA knows that I've been captured. My cover is still intact, and as far as the Syrians know, I still work for them. You would be wise to use me as a double agent, because I'm your best chance to get inside Syrian intelligence," responded Goran, with his elbows on the table and chin resting casually on his hands. "That's what I've got, now let's do a deal."

In the adjacent room, Manning turned to Sachs and said, "No way I'm letting him become a double agent. It would be ridiculous to think that he would honor any agreement. This man is a traitor and should be dealt with accordingly."

"It's not your call, Manning. I think we might be able to work with this guy," Sachs said, turning the knife. His guest had no leverage. Manning thought a call to the President might be necessary.

Samir's penis was attached to a specially prepared asbestos cord. His member was stretched until it appeared more like a deformed earthworm than a male body part. A hooded attendant fed the cord through the tubular shearers and led the tooth-laden device down the line to the highly sensitive flesh. Samir screamed in anticipation of the pain. Everyone in the camp heard his cries. The medieval apparatus tightened slowly around his manhood and Samir's screams turned into horrific pleas for mercy. Then silence; Samir passed out from the shock of his mutilation.

His comatose body was laid in the catapelta press, where he would be slowly crushed to death between two wooden planks. They repeatedly roused him with splashes of water so he could witness the process; death came painfully slow. Samir's instincts tried to override a reasoning brain that wanted to die, but he eventually begged for them to finish it. Fareed made sure the humiliation of his death equaled the severity of his transgressions and that the rest of the camp understood the consequences of being a Jew-lover.

Willy, Yussi, and Buji were on the way to Haifa Naval Base. During the hour and a half drive from Tel Aviv, the men discussed the upcoming mission. The three warriors savored the opportunity to work together on something that would certainly change the dynamics of the conflict.

Arriving at the Haifa Naval Base, they parked the SUV in a visitor's space and entered the building through the main lobby. After being greeted by the Naval Commodore in charge of the base he led the men into a conference room. They were introduced to a Mossad agent and an IDF officer who would jointly monitor the interview of Donald Murphy.

Willy left the room with the two Israeli officers for a briefing. He would learn everything about the events at sea and what was recovered from the failed mission. Meanwhile, a naval security guard led Donny into the interrogation room and handcuffed him to the metal table that was bolted to the floor. Buji immediately recognized Donny's resemblance to the man who came to his university office in search of Willy. Buji studied the POW and concluded the two men looked exactly alike. It was probably a fluke, but Willy needed to be alerted before the interrogation began.

"I'll be right back," Buji said to Yussi as he quickly left. He found Willy down the hall in a conference room with the door open.

"Excuse me, gentlemen. I need a few words in private with Mr. Cohen," Buji said with a smile not wanting to cause any alarm.

Once the agents cleared out, Buji said, "Willy, they just brought the prisoner into the interrogation room. It's probably nothing to worry about, but Donald Murphy looks just like the young man who claims to be your son, Trey Cowens."

"What?" responded Willy, as shocked at the connection as Buji.

"I know it sounds crazy, but this Irishman could be the American's double."

"Thanks for the head's up, Buji. It's probably just a coincidence," said Willy confidently.

The Israelis returned to continue the briefing with Willy. Buji left and returned to the room where Yussi sat alone reading e-mail on his smart phone.

"Hey, I need a favor old man," said Buji, interrupting Yussi. "Can you get me some deep background on William 'Trey' Cowens, an American from New York who recently entered Israel on a U.S. passport. We need his place of birth, the names of the parents and whether he has any siblings."

"Sure, can do. Why do you need the information Buji?" asked Yussi in a brotherly way.

"I can't tell you right now, but trust me on this one. How long will it take?" Buji impatiently inquired.

"Access to basic birth records...in an hour or two," Yussi responded.

"We need to know as soon as you find out anything. Understood?"

"No problem. I'll get right on it," answered Yussi who trusted Buji's judgment implicitly. Yussi left with his smart phone already dialing the Fischer Scientific office.

Willy entered the room with Buji watching from beyond the glass. Buji was right; Murphy appeared to be the double of the young man he saw at Omar's funeral. Willy purged those thoughts from his mind as he focused on the job at hand.

"*Cé na fok a bhfuil tú?*" (Who the fuck are you?), asked Donny in character, not knowing if his interrogator spoke Gaelic.

"*Raibh mé in ann a bheith do chara nó do namhaid is fearr is measa; tá sé de dhualgas ort.*" (I could be your best friend or your worst enemy; it is up to you), Willy responded in their common language.

"Impressive language skills, Mr. Mossad. Why should I talk to you?" Donny retorted in the Irish tongue.

"There's talking and then there's torture. I suggest you select the former because the later could derail any plans you might have to start a family. If you cooperate, I'll do what I can to help you. However, if you insist on playing the tough guy, my time's over and the professional interrogators will begin turning the screws."

"As an Irish national, I have rights. The Geneva Convention states that enemy combatants must be afforded the same rights as a prisoner of war." Donny was proud of his command of the facts. He had studied international military history his entire adult life and considered himself an expert.

"The UN Mercenary Convention clarified the Geneva Convention with regard to Unlawful Enemy Combatants. You must have missed that day in history class," Willy retorted as he got to the heart of the matter.

"Bullshit, I know the law. You're wrong, and you're an asshole."

Keeping his cool, Willy said, "You'll be interrogated as an Unlawful Enemy Combatant and tried in a military court. If you cooperate, I'll see what I can do to get you preferential treatment."

"And what if don't cooperate?" Donny continued the tough-guy, terrorist act.

"The consequences would be dire, and I can't predict what will happen to you," responded Willy, ready to begin the questioning.

"Once the British find out I've been captured, they'll make you turn me over to them." The thought of being turned over to the Brits scared the hell out of Donny, but he tried to conceal his fear.

"Even if Britain demands your return to stand trial for the murders they say you carried out, I don't think British-Israeli relations are in a place where we would jump to accommodate their request. You could spend the rest of your life in an Israeli prison awaiting trial. Many criminals wait their entire lives to be tried. Mortality rates in our prison system are double the norm, no surprise considering you're locked up with common murderers, international terrorists, modern day lepers, and crooked guards. Add squalid conditions to the equation and you have a breeding ground for prisoner-on-prisoner crime."

Willy waited for his words to sink in before beginning the questioning. He felt sorry for this young man, who appeared to be caught up in something much bigger than he bargained for.

Donny thought about Wolfe Tone, his capture and suicide in a British jail over two hundred years ago. He, like Tone, would not be afforded the rights of a prisoner of war. Since the day Trey told Donny they were related to the famous Irishman, Donny had reflected on his own life as an Irish terrorist. Was he going to jail as a fulfillment of his destiny to repeat the acts of his famous forefather?

Donny broke the silence. "They've got my girlfriend. The Syrians have Grace, and they'll kill her once they know of my capture."

"News of your capture could be accompanied by reports you are uncooperative and refused to disclose any intelligence." Willy hoped to loosen up his subject by appearing humane. "If you cooperate, I can try to get a prisoner exchange arranged for Grace's release. I can't guarantee anything, but it's worked in the past."

The two men sat staring at one another, both suspecting a connection deeper than interrogator and prisoner. Willy couldn't qualify the intuition, but the Irishman's likeness to the young man claiming to be his son was remarkable.

"I want to make a deal," said Donny. "But before I do, tell me who you are and why I should trust that you have the authority to grant me any of my demands?"

"You're in no position to be speaking of demands, and believe me, you should be grateful you got me and not one of those young officers." Willy responded with authority, knowing the men in question, who were listening, did not understand Gaelic.

"Look, I have information of value to Mossad and all I want in return is to get Grace out of Syria. If I can't get some assurance you'll try to rescue her, then you may as well end this right now because she's as good as dead," said Donny, who couldn't live with the grief of loosing her.

"We can have operatives try to locate her immediately. An aerial-drone can be dispatched to the area of the C10 camp. Once you give me the exact location, the aircraft will begin relaying high-resolution images, enabling us to see people clearly from 15,000 feet. If we can determine her exact location at the complex, our people will do the rest."

Willy could tell his bluff worked by the look on Donny's face. He blew the dust off his interrogation skills and began by saying, "You've got to speak English from now on."

Donny agreed and began to detail everything about the C10, Fareed, Syrian Intelligence, and the mission to assassinate the lead Israeli and U.S. peace negotiators plus the head of Fatah. He described the mission precisely and did not withhold any information.

When they finished, Donny again implored his captor to get Grace out of Syria. Donny offered to trade himself for Grace. Willy assured him the Syrians would prefer the return of a high-level operative held in an Israeli prison.

A recording of the English portion of the confession was transcribed for distribution to the IDF and Mossad. Willy translated the Gaelic on his way back to Tel Aviv. There was a lot of actionable information disclosed in Donny's confession, especially the location of the C10 camp and their collaborators in Southern Lebanon. The equipment used in the attack had been traced back to Iran. The guns, the boat, the rebreathers, the wetsuits, and other hardware were either manufactured in Iran or imported for delivery to Syria. Iran's international proxy army, Hezbollah, constituted one of the greatest threats to Israeli sovereignty and Donny's disclosures would assist Israel in balancing the threat on their northern border.

Chapter 45

Yussi, Willy, and Buji sat in an unlit, back booth at their favorite bar. On the drive back to Tel Aviv from Haifa, Yussi received confirmation of Trey's identity through New York birth records. Mary Stuart Cowens had twin boys on March 12, 1974.

They had talked about Willy's predicament for a little more than an hour. Willy was consumed by thoughts of Omar's death and the appearance of his twin sons. Until today, Willy had no children. Now he had two sons who were grown men, one a successful American banker and the other an Irish terrorist.

"What should I do? You are my best friends in the world; help me think through this mess," Willy said in an uncharacteristic moment of weakness.

"Get a grip," said Yussi, with the force only a friend can command. "If they're your sons, which by all indications they are, you've got to make an effort to know them. How many childless men are gifted a son this late in life? And you get two. You've got to go for it Willy."

Slamming his full drink on the table, Willy said, "Take me to Zach's house. I need to be with my family and meet my other son."

The men drove in silence to Willy's nephew's house. Willy recalled the day he left Mary. Could she have been pregnant the day of his callous departure?

William Joseph Cowens left for work on June 20, 1973, knowing he would never return to Buffalo or to Mary. It was difficult for him to go, but the time came when his Mossad *katsa* handler, an Israeli field officer known only as Buji, contacted him. Since his training and placement in deep cover, Willy had met his handler on only one previous occasion. They met in D.C. as part of the continuing education he received every three months. Buji had warned Willy that when the call came for him to become an active *kidon* assassin, he had to drop everything immediately and engage the mission plan. The call came, and Willy was ready.

He left work for lunch just like any other day, but it would be his last in Buffalo. His instructions directed him to the corner of Bush and Hudson Streets, where he deposited his car in the parking lot of a senior citizen's center. A Mossad *sayan,* assistant to the *katsa,* met him in a black Chevy Suburban. The *sayan* driver provided him with a Canadian passport, work clothes, and hardhat. They crossed into Canada over the Peace Bridge, which spanned the Niagara River, and cruised up to a Canadian Custom's checkpoint. Antennae, satellite dishes, bomb smelling sensors, and cameras crowded the roof and lane dividers as they approached the custom agent's booth.

Willy had become Conan "Mac" McGregor, a first generation Canadian, son of Lily and Ailean McGregor from Glasgow, Scotland. Willy's ability to take on the form and demeanor of this new character was magical. He transformed into Mac McGregor from the moment he learned his cover identity, replacing his Irish lilt with a Scottish tilt.

The customs agent asked why they were in the United States, how long they had been away, and where they were headed.

The *sayan* did the talking until the agent asked Willy a direct question. "Mr. McGregor, what kind of work do you do?"

"I'm a mason," responded Willy in his newly assumed accent.

"You're not from Canada, are you?" the agent fired back in an accusatory way.

"Well, I'm from New Brunswick. My parents came from Scotland originally," he responded with confidence.

After a thorough study of the documents, the agent returned their passports and waved them through. Willy, out of sorts from the three-minute encounter, concealed his trepidation as they drove toward Queen Elizabeth Way. This first undercover engagement with foreign law enforcement gave him a feeling of fear and elation all at once. He had officially entered the shadow world of international espionage and was on his way to avenging Eva's murder. Willy puffed up his chest and spread his knees in a display of manpower-comfort in the passenger seat. His body language told the driver he was in charge.

Once they reached cruising speed and well out of sight of border control, the *sayan* handed Willy an envelope, which he instructed him to open and read. It contained information on the next step of the mission, just enough to get Willy to a meeting with his *katsa* in Montreal. After memorizing the instructions, Willy burned the note in the ashtray, filling the car with white smoke. He rolled down the windows, the fog cleared, and he tossed out the contents of the ashtray. Willy had his initial instructions, but he still had no idea about the specifics of the mission. He would find out more tonight in "La Belle Ville."

The nameless driver and Willy settled in for a six-hour drive. The *sayan* hadn't said one word since he spoke to the customs agent. Willy tried to figure out his accent from the brief dialogue. He appeared to be a normal North American in his mid-thirties, a little overweight and totally unremarkable, anyone's son.

Willy's thoughts turned to Mary. He had left her that morning sleeping in their bed in Buffalo. He abandoned her without a word, not so much as a "good-bye" or "have a nice life." He was conflicted about the choices he had made. Then he remembered Eva and the parts of her the police found. Her hand attached to the violin she so cherished, her foot blown off her leg still in the shoe he had purchased for her the day before the concert, and her bloody mess of a head all still haunted him. The sacrifices of these last years would be worth all the deceit and subterfuge if he got a chance to exact revenge for Eva's brutal murder.

Mossad is an extension of the Israeli government and operates with the full knowledge of the Prime Minister. Executions and kidnappings require agreement from the PM. The Director of Mossad periodically presents a list of targets to the PM for final approval. Only the two officials are aware of the full roster; the file grew substantially following the Olympic Massacre in Germany.

"Operation Wrath of God" was conceived in the wake of the Munich debacle. The PLO terrorists who had been killed or captured—in the Olympic Village and at the airport—were just the tip of the iceberg. The Arabs who had a hand in the planning and supporting their fanatical acts would be hunted down and executed.

But as always, the Mossad would not rush into action. The Israeli intelligence agency created a profile on terrorists from information methodically collected by their minions. Each of these radical offenders would be followed for months. Eating habits and sexual proclivities were included in a long list of observable traits. They eventually uncovered predictable patterns of behavior. A strategy to intercept and kill the person would be formulated using this data. Once approved by the director and Prime Minister, the operational responsibility passed to a *katsa* handler who contacted a *kidon* assassin. The plan consisted of three main parts: acquisition of the target, execution (methods recommended but ultimately left to the *kidon*'s discretion), and extraction to a safe house.

Trying to act cool and collected, Willy shut his eyes as the driver cued up some music on the radio. "Let It Be" by the Beatles became a peaceful distraction.

Willy entered Zach's home, still thinking about the day he left Mary. He was dressed in black street clothes, only keeping the fedora from his Hasid costume. He was greeted by one of Milcah's sisters upon entering the house. She took his hat and directed him to where Zach sat on a stool in the great room. The expansive and modern home had French doors leading to a screened porch and patio. Excusing himself from the seating area, Zach approached the newcomer who seemed strangely familiar.

Here goes nothing, Willy thought, shedding his assumed Hasid identity. "I'm your Uncle William, Zach," Willy said extending his arms to embrace his nephew. Using his real name for first time in years was liberating. Willy had spent so much time underground, the simple act of honestly introducing himself gave him a jolt of pleasure.

"Thank you for coming. Omar missed you very much. I'm so glad you're here," Zach said, with a look of childlike surprise.

"I'm sorry I didn't get to visit him before he died. He loved you very much," responded Willy, wanting to keep the focus on Omar.

They spoke about Omar's last days and his passing. Then Zach said, "Uncle William, I have someone I want you to meet. Please come with me." Willy braced himself. He anticipated what would come next. Thoughts of having a son and leaving Mary had consumed Willy since seeing Trey at the funeral. He had interrogated his Irish son, and the time had come to face his American child.

Zach led Willy to his study on the other side of the house. They entered a room together. Books filled the walls, oriental rugs covered the floor, and an antique partner-desk anchored the center of the space. A leather couch and two overstuffed armchairs that surrounded a polished teakwood coffee table sat off to the side.

Trey was perched behind the desk checking his e-mail when Zach and Willy entered the study. He looked up and saw his father in person for the first time without the trappings of a Hasidic Jew. Their eyes met in confused recognition.

"Uncle William, I would like to introduce you to Trey Cowens. Trey and I met as a result of participation in a DNA ancestry project." The two men studied each other from an adequate distance. Neither of them spoke.

Sensing the need to circumvent the awkward silence, Zach continued, "We both contributed our paternal DNA to a public database. We found each other when the system matched us as immediate relatives. Trey came to Israel in search of information about his father's family, and found me." Both men stared at Zach as he continued to state the obvious.

Studying Willy's reaction, Zach added, "Trey had an opportunity to meet Omar on numerous occasions over the last month. Dad confirmed, separate and apart from the DNA match, Trey was his nephew and my cousin. Which leaves only one explanation."

Zach gave a knowing smile as he turned and left the room.

Trey came around from behind the desk and took a seat in one of the armchairs. Willy sat opposite Trey, a full coffee-table-length away. The light from the window behind Trey gave his figure an iridescent halo, a fitting effect for the son of the prodigal Israeli *kidon.* Still, no one spoke. The significance of the moment filled the room. Time froze for the father and son.

"How are you?" Willy asked in a nervous voice with his hands trembling.

"Fine," responded Trey bluntly, concealing all emotion.

"So you had a chance to meet Omar. He was an incredible man and a fierce defender of Israel," said Willy trying to inspire a conversation. "Both of us fought for the same cause, but in different ways."

Trey nodded his head to confirm his relationship with Omar but didn't say a word. Trey studied Willy with his arms crossed on his chest. His unblinking glare focused on Willy's whole form. Willy's outline became blurry, making him appear like an apparition that floated momentarily off the chair. He attempted to manage the fear with his brain but his heart pounded out of his chest.

"How's your mother?" asked Willy, unaware of her death almost four decades earlier.

Trey didn't answer; he just continued to stare. Willy became uncomfortable with Trey's silence. Willy had to remember this was not a mission. He didn't need to play a role or assume a false identity. He needed to be a father for the first time in his life.

"You've been through a lot since I left. I wouldn't blame you if you wanted me to leave and never see me again. But you're the one who came looking for me," concluded Willy, trying to sort through the emotional situation rationally.

Willy thought he had seen every look of fear and hatred imaginable as a *kidon* assassin. Once in the presence of a Mossad hit man, most marked men begged for their lives or began insulting Israel. Trey's demeanor differed from anything he had experienced; his face was transfixed in an emotionless gaze with his defense mechanisms on high alert.

"She died in 1974 giving birth to my brother and me," said Trey breaking his lengthy silence.

"I'm sorry, Trey. I had no idea," said Willy, shocked that Mary had passed away.

"Where did you go?" asked Trey, getting down to business.

"I'm sorry, I can't tell you," responded Willy, reluctant to disclose anything about the mission.

Trey continued to stare without responding to Willy's reticence. He hoped his father was uncomfortable, although it would do little to compensate Trey for a sterile childhood.

"She didn't tell me she was pregnant before I left," said Willy, not wanting to miss the opportunity to set the record straight. "If she had, I promise you things would have turned out differently. I might have stayed, but truthfully I can't say for sure." Willy sat back in his chair, paused to collect his thoughts, and continued in a measured tone. "I would've been responsible as your father, absentee if necessary. I would have been part of your life in some way. Son, please give me a chance to show you I can be someone important in your adult life, even if I wasn't able to be there for you as a child."

The word *son* echoed in Trey's mind. He had never heard that word in a sentence from anyone to whom he was biologically related. That single word began to dismantle Trey's anger and he started to accept this man as his father for the first time.

"What do you mean you didn't know she was pregnant? I assume you participated in the act that got her that way." Trey needed to know the truth, even if it hurt to relive the details of his mother's life before she died.

"We had marital problems, fighting all the time, not on the same page. I worked for your grandfather and wasn't happy with my job. As young adults will do, we had makeup sex often to relieve the stress. We tried to make the relationship work. I assume your mother got pregnant and for whatever reason didn't tell me before they called me into service." Willy wished he hadn't referred to makeup sex, the last thing a child wants to hear about his parents.

"'Called into service.' What the hell does that even mean?" Trey tried to contain his anger.

Willy considered the oath he had taken as a Mossad *kidon* not to disclose information on covert operations to anyone outside the organization. The current situation dictated he make an exception to that pledge.

"My marriage to your mother was part of a deep cover operation for the Mossad." Willy hesitated, overcoming his programmed reluctance to discuss the subject. "I was placed in the United States and asked to integrate into American society until the agency needed my services. I got the call in October 1973, and I left your mom and the United States." This was more information than Willy wanted to disclose, but the stakes were high.

"So you packed your bags and took off on some harebrained mission to save the world. How'd that work out for you?" Trey asked, reverting to a sarcastic stare.

"You can make fun of me if you want, but that's the truth. We can argue about how I handled the situation, but I had a job to do, and I did it," Willy said, holding his ground.

"What about your responsibilities as a husband?" Trey's face reddened as he considered his father's abandoned commitments. "Even if you didn't know about the pregnancy, didn't you have an obligation to tell her you were leaving? Even if the marriage was on the rocks, you still had a moral or ethical duty to tell her you were going."

"I couldn't, because it would have put her life in danger. It was not that easy, Trey. My obligation was to Israel. I made that decision when I came to the United States, and when it was time to leave, I had to disappear without a trace."

"Her life was in danger anyway. She died giving birth to your children, and she never had a chance to know her sons." Tears welled up in Trey's eyes as he thought about the mother he never had a chance to meet.

The intensity of Trey's pain was undeniable. Willy recognized the suffering etched onto his face. Trained to ignore the emotional cues of his enemies, he could skillfully override all human sentiment if necessary. This capacity was a requirement of his work. Willy's inherent parenting skills had atrophied over time; stunted by years of solitary living and neglect. He needed to exercise these emotional muscles or risk losing Trey. The time had come to plumb the depths of Trey's sadness in an honest and intense way. This was his flesh and blood. He decided to tell Trey everything about the mission that took him away. He needed to share his story with the people he hurt the most. Willy hoped his honesty would help him secure a future with his sons.

After being dropped off by his *sayan* driver at the Jacques Cartier Pier in Old Montreal on a beautiful, Canadian summer day in 1973, Willy took a taxi to 354 Rue Ducas and found his way to apartment number 404. As instructed in the first note, he found the key under the carpet at the end of the hall. The flat's living area was sparsely furnished with only a dining room table, four chairs, a love seat, and a TV. The bedrooms were just as spartan.

He tried to make himself comfortable by turning on the TV and sitting patiently in the love seat. As the minutes passed, his nerves ramped up in anticipation of his first *kidon* deployment. Moments later, he heard a key being inserted in the door, and without a knock, the door swung open. Buji was alone, carrying a bag of food Willy hoped was dinner.

"You made it," said Buji with a smile. "How was the trip? Any problems?"

"None, but I'm starved. I hope you have something for me in the bag."

"In fact I do. It's a local specialty called *poutine*. I've been craving some ever since I arrived in Quebec." Buji removed the contents from the grease-soaked bag, while asking, "Ever had any?"

"No, and it looks like road kill. What the hell is it?"

"It's lard-fried potatoes with curdled cheese and gravy. Have some."

Willy's hunger caused him to dig into the grease-enhanced mound of carbohydrates. The unique taste combination was more pleasing than he anticipated. He ate half of his portion before feeling the full mass of the congealed foodstuff in his stomach, causing him to stop. He waited for Buji to polish off his entire allotment before they spoke again.

A serious look came across Buji's face as he reached into his coat pocket and produced an envelope just like the one Willy had received from the *sayan* driver after crossing into Canada. Buji opened the envelope and removed the contents. He moved his chair next to Willy's so they could view the single sheet of paper together. They were all business.

Buji read the document aloud verbatim:

> *Ali Hassan Al-Husseini (a.k.a. Abu Hassan, a.k.a. Black Prince, a.k.a. Rayan Hariri) was the head of the Black September group that planned the Munich Massacre. He is a well-known Arab playboy who flaunts his family's wealth by driving expensive sports cars and throwing lavish parties in exotic locations. He obtained his education in France and the United States as an engineer. Al-Husseini was a very good student. His extremism can be traced to the death of his father at the hands of the Israeli Defense Forces somewhere north of Jaffa during the 1948 Arab-Israeli War. He returned to Syria and became involved with Yasser Arafat's Fatah organization, rising through the ranks in a short period of time. As the operations chief of the Black September terrorist group, he masterminded the Munich murders. Black September carried out his plan, which resulted*

in the death of eleven talented, young Jewish athletes at the Munich Olympics on September 5, 1972.

After the events in Germany, Al-Husseini surfaced in Paris, where he had facial reconstruction surgery and received constant protection from Arab handlers placed in Europe by Fatah. Full-color pictures of Abu Hassan before and after are attached. His features were dramatically changed, but he is still recognizable as the Black Prince by those familiar with his previous persona. He departed Paris when he realized Mossad was closing in on him.

Al-Husseini made his way to Casablanca where he boarded a Royal Air Maroc flight to Montreal, but not before a tracking device was inserted into his briefcase. Since his arrival in Montreal, a team of our communication technicians has easily tracked him. Abu Hassan currently lives in a monthly residence located at the Château Champlain Hotel.

His proclivities include beautiful women, expensive scotch whiskey, fast cars, an occasional snort of cocaine, and hatred of all things Israeli. He believes his facial surgery and relocation have given him a new life out of our spotlight, and he is free to act and behave as a newly arrived resident of Canada working for a French food company. Opportunities to acquire the subject will be many, but you must resist the temptation to execute him on sight. Study his daily habits and routines for months, if necessary, before formulating a plan to assassinate Abu Hassan.

The instructions ended; the rest would be up to Willy. He was visibly shocked by the identity of his target, while at the same time thrilled Abu Hassan was such a high level subject. He contemplated the many ways he could eliminate Abu Hassan. Poison, bombs, bullets, and knives were all worthy options. Willy would study his target with extra care and construct an execution plan that would cause both pain and humiliation.

"Any questions?" asked Buji.

"None for now," Willy responded confidently.

"The time *is* now, Willy. You're on your own until you call the *sayan* driver for your extraction. We've given you options for eliminating the target, but the situation will dictate what method to use. You have complete freedom to make those choices without fear of reprisal. Just be certain he is dead and the act cannot be immediately traced. Now, do you have any questions?" asked Buji.

"No, I'm ready," Willy replied in a firm, unwavering voice.

Willy's confidence inflated as he considered the days ahead. Assassinating Abu Hassan would not bring Eva back, but it would be the beginning of his quest to settle that score.

Willy continued, "And I will not let you or Mossad down. When the time is right, Abu Hassan will be dead."

Buji's face stretched in a wide smile as he stood to hug his compatriot. They embraced and concluded the hug with a kiss on both cheeks. Buji departed. Willy regained his composure from what was an emotional farewell by Mossad standards and moved to the window to view Buji's departure from the building. Buji was nowhere in sight, but what did he expect from a spook of his caliber? Willy reflected on his next move as he picked the key off the table and exited the building. He would scout the Montreal Underground and locate the entrance to Abu Hassan's building.

After a couple of hours together, Trey began to soften realizing it was best to listen without judging. The anger and sadness of being abandoned by his mother and father still haunted him, but he needed to file away his hostility and build a relationship with his only living parent.

Willy got out of his chair and moved to the corner of the couch right next to Trey. He placed his hand on Trey's arm and said, "I'm sorry, son."

Both men rose and embraced for a long time. They held each other as tightly as two humans can, not wanting to lose the connection of the moment. They were finally father and son, joined after many years through the science of DNA.

A knock on the study door, and Rachel entered. Seeing the two men in a soggy embrace, she walked over to the huddle and asked, "Is everything okay?"

Willy and Trey answered by parting their hug on one side, bringing Rachel into the scrum. The emotion of the moment caused Rachel to tear up. Willy's right hand rubbed Trey's bicep as if to verify his presence. The bulletproof *kidon* had met his match. Trey activated Willy's dormant heart in a way he never thought possible. The vacant space created by Eva's murder filled with an emerging love for his son.

Trey broke up the group hug by saying, "I have a twin brother. We were separated before we were two months old. We met for the first time in Ireland not long ago. Unfortunately, I don't know where he is right now. He left Ireland recently because of his involvement in a political situation."

"I know. We were introduced this morning in Haifa," said Willy in a mater of fact way.

Rachel covered her mouth and audibly gasped at Willy's response. Trey's reaction was more measured, but he was just as astounded as Rachel at Willy's revelation. They listened as Willy explained the situation with Donny and the failed raid on the Israeli coast.

Chapter 46

The Saturday following Omar's calling was a workday for Ari. Other Jews observed the Sabbath, but he used the "day of rest" to complete the assembly of the bio-bullet so it would be ready for delivery on Monday. Working on Saturday was a sacrilege to most faithful Jews, but Ari had a higher calling. The needs of his project superseded the dictates of his faith. Retuning a new temple to Jerusalem would assure Judaism's existence on the holiest of sites through the next millennium. He was convinced that without his intervention the destruction of his faith was all but certain.

Rachel had relented to meet with her brother at his home in Beit Jann rather than in Tel Aviv after a phone call the previous night. Ari said he had piles of work and needed to see his sister before she returned to the United States.

Trey was spending the day with his father. Rachel knew the two men needed some time alone. After almost forty years without any contact, they had a lot of ground to cover. She hoped they would seize the opportunity and find a way to become family.

Ari greeted Rachel in the drive as the Lincoln Town Car from the hotel came to a stop in front of his house. The driver opened the rear passenger door; Rachel swung her legs to the ground and stood to greet her brother. He looked like a mad scientist more than ever. With long grey-streaked hair, a week-old beard, and his ribcage showing through a tattered maroon T-shirt, Ari hugged his sister. He stunk like a stable hand after mucking out stalls on a hot summer day. The stench elicited a spontaneous comment from Rachel.

"Ari, you reek to high hell. What is going on with you? I can count your ribs through your T-shirt. When was the last time you ate? I'm making you a meal before we talk about anything." She walked by her brother and pushed her way into the house.

She went to the refrigerator where she found some old vegetables suitable for resurrection into a meal with rice and spices. But first she took some very ripe fruit, which included a black banana, and combined it with ice, yogurt, apple juice and protein powder in a blender to make a power shake. This would get Ari started.

"Here, take this into the bathroom with you. I'll prepare a meal while you're in the shower. For God's sake, Ari, you're a mess and the house is a wreck. I can't believe you've let yourself get this way." She was almost in tears as she listed his hygienic transgressions.

"My work..." was all he could get out of his mouth in defense of her accusations.

Rachel interrupted, "Your work will mean nothing if you're dead. Or is it your goal to become famous posthumously?"

"No, I'm losing weight so I look slimmer on television for the upcoming season of *Israel's Idol,*" joked Ari as he turned toward the bathroom and headed to the shower.

Ari suffered from a mania of the highest order. Professionally, Rachel knew all of the symptoms of full-blown mania, and Ari was a poster child for the condition. Ari's preoccupation with thoughts and plans caused him to neglect his physical needs. She had seen him go for a year or two as a completely normal and successful geneticist only to have his manic side erupt in outbursts of creative energy. Over the years, each event took Ari deeper into a delusional world of grandeur where he became suspicious of others, even his sister. Rachel would never give up on Ari even though all of her attempts to get him help in the past had been rebuffed.

Ari and Rachel sat down for a meal in a real home, as disheveled as it was, for the first time as brother and sister in over two years. Rachel remembered the last family meal they enjoyed together at their mother's house, one week before she suddenly died. The menu included brisket, *lokshen kugel*, *matza* ball soup, carrots, turnips, and an assortment of homemade strudel and cheesecake for dessert. Rachel's rice and veggies was a far cry from her mother's parting meal, but still a family dinner. Ari dug in as though he hadn't eaten in days, which probably wasn't far from the truth.

"Ari, you have to take better care of yourself. Your work isn't so important that you can let your heath suffer. Please promise you will try to do better. Do I need to move in here and be your maid, cook, shopper, and nanny?" she said, tongue in cheek, but with the force only a sister can command.

"You're right. I'll do better. Things will slow down shortly, and I plan to take a break from the lab soon." He asked for a second helping. Ari always liked when his sister cooked for him. She could make road-kill into a three-star meal by adding a little garlic, crushed red peppers, and onions. He consumed seconds and wiped his mouth on his shirtsleeve.

"Not the sleeve. You're not an animal, Ari." Her frustration grew, but she bit her tongue out of love. "Look, there are cloth napkins right next to your plate. What am I going to do with you?"

Piling the dishes into the sink, they retired to the back patio that overlooked verdant vineyards and orchards. Rachel would return to the United States soon, and Ari needed her help before she left. She was the only one who could do it, and he was desperate for her to agree. He launched into an explanation of Zadok's eggs and the procedure to germinate Ari's most outrageous ambition.

"You want me to have whose baby?" Rachel was incredulous at the suggestion that she carry Zadok's embryos in her body.

"Calm down, Rachel. This is my life's work and you are my sister. I need you to help me create the next leaders of the Jewish faith. Don't you see? The weakness of the Israeli citizenry has gotten us into this current crisis. We require leaders with the resolve of our ancestors, not ones who cave in to threats that will lead to our extinction. Who will stand up to the Jew-hating societies around us?" Overly animated as he discussed his work, Ari scared Rachel while exciting her at the same time.

"Ari, you need help. This is just absurd. You can't be serious about this whole Zadok thing. I'm calling Trey. Maybe his cousin Zach knows someone locally who can sort these issues with you. As your sister and as a psychiatric professional, I implore you to consider therapy before this craziness becomes a full-blown psychosis." Rachel's discomfort increased, fearing Ari was already detached from reality and headed down the same path as their father.

Ari did not relent. His passion for the science overrode all sense of boundaries and sanity. He made his case over and over again. Rachel listened as he described the implantation procedure, making it seem like a simple visit to the gynecologist. He also railed on about how the future of Israel rested on the premise that strong leaders would emerge from the pure DNA of ancient, Jewish trailblazers.

Rachel looked at him, not listening. Her mind wandered back to their childhood summers in New Hampshire at a rented lake cottage. They were children, four years apart, loving each other's company. Ari always included his little sister in his daily outings. He had boundless energy for all things in nature and how they could be manipulated. The simple act of splitting an earthworm in half and watching it reconstitute as two separate worms amazed and captivated Ari. This began his fascination with biological science.

Rachel was proud of his success as a geneticist and CEO of his own multinational company. But she feared for his life. If he lived through these scientific travails, he might still be sentenced to the same aberrant existence as their father. The similarities were stunning. Rachel would not lose her only blood relative, and she suspected her intervention was Ari's only hope of survival.

"Don't you think God would have a problem with you changing the recipe for human creation? I imagine He would take issue with your approach." Rachel laced the sarcasm with a plea for Ari to reconsider.

"God gifted me a brain, and that same brain conceived the plan. My scientific studies confirm the relationship between undiluted, Jewish DNA and exemplary brain function. My intellect placed the DNA of a venerable Jewish pioneer in a blank female ovum. The resulting child will be just as human as you or me."

Ari's campaign was getting to Rachel. She thought seriously about what would happen to him if she rejected the proposal. She asked herself, *Who would receive the fertilized eggs if I don't? If I refuse, will I loose Ari, the only family I have in the world? And, what about Trey, don't I have a responsibility to him?*

"I'll do it," stated Rachel emphatically. "I'll carry this child in my body, but you have to bless my marriage to Trey, and he must never find out that the baby is not his. If you will agree to my terms I will give birth to the future of Israel."

Rachel had concluded that if she spurned Ari's proposition he would select the one-legged skank, Ziva, as the recipient of the embryos. That was not going to happen. Besides, Trey was going to be a great father.

Ziva arrived at Ari's house for a meeting that had been scheduled for five o'clock in the afternoon. Ari had asked her to come to his place so they could catch up on some Genoshalom paperwork. He had not been to the office all week, claiming he needed time alone in his home laboratory to finish the project for Colonel Fischer. Ziva parked her car on the street and walked to the front door with her briefcase in hand. As she approached the door, she noticed that it was open a crack, very unusual for Ari who was a safety freak by nature. Just as she was preparing to enter the house and chastise Ari for lax security, she heard a woman's voice. Ziva stopped in her tracks and placed her ear near the opening so she could determine who was with Ari.

Ari was in a conversation with his sister Rachel. *What is she doing here?* Ziva asked herself. *I better not go in until they're done talking.* She was not one to shy away from an opportunity to eavesdrop. Ziva carefully pushed the door open a few more inches so she could better hear the exchange between brother and sister.

"Alright Rachel, no sex for two weeks, no heavy lifting and don't worry about spotting; a little bleeding is normal after a successful procedure. After fourteen days we will do a standard pregnancy test to determine if the implantation was a success. Do you have any more questions, my darling sister?" Ziva was overhearing Ari deliver the standard post-op do's and don'ts to an IVF patient.

That bastard implanted my eggs in that bitch's uterus, thought Ziva as she struggled to hear Rachel's response.

"I'm scared as hell Ari. You have to promise me that from now on you will always be there. No more hiding in the laboratory and telling everyone you are in Indonesia. Is it alright to go on an airplane?" Rachel asked, knowing that she had to return to New York soon.

"Flying is not a problem, but yoga is out for at least one month. You are an amazing woman Rachel. I love you more than any brother could love a sister. I promise to be the best brother, uncle and godfather on the planet. I will always be there for you and the child."

Ari, how could you do this to me? I have devoted my life to you and your aspirations. And this is how you show your gratitude? You let me believe the embryos would be implanted in my body and together we would be the High Priest and Priestess of the Jewish people. I never would have agreed to let you have my eggs if I knew they would be given to your slut of a sister, thought Ziva. She also realized that she could do nothing for at least nine months if she wanted to be in *her* child's life. She needed to collect herself and push her way into the house as though nothing had happened.

"Ari, I'm here. Hey, you left your door open. Oh… hi Rachel, I didn't know you were here," Ziva brushed by Rachel, intentionally bumping her with a shoulder while on her way to the dining room table where she began spreading out the papers.

Ari had ordered a car to take Rachel back to Tel Aviv. The limo appeared in the driveway right on queue. Rachel gave Ari a big hug, she said goodbye to Ziva and exited through the front door.

"Did you have a nice visit with your sister?" Ziva asked, still in character.

"Yeah, it was great to spend some time with her before she goes back to New York," Ari responded, clueless about Ziva's discovery.

"Let's get to work on these documents," Ziva said in a take-charge voice, never showing any sign of being upset. Her body was going through the motions while her mind contemplated what she should do next.

Chapter 47

Over the course of the next two days, Willy and Trey spent hours talking and sharing stories of their separate lives. Willy wanted to know everything about Trey's personal interests and his work on Wall Street. So much had been missed and each wanted to hear every detail. Their parental-filial exchange defined a new relationship, unfamiliar yet comfortable for both men.

Trey's curiosity regarding Willy's work and the mission that called him away from his family consumed a good deal of their time. Willy reconciled himself to the fact he must be totally honest with his son, regardless of his oath to Mossad. The truth would set them both free. So, Willy continued to relate the mission that targeted Ali "Abu Hassan" al-Husseini as revenge for the atrocities Black September committed at the Munich Olympics. Trey listened, as Willy broke all of Mossad's rules of confidentiality by telling him the complete, unabridged story about the mission that caused Willy's hasty departure from Buffalo in 1973.

Abu Hassan's suite at the Chateau Champlain Hotel was as grand as his status in the eyes of Fatah's leaders. The expensive abode was a trapping of his new life in Canada, compliments of Yasser Arafat's vast financial network. Whatever Abu Hassan wanted, the hotel provided by simply summoning the concierge. The champagne flowed, as did the nightly parade of attractive women.

A significant weight gain further transformed his overall appearance. No exercise and up to five meals a day bestowed him with an extra fifty pounds. The French-influenced Canadian cuisine, high in calories and carbohydrates, and the endless river of scotch, principally sugar converted into a brown liquid, had morphed a handsome, athletic man into a pasty-faced slob. And his sexual habits were changing too.

His fat-cat diet, drugging, and drinking routine began to affect his ability to get an erection. Embarrassed more than once while attempting to perform sexually with a willing young beauty, he looked for other ways to heighten his satisfaction. That's when he met Felix.

Felix Ricard was a strapping young man who stood 6' 3" and weighed two hundred pounds. He was the manager of the hotel's fitness center and met Abu Hassan during one of his rare trips to the hotel's swimming pool. Abu Hassan had previously been passionate about swimming. While studying in Paris, he swam the English Channel on a bet with a classmate. He won the race and the prize, which was the completion of a term paper by the loser. Now he swam to counter a hangover.

The two men became friendly over the course of a few weeks and ended up meeting for a drink at a bar a fair distance from the hotel after Felix got off work. Nervous about being seen with a hotel resident, Felix arrived early for their rendezvous. He wore a hat and sat at a table near the rear of the establishment. When his guest arrived he gave a slight hand signal indicating his location in the back. Felix was very interested in this man.

"Good evening, Felix. Why are you sitting way back here when all the action is up front?" asked Abu Hassan.

"It's against company policy to meet socially with any of the residents or guests of the hotel. I could lose my job if the wrong person spots us together." He really didn't give a shit, Felix enjoyed the rush of breaking all rules, hotel or otherwise.

"I guess that begs the question of what you mean by 'meet socially.' We could be two buddies getting together for a beer after a hard day's work, or we could be two guys looking to jam our hard cocks up each other's asses. What's it going to be?" Abu Hassan queried. A wide smile appeared on his face, soliciting confirmation from his tablemate. He was surprised at how aroused he got by merely saying those words.

"I personally prefer the hard cock option," responded Felix without hesitation.

After a few rounds of drinks and some appetizers, Abu Hassan paid the bill. With the fragrant funk of two men in heat in the air, they departed separately with a plan to meet at Abu Hassan's suite in one hour. Walking back to the hotel, a late summer chill blew up the cavernous street right into Abu Hassan. He arrived at the front entrance of the Chateau Champlain and pushed his way through the oversized revolving door. The heat of the interior welcomed him back home. His courage waning, Abu Hassan stopped in the lobby bar for a double scotch, which he carried to his suite. He was nervous about his decision to experiment with another man. He had never crossed that sexual line, but he thought about it often. He was excited that he was going through with it and the booze balanced his nerves temporarily. A soft knock at the door indicated Felix had arrived. It was time to get it up or shut up; he prayed he could get a boner.

Willy had entered the suite only moments before Abu Hassan's return. He had watched Abu Hassan's every move for more than a month and had decided tonight would be his last. Willy heard a cardkey fumbling in the suite door and hid in the bedroom closet when his mark unexpectedly returned. The louvered door of the closet permitted a view of the floor as Abu Hassan entered the room to discard his coat and shoes. Willy heard a knock on the door. A burst of adrenaline pulsed through him as he considered how a second person would alter his plans. He was surprised to hear a man's voice as Abu Hassan and his guest settled into a conversation in the adjacent living area. Their dialogue was mostly garbled, but he could make out an occasional word or phrase. And then they went silent.

The two men made their way into the bedroom. Willy saw four feet moving across the carpet. He recognized the sound of belt buckles clanking as they hurriedly removed their clothing, which Willy could see piling up on the floor. A strained squeak from the box springs signaled their presence on the bed. The groaning started and the squeaking increased as the sexual energy in the room grew. Willy could smell the two men as a combination of body odor and alcohol fumes made it through the closet door. Willy considered his options as the foreplay continued on the other side of the barrier. Then he heard gasping. One of the two rodents was struggling to get his breath while the other moaned like an animal in heat. Fearing that Abu Hassan would die at the hands of someone else, he opened the closet door a crack to catch a peek at the amorous activities. What he saw shocked him.

Abu Hassan was face down tied to all four bedposts. He had a belt cinched around his neck that was held by Felix. They were both lost in the bliss of erotic asphyxiation. Willy had heard about this form of paraphilia where one person restricts blood flow to the brain of their partner while performing anal intercourse. Temporary asphyxiation was used to treat erectile dysfunction in the old days after it was discovered that hanging victims maintained erect members long after death. He fought the urge to vomit. Dealing with pheromone festooned ass-freaks had not been in the *kidon* training manual, but he would improvise.

Willy silently left the confines of the closet and positioned himself at the foot of the bed. Neither man noticed his presence. He continued to watch in disgust as Felix went at Abu Hassan's ass with fierce thrusts. After a minute or two, Willy had had enough. He reached into his coat pocket and removed a syringe already loaded with his preferred poison. Shellfish toxin was totally organic and untraceable in an autopsy. He inserted the needle into Felix's exposed buttock as he prepared to launch another assault on Abu Hassan's asshole. Feeling the needle prick, Felix turned to see Willy standing with an empty syringe pointed at the ceiling. He tried to form the word "Why?" as he fell forward onto the back of his new friend, Abu Hassan.

"Get off me you stupid fuck," yelled Abu Hassan under the considerable weight of the dead trainer. He was unable to extricate himself from beneath Felix's body. Abu Hassan struggled to get air in his lungs as Willy stepped around the side of the bed so he could be seen. The belt around Abu Hassan's neck had fallen from Felix's grasp and was now being held by Willy's surgically gloved hand.

"Who the fuck are you?" barked Abu Hassan as though he couldn't get the words out of his mouth fast enough.

"I'm your very own Olympic nightmare, Mr. al-Husseini," replied Willy still firmly gripping on the belt.

Abu Hassan immediately realized he was in the presence of an Israeli assassin. He tried to scream, but Willy's hold on the belt tightened with his every effort to call for help. "Don't try to call out or I'll end it right now. I would prefer to prolong this so we can discuss your long list of crimes against Israel."

"Fuck you," was all he could choke out before Willy yanked the belt, squeezing Abu Hassan's neck to less than half its normal size. His eyes began to bug out as his struggle to free himself intensified. Willy decided to end it, and with a firm tug on the leather strap, he felt the vibration of snapping vertebrae. The Black Prince's body went limp.

Willy took pictures of the dead trainer lying on top of Abu Hassan's strangled carcass. Images of the nude men would be disseminated in the most harmful manner possible, sending a message to Arafat and the entire Arab world that no act against Israel would go unpunished.

He let himself out of the suite looking both ways down the hall to assure his departure went undetected. Using the stairs he found his way to the ground floor and a side exit that led him to the street. Everything was going according to plan. The authorities would conclude the men died from their sexual activities, never suspecting murder by a third party.

He located a pay phone a few blocks from the hotel and called the number of the *sayan* driver provided by Buji. They spoke briefly, agreeing on a meeting place in ten minutes. Willy would be leaving Canada on a late night flight. His *kidon* cherry had been broken. The first assassination had been flawless. He would be hunted as the man who killed one of the world's most revered Arab terrorists. Radical Islam would not sleep until the perpetrator of Abu Hassan's murder was brought to justice.

"Are you alright?" asked Willy, concerned that the description of his first assassination may have been too graphic.

"Yeah, I think so. It's just that…I'd created an illusion of you being a famous person who did normal things like curing cancer or fighting child sex trafficking. I guess kids without parents just create a fiction, anything to fill the void. But, I never could have imagined this," said Trey, reservedly pleased that he finally knew the truth about his father's departure.

They continued to talk about their separate lives well into the night, becoming more like father and son as each hour passed. The two men lost track of time as they conversed across a wide range of topics. Time had been their enemy until now. They had a lot of catching up to do and time was finally on their side.

Trey was grateful for the chance to know his father and alarmed at the same time. Donny had murdered at least 15 people that Trey knew of and Willy, the self-professed king of the *kidonim*, had killed scores more. It troubled Trey that these two men, his father and brother, had taken so many lives while showing no outward signs of remorse or guilt. How could someone become so desensitized to the taking of a human life? Trey hoped they were both engaged in an internal, moral debate about life and death.

Chapter 48

Samir's earthworm would not reconstitute itself. It was now a mutilated and flaccid appendage, unrecognizable as a penis. Of course, this mattered little, since he was dead. Fareed's men crated the body for shipment to Samir's family, who were notified of his traitorous activities. The shame brought on his family was immeasurable. He would be buried in a private ceremony attended only by his wife and daughters. They would endure the consequences of Samir's actions in his absence by being excommunicated from the mosque. They would be forced out of their home by neighbors who refused to live next to the family of a Mossad spy. This was considered the biggest breach of Muslim custom; collaborating with the Jews made you a Jew. No self-respecting Muslim would ever live next to a family whose patriarch was such a consummate snake.

Goran's negotiations with his interrogators turned out better than Samir's. With his penis and cover intact, Goran began to establish himself as a double agent for Mossad. His captors warmed to the idea after he told them about his recruitment in the UK and his relationship with the Syrian President and first lady. Goran's name-dropping got him a lot of attention in Pimi's office as well. Israel sought to uncover other traitorous agents in the ranks of the Syrian intelligence community. If Syria was able to turn a CIA officer with a cash offer, then it stood to reason many others existed. It would be Goran's job to find and expose them.

Mark Manning initially resisted this approach, wanting to draw and quarter his impertinent underling. Once the logic of using him to further their mutual interests sank in, he conceded and agreed to the plan. As a U.S. citizen, Goran had rights that went beyond a foreign fighter's legal protections. The U.S. system would grant him legal council and the right to a jury trial. Finally, Manning considered the hit his reputation would take once it became known that a high-ranking CIA official spied for the Syrians. The politics of survival and a healthy dose of professional vanity dictated he cut and run.

"Take him. I don't want to see him again, and I hope he eventually gets what he deserves. He can be replaced at the CIA, but the CIA can never replace Israel. Gentlemen, I leave the traitor in your capable hands. Good luck trusting him. I don't." Manning turned to depart the conference room as Sachs rose to say good-bye.

"Mark, you're making the right decision. He's a liability we can manage. We oversee a number of double agents around the world who provide actionable information daily. I assure you Goran will fit in nicely, but if he doesn't we have people who can terminate the relationship without prejudice. Have a safe trip home. We'll be in touch." The two men shook hands, and Manning was out the door.

Donny's situation was more delicate. He didn't have the choice to continue as a double agent with the Syrians. News of his capture had gotten back to Syria and the C10. The Israelis knew that trying Donny as an enemy combatant would not deter others from throwing in with the Arabs against Israel. So rather than wasting the resources in court they needed to come up with a strategy to trade Donny for something they wanted.

Ireland had incarcerated an Israeli "diplomat" who was actually a Mossad intelligence officer. The perpetrator would normally be sent back to his home country with a public tongue-lashing; however this operative had infiltrated Ireland's M-2 Military Intelligence Branch. The spoils of his efforts were the names of all British MI6 and U.S. CIA counterintelligence agents in joint operations with Ireland's M-2. Mossad wanted its supposed diplomat back, and the British wanted Donny returned to stand trial for orchestrating the assassinations.

A deal was proffered through diplomatic channels, and an exchange negotiated out of the media spotlight. Neither country wanted the world to know the way backroom wrangling enabled those who committed crimes on foreign soil to walk out the backdoor to the safety of their home country. Everyone played by the same rules, albeit for different reasons: If you have something we want, name your price and settle on terms for an exchange that is politically acceptable. Next, assume the media will find out, agree on your story with the counterparty, and stick to it like white on rice.

These were the rare times countries in conflict could agree on protocols and be motivated to deal with each other. Donny would be returned to Dublin after a trade for the Israeli envoy on the tarmac of the Vienna Airport. The Irish would decide how to handle his case with the British authorities.

Chapter 49

"Operation Trojan Stallion" was wisely conceived by Willy, Buji, and Yussi as a way to decapitate the command and control structures in the region. The targets were the President of Iran, the Chairman of the Hamas Political Bureau, and the President of Syria. Removing these despicable Muslims would create a temporary leadership vacuum Israel could use to its benefit.

Willy selected the leader of Hamas as their first target. He would deliver the lethal dose while Yussi's team of *sayan* helpers planted evidence pointing to tribal forces as the perpetrators. If all went as planned, Israel would begin to climb out of the penalty box of international espionage and regain its rightful place at the apex of world intelligence.

Ari met the three principals at Yussi's bug-free condominium. Operation Trojan Stallion was a go and Ari's ammunition was ready for delivery. Willy and his team were anxious to re-enter the fight. The chairman of Hamas would be the first to die.

"Our contacts in Gaza and the West Bank have identified three *sayanim* embedded in the Hamas organization. They will be working at the wedding of the Hamas leader's daughter next week. Two *sayanim* are on the catering staff and one is part of the security detail. The brilliance of this execution method is that food security measures will fail to protect him," Buji said, gratified at how the plan was coming together. Willy's return energized both he and Yussi at a time when they should be trading in their guns for beach chairs, but they weren't missing this chance to line up with Willy regardless of their advanced age.

Ari watched in amazement as his hosts reviewed the methods of delivery for the final two targets. The commitment of these patriots was an inspiration. Ari's pride was evidenced by his satisfied silence as he listened to the plan to infect the Iranian and Syrian leaders. Yussi's private network of *sayanim* would be crucial to the success of their plan. These *sayanim* were highly placed within the administration of their host nation. As trusted aides or military types, they had the necessary access to the target's immediate environment.

Ari removed the weapons from his briefcase and placed three 4" x 4" x 2" Styrofoam boxes on the coffee table. Each box was color coded with a single dot: green for Hamas, red for Syria, and yellow for Iran. He opened one of the boxes to reveal the bio-bullet in an unbreakable glass vial also marked with a matching colored dot. A syringe would be used to draw the material from the vial for dissemination into the immediate environment, but it was not necessary to inject anyone directly.

"Doctor, what is the best way to make sure we infect the right person?" asked Willy.

"The material was designed to be odorless, tasteless and colorless. It can be injected into fruit, like a whole pomegranate or melon. Water or any beverage makes for a good delivery medium," Ari said, very pleased at how the meeting was going. "Other people can enjoy the tainted food or drink without harm. The mixture can also be broadcast through the air by injecting it into a water-mist fan commonly in use at outdoor functions."

Willy turned to his partners and said, "That covers it for me. Do you guys have any questions?" Both Buji and Yussi shook their heads.

"Thank you gentlemen for letting me take part in the making of history. My work in the laboratory normally serves a constituency limited to people looking for lost relatives or genetically modified seeds. Today I feel like I'm part of something much greater. I trust you will carry out the mission with the same professionalism you have demonstrated over the last few weeks. I expect our work will result in a more secure and safe *eretz* for all Israelis. Thank you again," said Ari, visibly moved by the meeting.

"I never thought it would come to this," said Willy, looking uncharacteristically forlorn. "Why is it, when all the chips are down, our leaders crawl into their little political caves and leave it to the true defenders of Israel to do their dirty work? It's bullshit that we have to risk our necks to bail them out again and again."

No one needed to be reminded of the countless times Jewish mercenaries had taken situations into their own hands. Willy had no patience for the religiously motivated zealots who were hijacking Israel's national conscious, or archeologists who dug for evidence of God's gift to the son's of Abraham. And Pimi did not have the political capital or will to stand up to Jewish liberals and Israeli Arabs when it came to truly protecting the country. Willy and the men in this room would do the government's job.

"One last question, Dr. Kohen. Have you uncovered any other medical conditions from the Summit samples?" Yussi inquired, still not over the premature release of the Saudi King's affliction.

"Yes, the King of Brunei is a hermaphrodite," Ari offered, knowing clarification would be necessary.

"He's a bleeder?" asked Yussi.

"No, that's a hemophiliac, Colonel," said Ari with a chuckle.

"Do you mean he is both male and female? A shemale?" asked Buji.

"Yes, someone with this condition has both ovarian and testicular tissue. Their external genitalia are often ambiguous. My review of pictures of the King confirms the DNA results. He's a true hermaphrodite who attempted to surgically reverse his biological condition, but you would have to see him disrobed to be sure." Ari was enjoying this opportunity to show off his scientific wares. The men looked at him with their mouths slightly ajar and their eyes wide open.

Ari continued, "Hormone therapy can only do so much to conceal the condition on the outside. I can guarantee you that this person got a shit sandwich from Allah at birth. It can't be pleasant to be a King with a clitoris."

Chapter 50

Rachel and Trey were back in the hotel waking up after an evening of deep conversations about everything from Trey's father to Rachel's brother. So much had taken place during the past month. Rachel had returned from the five-day visit with her brother in Upper Galilee the day before. Her initial plan to go up to Ari's house for one night and return to Tel Aviv the following morning got shelved once she saw Ari's mongrel-like appearance and the condition of his home. She and Trey agreed her brother needed her. Trey encouraged her to stay as long as she needed and even offered to come up if he could help in any way. She said that she could handle it and wanted some time alone with Ari. Trey loved Rachel's maternal instincts and her commitment to family.

Now Rachel and Trey were together. They had taken the previous day to shop and linger in sidewalk cafes. Rachel would return to the United States on a flight later that day while Trey decided what he would do next. His father had disappeared again, but this time he left a note.

> *To My Son Trey,*
>
> *I am sorry to leave so abruptly. My country has called on me once again, and I cannot ignore my duty in this time of crisis. However, my work should be completed in a matter of months. We will be together soon to continue our journey*

of personal discovery. I regret the time we have been apart, but the times we have to look forward to have a unique value that must not be squandered. A father rarely has a chance to make things right with his children. I intend to be the exception and be part of your life now and forever.

Let Zach know how you can be reached, and I will call as soon as my work is done. I hope you will be at your home in Ireland because I need to be there for your brother when he stands trial. Grace has been rescued from Syria and I understand she will be tried with Donny as a coconspirator.

Dtí sin mo mhac, a bheith sábháilte, shaol grá agus an fhírinne a lorg —Until then, my son, be safe, love life, and seek the truth.

Love,

Your Father

Trey read the letter for the third time and folded it into his pocket. A twinge of abandonment at his father's sudden departure washed over him, but at least this time he left a letter. After hearing Willy's story, he couldn't blame him for his fatherless childhood. Willy claimed he didn't know Mary was pregnant when he left. Trey gladly took him at his word for an opportunity to know his father as an adult. *Water over the dam* was the phrase that popped into Trey's head. Father and son made the most of their time together; dinners and runs in the park helped Trey get over his hostility. He would try like hell to be part of his father's life and not harbor any resentment about the past. The reconciliation tour would resume when they were together again.

Rachel rolled over in bed and noticed Trey at the desk, deep in thought. She interrupted him by saying, "You know I love you, William John Cowens, and I'm going to spend the rest of my life with you. Like it or not, I'm yours."

Trey came over and sat on the bed. He wanted her in his life in the worst way.

"I love you more than you could ever know, Rachel."

Satisfied with his response, Rachel got down to business. "When I get back to New York, I'm planning to sell my apartment, and wind down my psychiatric practice. After which, I'll join you in Ireland for the life we both deserve. Promise me we can return to the cottage in Letterkenny to continue our love-making in the glow of the fireplace and beneath the ancient oaks." Rachel was upping the ante considerably, and Trey was all in.

Trey loved Rachel in ways he never thought possible; her soul spoke to him with an intimacy he had not experienced with anyone else. Would they really spend the rest of their lives together? Doubt crept into his mind as he thought about the meaning of such a commitment. Trey had failed at every relationship he had attempted. What would make this different?

They walked to a family-owned cafe recommended by the hotel concierge. At seven a.m. the place was almost empty, so they had their pick of tables; they settled in by the window. A very attractive twenty-something woman came with coffee and menus. The sheer beauty of their waitress briefly distracted Trey; this didn't go unnoticed by Rachel.

"So you like young Jewish women do you?" She smiled, having witnessed his man-gaze in full x-ray mode.

"Guilty as charged," Trey said, a little sheepish at being caught leering at the much younger woman. He leaned across the table and gave Rachel a kiss on the cheek. "I was just comparing your beauty to hers, and you are the winner, hands-down."

"Stop the bullshit and decide what you are having for breakfast," Rachel urged wryly, redirecting the topic to their stomachs.

They both consumed a huge meal. Trey was impressed at her ability to put away the food. For such a fit, young woman she ate like a man, even poaching some of Trey's neglected toast. They settled the bill and ordered coffee to go for their walk back to the hotel.

Rachel packed while Trey read the news and checked his e-mail. He was a lifetime removed from the chaos of his former career as a major player on Wall Street. He ran through the changes of the past months in his mind. Work no longer defined Trey. He had begun to get in touch with himself in a deep and meaningful way. He had a father, a brother, a cousin, and a lover who had not existed six months before and it was Rachel who had inspired it all. Whatever he would do he would do it with Rachel.

The hotel provided a car for their ride to the airport. Trey and Rachel sat silently in the backseat for the fifteen-kilometer drive in midday traffic. Rachel's head rested on Trey's shoulder. His hand found hers as her chest heaved and droplets of tears began to appear on Trey's suede jacket. They would be apart for at least a month while she concluded her business in New York and he found his way back to Ireland. His stomach turned at the thought of the separation. Was this how love felt? Why did it hurt so much? Would they be together, or was this just a cruel joke?

They arrived on the departure level of the airport terminal. The driver popped the trunk and opened the rear door. Trey tried to release her hand but she did not let go.

"Don't you ever leave me, Trey Cowens. We're a great team. Hang in there for another month, and it will all make sense."

Wiping tears from her eyes, Rachel stepped out of the car onto the curb. Trey came around the back of the car to help attach her briefcase to the roller-bag before they made their way into the terminal.

Trey removed a baseball cap from his coat pocket. He wanted to avoid the hassle of being recognized by Israel's highly developed facial recognition systems. They continued to hold hands as they walked through the terminal. Trey rolled the bags to the first class counter. They were greeted by a friendly airline agent who asked the Israeli flight security questions. She issued a boarding pass and gave the couple directions to the security screening area.

Trey and Rachel's hands were locked in a death grip, neither one willing to be the first to let go. As they approached the door an officer said, "Sir, you have to go back; you're not allowed in there without a ticket."

Trey released Rachel's hand and pulled her into his arms for one last embrace. They kissed like Parisian lovers for everyone to see. They were alone in their thoughts about their love for one another and their future. Trey reluctantly released her and took a step back while placing the handle of the roller-bag in her hand. Before she disappeared behind the wall Trey said, "You're on your own now, my love. See you soon."

Before entering the screening area, Rachel turned to Trey and stated with authority, "I better not be on my own because I'm pregnant. We're going to have a baby, and I'm certainly not raising this child alone." Then she was gone, disappearing behind the security wall, leaving Trey to contemplate the gravity of her parting statement. *Baby! Whose? Mine? Did you just say we are having a baby? No way...yes way!*

Shaking himself out of the baby haze, Trey noticed four well-polished shoes in his line of sight just under the bill of the baseball cap. He looked up to find two uniformed officers from the Israel Police Department staring at him. Trey was feeling nauseous as one policeman asked, "Sir, may we please see some identification?"

Rachel found thirty-nine A, a window seat located about halfway back in the economy section of the EL AL Boeing 747-400 bound for New York City. The image of Trey's face reacting to the news of her pregnancy played over and over in her head. Most of the guilt she had about deceiving Trey was vanquished by her total commitment to Ari and the future of Israel. The four nights she had spent with Ari after the procedure were the best of her entire life. She felt a love and closeness to Ari not experienced since those summer days in the New Hampshire woods. Once the embryos were in her body, Ari's demeanor transformed into the loving brother she had lost many years before.

As children, Ari had shielded Rachel from her father, the monster in the basement, by distracting her with science experiments or word games. The closeness they shared for those years under their parent's roof was lost when Ari left for rabbinical school. Rachel's father began assaulting her both mentally and physically, subjecting her unspeakable humiliations. Her mother was complicit in these acts by not intervening, but Rachel did not blame her knowing that she would be beaten to death if she tried to stop the molestations. Rachel was able to deal with her father's behavior through self- hypnosis, inducing a trance-like state that allowed for dissociation from her body. In those moments she had called on an image of Ari for the strength to endure the pain.

Her phone rang; it was Trey calling from the terminal. She hit the red "Ignore" button on her iPhone and tried to focus on Ari and the next nine months. There would be plenty of time to fix whatever problems she had caused by leaving Trey hanging with the news that he was going to be a "father". It was true that he would be the father on paper, however it was the Father, the Creator of all mankind who was directing this plan and He would raise this child. She was now a vessel for the future of the Jewish people, a people in desperate need of leadership.

She saw herself as a modern day version of the biblical Hannah who had been impregnated with an intervention from God. The price of this holy assistance was Hannah's promise to dedicate the unborn child to the service of God. A boy was born and given into the care of Eli the priest who raised him within the confines of the Temple. This is the story of Samuel, one of the holiest and most revered men in the bible. Rachel as Hannah was an analogy used often by Ari the past week, one that echoed in Rachel's soul.

Her phone rang, again. It was Ari calling from his office. She picked up and said, "Hello brother, how are you on this wonderful day?"

"Fine. Did you tell Trey about the pregnancy before you boarded, like we discussed?" Ari asked, getting right down to business.

"Yes, I told him just as I was passing through the security barrier," Rachel responded with pleasure, having executed Ari's instructions to the letter.

"Oh, good. I was worried that you would chicken-out. How are you feeling?" Ari asked, being brotherly only after confirming that his directive had been carried out.

"My lower back is really sore," Rachel said, pleased that he had asked about her health. No one could make her feel better than Ari, he had protected her as a child and she loved his attention as an adult.

"Your back pain is probably associated with the procedure and completely normal. Call me when you land in New York."

"Have you told Ziva yet?" Rachel asked, following up on Ari's pledge to let her know about his decision.

"Not yet. She hasn't come into the office since you left. I'll tell her as soon as I see her, but don't worry about Ziva. I can handle her."

"Are you sure Ari? You know that she's crazy. I wouldn't put it past her to do something radical."

"Rachel, I said don't concern yourself with Ziva. I have it under control. Alright?"

"If you say so, but…"

"Not buts, I'll handle it. You just focus on eating and sleeping like I told you, and no yoga for thirty days. Understood?" Ari's pleadings about her diet and the need to sleep at least eight hours per day had been drilled into her head the whole time she was at his house.

"How about bungee jumping, is that allowed?" Rachel needed that jab to even things out with her brother.

Ari laughed and they said their loving goodbyes. Rachel hung up and tried to get comfortable for the ten-hour flight to the US. She was already antsy and they had not even taken off, it was going to be a long trip.

Seated three rows behind Rachel, in seat forty-two A, was Ziva Wolfson.